ENDGAME

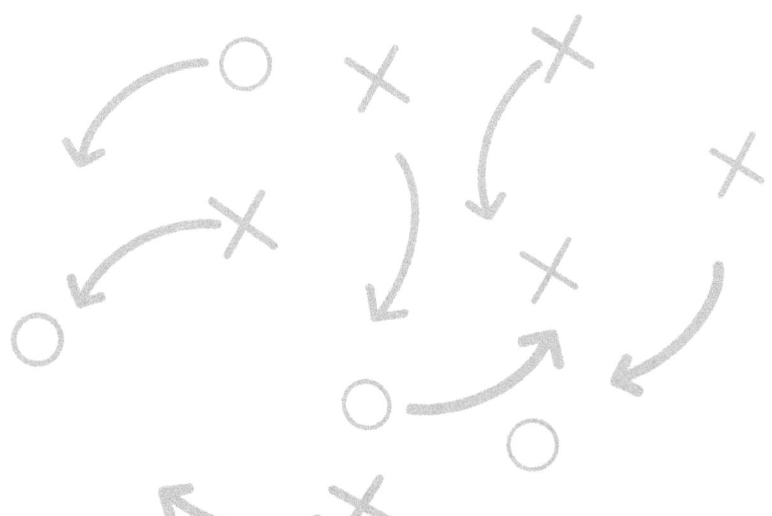

Jennifer Froh

Wilted Wallflower Books
Mustang, Oklahoma

Endgame

Copyright © 20226 Author Jennifer Froh

Published: Wilted Wallflower Books

Cover Design: Author Jennifer Froh and a collaboration with Beverly Sigmund hand painted art

ISBN: 979-8-234-04568-

For the thrill of forbidden plays, fiery passions, and wild hearts, refusing to follow the rules.

A little note to my readers

This book contains strong language, sexual content, and hints of violence. You may also find heart-stopping chaos, cowboy hats, and assless chaps are optional, but recommended.

Hold onto your cowboy hat, because Jax in assless chaps may have your drooling. However, if spice or hints of spice is not for you, I have highlighted a few scenes you can skip if you would like. (Please note these may not be all the scenes that talk about, have, or hint at spice.)

TAYLOR
12
FUMBLE

CHAPTER 1

JAX

"What's your poison?" the bartender asks, leaning over the bar.

She is wearing a tight, thin, white shirt that is sheer and cut too low, revealing her ample breasts supported by a black bra. As she leans further, her chest rises, making her assets even more on display. I am not disappointed with the view, but after what I walked into before coming here, I would rather not be hit on, even if she is doing her job and trying to get a good tip.

"I'll take a whiskey, double neat," I order the first thing to pop into my mind.

I don't typically order whiskey because one of my best friends, Poppy's father, was an alcoholic, and whiskey was his drink of choice. However, I want to feel like whatever I am drinking is going to sear the taste of Lilah right out of me. I don't ever drink my feelings away, but for a little while, I want to forget the image of my now ex fucking another guy in my bed. If drowning the mental image of her getting pounded by him from behind and sounds of her calling out this dicks name as she thoroughly enjoys herself will help me get through this night, I don't see anything wrong with my plan.

I put the whiskey glass to my lips, tipping back two large gulps of the strong amber liquor, emptying my glass before the bartender has a chance to walk away. She refills my drink and props her chin in the palm of her hand.

"Rough night?" She asks with only the right side of her mouth lifted into a sad smile.

I still think she might be looking for one hell of a tip unless she wants someone to help warm her bed after her shift. I do not want to

"

take her home, nor do I want to go home with her, but if she were wearing a giant nightgown with her hair in curlers, I would still tip her well. I don't think I can get it up with the image of Lilah still ingrained in my mind.

Lilah has always been a wild, carefree party girl. Hell, she still is, but I thought she stopped hooking up with random guys after we got together. I don't think she thought about what I had to go through to be with her. She is my best friend, Lewis's sister, and to think of the massive fights I've had with him about me wanting to date her makes my blood boil even more.

"Yeah, you could say that." I sip my whiskey, enjoying the taste more than the burn.

The burning sensation I once craved is gone, but the need for a buzz I know I will eventually get will take over, which may help me forget about this evening or only make me feel worse. I guess only time can tell, and I'm here to at least try to drown my problems away so I can go into the fight I know I will have with her tomorrow. I don't want to be burning with rage when I talk to Lilah, so I am going to sit here until I need to call Poppy for a ride home.

"You want to talk about it?" The beautiful bartender smiles, showing off perfect white teeth between her red, pouty lips.

Before I can say anything, I hear my name being called over the loud country music playing through the bar. I tense as Lilah sits on the stool next to me. I came here to get away, not for her to follow me. Plus, I don't want to have this fight now, especially in a crowded bar.

"What?!" I snap, not bothering to hide my irritation.

Lilah turns her body in my direction. "Jax, please let me explain…" Lilah trails off when I slam my glass down on the bar, and the bartender, who hasn't moved yet, gives me another refill. "Oh, I'll have a…" Lilah stops talking when the bartender moves to the customer on the other side of me.

She doesn't move far, so I'm guessing she wants to know what is bothering me so badly that she feels the need to eavesdrop. I down my full glass of whiskey and wipe away the stray drops off the side of my mouth. I know I am going to regret this in the morning, but I don't care. I will take the hangover instead of feeling my heart break right now.

"I think we should talk about this. I mean, we've been together almost over two years now, and we've been friends since we were kids." Lilah whines, sounding pathetic, but I'm not surprised she doesn't stop talking. "I graduated from college last May, and I want to experiment more, because I may not get the chance before you graduate." She says this like I am the one to blame for her cheating on me.

"If you want to experiment more, maybe you should at least have the decency to talk to me about it or break up with me first. I don't know why you thought I would ever be okay with you fucking someone else, especially in our bed." I spit my words at Lilah like they are venom, making her flinch. "How long have you been cheating on me?" I slam the rest of my drink back.

The busty bartender immediately fills my empty glass again, but this time she leaves the mostly empty bottle behind.

Lilah's eyes water as she shakes her head, looking away from me for the first time since she sat next to me. I know I will not like what she has to say based on her reaction to my question, but the tipsy part of me wants to know. This can't be the only time she has chosen to do mattress gymnastics with someone else, while we've been together, after all, she was brave enough to bring them home. I wonder how many other guys she invited into my bed. My blood boils from the image of another naked man in my bed, and I now have the impulsive thought to burn my mattress.

Before Lilah can answer, I feel a warm hand touch my arm. I turn in the direction of the welcomed distraction. She is wearing a pair of dark, washed jeans, a shirt with buttons down the front showing her perfect chest, and cowboy boots. This girl doesn't know she broke the angry spell I was under from Lilah and the whiskey, but frankly, I think it was much needed.

"Buy me a drink?" She asks, raising a perfectly drawn eyebrow.

I turn my back to Lilah, giving this girl my full attention. If she wants to experiment and play games, I will stoop down to her level, but I won't hide what I'm doing.

"What would you like?" I smile even though my heart feels like it is going through a blender right now.

Buying this girl a drink will not help me feel better, but I'm hoping it will make her mad enough to leave.

Lilah huffs, so I can only imagine she is now crossing her arms over her chest. "JAX! WE NEED TO TALK!"

I don't respond to her. Hell, I don't even turn back to her. I know this is pissing her off. She groans, confirming how unhappy she is with me. I feel her move at the same time, the sound of a stool scraping on the bar's floor, making the hair on the back of my neck stand. I glance over my shoulder, watching Lilah struggle to get off the stool until she knocks it over before storming angrily out of the bar.

I would put money on her going home and waiting for me to finish what she has to say, but I won't be talking to her tonight, because avoiding her sounds better than fighting with her when I am drunk. Maybe we can talk when I am sober, and I've had some time to cool off, but if she hasn't figured out our relationship is over by now, she will in the morning.

The girl's cheeks flame bright pink as a deep blush travels down her neck. My eyes snap back to her beautiful face, and her pouty lips are parted, making her embarrassment even more obvious. "I would love a vodka cranberry."

The least I can do is buy her a drink for unintentionally helping me get rid of Lilah. My original plan wasn't to get her to bed. She doesn't talk; in fact, she sits there glancing at me every few seconds. I turn back to my empty glass with the images of Lilah leaving here with her hands balled into tight fists, her mouth smashed into a thin line, and her breathing hard and fast.

I thought we were happy, and maybe we were, but it doesn't excuse Lilah for sleeping around and thinking what she was doing was okay. I mean, we live with each other now, you know, building a life together. You would think if you wanted to "experiment," as she said, talking to your partner would be a good idea. Right? Lilah never said a thing, and I doubt I would have ever known if I hadn't caught her in action.

Memories flash through my mind of the day I told Lilah I had feelings for her. Lewis was furious, but I told him I never made a move on Poppy out of respect for his feelings for her. He kept saying how he called dibs on Poppy a long time ago, but this is different, because Lilah is his sister and Poppy isn't mine. I see Lewis's point, but it doesn't mean I agree with it. If I did, he wouldn't have eventually given me the thumbs up to date his sister. I had chased her for a couple of years, and when she finally agreed to let me take her on a date, I thought I was the luckiest guy ever.

The bartender comes over, interrupting the memories, which are souring my mood even more. I fill my glass full of the rest of the whiskey, and the bartender takes the bottle, tossing it in the trash. The girl next to me clears her throat like I need a reminder I promised to order her drink, but the overwhelming scent of her perfume makes her hard to forget.

"Can I get a vodka cranberry for my friend?" I ask, and the bartender smiles, glancing at the stranger next to me.

"Of course," she says, grabbing a glass and making the simple drink before walking to another customer.

"Thanks," The girl says, turning in her stool to face me.

Her knees brush against my thigh. She has subtle curves men go crazy for, with a slim waist and creamy-looking skin, which I'm sure is buttery soft. She is a bombshell of a woman, with a map of freckles traveling down her neck, disappearing into her shirt. Any man would do almost anything to follow the path, hoping they lead to the sweetest of treasures. Even though she is sitting, and I can't get a good look at her ass, I know from the way her jeans hug tightly to her hips and thighs that she has a nice, round butt. She could be the perfect distraction I need for the night.

As if she is reading my mind, she boldly asks, "Do you want to get out of here? Maybe find somewhere a little more private."

A wide smile slowly stretches across my face. "How about I play you in a friendly game of pool?"

"Okay, but what do I get if I win?" She hesitantly asks.

"You can have me for one night, but if you lose, you get a free drink." I lean on the bar, raising my eyebrow at her challengingly.

I don't tell her we won't be going back to my place, and we will have to figure out a way to get to her place. I wonder if she is okay with fooling around in the back seat of my truck, because I am too drunk to drive home.

I tip the full glass of whiskey back, emptying the amber liquor in four large gulps.

"Perfect, we can go back to my place." She turns away from me, leaving her full glass behind on the bar.

I follow her to the pool tables, checking her ass as she walks ahead of me. She is very attractive, and I'm not going to be disappointed in her being the first woman I sleep with since I've been in a relationship with Lilah. My eyes travel over her body for the second time, and a small twinge of betrayal sweeps through me.

"Deal," I say, even though I know I'm not in the right headspace to do this.

I begin racking the balls on the pool table as she looks for which pool stick she wants. I focus on what I'm doing and not my beautiful opponent. I know if I think about this too much, I will not go through with this.

"I should warn you, I am pretty damn good," she puts the bottom part of her pool stick on the floor, holding on with only her thumb and pointer finger, circling the slim shaft of the pool stick.

She could do something suggestive, but I could be the only one with filthy things running through my mind right now.

"Good, I love a little friendly competition." I take the triangle rack off the table.

The amber liquor I was downing is now catching up to me, making me feel a little more than good. I wave my hand, telling her she can take the first shot. She leans over the table, but the only thing I can focus on are her tits threatening to push past the buttons on her shirt. I am so distracted I barely notice she sinks four balls, two solids and two stripes.

"Solids," she calls out, walking around the pool table.

I'm not surprised by her choice, but I wonder if she will call out her intended shots. She leans over the table, lining up her pool stick. I am distracted yet again by her breasts, trying to push out of her top to notice she has sunk the ball into the corner pocket. She straightens back up, biting her pink pouty lips. She walks around the table, but she doesn't look up at me as she tries to figure out what she wants to do next. I watch her hips sway seductively as she stops in front of me, leaning over the table, giving me a perfect view of her ass. As any man would do, I take this opportunity to check her out.

She makes shot after shot until she finally misses the second-to-last ball she has left. I am extremely impressed, but I am also turned on as I watch her, like a cobra hypnotized by the confidence oozing from her. She looks up at me from under her lashes with a smile so big you can see all her pearly white teeth. I finally get to play instead of watching her bend in various positions, which is honestly making my filthy mind run wild. Don't get me wrong, I normally love seeing girls bend over in different positions, but they usually have far less clothes on, begging for my touch.

I finally get to have my turn, and I have an easy shot lined up, and I sink the ball with ease. I am going to have to try hard to throw this game unless we both decide to say "fuck it" to the bet, and I let her take me to her place. I sink four of my balls before I intentionally miss the next pocket.

She pats my shoulder. "You want to get a couple of shots before we go back to my place?"

She looks me up and down, so I do the same. I'm a thirsty man ready to quench his thirst, but nothing behind the bar will do, because the only thing I want at this moment is the beautiful woman standing in front of me.

"Yeah, I'll get us a car." I pull my phone out of my pocket.

We walk to the bar, and she loops her arm in mine, giggling. "I can drive."

I look down at her. Her eyes are clear and not glassy, and I never saw her take a drink, but I would rather be safe and get a car.

"Not after you have those shots, besides, the car will be here in fifteen minutes."

We go to the bar, and I order us both tequila shots each. She turns in the stool to face me, and she smiles big before I feel her hand on my knee, travel up my thigh. I swallow hard. Thankfully, the bartender places four shot glasses in front of us. I slide one to her, before we clink the glass, and we put the cold cup to our lips, shooting back the gold liquor to do the same thing again.

"Another round?" the bartender asks.

"Fuck it, let's do it." I smile. "Can I close my tab after?"

"Of course." Our glasses are filled again, and I take both shots back-to-back.

After I pay walk through the crowded bar, not talking to each other as the sound of loud country music blares through the bar, and the sound of her boots tapping on the pavement. The noises are grating on my last nerve and should be a sign that this is something I shouldn't do, but not enough for me to go home right now.

The girl tells the driver her address, and if I were paying more attention to her, I would know where she is taking me. I look out the window at the blurry buildings passing us. I blink again and thank myself for knowing better than to get behind the wheel. The car pulls up to the curb of an apartment building, a couple of units down from mine. At least when I leave, I can walk home and have Poppy take me to my car tomorrow.

I follow the attractive girl from the car to her apartment, checking her ass out as she walks. She lives on the first floor. I am severely glad I don't have to try climbing stairs, given how drunk I have gotten. She stops at a door, I grab her hips, I lean down, and I kiss her neck. She tries to unlock her door, but misses a few times, giggling as the alcohol she drank swirls in her head, making her feel good.

She manages to get the door open, stumbling on her feet.

"Sorry, my place is a mess. I moved in a few days ago." She slurs, informing me, looking, and sounding more like a drunken mess as time goes by.

I step inside and look around her tiny apartment. The living room is cluttered with boxes, and from the size of the place, I'm guessing it's a one-bedroom. The walls are painted the same ugly beige as mine, but her kitchen is a decent size for one of the smaller units.

These apartments are nice enough, but they're still college housing, which means the rent is pretty reasonable. Poppy, Lewis, Lilah, and I share a two-bed, two-bath. I have the master bedroom since my parents cover most of the rent, even though I offered it to Poppy first. Lilah was annoyed that I did.

I glance down at the stained, oatmeal-colored carpet and silently thank my parents for convincing the landlord to put in hardwood floors for me.

I feel her touch my back, lightly moving her arms around me. My stomach muscles twitch from the soft touch of her hands as they rest above my belly button. I feel her body press against mine, and my drunken mind instantly thinks about how nice her boobs feel pressed against me. Regret claws at me for a moment until I remember, no matter what I do tonight doesn't change how Lilah and I are breaking up. I should probably wait until she knows too, but the anger and jealousy mixed with the whiskey pumping through me make staying a lot easier. I turn around, looking down at my pretty one-night stand. For a moment, I forget what to do with my hands, but my momentary forgetfulness doesn't last long. The girl's hands move up my chest until she grabs a fistful of my shirt near the collar. My hands move to her hips, pulling her closer to me.

"Do you want to give me a tour?" I smirk down at her, letting her know we should move this shindig to her room.

"Yeah, my bedroom is this way." She pulls my shirt roughly, but not enough to move me.

I follow her to her room, but she keeps her firm grasp on my shirt.

I hope she thinks this is cute and not I am going to bolt as soon as she lets go of me, because if I were going to stop, I would have gone home as soon as she pulled into the same apartments I live in. Her bedroom door is open, and once we are next to the bed, she lets go of me. I look down at her again as Lilah's face flashes in my mind. I sigh heavily before I pull my shirt off, tossing the soft fabric to the side.

My fingers go to the girl's button-up shirt, slowly freeing each button from its hole. As I unbutton the girl's shirt, I reveal that a black, silky-looking bra is too small for the heavy breasts. I like the look of her tits hoisted up, but I can't wait to set them free. I get the last button undone, slowly move the shirt off her shoulders, and down her arms. As my hands glide down her arms, goosebumps appear on her skin.

I lean down, kissing the stranger before I lift her onto her bed, making her squeal. I unbutton the fly on my jeans, ignoring the fact that I am going to wake up in a few hours regretting what I am doing. I lay down on the girl, pressing her into the firm mattress.

"I hope you're ready for one hell of a ride," The girl hooks her leg over my hip, pushing her body into mine until I am on my back and she is on top of me.

Even if I'm not ready, there is no way I am going to let this stop now.

A high-pitched squealing of "Shit!" wakes me up.

I sit up so fast the room begins to spin, making my head pound harder as the whiskey from last night comes back to kick my ass with one hell of a hangover. I look around the strange room as the memory of walking in on Lilah being fucked by another guy slams painfully in my mind. The rest of last night plays like a slow-motion movie in my head. Fuck, I need to get my truck from the bar. I know Poppy will take me, but I might spare myself some embarrassment by taking the walk of shame.

I look around the room with boxes scattered around, as the sound of the shower running from the bathroom. This is my chance to sneak out while she is busy, and I won't have to be a bigger dick by not giving my number or rejecting her if she asks to do this again. I get out of her hard bed and gather my clothes and shoes are scattered across the messy bedroom. As I walk through her living room, I clumsily put on my clothes as fast as possible. Once my last shoe is on, I open the door, getting blinded by the rising sun.

I jog along the sidewalk to my apartment building, and Lilah's SUV is in the spot she normally parks in. Shit, I was hoping she wasn't going to be home. I was too drunk to fight with her last night, and this morning I'm too hungover to have the energy to break up with her. The good news is I don't see Lewis's Jeep, so I know he's already left for the gym, but Poppy's Mini is parked in her usual spot. Even though I don't want to break up with Lilah right now, putting this conversation off for later sounds worse.

I take a deep breath. This feels harder than I thought. Not only are we breaking up, but I am going to have to tell Lilah she is also going to need to find somewhere else to live.

"Jax!" I hear my name being called by my best friend, Poppy.

I look up to see her walking in my direction. She is wearing leggings and an oversized shirt with our school's logo across her chest.

"Hey." I try to plaster on a smile as I walk to meet her, so we don't have to yell through the parking lot.

"Where were you last night?" Poppy cups her hands around her eyes.

"I needed some time to myself." I shrug, looking down at Poppy. "Can you take me to get my truck later?"

Her eyes are bloodshot and puffy. I know she has been crying, which means she and Lewis were fighting again.

"Is everything okay?" she bites the corner of her mouth. "Did you and Lilah get into a fight, too?"

"Something like that." I look away from Poppy. "I got drunk and couldn't drive home."

"Oh, I ask because I could hear Lilah crying last night. I didn't know if I should go talk to her, so I hid in my room until Lewis came home." I look back at Poppy. "Yeah, do you want to go get it now?"

My jaw ticks as I begin grinding my teeth. I don't know what to tell Poppy. Lilah is her best friend and Lewis's sister. I don't want to say anything could hurt Poppy. I also don't want her to feel like she must take sides.

"I need to talk to Lilah first." I rub the back of my head. "I walked in on Lilah with another guy last night."

Poppy gasps, wrapping her arms around me and burying her face in my chest. I feel her hands rub up and down my back as she tries to comfort me.

"I'm so sorry." Poppy's small voice is muffled, but I can still hear how sincere she is.

I put my hands on Poppy's shoulders, lightly pushing her off me. I don't want to talk about this, and with Poppy holding onto me like she is trying to squeeze the pain out of me, making the hurt I've been trying to push away harder to ignore.

"I'll be okay." I smile weakly. "I seriously need to go talk to Lilah. I'll see you later."

I move past Poppy, and thankfully, she doesn't try to say anything else. The closer I get to my apartment, the more tense my shoulders become. My stomach turns, making me want to vomit, but I'm not sure if the sickening feeling is from my hangover or having to confront Lilah. I think I would rather have someone punch me in the face right now.

I open the door to a quiet apartment and the familiar smell of Lilah's and Poppy's perfumes. The smell is too overwhelming right now, making me dizzy.

"Jax! Is that you?" Lilah hollers from the back of the apartment, where our room is.

I slowly walk through the living room. I don't think I can reply, because my voice will come out sounding broken. Lilah walks out of the room, and the sight of her in a tiny dark green dress leaves nothing to the imagination is like a punch to the gut. She has a pair of heels in her hand, making me wonder where she is going in a dress like that.

"Going out?" I ask, crossing my arms over my chest.

She tucks some of her perfectly curled hair behind her ear. "Yeah, the girls and I are going to hit the town later."

"Hmm…" I look her up and down.

I don't believe a word she is saying, because she wouldn't be this dressed up so early in the day if she was going out later. She would never be caught dead going out in the same outfit she wore all day. This proves to me that breaking up with her is the right thing to do. Even if I could forgive her for cheating on me, I don't think I could ever trust her again.

I step around Lilah, walking into my room. "I think you need to start looking for another place to live."

"Jax," Lilah grabs my hand. I look back at her, resisting the urge to pull away from her. "Can we work this out?" she asks, her voice breaking.

I look back at her and find she is red in the face as tears well in her eyes. I know I am hurting her, but walking in on her naked dancing with someone else is destroying me.

"No, we can't." I shake my head.

"All I wanted to do was experiment some." She rolls her eyes.

I walk away from her and start taking the sheets off the bed. "That's what you said last night." I throw the used bedding to the side. "I'm sorry if not wanting to share my girlfriend is a bad thing. I don't even know what you mean by experimenting, because keeping it a secret feels a lot like cheating to me."

Lilah huffs. "I didn't think you would want to know the details. Would you have reacted the same way if you walked in on me with another girl, or would you have wanted to join us?"

"I would have reacted the same way, because you kept it from me. If you wanted to try new things, we could have done it together." I cross my arms, looking down at my bed. If I could burn the mattress, I would.

"I know, but doing some things with other people has a different feeling..."

I turn around, facing Lilah, cutting her off. "Exactly, it is cheating, because there are feelings involved."

"What would have happened if I told you I wanted to sleep with other guys but wanted to stay together?" Lilah narrows her eyes at me.

"I would have broken up with you, but with no anger mixed in."

"Why? I'm not angry. I'm hurt you don't want to accept this part of me." Lilah screams, trying to make me feel guilty or something.

"I'm hurt you thought I would be okay with it, and you started experimenting with who knows what without telling me. You could have exposed me to God knows what, and I wouldn't have any idea. You thought you were trying new things and new people, but to me, you were cheating."

"Can we please move past this? I don't want to break up." Lilah is now fully crying.

"Let me ask you one thing." My hands ball into a fist at my sides. I'm trying so hard not to yell at her. "Would it hurt you if I were sleeping with other girls without you knowing for the same amount of time you were experimenting?" I say holding up air quotes when I say "experimenting."

Lilah gasps, her face paling at my words. I hate myself for spitting back in her face, but I need her to understand how I feel.

"You're being difficult and dramatic." Lilah tries to take a step towards me, but I take a step back. "I never meant to hurt you."

"But you did." I cross my arms over my chest, shifting my weight from foot to foot. "I can't keep doing this. I'll sleep on the couch until you can find a new place to live." I sit on the mattress as Lilah runs out of the room sobbing.

A part of me wants to chase after her, so I can comfort her, but I can't. I know I won't forgive her, but I don't like how to upset she is, but I can't get over the choices she has made when she didn't even consider mine.

After some time has passed, a soft knock on the door makes me tense. I'm not exactly sure, because I have sat on my bed with my head in my hands.

"Jax, are you ready to go get your truck?" The door slowly starts to open, and I can see Poppy's light blonde hair.

She is petite with no real curves to her. She is gorgeous and doesn't need the sexy little curves to drive men wild, because she looks like a little doll with her pale skin and big doe-like eyes. There was a time when I would love to make her mine. However, is impossible now.

"Sure, I'll meet you there." I stand up, but before I can take a step, Poppy walks up to me.

"Jax, I am so sorry about what happened between you and Lilah." Poppy wraps her arms around my waist. "She called me and told me you broke up with her. She wasn't forthcoming with the details, but after some prying, she finally caved. What she did was awful."

I tense. "I don't want this to ruin your friendship with her."

Poppy steps back, looking up at me. "I'm not going to lie to you or her. What she did to you and how she has clearly hurt you makes me so mad." Poppy balls her hands into tight, white-knuckled fists. "There are no excuses for cheating, even if the other person doesn't see it that way."

Poppy and I agree, probably more than she will ever realize.

"Yeah, but there is nothing I can do about it now other than try to move on." I walk out of my room, and for the first time in a couple of hours, I can breathe a little easier. "Let's go get my truck."

"After, do you want to go get tacos?"

I don't want to go anywhere. If I'm honest, I also don't want to be stuck in my room with all the memories I have with Lilah in here. includes the most recent events. However, I know Poppy is secretly worried about me, and getting out in a more productive way than last night couldn't hurt, right?

"Yeah, tacos sound good." I follow Poppy through the living room and out to her little car.

"Let's bring your matchbox car back here after we get my truck." I chuckle darkly.

I don't feel like myself in half to get in her car. I'm a tall guy, and riding in her car is not comfortable.

"That's fine. I know you don't like being in my car." Poppy unlocks the door.

"Should we call Lewis and see if he wants to meet us?" I get in, almost hitting my head on the roof of her soft top.

Poppy has a bright cherry red Mini convertible, and I couldn't picture her in a different car. She is so cute sitting in the driver's seat. Her fingers flex on the steering wheel.

"Um, we kind of got into a fit and he left last night. He hasn't come home since."

Lewis and Poppy have been fighting so much lately, and I hate hearing the hurt in her voice.

"Well, we will have a better time without him." I put my hand on Poppy's thigh.

"Yeah, you're probably right." Poppy turns the radio up.

That was her silent way of telling me she doesn't want to talk about Lewis right now, and who am I to argue, because I don't want to talk about Lilah right now.

CHAPTER 2

POPPY

The front door slams shut, making me jump. Growing up with an alcoholic father who liked to take his anger out on me, unexpected noises like doors slamming can trigger me. More times than I would like to admit, I am sucked into a memory from things, taking me out of reality and back to my father, Jack's, house in the most horrific and terrifying time in my life. I don't know if Lewis or Jax is home, but either way, they are stomping way too loudly. The closer the footsteps get to my bedroom door, the more my music theory homework begins to blur, and I get sucked into one of the many horrific memories I have when I lived with my dad.

He would come home in a drunken rage, ready to take his anger out on me. My stomach churns, and my whole body goes rigid, waiting for the door to fly open, banging against the wall. My dad would stand on unsteady feet in the doorway, backlit from the hall light. He would sometimes stay there, building on the fear that was already clawing at my heart, to stumble away, because he was too drunk to punish me, or he wanted me to know he was home. He was taunting me, letting me know he could do whatever he wanted, including terrorizing his daughter. Sometimes were worse than when he would come home to scare me, because he would come into my room and beat me, punishing me for whatever he thought I did wrong, even if I didn't do anything at all.

I hated the life I had when I lived with Jack. Some nights, I would lie awake wondering if things would have gotten bad if my mom had never gotten sick and passed away from breast cancer when I was ten years old. I know asking myself isn't healthy, because I can't change the past. However, I did get out, and I have a lifetime of thanks to give to Jax and his family for saving me.

I shake my head, trying to clear the fog clouding my current reality. Sometimes getting out of the clutches of an anxiety attack is easy, while other times the world around me slips away, making escaping the darkening feelings and memories impossible to come out of. I can make out Lewis's voice from either the kitchen or the living room, but I can't tell what he is saying from the sounds of my dad's expensive loafers tapping on the hardwood floor. I know he isn't here because he is dead, but the reminder doesn't stop the tears from falling down my face as fear churns in my stomach. I bet he is calling to get a flight to go visit another college, because he says he has been unhappy with this school. We are going into our senior year of college, and he still tries to blame me for him not going to his dream college, but I was the one who told him to go, and we could go long distance, but he didn't want that either.

We fight about this all the time, and I am tired of fighting. Sometimes having a big-shot football player as a boyfriend sucks.

"Poppy, you home?" Lewis hollers, sounding way too cheerful.

"I'm in our room!" I yell back, closing my laptop and notebook.

Lewis struts into the room with a sandwich in one hand, and he tosses his gym bag towards the closet with the other. "You will never guess who called me after I got out of the gym."

"I'm guessing a school based on how excited you are." I pull my knees up to my chest, hugging my legs.

"Yeah, but this is the school I have been waiting for, you know, my dream college. I never should have turned them down the first time." Lewis takes a huge bite out of his sandwich. "They are offering me a walk-on spot on the team and a damn good scholarship," he says between bites. "This is my last chance to get on the team. We are graduating after this year. I already put my eligibility out to play pro, and I need a better team."

I nod, unsure what to say. No matter how I answer, it'll turn into a fight. He knows I don't like him looking into other schools, especially during preseason, which has already started, and it doesn't feel right for him to leave the team now.

But that's not the only reason I hate the idea. It's just the easier one to admit. How am I supposed to tell him that his search for something better, his way of trying to make himself happy so we can be together, is also hurting me? I rest my chin on my knees. "I'm happy for you…"

I pause, trying to wrap my head around the things he is saying. I hiccup, trying to fight off the strong emotions bubbling in the pit of my stomach. "This is what you've always wanted," I whisper.

Lewis's head jerks in my direction. "Don't start this shit now. I'm in a good mood, and I don't want you to ruin it." Lewis snaps at me.

I wince at Lewis's harsh tone. I thought I was saying something nice. I wasn't lying, I am happy for him, but I'm sad for me. I have some serious doubts about whether our relationship will be able to withstand the distance now. We've had too many issues in the past couple of years, and I think being apart is going to ultimately break us. Lewis is my first love; he was my first everything, but I'm slowly learning that sometimes you must let love go. I wish I were brave enough to tell him to go follow his dreams, because I want him to be happy, even if that means we are not together anymore.

"Lewis, I am genuinely happy for you. I know you've wanted to go to this school your whole life, and I want you to do it, but I hope you will be happy, but you act like this decision doesn't affect me, too."

Lewis yanks open the closet door, pulling down a small suitcase from the top shelf. I flinch when he slams the luggage down on the bed. He looks at me with narrowed eyes, putting his hands on his hips. "What do you expect me to say, Poppy? I came to this damn school to be with you. I hate it here, and I am not happy." The way he spits his words at me makes me flinch with every syllable, making me regret saying something.

I watch silently as he begins taking clothes out of the drawers, tossing them toward his suitcase. I know I made him mad, but I feel like he doesn't care about me anymore.

"I'm sorry," I mutter, putting my head down on my knees, hiding the tears falling down my cheeks. "How long are you going to be gone?" My voice cracks, so I know Lewis can hear me crying.

I don't look up, but I can hear Lewis moving around the room, still packing his bag. "Well, it depends. I want to take this offer, but I want to get a feel for the team, because moving like I'm a huge risk, and I want to make sure I am making the right decision. If that is the case, I may have to look for a place and register for classes." I look up as I watch Lewis zip up the suitcase. "I don't know how long that will take."

He may not realize what he said, but he confirms he's not considering me in all of this. I'm not saying I don't want him to go, because the last thing I want to do is hold him back. My stomach churns again, because maybe we've been holding each other back this whole time, and I'm now realizing. His moving to another college and state might be what we need for us to soar. My heart thumps painfully in my chest at the thought of what it could mean.

"I'm going to miss you," I whisper.

Lewis sighs, "Can we drop it? I don't want to fight." Lewis moves his suitcase by the door. "There's a frat party tonight, and I would like to have a good time."

I get out of bed and walk to the bathroom door. "I have a lot of homework. How about we go to dinner, and after, you can go to the party?"

This wouldn't be the first time I'd declined to go to a party with Lewis.

"If that is what you want, but this could be our last party together since I'm hoping to transfer." Lewis gives me a half smile.

"Alright, I guess I can go to the party for a little bit, and I can get a ride home when I am ready to leave."

Lewis walks up to me with a half-smile. "Thanks."

Lewis's eyes glaze over in a lust-filled haze. I know what he wants as he slowly bends to me. I haven't seen that look in quite some time, but the one I miss is the one you read about in books or see in movies, the one making you feel like you're the only girl in the world. The more we fight, the less I feel like that with Lewis. His left hand moves to the back of my neck as his right one finds the small of my back, holding me close to his body as he leans down, kissing my neck.

"Lewis," I sigh, putting my arms around his neck.

He bends down some more, kissing me deeply. Lewis has always known how to kiss me so that my toes curl and the world around us disappears. Lewis guides me to the bed, and when the back of my knees hit the soft sheets, he gently lays me down. Lewis lies on top of me, his weight pressing down on me, and he moves some hair off my face.

"I love you," Lewis says, kissing me.

The music is blasting through the speakers so loud the bass feels like it is vibrating my bones. I've been at the party for three hours after Lewis made love to me. Jax and Lewis are probably wasted, so I'm waiting for them to tell me they want to go home so I can drive them. I slowly walk up the stairs, passing a bunch of drunk sorority girls who are not paying attention to anyone around them. I hear one say Jax's name, so I am thinking she is trying to get enough liquid courage to hit on him. Little does she know that he would probably take her and her friend to a room to help him forget about Lilah.

I finally find the end of the restroom line and lean against the wall. I pull my phone out, mindlessly doomscrolling, trying to ignore one of the girls in front of me with messy hair and smeared makeup as she gets out of bed with a guy.

"Yeah, Lewis knows what he is doing, and he is wild. Best sex I've ever had," the girls giggle. "I'm surprised he agreed to fuck since I know he has an annoying little girlfriend."

Please tell me I'm not hearing them correctly.

"Yeah, and she has the stupidest name ever. Can you believe she is named after a flower?" The girl's friend who hooked up with Lewis says, flipping her hair.

I try to fight back the tears threatening to spill out of my eyes as they continue to talk about Lewis and how he cheated on me. I don't care about them insulting my name, because I love my name and the meaning behind it. However, hearing what Lewis did, especially after practically forcing me to come here, stings worse than if they had slapped me in the face.

"I told you when I hooked up with him a couple of weeks ago, you would have no issues getting him to bed."

How can two people be so cruel, but I should say three, because Lewis agreed to go to bed with them. I mean, I shouldn't be this surprised since I've had suspicions; he's been unfaithful for a while. I quickly pull up the group chat I have with Lewis and Jax. I text them I'm not feeling well, and I'm going to get a car to go home, but to call me when they need a ride.

I try to move past two girls without them seeing me, but Walsh moves down the hall with his girlfriend, Lidia, next to him.

"Hey, Poppy, are you okay?" He asks, making the two girls Lewis cheated on me with, turn around.

Their jaws drop as they see my red cheeks and tears in my eyes, but I try to avoid looking at them.

"Ugh, yeah. I'm not feeling well." I say, leaving the line.

"Oh, if you need to go home, we'll make sure Lewis and Jax get home." Lidia smiles warmly.

"Do you need a ride?" Walsh asks with his eyebrows knitting together.

"Oh, no!" I shake my head. "I have a car waiting for me out front." I lie easily.

I walk away, not waiting for them to reply. I can feel the eyes of all the people around us on me. A couple of other girls smile at me with wide, knowing smiles, as if they are trying to hint that those two weren't the only ones Lewis has hooked up with. I walk down the stairs. When I get to the bottom step, I hear some chick in a tight black dress talking to her friend say Lewis's name. I stop out of sick curiosity when she says she hooked up with Lewis, and he has been sleeping with some girl at a Texas college whenever he gets the chance.

My heart stops, but when it starts pounding again, a sharp thump in my chest is almost painful enough to bring me to my knees. I can't stay here and listen to this anymore. How could I be so stupid? I never realized Lewis had been cheating on me this whole time. I would bet the girl in Texas is probably Lana, so does this mean he's been cheating on me since we started dating?

A massive sob stops in my throat, making me choke. The people and the house around me feel like they are closing in on me. I need to get out of here before I throw up all over someone.

I run past a bunch of drunk college students who are either drinking, talking, dancing, or making out as I try to hold down the vomit burning my throat. I guess his leaving is a good thing after all.

I run past two people not paying attention to who is around me, but Jax's voice stops me in my tracks. "POPPY!" I turn around, and his jaw ticks when he sees me crying. "What's wrong?"

"I'm not feeling well, so I'm going home." A wave of nausea passes through me.

"Come on, I'll give you a lift. I haven't had anything to drink yet." He reaches into his pocket, grabbing his keys.

"Are you sure?" I hiccup.

"Yeah, I figured you would want to go home before Lewis and me. Turns out I was right." Jax throws his arm over my shoulder.

"Thanks, Walsh said they would give you guys a ride home if you would like.”

“Nah, I’m going to come back, but I don’t plan on drinking. I am going to hit the gym for team workouts in the morning.”

Jax helps me into his truck, and after I buckle my seatbelt, I lean my head on the cool window.

“Do you and Lewis want to go get breakfast in the morning?” Jax turns the country music he was listening to down so he can talk.

“I will, but Lewis is leaving to go tour a college in Texas in the morning.”

Jax cusses under his breath. He is not happy about Lewis wanting to leave the team and school, but he isn’t going to stop him.

“Cool, I’ll be home from the gym around ten.” Jax pulls up to the curb in front of our apartment building. “Call me if you need anything.”

I climb down, turning toward Jax. He’s my best friend, and I couldn’t imagine my life without him now. “You do the same.” I close the door and walk up the stairs to my apartment.

I unlock the door and step into the dark, quiet living room. I can smell Lewis’s cologne lingering in the air, and tears pool in my eyes again at the thought of him and what the girls were saying replays repeatedly in my mind. I don’t have the actual image of them, not like Jax does with Lilah, but I can still picture it in my head.

UGH! What am I supposed to do now?

I don’t want to fight with Lewis, but I don’t know if I can keep this information to myself. I change into a dark green sweat suit and climb into my bed with a million questions burning in me. I want to know how long he has been unfaithful, even though knowing will hurt too. What if he wants to move to another school as an excuse to break up with me?

I lay there letting the tears free-fall, soaking into my pillowcase. My heart is breaking because Lewis has done something I can’t forgive. I don’t know how I’m going to handle this, and I don’t know how I will ever be able to trust him again. I guess I need to answer the question like a flamethrower to the heart, because maybe I can decide what I should do next.

I continue to lie in bed, curled in a tight ball, trying to think of what I should do. There isn’t anyone in my life I can talk to about this, because they are all connected to Lewis somehow, and this can hurt them, too.

Around three in the morning, my bedroom door softly opens, and a light from the hall spills onto me. Thankfully, my face is covered, and Lewis can't see that I'm still awake. He doesn't go to the bathroom to shower like he normally does. Instead, I peek from under the covers, watching as he strips down to his underwear before climbing into bed behind me.

He pulls me into his arms after he gets settled, and he buries his face in my hair, inhaling deeply. "Lan…" he slurs to a stop before sighing. "Poppy."

Pain squeezes my heart, and I bite my tongue to stop the cry threatening to rip out of my throat. I don't think Lewis knows how much he hurt me right now, not from almost saying another girl's name, but he also reeks of perfume that doesn't belong to me.

Maybe Lewis going to Texas for who knows how long is for the best. Lewis's deep snores fill the room, giving me the perfect opportunity to silently cry. I want to climb out of bed and sleep on the couch, but that could start another fight with Lewis in the morning before he leaves.

Lewis eventually turns in his sleep, and I am no longer feeling trapped in his hold. I feel like I can breathe a little easier, even though sleep never comes. Maybe after he leaves, I will be able to sleep for a couple of hours before I go to breakfast with Jax.

But the only question remaining is: What do I do now? From repeating in my head, and honestly, I think I'm going to have to do something hard, but I've been through worse, and like Roxi, Shane, and my therapist keep telling me, I need to do what will make me happy, no matter how hard it may seem.

I've been through so much not to live the life I want. Constantly fighting with Lewis is not it, because I spent too much of my life fighting, and I think the time has come for me to let him go. I'll give myself the time Lewis is away to figure out exactly how to close this chapter in my life, and when he returns, I will hopefully be a new and stronger version of myself. I know I can gather the courage to stand up to my first love. I need to tell him this isn't working and we need to take time apart from each other. If I do this right, we can end on good terms.

I roll onto my stomach, holding onto my wet, tear-stained pillow. I heave a heavy sigh, close my eyes, and try to think of the good times. It takes me back to the summer after we graduated high school, when

Lewis was traveling with his family a lot, and I spent most of my time with Jax until I drift into a restless sleep.

CHAPTER 3

JAX

Lana's voice is grating on my everlasting nerves as she talks about how the other girls look in their semi-formal dresses. The only students at the dance who are fully dressed up in actual formal attire are the ones on the homecoming court, but in my opinion, they did too much. Don't get me wrong, Lana looks damn good, but she went way too overboard and looks like she is going to prom instead of a football homecoming. Even though in our town, this is as big a deal for everyone as prom.

Then there is Poppy, who looks like the sweet little flower she was named after in her simple red dress. When I say it is backless except for a sexy little X, which I think are the straps of her dress, I wanted to reach out and touch her soft, pale skin has some freckles peppering her skin, but sitting among the freckles are some pink or white scars from what look like scratches I would assume are from her father. She did some kind of wavy hair thing I'm sure took her and my mom a long time to do this afternoon, but she still looks like Poppy, only sparkly. If she looks this amazing now, I can only imagine what she will look like at prom in a much more formal dress, but I guess what I think of Poppy doesn't matter because she is not my date for the dance, since she is my best friend's girlfriend.

Lana and I didn't want to come together, because she wanted Lewis to be her date, and I think for more than the fact he is the captain of the football team. As for me, I can't stand her, but Lana had cornered me at school last week and said we needed to come together because it would look bad if we came alone, since we are on the homecoming court. I was stupid enough to let her talk me into coming with her since I couldn't come with either of the girls I wanted to bring. One of the girls is obviously Poppy, and she is off limits for more than being my best friend's girlfriend, but I can't think about it right now. The other girl is Lilah. who is also my best friend's sister. Lewis doesn't want me to go out with his sister for some reason. Why can't I like a girl without there being any kind of complications?

As if right on cue, Lana whines for what I think is the third time in like ten minutes now. "These girls look as if they are at a normal dance and not a winter formal," she picks up her punch, taking a small sip, puckering her lips, scrunching her nose as if her drink was sour or spiked with something strong.

I chuckle, "They are dressed nicely, you're the one who looks like she belongs at prom or a snooty red-carpet event instead of a homecoming dance in a high school gymnasium." I roll my eyes, turning away from my date, searching the gym for Lewis and Poppy.

I can't help but wonder where the hell they are. I made Poppy promise me that she or Lewis would not leave me alone with Lana for a long time. I don't know if I should be worried about them not being here yet or not, because the police still haven't caught Poppy's abusive father.

Lana huffs, crossing her arms, looking away from me. I bite my lip to hide the satisfied smile I feel from ruffling her feathers. This confirms my thought from earlier; I should have come without a date. Maybe Lana will get tired of me and ditch me for some other unsuspecting guy. Maybe I can even find a cute girl to sneak out to have a good time with until I must meet up with the team at the diner for our after-game tradition in a couple of hours.

"JAX!" I roll my eyes at the whiny sound of my name. "I WANT TO DANCE!" Lana screeches in my ear.

I reluctantly turn my attention back to her. Lana has her eyes on her friends, who are several feet away, dancing, if you want to call the grinding thing they are doing. How do I tell her nicely to go dance and leave me the hell alone? I'm not typically an asshole, but there is something about Lana that makes me want to be a dick to her. I don't know how Lewis could stand hooking up with her for as long as he did.

My phone vibrates in my jacket pocket, saving me from having to go dance with my date. Poppy's name and a picture of us at a college football game we went to with my parents' names flashing across my screen.

I glance up from my phone at Lana. "Go ahead, have fun, I have to take this."

I jog to the nearest door, busting through the heavy metal double doors, and I walk into a hallway decorated with posters and banners in our school colors. My ears start ringing from the music I can still hear on the other side of the heavy metal doors that lead to the gym.

"Hey, where are you guys!" I yell into the phone, or at least it sounds like I am yelling, because my ears are still ringing like I left a concert, and I can't hear anything right.

I move further away from the gym doors, trying to see if it will help me hear better, and that's when I hear some grumbling in the background. But I still can't tell what is going on from the static buzzing from Poppy's side of the phone.

Another unrecognizable grumbling sound comes from the other end of the phone, "What did you say?" I try to yell a little louder.

The sound of the music from the gym blares through the hallway, momentarily distracting me from my one-sided phone call. I turn around, and the sight of Lana walking out of the gym holding hands with Drew makes me chuckle. I should be pissed my date is going off to hook up with one of my teammates, but I'm more relieved than anything, because this means Lana can be his problem for the rest of the night, and I can find someone else to entertain later, but first, I need to figure out what the hell is going on with Poppy and Lewis.

My relief from not having to deal with Lana's drama vanishes as the sound of Poppy's high pitched blood curdling scream fills my ear.

I can hear her loudly yell, "HELP!" There is another crackle of static, the hairs on my arms stand, and I hear Poppy wail, "DAD! STOP!" Some more static, and something else, "par…" static, "lot…" before the phone call drops with an annoying beeping sound.

Would her dad actually come to the school with the risk of being caught? He has a warrant out for his arrest for missing court, among other charges I can't get into right now. What did Poppy mean by "par lot"? As I'm trying to figure out what she was trying to tell me, I try to call her again. Each time I dial Poppy's number, the call doesn't go through. I try to call Poppy back, but the call goes straight to the sound of the automated voice "your call cannot be…" I hang up and try calling one more time, but I'm greeted by the same message.

"SHIT!" I kick a trash can nearby, making it fall over and slide across the floor, leaving a small trail of trash behind.

I run back into the gym, desperately looking around for an adult. I push past a group of students who have gathered by the gym doors, and all of them begin yelling different things at me. Finally, I spot Coach Denver.

I start weaving past students, dry humping each other on the dance floor, desperately trying to get to Coach Denver as fast as I can, but in my frustration and haste, I begin shouting, "Move!" at anyone who won't get out of my way.

I pass a table full of cute girls, I would normally stop and chat up until one of them agreed to leave with me, but right now I don't have the time because I know Poppy is in trouble.

"Coach," I try yelling over the music, but he doesn't look in my direction. I holler a few more times before he finally looks my way with a wide smile splitting his face in two, making the skin around his eyes wrinkle.

"Jax, good game tonight. You played..." Coach Denver starts cheerfully, but I cut him off.

"Coach, I got this weird call from Poppy. I couldn't hear everything she said, because she was screaming, but I think she said her and Lewis are in the parking lot and something about her dad." Coach Denver's smile fades as he realizes what I'm trying to say.

One day after school, and the parking lot had cleared out, Poppy was walking to the field to watch Lewis and mine's football practice, her father grabbed her and took her to a classroom to beat her almost to death. She managed to call my father for help, and when they called asking for a staff member to help, Coach Denver didn't hesitate. He ran out of practice and stayed with her until the ambulance drove away.

"Jax." Coach Denver puts a hand on my shoulder, clearing his throat. "Call the police and your parents." Coach drops his hand from my shoulder and jogs away from me.

I watch from a distance as Coach Denver goes to the group of other teachers, and the principal, whom I didn't notice, was over there. I wish I knew what he was saying to them, because all their smiles fall before every adult in the little circle practically sprints to the emergency exit leading to the student parking lot while Poppy's science teacher calmly walks to the stage.

I stand there trying to figure out what I should do. I know I need to call the police officers and my parents, but I'm fighting the urge to run out of the emergency exit to find Poppy for myself. The music stops playing, and the crowd of teenagers groans.

Mr. Franks walks to the microphone, clearing his throat. "Students, I need you all to stay calm, but we are now in a lockdown. Please find a seat, and once things are under control, the dance will continue." Mr. Franks moves from the mic stand, taking the microphone with him.

He begins walking around the gym, directing my classmates where to go, but I know the last thing I can do right now is sit in one of these uncomfortable chairs. I look around the gym trying to decide what I should do first, and the exit sign glowing in the distance is calling my name.

I begin walking toward the exit, but I don't get too far, because Mr. Franks sees me, saying loudly over the intercom, "Taylor, find a seat!"

I shake my head, pushing past everyone who is now walking in the direction of the tables, not paying attention to who I am shoving past.

I hear a few shrieks consisting of "HEY!" or "WATCH IT!" being yelled at me, but I don't have time to stop or apologize.

I shoulder past another crowd of people near a table, running into one of my teammates. He doesn't yell at me, but he and the other guys he is talking with begin to follow me, calling after me. They keep saying things like "Jax, what's up?" and "Are you okay?"

Before I can get through the doors leading to the parking lot, one of the guys pats me on the shoulder. "Jax, what's going on? You look like you're ready to start a fight?" Brandon asks with his thick black eyebrows scrunched together. At least he isn't pissed I angrily pushed past him.

"All I know is Poppy is in trouble," I say, busting through the heavy metal door, which leads to a parking lot, not caring what anyone has to say right now.

When I walk into the darkness of our school's parking lot, adrenaline begins to pump through my blood. I look around, but I don't see Lewis or Poppy. Hell, I don't even see the teachers. I'm beginning to freak out, hoping like hell we can find them before it's too late.

"Jax, what can we do to help?" Brandon asks as the rest of the football team, minus Drew, circles around me. We huddle like we would on the field. "Is Lewis with Poppy?"

"Yeah, Lewis is with her." My jaw ticks from the jealousy burning through me at the reminder that my best friend is with one of my dream girls.

I know I shouldn't be jealous of Lewis and Poppy, because he is my best friend, but Lewis and I both have had a crush on her since youth football. I remember she would come with her mom in a little cheerleading costume, her long, pale blonde hair braided down her back, tied with little red ribbons on the ends, yelling and cheering for Lewis and me on the sidelines. All three of our moms were best friends before we were born, so they used our games as an excuse to hang out even though they didn't need one. They would joke about which of their sons would marry Poppy since we are all so close in age.

I look around the parking lot. "POPPY!" I cup my hands around my mouth, yelling, "LEWIS!" They must be somewhere around here, right?

We walk past a row of cars, and I hear a few more voices close to me echo their names. Brandon and the rest of the team are following me. I can tell they are going to stay to help look for Lewis and Poppy, not knowing what is waiting out here. If I'm being honest, I don't either or scares the shit out of me. We begin walking through the parking lot, scattering around different cars as we search for Poppy and Lewis. I round my truck, and I can see the teachers walking in between the vehicles as they holler for them as well.

This parking lot isn't big. Where the hell can they be? I cup my hands around my mouth again, yelling their names. Panic is gripping my pounding heart, making me wonder if this is a fraction of the fear Poppy has lived with since her mom died. That thought makes me want to find her more, which I didn't think was possible.

"Poppy!" The teachers turn in my direction when they hear me.

Principal Lester walks up to me with the look of pity etched on her normally soft features. "Jax, I need you and the rest of the team to go back inside to the gym."

I open my mouth to argue, but stop when Coach Rufis joins us, "Son, you do as you're told. This situation is not safe for anyone involved, and we can't risk any more students getting hurt." Coach Rufis pats my shoulder. "The school is on lockdown. You guys will be safe there."

I shake my head. "Sir, I don't mean any disrespect, but I can't go back to the gym and sit around, waiting to see if my best friends are okay." I cross my arms over my chest, trying to stand my ground.

"Jax, what would help right now is for you to do as I asked in the gym." Coach Denver joins us. "We need you to call the police and your parents."

"Fine, but after I am still going to look for Lewis and Poppy." I begin pulling my phone out of my pocket.

"Make the calls," Principal Lester sighs, "The rest of you gentlemen need to go back to the gym and are not open for negotiations." Principal Lester begins to turn around but stops.

"Yes, ma'am," Brandon lifts one side of his mouth, but I know for a fact he and the rest of the team aren't going back to the gym either.

"Brandon, will you call the police, so I can call my dad?" I unlock the screen of my phone.

The sooner we get these phone calls done, the faster I can continue to help look for Poppy and Lewis. Knowing as much as I do about Jack, Poppy's father, I know we can't waste time because at any moment, he could lose control and hurt them. For the first time tonight, I am happy Poppy is Lewis, because he will do anything to protect her.

"Jax." My dad yawns into the phone.

"Dad, I don't have much time to explain, but Poppy is in trouble. We are trying to find her and Lewis in the parking lot at school." I say in a rush, hoping he can understand me.

My dad, who is normally composed, curses under his breath before yelling for my mom. "We are on our way." We hang up without saying goodbye, and I watch as my teammates spread out once more, looking for Lewis and Poppy.

My teammates kind of have a hint of how dangerous Poppy's dad is by seeing her bruises a couple of months ago, but she and her father are the only ones who truly know all the details of what has happened to her. That is, if his drunken ass can remember.

I can still only guess how bad it was at home with him, because I saw what she looked like the day she moved in. I saw her, and I knew she needed to get out of there even though she tried to lie to me about why she was so beat up the day I found her. I also witnessed her father harass her on more than one occasion. She was living with us when her father showed up at our school, and he put her in the hospital. The sight of her broken and bleeding in her car after she tried to find somewhere safe to hide almost destroyed me.

I pass a truck, and my frustration doubles when I still can't find them. Even though time feels like it is frozen and hours have passed since I got Poppy's phone call, I know we haven't been looking for them all that long.

I round a silver SUV, "Popp..." I begin to yell again, but I stop dead in my tracks.

The sight in front of me makes me want to vomit. Poppy is standing in her pretty little red dress with her perfect back exposed, begging to be touched. Her hair is a rumpled mess of knots, and her makeup is staining her flawless pale skin as tears stream down her horror-struck face. Even locked in the state of terror, she is still the most beautiful girl I have ever seen.

I look in the direction where Poppy's wide, tearful eyes are locked in place. She looks like a deer stuck in headlights with wide eyes, her mouth dropped open like she is screaming silently. Lewis, who is wrestling on top of Jack, is not something I was expecting to see, but as if this scene isn't bad enough, Jack has one of his arms raised, aiming a gun right at Poppy. My heart pumps harder and painfully in my chest as my blood rushes through my veins, making me feel more anxious.

I lift onto the balls of my feet, and I begin to charge in Poppy's direction. I get the same feeling I do at the height of football games when everything around me is moving in slow motion or time feels like it has stopped completely. As I speed closer to Poppy, I can hear the slur of curses coming from her father, but the smells hit me like a brick wall, making my stomach roll. They are strong and foul enough I feel like I can pass out from the stench. I don't think I will ever be able to forget the smell of vomit mixed with stale cigarettes, body odor, and Poppy's sweet perfume.

I feel my arms go around Poppy's small body, and at the same time, I hear a deafening pop come from my left.

I roll over onto my back in bed, putting my pillow over my face, trying to drown out the echoes of my screams and the sound of the gun going off in my head. Like most nights when I dream about being shot, I wake drenched with sweat, my heart pounding so hard it is going to come out of my chest.

"Fuck," I curse under my breath at the soft sound of Poppy's tiny feet walking on the wood floor in the hallway.

I hate waking up Poppy when I have a nightmare, because she knows what I'm dreaming about. I try not to make her feel more guilty about that night than she already does. Poppy is the type of person who would gladly sacrifice herself before anyone she cares about got hurt, but none of us would ever allow that. What I told her when I woke up in the hospital was true. Everything we did and went through was worth saving Poppy. Still, the night of the winter formal changed all of our lives.

I try to focus on the silence in my room, but the sound of the gun haunts me even as I sit up in my bed trying to get a hold of myself. Poppy is coming in here to see if I'm okay, but I don't think I will be able to act like I'm still asleep when she comes into my room tonight. I know she is going to crawl into my bed and comfort me until she falls asleep, while I try to fight the raging hard on, I get whenever she is in my bed. My heart begins to pound with sheer anticipation of getting to feel the soft skin of Poppy's arm touching mine as she lies too close to me, her sweet perfume enveloping me in a warm hug, and the lulling sounds of her soft snores as she sleeps, driving me crazy. Every time she holds me like this, I fall more in love with her, and I can't seem to help it.

I've always had feelings for Poppy, but I never acted on them out of respect for Lewis. I followed bro code even when I didn't want to. After she moved in, and I saw my parents wanted to include her in the family, I tried to change how I felt about her again. Each attempt was tough, but I started dating Lilah, and as our relationship grew, I found myself gradually forgetting my feelings for Poppy again. Until Lilah and I broke up a couple of months ago.

I remember a day when we were in middle school, Lewis lost it in the locker room after hearing one of the guys on the team say he was going to ask Poppy to the upcoming dance. Lewis yelled through the whole locker room lobby no one is allowed to ask Poppy out, and he told everyone to spread the word around school. I don't think his behavior in the locker room was right, but I never told him how I felt.

I guess I was hoping I would eventually find another girl who would capture my attention as much as Poppy always did. I was falling deep for Lewis's older sister, but after we broke up and Poppy started coming into my room after I woke up from a nightmare, those old feelings began to resurface, and I am finding it harder to bury them again.

I know I can't have her since she is with my best friend, Lewis, but she has been one of my biggest temptations since I learned what girls and sex were.

Poppy knocks once on my bedroom door. She has started coming into my room after I wake up screaming from a nightmare, a couple of weeks after Lilah and I broke up. Sometimes, she waits in the hallway like she is debating whether coming in here is the right thing to do, and other times, I wonder if she is listening to see if I have a girl over. The door opens, interrupting my thoughts. After a couple of minutes, Poppy finally walks in without saying a word.

My eyes watch her as she tiptoes around my bed, almost like she is afraid someone other than us will hear her in my room. Lewis is gone again, trying to get on a football team at another college, and we don't know when he'll be home.

Poppy turns around to sit on my bed, and I watch her every move. My eyes burn, needing the sweet relief blinking would bring, but damn it, she came in here wearing a barely-there silky dark blue nightgown falling right at the curve of her small but delicious-looking ass. Seeing her in these tiny pajamas, I'm instantly reminded of the time I was a senior in high school at lunch with the boys, and I joked about telling my parents Poppy was a ten and had a body made for fucking. I never actually told my parents, but damn, I was right, and I would give anything for the chance to have one night with her. I'm not stupid, I know I will never get to, which pisses me off sometimes.

I'm still sitting up, so I lift my white comforter for Poppy as she climbs into my bed. I lay back down, trying to quickly get comfortable as Poppy gets under the blanket, rolling over until she is holding me, putting an arm over my stomach, and hooking one leg over mine. Her body feels good and fits perfectly against mine. I put my arm around her back, resting my hand at the small of her back.

Poppy hasn't always come in here wearing sexy little nighties and cuddling up to me like this. She started this sometime in the past couple of months, when she and Lewis had started fighting a lot more. Around that time, Lewis had become more serious about looking into transferring to a new college. I think she might be feeling lonely and wants to comfort herself, too.

Our coach is pissed at Lewis and rightfully so. The only times a player should leave our team early is if they get injured, kicked off for various reasons like academics, or if they are going to go pro, but you never leave for another college team, like Lewis wants to do. He doesn't even have a legit reason for wanting to leave, other than he never wanted to go to this school. He had the opportunity to go to the school he wanted when we graduated. The scholarship was better than the one he got here, but he didn't want to be away from Poppy.

Poppy begins rubbing lazy circles on my stomach next to my belly button with her finger, and my body begins to burn, begging me to tell her I need more of her gentle touch. Her soft skin and light touch help me forget about my nightmare, but make warmth swirl in my stomach, replacing the image of Jack with a gun pointed at Poppy with dirty thoughts of all the things I want to do with Poppy right now. I keep reminding myself she is completely off-limits, making her even more tempting. My body tenses, and my blood begins to boil at the slow anger taking over me from wanting someone so much but knowing I will never get to have her.

"When is…" I clear my throat. "Lewis coming back from looking at whatever college he went to tour this time?"

I know asking about Lewis will make her move away from me, even though that is the last thing I want. I desperately need a few extra inches of space from her because I can't think clearly with her close to me, and the last thing I want to do is say or do something stupid.

Poppy stiffly rolls over to the edge of the bed with her back facing me. She pulls the bedspread over her head. I know I fucked up because the last time I put my foot in my mouth, she moved a couple of inches away from me, but this time, she covers herself, hiding under my comforter.

"I don't want to talk about Lewis right now." Poppy's voice is muffled by the blanket covering her face. "If you want to talk, we can talk about the nightmare waking up both of us," Poppy finally pulls the blanket up off her head, tucking the soft material under her chin.

For the first time since she tiptoed into my room and crawled into my bed, I see her beautiful, pale face, and she is looking up at me with red, puffy eyes, and I know she has been crying for a while.

"Shit," I curse under my breath.

I know when to put my foot in my mouth sometimes.

"Maybe we should try to get some sleep," Poppy yawns, turning away from me again.

I know Poppy originally came in here to comfort me, but she looks so sad now. I want to make her feel a little better. I pull Poppy into my arms until I am the one spooning her. Poppy readjusts herself a little, but when she moves, her velvety soft hair brushing against my bare chest tickles my nipples, and her soft silk nightgown against my skin feels so good. I know Poppy isn't trying to tease me, but that doesn't stop my body and mind from responding in ways Poppy would be embarrassed about.

I bite on my lip to keep the moan building in my chest from slipping out. I haven't been able to get her off my mind since she came into my room and I saw her in her little nightgown, which hits the curve of her ass.

I need to blow off some steam at the gym or get laid. I know some of the guys on the football team are going to a frat party tomorrow night. I should go somewhere to find a girl or two to help me get Poppy off my mind for a little bit.

The sound of the front door slamming closed makes Poppy jump. "Poppy!" Lewis yells, slurring his words.

Poppy curses under her breath, which is surprising, since she doesn't cuss a lot. "Shit, he's home."

"POPPY!" Lewis's voice is closer, so I'm assuming he has quickly made his way to their room, but his yelling isn't what pisses me off; he is slurring, meaning he came home smashed.

He should know better than to come home wasted and yelling like this. Poppy's dad was a drunk and took his anger out on her, so I know she is probably replaying some of what she went through in her mind with how tense and rigid she is right now lying in my bed.

Poppy once told me that when Lewis comes home like this, he tries to say he goes to the bar, because it helps him clear his mind, but all it does is remind her of her dad coming home drunk and yelling in full rage, ready to take his anger out on his daughter. I think he is building walls and pushing Poppy away. Could he be trying to get Poppy to break up with him before he moves to another college, so he doesn't have to do it himself?

Lewis has been pretty outspoken to me about how pissed he is about playing for a subpar team. I know he still feels, but our team is one of the few that acts as a true team on and off the field. However, we are a division one team, so I never understood what he meant by subpar. We were almost undefeated last year, and I know a lot of this is thanks to Lewis, because better players are signing on so they can be on the same team as him.

Poppy talks to me a little about her relationship and what they are fighting about, but she doesn't want to make me feel like I need to pick sides. I get that, but it doesn't stop Lewis from bitching about how Poppy has been on his case a lot lately about him wanting to leave.

"Jax," Poppy's sweet whisper takes over the grumbling in my head. "I can't see Lewis when he is like this," Poppy sniffles and wipes her nose with the back of her hand. "When he comes home like this, I can't help but be reminded of my father," she whimpers, confirming exactly what I thought.

"What do you want me to tell him?" I pull away from Poppy.

Apparently, I'm willing to do anything for her, including lying to my best friend.

Talking to Lewis is the last thing I want to do right now, but I'm selfish enough that I would rather talk to him than risk Poppy leaving my bed to go to the one she shares with him. I sit up, turning my back to Poppy. I feet hit the soft rung under my bed. I am thankful some mornings I don't have to step on cold hardwood floors first thing in the morning.

I hear the blankets rustle behind me. "Jax, I don't care what you say, make up something, please," Poppy sniffles. "I think if I see him right now, I will say something I can't take back."

I look back at Poppy one more time before I leave my room. I can't believe I'm doing this. I walk the short hall to Poppy and Lewis's bedroom. The door is wide open, and what I see shocks me. Their usually tidy room looks like a tornado went through it. Lewis is digging through their dresser, throwing clothes around. I try not to laugh because he looks like a child searching for a toy in his toy box. When they don't find what they are looking for, they throw what they don't want like it's on fire.

Lewis opens another drawer and begins tossing brightly colored pieces of fabric behind his back. Something bright red flies toward me, and I catch the soft fabric. After a quick inspection, I see I caught a bright red lace thong. I ball them into a fist, and the devilish thought of keeping them sears in my mind, making focusing on why I came in here in the first-place slip from my mind. Lewis still hasn't noticed me, because he is tossing things around with his eyes narrowed and his lips smashed in a thin line. He is huffing and puffing, tearing his way through the room like a raging bull in a China shop, not caring what kind of mess he is leaving behind.

"What's up, man?" I ask, Lewis freezes before turning toward me, red in the face. "Trying to wake up the entire apartment complex?" I raise a single brow.

"Where's Poppy?" Lewis slurs, swaying on his feet, struggling to stay standing from how intoxicated he is.

"I think she mentioned something about girls' night with my mom, but I don't remember." I shrug, trying to make it look like I don't know where she is, even though she is snuggled safely in my bed right now.

"She's been going back home a lot." Lewis sits on the foot of his bed, running a hand through his hair before propping his elbows on his knees, putting his head down in his hand, "She doesn't want to be around me right now, but I guess I don't blame her." Lewis mumbles almost to himself, but I know he is talking to me.

"I'm not going to disagree with you, man." I lean against the door frame, "I'm saying, as your friend, coming home drunk and angry like this is not cool. You know as much as I do about what she lived through with her father. Her not being here is probably a good thing."

"Shit, I didn't mean to get this wasted, but I got the offer I've been waiting for, so I went out to celebrate. I got a little carried away. This is my dream school and team. I've worked my whole life to get in, and I'm not wasting a second opportunity." Lewis looks up at me, and I see his eyes water and some of the color from his face drain, making his normal tan skin look a little paler, "I don't want Poppy to come with me, and I don't want to do the long-distance relationship thing. That is why I came to this school in the first place." He smashes his mouth in a thin line.

I can tell he is stressed about this, and he is handling everything poorly. I feel for him, but I also know they are miserable living in the same state now.

"You've got to do what you think is best for yourself," Lewis nods his head as if he understands what I'm saying, but from the glassiness of his eyes, I doubt he can understand what I'm trying to say to him. "To be fair to Poppy and stop stringing her along. You two have been together since senior year, and after all you guys have been through, I think you two deserve to have an honest conversation about what you want."

"I get it, I'll think about everything tonight." Lewis sighs, "I have to leave in the morning, so I may text Poppy and see if she can come home so we can talk."

"Since we are being honest, I want you to know I'm pissed with how you're leaving the team," Lewis opens his mouth to say something but from the way my eyebrows are pushed together, the firm set of my mouth, and the way I am talking through my teeth, he is smart enough to shut his trap, "I won't back you up on this with the team, but I'm not going to stop you if it means you'll finally be happy."

Lewis mumbles something, but when he talks this time, he speaks a little louder for me to hear him say, "I understand." I turn to go back to bed, but Lewis's words stop me: "I've been a shitty friend, and I'm sorry, man."

I look over my shoulder at someone who used to be my ride or die best friend, but if I'm being honest, since coming to college, I've felt our friendship drifting apart. I'm tired of feeling like a chick talking about our feelings when I want to punch the guy and move on.

"We're good, man, try to sleep the whiskey off." I leave him there and walk back to my room with Poppy's panties still balled up in my fist.

I can hear him start moving around his room again, but he is at least a little quieter. I know he is angry about how college here has gone for him, but he is making all of us miserable as well. Lewis has changed since we came here. He was always a serious no-bullshit type of guy, but lately, the humor he did have seems to have disappeared.

Poppy doesn't stir when I quietly open my bedroom door, feeling relieved she has fallen asleep before I came in here, which means I can stash her little thong in my underwear drawer without her knowing. I walk to my dresser, tucking her panties under my boxer briefs for safekeeping before I go to the side of my bed, lying down on my back with my hands under my head. I know now more than ever she is going to need me tomorrow. Even though Lewis was drunk, I could tell he was serious when he said he wanted to end things with Poppy.

I roll over onto my side, spooning Poppy, and I hold her, because there is a chance I will never get to have this again. My heart thumps in my chest. I love having Poppy in my arms; she fits perfectly into me, almost like she is my missing puzzle piece.

I don't know what tomorrow is going to mean for Poppy and Lewis, but I do know I want to be here for her in case Lewis was serious about ending it with her. His wanting to move is already crushing her, so I can only imagine what breaking up with her will do.

Poppy shifts in my arms, whimpering my name, sounding heartbroken already. I pull her closer to my chest, and I put my head in her neck, inhaling the sweet scent of vanilla. The scent of her lotion or soup goes straight to my head, intoxicating me. Poppy is the type of woman a man can get intoxicated with, and I want to be that man, and for a moment, I almost forget that she is in a relationship with my best friend, but I can forget that, because I will never knowingly allow myself to be a part of someone cheating on their partner.

I pull the comforter over our shoulders and lie there until Poppy's light snores lull me into a deep sleep.

TAYLOR
12
REBOUND

CHAPTER 4

JAX

I blindly reach over, finding the sheets where Poppy was last night, cold. I don't know when she got up, but my stomach falls, and disappointment claws at my heart. I know why she left. She doesn't want Lewis to know she spent the night with me last night while she was avoiding him.

"LEWIS! YOU CAN'T LEAVE LIKE THIS!" Poppy cries out, almost like she is in pain, but I'm pretty sure she is.

I don't hear anything for a second, but I throw my comforter off my legs, and it goes flying across my room, but that is the least of my problems right now. I have a feeling Lewis broke up with Poppy. Lewis hinted at it, but I didn't think he would go through with it.

I get out of bed, and as soon as my feet hit the thick rug over the hardwood floor, I take large steps to get to the living room quickly. I see Lewis's mouth moving, but I don't know if he is talking to Poppy softly or if what he is saying is being drowned out by the ringing in my ears from the headache, building from the liquor I drank last night, but whatever he says causes Poppy to fall onto her knees, crying out in pain like she was slapped in the face.

Lewis looks down at Poppy's trembling body curled in a tight ball at his feet for a long second before he grabs the two large suitcases by the door and storms out of our apartment, slamming the door behind him. I blink the sleep and disbelief of what I saw from my eyes. If Poppy weren't crying on the floor right now, I wouldn't believe Lewis did break up with her.

"Fuck," I run my hands through my hair.

Damn, my mind is spinning from the liquor, but also from the fact that my best friend broke the heart of the girl of both of our dreams, and he was stupid enough to leave her here with me. However, Lewis doesn't know that my feelings for Poppy have been getting mixed up lately.

All I can hear in the quiet living room is soft hiccupping from Poppy sobbing and trying her hardest to breathe through her breaking heart. I walk with slow, careful steps toward Poppy. The closer I get, her sobs become louder, shaking her body even more.

"Poppy," I whisper, trying to keep myself small, so I don't scare her.

I crouch down onto the balls of my feet and lightly place my hand on Poppy's trembling back. She tenses from my light touch for a moment before she looks up at me with glassy, bloodshot eyes, and her face wet with tears. I know I shouldn't find her beautiful when she is hurting like this, but I do.

Poppy looks up at me through her wet lashes for a few moments before she falls into my chest. "OH! JAX!" she cries, wrapping her arms tight around my neck.

I rub my hand down her back, whispering, "SHH. I'm here," I repeat, trying to reassure her everything is going to be okay.

"Jax, he left me." Poppy sniffles and rubs her face on my bare chest, smearing a mixture of tears and hot shot on me. "Lewis took the spot on the football team he wanted in Texas. I mean, they've wanted him since we were in high school, so I shouldn't be surprised he is going now, but I didn't think he would abandon me and everything else in his life to go." Poppy hiccups. "Why didn't he go when they offered it to him senior year, because maybe breaking up wouldn't have hurt this much back then?"

"I don't know…I clench my jaw to keep from saying something stupid, because how do you say this would hurt no matter what, but when you're ready, I want to make you mine, even though I know I can never say those words out loud.

I see red as I look down at Poppy crying over Lewis. She has cried over too many people in her life, and she shouldn't be doing it now. Poppy deserves nothing but happiness, and I know this hurt and heartbreak will eventually fade, but she deserves better than what life has given her. I thought she was finally getting it, but something always seems to happen. Still, she finally has a family with mine who loves her.

"Jax, I feel like a fool. I thought he would want to try long distance before breaking up. I mean, we were together since senior year."

Poppy moves away from me, wiping at the tears rushing down her face.

"Is that what you would want? I mean, do you want to have a long-distance relationship or uproot your life to transfer to a college you never wanted to go to?"

Poppy looks away from me, but I can still see her cheeks pale a little highlight the pink splotches on her face from crying.

"No, but wouldn't talking about it be better than him telling me he wants to go to a new college with no baggage. When he said those words, it felt like he was saying I'm the one who is responsible for holding him back." Poppy hiccups as new sobs wrack through her. "Jax…" She is talking so softly that I can't hear what she is saying.

"He was successful with his class and football here. He thinks this college and team don't have what he needs to go pro." I sigh. "I don't know why he wanted to break up with you, but he is foolish to think he can find someone better." Poppy wraps her arms around my neck, lying her head back on my chest. "Let's get you back to bed." I loop my arms under her legs and the other around her back, lifting Poppy into my arms, cradling her close to me.

"Jax?" Poppy whispers, laying her head on my chest. "I don't want to go to my room. Can you take me to your bed?"

The devil in me puffs up his chest, happy and a little too excited. Poppy wants to go to my bed, but this feeling doesn't last long, because I know nothing is going to happen. Poppy's heart is breaking, and I want to be there for her, even if I can't have her the way I want. I am willing to settle for a sad slumber party.

I walk to my bed, softly lying Poppy down. She rolls to her side as I pick up my comforter, I threw on the floor when I ran out of my room at the sound of screaming. I tuck her into a tight cocoon. I climb into bed from the other side, and before I get comfortable, I pull Poppy's shaking body into my arms. I want to tell her she is going to be okay, but I don't think anything I say or do will be comforting since her heart is breaking into a million little pieces.

Poppy's body continues shaking as she sobs loudly. I want to tell her she will be okay, but I know she doesn't want to hear right now.

Poppy perfume fills my space, overtaking my senses. Lust surges through my body, and let me tell you, there is nothing worse than poking a beautiful girl in the ass with your boner as she cries her sweet heart out over another guy.

I need to think of something to calm the growing erection in my boxer briefs, but damn, there are only a few things I can think of to help the growing problem between my best friend and me. You would think seeing someone you care about breaking would be enough to kill the mood, but I guess I'm sick and twisted enough that I still want her even at the worst time.

I could think of Lilah, but those thoughts will only piss me off because of how things ended between us. Even though she was the only girl who could make me forget about my feelings for Poppy, every time I think of her, all I can picture is her in bed with someone else.

Shit, I need to think of something funny fast, because I'm starting to feel my blood boil with red-hot anger from the little thoughts of Lilah, I allowed myself to have. However, thinking those brief thoughts did absolutely nothing to tame my hard-on.

Poppy shifts, brushing up against me, and my eyes widen at her sudden movement. That one simple move almost snapped the last bit of control I have left. I need to think of something fast.

Memories flash through my mind of the last few years until the image of me in assless chaps dancing on a coffee table could have easily buckled under me at a party makes me want to laugh.

This was during rush week, and it was torture. I had to wear the ridiculous costume. I pledged to the same fraternity my father was in during my freshman year, making me what they call a legacy. My fraternity didn't do any real hazing, but they did like to see if you would do anything for our fraternity and your brothers. That's where you would have to do some tests and wear whatever costumes they wanted when pledges had to go to parties and events, so maybe there was some hazing, not like you see in the movies.

My brothers had me wear a fuchsia pink man thong, bedazzled heart pasties, a pink cowboy hat with a feathered rim and a little silver tiara attached, white cowboy boots, and white fake leather assless chaps. The worst part of my get-up was the pink cowboy hat with a white feather trim and a matching feather boa scarf thing, because they were so fucking itchy.

I should have been humiliated wearing that shit for a week, but I wasn't. I was proud to do this with my fellow pledges and for my brothers. The only thing hard about the whole week was constantly being turned down by Lilah, because she was too embarrassed to be seen with me while the goods were practically on full display.

In the most un-humble brag, I did rock the fucking outfit, and even though I was trying to get with Lilah, I still managed to get plenty of ass. At first, I felt like shit sleeping with other girls while I was trying to get with Lilah, but I know for a fact she was hooking up with other guys too, because I had seen her at parties come out of rooms with other guys looking freshly fucked with smeared makeup, and ruffled hair.

Thankfully, I begin to feel a little calmer the more I think about rush week. Poppy is also not shaking as badly, so she is beginning to calm down enough to go back to sleep. I tilt my head as far back as I can to my bedside table, seeing my alarm clock read 6:00 in the morning. I didn't realize what time it was when Poppy woke me up from her screaming. I yawn, lying my head back down, thinking about one of the first parties my frat hosted.

I was so stressed because Poppy and I had been partnered to man the bar during one of our bigger parties. I think dressing in assless chaps and a man thong helped Poppy feel a little more comfortable in hers, because, as I said, my costume left nothing to the imagination and was uncomfortable with how restricting the underwear was. At least I'm proud of the package I was blessed with but combine that with the tight man thong I was bursting at the seams, especially at the sight of Poppy in her costume she had to wear when she rushed for her sorority.

She was dressed straight out of a porno or music video from 2002, and she left guys drooling in her wake. Poppy looked sinful in her matching cowgirl costume, including the assless chaps, but she was in a teeny tiny string bikini in the same color as my man thong. She had her hair in pigtails, and she was always sucking on a damn lollipop.

I asked her about it, and she shrugged, saying it was part of her costume, but I wasn't prepared for the question she threw back at me. She looked me dead in the eyes, and I quote, "Does it bother you?" I wanted to tell her, hell yes, it does, because watching her pop the damn sucker in her mouth and sucking on it was a major turn-on.

The first time Poppy saw me in my sexy cowboy outfit, her face turned a deep shade of red, but looking back now, I don't know whether she was blushing because of her costume or mine. She would look anywhere but at me. However, when she thought I wasn't paying attention, I would catch her trying to check me out without me noticing. I could have sworn I saw the sexy, hungry glaze in her eyes. I know she liked what she saw, and I have to say I enjoyed the view of her, too. At first, I thought it was fucking awkward catching her checking me out, but the more she did, I would find myself looking at her pale skin, begging for my touch. I started to crave looking at her so much I volunteered to work extra parties, and I knew she had to work for her sorority.

I pull Poppy closer to me, burying my face in her long, soft hair, inhaling deeply. "Shit!" I groan in my head. Poppy smells so good.

I feel myself growing more aroused than I was before, and I doubt anything in this world could deflate my erection now. Poppy squirms against me enough to make me hiss through my teeth.

"Jax, can we get drunk?" Poppy's low, raspy voice breaks through the cold silence in my bedroom.

"Fuck, yeah." I don't hesitate to jump out of bed, getting some much-needed distance between Poppy and me.

I go to the kitchen and the first thing I do is go to the sink, turning on the cold water, and I splash the water on my burning face. I should take a freezing shower but getting drunk sounds even better. I open the refrigerator door, not thinking about how early in the morning we are going to drink, and I grab the bottle of wine we always keep here for Poppy. She isn't much of a drinker, but when she turned 21 earlier this year, my mother took her to a wine tasting at a winery here in Broken Bow, Oklahoma. Thankfully, there is some tequila left over from when we made margaritas from taco Tuesday a couple of nights ago, or I would have to drink wine. I grab a couple of glasses, and for a second, I think I should let Poppy sleep in my room, and I do the right thing and take the couch.

When I get back to my room, I try to hand Poppy the bottle of wine, but she takes the bottle of tequila out of my hand, pulling the lid off. "I don't want to get wine drunk." Poppy takes a large swig, which makes her face scrunch up as she winces from the strong taste.

I sit on the floor, propping my back up against the side of my bed. Poppy climbs off the bed, sitting beside me. She takes another drink from the bottle before handing it to me. When I raise the bottle to my lips, I can hear the liquor swish in the bottle. I gulp a large drink of the tequila. When I hand the bottle back to Poppy, I wipe the excess from my mouth. She takes two more small drinks, wincing each time from the taste.

We silently pass the bottle back and forth to each other, taking large gulps until there is not a drop left. I lean my head back, and the ceiling starts to spin. I clumsily try to get off the floor, stumbling to the bathroom. Poppy was sitting so close to me I could smell her shampoo again, and in my drunken state, the lines I put between us were beginning to blur again. I can't allow myself to have these feelings for Poppy again, not after my family took her in.

Once I'm locked in the bathroom, I splash some cold water on my face, cooling my blazing hot face enough to feel like I'm not going to burst into flames. With the wall and door separating Poppy, my drunken, hazed mind begins to clear, and the lust I am feeling for Poppy starts to slowly fade. If I can stay in here until she passes out, I will be fine.

"Jax! Come to bed!" Poppy slurs loudly.

I don't move. I should do the right thing and sleep the booze off on the couch, but thinking about the feeling of Poppy's warm body pressed against mine will always win the war over me doing the right thing. Fuck, why do things have to be so complicated?

When I go back to my room, I find Poppy curled in a tiny ball on my bed, facing me. Her eyes were heavy with exhaustion and barely open. I walk over and again I think I should go sleep on the couch, but seeing Poppy's face cast in shadows, the sadness clouding her eyes, and the soft, slow breathing sound filling the air makes the pull to hold her in my arms again stronger and impossible to ignore.

I curse to myself as I lie down on my back with my hands crossed on my stomach next to Poppy. I'm trying to be extremely careful not to touch her. Poppy tucks her knees up to her chest, giving me more space to think clearly, which is difficult between the alcohol rushing through me and Poppy's sweet perfume filling my room. I feel the bed shift next to me, and small, cold hands wrap around my wrist.

"Jax," Poppy hiccups, "Can you make me forget everything?"

The room around me disappears, and the reason why I can't make a move on Poppy blurs again at her sweet request. I have a feeling I know what she is asking, and I don't know if I'll be able to resist her if she asks me for what I want more than my next breath.

"Poppy, we can't." I blink, making the ceiling look blurrier.

"I want to know what it feels like to be with someone other than him." Her desperate whine makes resisting her harder.

I don't want to be another reason Poppy is hurting right now, but I also don't want her to regret something when she sobers up. Poppy's hand moves from my wrist. I look at her, and she is looking at me with wide eyes and pink cheeks. She looks so beautiful and telling her no feels impossible.

I open my mouth, but I stop myself from denying both of us what we want by moving on top of her. Poppy's eyes widen, and she gasps, looking shocked. I don't think she was expecting me to give in to her.

I'm looking down at her, my eyes sparkling with drunken mischief, but the way Poppy is looking up at me, blinking fast, biting down on the corner of her bottom lip, turns me on more.

"What do you want to feel?" I smirk down at her, pinning her arms under me.

"Jax," Poppy sighs, squirming under me, trying to free her arms.

Poppy moves her hands to my shoulders. Her soft touch is almost too much for my liquored brain to handle. I sit back on my knees, and I grab her by the wrist, pinning them above her head.

"What do you want?" I ask, moving until I'm lying back on top of Poppy, but I never let go of her wrists.

"I want to feel you." Her chest rises as her breathing becomes heavy.

I watch as her small chest moves up and down with every deep breath she takes. I want more than anything to take her shirt off and feel her skin to skin.

I lean down close to her ear, whispering, "You have no idea what you're asking for."

I try to warn her away from what she is asking, because she doesn't know what she is getting herself into. I know she thinks she does, because she can feel my erection poking into her, but I know for a fact she didn't go too far past the basics with Lewis. He would complain when he was drunk. Poppy didn't like to experiment in bed. I can do the basics, but I like to do more, and she was never up for going beyond what she was comfortable with.

I feel four cold fingers brush on each of my hip bones, Poppy's fingers curling into the waistband of my underwear. A strangled-sounding groan forms in my chest. The urge to touch her grows stronger. Poppy smiles boldly at me with a wide smile plastered on her sweet face. Even though she looks confident, her pink cheeks are telling me she is also nervous, if not unsure, this is something she wants to do.

I continue looking down at Poppy, trying to figure out my next move. Should I be selfish and do what we both want, even though we shouldn't, or should I be a gentleman and sleep on the couch? This is the hardest choice I've ever had to make. Well, second to jumping in front of a bullet for her. I never had to second-guess if saving her was the right thing back then, like I am now. I push up, ready to tell Poppy we can't do this, but she makes the decision for both of us by pushing her hand into my underwear, wrapping her small fingers around me, and squeezing lightly.

I squeeze my eyes tightly. "Poppy, we shouldn't do this." I clear my throat, trying to hide the strangled moan from a man who is fixing to give in.

Poppy's blush deepens. "Jax, please, I want this." Poppy sounds so sweet.

Only a devil would give in to an angel when she is desperately asking for something that can blow up both of our lives, but hers more than mine. However, I know I can't deny what she wants now.

"Fuck it," I lean down, kissing Poppy's cheek, slowly making my way to her lips, trying to prolong the only time I'll ever be able to have her for myself, and I want to make this moment last as long as I can.

Poppy lets go of me, and her small hand leaves my underwear. She cups my cheeks, holding my face for a few seconds before she starts kissing me deeply. Poppy tastes sweeter than anything I've ever had in my life. I know from this one kiss I will be addicted for life.

Poppy moves her hand from my face, lightly caressing my shoulders with her fingers as she makes her way down my back, tickling me. I shiver when her hand flattens on the small of my back. She pauses long enough to nip at my lip before her hand dips into my underwear again, but this time she cups my ass with her hand.

I move my hand down Poppy's soft thigh, hooking her leg around my waist. Poppy wraps her other leg around me, caging me in between her delicious thighs. I take my hand off her leg, slowly caressing her silky-smooth skin, moving my hand up her slim body until I reach the hem of her oversized t-shirt, which is almost as soft as her skin. I pause, looking down at her slim body before I slip my hand under the thin fabric, slowly revealing the pale skin of her stomach.

"Your skin is so soft." I dip down, kissing her neck sloppily. "You feel like heaven," I say, knowing we haven't even got to the best part.

I start kissing Poppy's neck again as my hands move up her body, slowly revealing more of her creamy skin. My hands move over her ribcage, and my body hums with excitement as every inch of skin appears. I could burst when my hands cup Poppy's small but perfect breasts. I move my mouth down as I lower my head until I'm a couple of inches away from her little pink nipple. The sudden realization of what I am doing slams through my lust-filled brain.

"Poppy." Goosebumps appear when my hot breath fans over her warm skin.

Poppy's hands fist my hair, and she pulls me close to her body. In my poor attempt to lick my drying lips, I end up flicking my tongue on Poppy's nipple, causing her to gasp.

She moves her hands from my hair, and I feel the thin fabric of her shirt move. She leans up a little, pulling her shirt over her head, tossing it to the side. When Poppy lies back down, her blonde hair fans out over the pillow, making a halo around her. I lean back, pulling Poppy's tight leggings off her, leaving her in a pair of white panties.

The deep red blush on Poppy's cheeks travels down her neck and over her chest. I want nothing more than to take a picture of how sweet and sexy she looks under me, but I won't. I'm going to memorize every detail of this. I want to engrain all of Poppy like this in my mind. I want to remember all her sweet sounds. If I can only have her once, I need to sober up quickly, so this night can stay with me forever.

I lean down and pull one of her nipples in my mouth, sucking hard. Poppy's back arches, and she grabs my hair, holding me to her. I tease her other nipple by rolling the soft tip between my thumb and pointer finger, making her moan a little louder.

Doubt creeps its way back into my drunken lust-filled brain. I will give her one more chance to say no. I lean above her on my elbow, a few inches from her face. I know she can feel my breath on her, but she doesn't say anything. She looks up at me with a small smile playing on the corners of her mouth.

"Poppy…" I whisper, looking into her eyes.

"Jax," she puts her hands on my face, holding my gaze to hers. "Please, don't stop." Poppy's desperate voice is slurred.

The way she sounds, and the glassy look of her bloodshot eyes, should be enough to tell me she is too drunk to do this, but the pleading in her voice breaks my heart, because I want to give her everything she wants.

Poppy kisses my cheek to my chin before lying back down on my pillow. I hope her smell never leaves the fabric of my pillowcase after tonight.

I lean down, kissing Poppy as I enter her slowly. HOLY SHIT! She is so fucking tight and scorching hot. I stop for a few seconds, breathing hard, feeling like I am going to explode. Damn, I feel like a teenager discovering sex for the first time. The sudden need to move again overcomes me, and I thrust the rest of the way into her.

I break our kiss, looking down at Poppy. I find her hands, bringing them back above her head so she doesn't touch me. I pin her there with my right hand as my left hand travels down her body, slick with sweat, making her shiver from my touch.

"JAX!" Poppy cries out, arching her back.

My fingers find her slick clit, swirling around, applying the perfect amount of pressure, making her pleasure climb higher without her falling over the edge. I keep pumping my hips, moving faster, causing Poppy to scream louder. Each time I feel Poppy about to let go, I back off long enough to prolong this moment as long as I can.

Poppy moves her hands from my ass to my shoulders, digging her nails into my skin. The bite of pain makes me grunt as my pleasure intensifies. I move faster, letting Poppy come while I let go with her, but for the first time, I don't feel satisfied. I want more, and I know I can't have it.

I roll over onto my back, and Poppy follows me, laying her head on my sweaty shoulder. "Jax…" she says breathily, but I cut her off.

"We can never, and I mean never, do this again." I sit up, and Poppy moves her head off me.

I try not to look at Poppy as I grab my underwear off the floor and leave her alone in my bed, because if I do, I will regret my words more than I already am. I go to the living room and sit on the couch, looking up at the ceiling. A few minutes later, a door slams. Fuck, I pissed Poppy off. I feel like a jerk because I know Poppy was feeling the blissful high you get after sex, and I ruined it for her. I never intended to hurt Poppy with how I handled things, but she doesn't know how much saying after I wanted to bask in what we did hurt me too. However, I do know I made her pain feel ten times worse, and I would do anything to take it back, but I can't.

I walk back to my room, and I feel like I've been sucker punched in my chest, because I can hear Poppy sobbing in her room. I don't stop even though I want to burst into her room, begging her to forgive me and my stupid mouth. I hope one day she will be able to see I was right, even though I handled everything wrong, and I am not going to blame the alcohol, because this is all on me.

I lie in my bed feeling alone in my room for the first time since Lilah and I broke up. I sigh and sit up. I'm still too drunk to go to the gym to blow off some steam, and I'm too angry to sleep. I fucked up this time, and I don't think there's anything I can do to fix it. I climb out of bed and stand in front of Poppy's bedroom door, listening to her sob.

I knock once before I walk in. "Poppy…" I say, looking into her dark room. "I'm sorry, I hope you can forgive me."

She doesn't say anything as I close her door, going back to my room to wait for myself to sober up enough to go to the gym.

CHAPTER 5

POPPY

My body is stiff and sore from this morning's activities with Jax and from lying for hours curled in a tight ball, crying after he said the one thing a girl never wants to hear after having sex with someone. The fact that I used Jax this morning for ammunition to hurt Lewis one day makes me sick to my stomach. At first, I wanted to see what it was like being with someone other than Lewis. I felt like I could ask Jax since I feel safe with him. I instantly regretted my intentions of sleeping with Jax, but he said those hurtful words, and I felt like I made the wrong choice and forced him to do something he didn't want to do, so the way he reacted is my fault.

I never fell asleep after I left Jax's bed, but the image of him on top of me and the sounds he made has not left my mind. I clench my thighs, replaying one of the hottest sexual experiences of my life. I wouldn't say I had bad sex with Lewis, but now I've been with someone else, I feel like there was no passion between us. There was always excitement, of course, but not as much fire as there was with Jax.

Lewis was my first crush, my first boyfriend, and my first love, but he started as the boy next door. He became my best friend until my mom died, and my father forced me to stop being his friend. Anytime I pictured my future husband, I would picture him with Lewis's good looks. I always liked his messy, dark brown hair with a perfect square jaw and the perfect amount of stubble, and he had always been tall. By the senior year of his school, he had hit 6'2" with broad shoulders from working out and football. Don't get me wrong, the other girls fell for his good looks, and most of them benefited from his Playboy ways.

Then there's Jax, who was always the carefree guy who liked to crack jokes, mostly inappropriate ones, but he still makes me laugh more than anyone else I know. He is also a playboy type, but loyal to whoever he is in a relationship with. He is handsome in a completely different way than Lewis. Jax has deep blue eyes I want to swim in. His dirty blond hair is longer on the top and faded on the sides. He has cleaned it up some as he's matured. Jax is tall like Shane, standing at 6'4" with harder muscles, making him look like a big teddy bear.

I know comparing them is wrong because they are completely different. Growing up, my crushes have always been one of them. When Lewis would be mean to me after my mom died, Jax would always be nice to me. Anytime I was paired with either of them for school projects, I would always refuse to meet outside of school. Jax was the only one out of the two of them who would do his part of the work on his own; Lewis would push it off on me. Lewis started as my best friend, he became my bully, my boyfriend. I sigh, thinking now he is my ex.

The last couple of days have been a living nightmare full of overthinking and heartbreak, especially after I had made up my mind about where I need my relationship with Lewis to go. It was hard to come to terms with learning how much Lewis had been unfaithful to me. I know I can't trust him anymore, and I don't want to be with someone if I can't trust them with my whole heart. I didn't have the chance to talk to him about breaking up and trying to end things on good terms, because once he woke up, he grabbed his suitcases, turned to me, and said he didn't want to be with me. Well, he didn't say it nicely, and he felt the need to let me know he is interested in someone in Texas. If I am correct, I would think the girl is Lana, and she had been a major bully to me when I started dating Lewis, but to be fair, my whole life was changing when I got together with Lewis.

We've been through so much for him to tell me he is going to a new college, and he wants no strings when he goes. I tried to stop him from leaving, but he kept getting angrier when I tried to say anything. He kept saying, "I don't want to fight about this." When all I wanted to do was tell him I understand why he needs to go, and all I want is for him to be happy. I wasn't going to ask him why he cheated on me or what I had done to deserve that. I don't think the answer would have made me feel better. Sleeping with my best friend after getting drunk was also not the best idea since we were both drunk and not in the right headspace. Everything with Jax felt so natural, and I never felt more seen and beautiful in my entire life than when Jax had me pinned under him. I felt so comfortable with him; I felt like I could have done new things with him more than I ever could have with Lewis.

I wish I could talk to someone about all of this, but everything is so complicated. After all, Jax and his family took me in when I needed a new home with zero hesitation, and my only friend is Lilah, Jax's ex-girlfriend. I grab my phone, unlocking the screen, and scroll on social media until I finally do what I should have done from the moment Lewis and I broke up. I call the only other person I can think of, and like she normally does, Roxi picks up after the third ring.

"Hey, Poppy." I hear water being turned off.

New tears fall down my face when I hear her comforting voice. "Roxi!" I cry into the phone as the pain begins to clench at my heart again at having to say the words of Lewis and me breaking up out loud.

"Poppy, sweetie, what is wrong?" Roxi's voice cracks.

This familiar sense of panic I hear from Roxi is because this is unfortunately not the first time I've called her crying.

"Can I come home for a couple of days?" I hiccup.

"Of course, you can." Roxi gasps for air. "Poppy, what's wrong? Are you hurt?"

I climb out of bed, grabbing the first t-shirt and pair of leggings my hand touches. I toss them on my bed with clean underwear and a bra.

"No, I'm not hurt." I hiccup again as a new sob overcomes me.

I lean on the bed as the look on Lewis's face pops into my mind right before he walks out of the apartment for the last time. The emotions surging through me are starting to feel unbearable again, because I don't want to say the words Lewis and I broke up out loud.

"Poppy, can you please tell me what is wrong?" Roxi's voice shakes, but she is talking in a low tone, trying to sound soothing and not panicked.

"I..." stop, choking on a sob.

"Shane!" I hear Roxi yell, but not loudly, which makes me think she pulled the phone away from her ear.

"Lewis..." I hiccup. Trying to get the words out is harder than I want them to be. "Broke up with me." I start crying harder.

"Oh, Poppy." Roxi sighs. "Let me come get you. You seem far too upset to drive.

I can hear Shane ask Roxi what's wrong, but she doesn't reply to Shane. I'm guessing she is holding one finger up to him, trying to tell him to give her a minute.

A door somewhere in the apartment slams, but I don't know if Jax is coming home or leaving; either way, it doesn't matter. Even though I want to stay here with Jax, I know I need some space to clear my head from everything. Especially with Jax, because I need to figure out a way to make things right between us again.

"I need to get out of this apartment for a couple of days, if that is okay?" I hiccup.

"Of course." Roxi sighs.

"I am getting ready now, and I'll text you before I leave." I set the phone on my dresser, turning my speaker phone on long enough for Roxi and me to finish our goodbyes.

I pull my sweats off that I changed into this morning before Lewis woke up, tossing them to the side with my underwear. I shiver as the cold air from the air conditioning hits my skin. I slip into a pair of comfy boy short panties, and I pull a bralette onto my shoulders and clasp the little claw clasps together. The door opens wide. I turn around, and I find Jax in the doorway, looking at me with hungry eyes.

"Shit, sorry," Jax mutters, but he doesn't turn around or hide that he is still checking me out, leading me to believe he is anything but sorry he walked in on me in nothing but my underwear.

I turn around, grab my shirt, pull it on, and I tug my leggings on, while I can feel his eyes burning into me the whole time I get dressed.

"I'm going home for a couple of days. I can't be here right now." I say, pulling my long blonde hair out of my shirt.

I turn to Jax as soon as I'm fully clothed. I notice he is leaning against the doorframe with his hands in his pockets. He used to do it when I moved in with his family. "I understand, but you're pretty upset. Do you want me to drive you home?"

How do I tell him I'm not ready to talk to him yet, and being alone in the car with him might be awkward, because now I have to get over my breakup and the sting of his words? I don't regret sleeping with him, the reason I asked, and how things are between us right now.

"No, I think the time alone will be good for me." I sit on the edge of my bed, slipping on my socks and tennis shoes, still feeling Jax's eyes burning into me. "I need to think about some things."

"Poppy, I am so fucking sorry for what I said." Jax's voice is soft, but he is looking at me with his mouth turned down in the corners. "I shouldn't have said what I did." The normal, silly, carefree Jax isn't the man standing in front of me, and I want him back. "I freaked, and I am here to own up to it."

I grab my purse. "No, you shouldn't have, but I shouldn't have pressured you either." I walk to the door, and he moves out of my way. I walk into the living room before. "Do you…" I take a shaky breath, turning around to face him. "Um, do you regret it?"

He begins shaking his head. "No, god, no. Trust me, I have wanted to do that for a long time, but damn it, Poppy, you were broken up with, and we were drunk."

I shake my head. "Maybe we shouldn't have done that, but Jax, after what you said, you ruined one of the best moments of my life." I feel my face heat, and I know I must be as red as a tomato from my confession.

"I'm so fucking sorry. If I could take it back, I would, but there is too much in our lives making what we did messy and complicated." Jax takes a few steps toward me, but I take a step back, shaking my head. "Poppy, you have no idea how much I want more of you, but it could hurt so many people."

I can hear the hurt in his voice and a storm of hurt in his beautiful blue eyes, holding me captive. I know he is sorry. I can hear the desperation in his voice. "I know, but I need some time."

"This isn't going to change anything between us, is it?" Jax's eyes are wide, and his hands ball into a fist.

I can hear the desperation in his voice, and like him, I don't want this to change anything, either, but I think things need to be a little different; I need to figure out how. I don't want to pretend this morning never happened, but I need to figure out how to live with this morning's sexcapade being the only time I get with him. As much as I hate to admit it, he is right; this is complicated.

"I hope not." I open the front door. "I'll be home in a couple of days."

I walk out the door, leaving Jax in our apartment. I can feel the distance between us. I want to talk to Roxi about what I did and how everything has changed, but I'll keep this morning between Jax and me to myself.

Roxi is waiting for me in the driveway when I pull up to the house. I park, and as soon as I get out of my car, I run to the woman who has been like a mother to me for the past few years. I can't ever repay Jax,

Roxi, and Shane for taking me in after Jax saw me after one of my father's punishments. They saved me by giving me a safe, loving home where I felt welcomed, and I have been treated like family ever since.

They never made me feel like I was unloved or a burden, even after Jax was put in the hospital because of my father. They took guardianship over me and tried to adopt me, but I aged out before anything could happen. I understand what complications Jax is talking about, but he handled everything wrong, and so did I. I need to keep reminding myself, because it takes two to mess up the way we did.

"Shane is going to get us pizza, and I have the den set up for movies and spa night." Roxi hooks her arm in mine.

When we walk into the foyer, I am hit with the familiar clean scent of home. It feels so good to be back here, but I wish more than anything I didn't have to come back, because my heart is breaking.

"Thanks." Tears begin to well in my eyes.

We walk to the den, and I can't help but be reminded of all the times I would hang out with Lewis and Jax in here. This is where I had my first date and my first make-out session. I also learned to play video games on the big screen, and Jax would stay up late with me when I was too scared to go to sleep, because of the day's events, while my dad was alive. Jax would even come down here with me after I woke him up screaming from a nightmare. We would watch movies until we fell asleep.

"We don't have to talk; we can watch rom-coms or sad movies and cry if that is what you want to do." Roxi goes behind the bar and pulls a bottle of wine out of the fridge.

I don't want to drink because I helped Jax drink a lot of tequila early this morning, but a glass of wine will help me feel better. Something in me feels wrong. I bet Jack, my dad, would say before going to the bar to get wasted, and come home to take his anger out on me. He drank his feelings until he had nothing left but fury blazing through him. I don't want to rely on alcohol to comfort me as Jack did. I always want to do the right thing, but sometimes you have to bend the rules, right?

I smile weakly. "That sounds good. Being at home is hard. My bed and room don't feel right with Lewis not there, which is crazy, because we broke up this morning." I hiccup again, feeling like I vomited words and emotions all over Roxi.

"If you need to move, you can. We haven't told you guys about it yet, but we rented the unit next door, so we could have a place to stay if we don't want to drive back home after a late game, your concerts, or visits." Roxi faces me. "Before you got here, I told Shane if you need it, you can have the apartment for as long as you need it."

I'm honestly surprised they didn't do this earlier. They usually rent a hotel room if they want to stay close to the school instead of driving home.

"How many rooms?" I ask, picking up a freshly baked brownie with peanut butter swirled in it.

"There are two rooms. It has a similar layout to the one you live in now." Roxi hands me a napkin.

I bite into the warm, gooey brownie as Shane walks into the den. "Pizza is here."

He walks around the sectional, setting the pizza box down on the ottoman with some paper plates. Before he leaves, he kisses us on the head. "Thank you," Roxi and I say at the same time.

"Let me know if you two need anything else," he gives me a sad smile.

Shane leaves us alone for our girls' night. Roxi opens the lid to the pizza box, and the smell of garlic and Italian spices fills my nose.

"I think I would love that. At least for a little while." Roxi hands me a plate. "You know, until the breakup doesn't hurt as much.

"You are welcome to live there as long as you want. We'll go shopping and get things set up to make the apartment feel like home. It will be okay if you don't want to move back into your apartment. However, if you want Jax to be your roommate, he may be happy to make the switch, especially after everything that happened between him and Lilah there." Roxi crosses her legs once she gets settled on the couch. "But I'm afraid to say your first heartbreak usually hurts the longest and hardest."

I don't want to tell her I'm also hurting because of Jax, and I do not want to live with him right now, either. I don't think she will handle the news of Jax and me having sex well, but by leaving out information. I feel like I'm lying to her. We've always been able to talk about everything, even the hard and uncomfortable things, but I think her son's sex life is one of those off-limits topics.

"I think I need some time alone, but when I'm ready, I promise I'll talk to Jax about switching to the new apartment." I can't look at Roxi when I say this. I look away, taking a large bite of pizza, and when I swallow, the greasy food hits the bottom of my stomach like a rock.

Roxi and I talk during dinner, and she can get me to laugh. Even though I can't stop thinking about how I am going to break the news about my moving out to Jax, I still manage to pay attention to Roxi.

My heart still hurts, and my ego is bruised from Jax's words, but I know I am going to be okay. This isn't the hardest thing I've had to overcome in my life. I have learned that if you have the right people by your side, you can overcome almost anything.

I know by the time I go back home; I will forgive Jax for what he said. The funny thing is, when I was a freshman in high school, I had given up on my crush and my hopes of being lucky enough to be with Lewis, because of how mean he could be to me sometimes. I know at the time, he had his reasons, but to me, I was wishing he would stop, because I was already hurting, and he was adding to it. Eventually, my feelings shifted, and I started crushing on Jax, which was confusing back then. He was Lewis's best friend, but I always thought he was cute and funny.

"Poppy, are you okay?" Roxi looks at me with her perfectly painted eyebrows scrunched together.

"Yeah," my voice cracks. "I'm thinking of when I moved here."

"I can see how that can be sad." Roxi nods, agreeing with me.

"I had a family and two best friends when I came here, and now I only have one friend." I begin crying hard, and Roxi moves, pulling me into her arms. "I lost more than my boyfriend; he was also my best friend."

I don't say how I think I might have lost both of my best friends in one day, because it is a can of worms I don't want to open.

"Maybe one day you two can be friends again." Roxi rubs her hand up and down my arm, comforting me. "It does happen, but the sting and the hard feelings must heal, or they will continue to come between you. Did Lewis tell you why he wanted to break up?"

I'm not telling her he has been cheating on me, because I don't want her to think anything bad about him. Roxi is best friends with Macey, Lewis's mom.

I nod, wiping away the tears from my face. "He took the spot on the team in Texas that he has always wanted to play for. He left his team with me, not caring how this would affect us."

"I don't know why he would do something like this." Roxi adjusts herself a little. "This doesn't seem like the Lewis I have known since he and Jax became friends when they were in youth football."

"I mean, we have been fighting a lot lately, but I thought it was because we didn't see eye to eye about him looking at other schools.

It wasn't until he broke up to me that I thought he might have been picking fights to make breaking up with me easier for me." I close my eyes, not wanting to see her reaction.

"Maybe, but is it fair to assume unless there was more going on I didn't know about?"

I groan. "I didn't want to tell you this, because I didn't want you to think differently of him or for it to come between you and Macey…" I stop as Roxi sits up, facing me, giving me her full attention.

"You can tell me anything, and if things change, they change. They did when I found out what happened between Lilah and Jax."

"Well, before we broke up, Lewis and I went to a party, and a couple of girls were talking. Long story short, I found out he has been cheating on me…" Roxi gasps, making me pause for a second. "I don't know how or for how long, but I had planned to break up with him, but when he did, he was so nasty about it. I don't know what hurts more, the way he broke up with me or the fact that our relationship is over, and we won't be friends now."

"Poppy, I'm so sorry." Roxi hugs me. "I think you were already hurt when he broke up with you, intensifying the pain."

I guess I never paid too much attention to Roxi and Macey's relationship after Jax and Lilah broke up, but it would make sense for things to be different after your kids break up. If Jax found out Lewis was cheating on me, how would that make him feel? Would they stay friends? This breakup is messy and complicated, like everything else in my life right now. What have I done?

My phone chimes, and I see Jax's name on the screen. I read the message.

Jax: Let me know if you need anything.

Another message pops up.

Jax: Also, I am sorry for what I said.

I set my phone down, turning my attention back to Roxi. Tears fill my eyes.

"Poppy, everything will be alright." Roxi lays her head on mine.

I love that I get to have her as a mother figure in my life, but being with Jax could ruin that, confirming the mess I made of my life. You never think of how your choices can affect other people's lives until they do.

"Why does it feel like everything is falling apart?" Tears dip onto Roxi's shirt.

"Your whole world has been turned upside down. Lean on us, and eventually everything will be okay." Roxi smooths my hair down.

I guess she is right. I need to lean on them, including Jax, because moving past my heartbreak is going to be hard. And I'm hit with the double whammy of trying to figure out how to deal with making a mistake with Jax, even though I never want to think of what we did as a mistake, because I have never felt that good in my life.

CHAPTER 6
JAX

Things with Poppy and me are tense. Ever since she came home from my parents' house, she barely looks at me when we are in the same room, which doesn't last long, because she always finds a reason to leave. I know she is still mad at me for what I said after we hooked up, and I don't blame her. I am still kicking myself for being so stupid. Every time I try to talk or apologize to her, she storms away from me with tears pooling in the waterline of her eyes. I have many regrets about that day, but sleeping with Poppy is not one of them.

"TAYLOR! GET YOUR HEAD IN THE GAME!" Coach Harrison blows his whistle, making the shrill echo through the practice stadium.

I jump back to my feet. "What the fuck, man, which is an illegal move!" I push Zach's shoulder pads.

Walsh grins widely at me, putting his hands out, silently asking me what are you going to do about it?

"Walsh! I don't want to see shit on my field again! You could have benched my player with illegal move," Coach Harrison jabs his finger in Walsh's direction.

Walsh is a damn good football player. He pushes the boundaries at practice and takes a lot of heat for it, but during games, he plays clean, and I am lucky to have him on my team.

"Who is in your head, because when you're on the field, you need to focus?" Walsh grins at me, wiggling his eyebrows, but I can tell he is serious because he wouldn't have asked if I was distracted during practice.

Walsh is a straight-to-the-point kind of guy, even off the field, but he knows how to have a good time. Outside of Lewis and Poppy, he is my best friend. When Lewis told the team he was leaving, Walsh was livid; the whole team was. I don't blame them because I was not only mad but also felt betrayed.

"Hit the showers!" Coach leaves us on the field, shaking his head, tossing his hands in the air, grumbling under his breath.

He has been in a piss poor mood since Lewis walked off the team. The whole team has been acting out, and our spirits are down. We are trying to figure out how to be a team again. Unfortunately, for the team, Lewis was one of the leaders; he helped build the team into what it is now. I don't know how much longer I'll be able to wait for the captains to get their shit together before I step in and knock some sense into my brothers. Even though I am rumored to be a captain next year, I still refuse to fumble our way through this season. We were a strong team and hard as shit to beat before Lewis left, and we will continue to be that way even after him. We need to let the sting of the betrayal heal some more.

I pull my helmet off, running my hand through my sweat-soaked hair. I glance at the stands, secretly wishing I were one of my teammates who has a girl waiting up there for them. Lilah never came during practices; she always claimed to be studying, but I eventually learned she used the time to hook up with random guys.

I stop short when I see Poppy sitting in the stands. Her head is bent down, looking at a book, one of her hands raised, twirling a pen in her fingers. I would bet she is either doing homework or working on a song she is writing. Poppy came to a few practices for Lewis, but she stopped when they started fighting. She kept saying it reminds her of the day her dad came to our high school one day. You see, her dad was furious with her because I found out what life was like at her father's home. At one look at her swollen and bruised face, I knew she needed out of there. When Poppy came to live with us, we thought this was the end of her pain and suffering, but I am sad to say, we were wrong. He somehow managed to come to the school, and he grabbed her when she was coming to sit in the stands during practice. He dragged her to an empty classroom and beat her within an inch of her life. She said she could see the hatred he had in her eyes, fueled by the stench of whiskey oozing out of his pores.

I jog to the railing of the stands. "POPPY!"

She jumps a little, looking up at me with pink cheeks and wide eyes. "Can we talk?" she yells with her hands cupping her mouth.

She looks cute with her pen pressed between two fingers, but the light beaming down on her highlights her beauty more.

"Sure! Let me go get changed." I turn quickly, jogging to the tunnel leading to the locker room, not waiting for her to respond, because it might give her time to change her mind about finally wanting to talk to me.

This is the first time Poppy has wanted to talk since the morning I put my foot in my big mouth. She has been avoiding me, and I want things to be normal so bad I'm almost to the point of getting on my knees begging her to forgive me.

After about 30 minutes, I exit the locker rooms. Poppy is waiting for me in the hallway as she would for Lewis when she came to his practices. Seeing her standing there feels like someone sucker punched me in the gut as jealousy swirls in my stomach. I hope she isn't about to tell me she is getting back together with Lewis.

"Hey, I want you to know I've thought a lot about things, and I talked with Roxi about my breakup. I have decided I can't live in the apartment after everything. I need to start fresh in a new place." Poppy shifts nervously, but she never looks away from me. "Shane and Roxi are here to help me move. I need some space from all the memories I have with Lewis..." Poppy looks away from me, but not fast enough for me to see her eyes are starting to water. "And with you."

Poppy not being able to look at my feelings is like a punch to the gut.

My jaw drops. What does she mean she is moving out? "I don't want you to go." I can't believe I'm trying to plead with her to stay right now, because I know there's nothing I can say to make her stay.

"I need some more time. Let's plan to go to dinner in a few days, and we can talk." She crosses her arms over her chest, looking up at me under her lashes, which are wet from tears. "I do miss you, you're my best friend, but being around you is too much right now."

I suck in a sharp breath, and the air feels like fire, making me wince. I can tell how sad she is, and I know she isn't sleeping from the dark circles under her eyes. I want to pull her into my arms, but if she doesn't want to talk to me, she doesn't want me to hug her.

I clear my throat. "Ugh, dinner sounds great." I force a smile. "If you want, I can come help you move."

Her head whips in my direction. "Jax..." She starts to say something but stops herself.

"Poppy, I..." she shakes her head before running to the parking lot.

My heart begins to pump faster, sweat forms on the back of my neck, and my shoulders tense. Why do I feel like Poppy broke up with me? I kick the wall before walking to my truck. I wait until I don't see Poppy's little car anymore before I go home.

The drive home is short and does nothing to help me calm down. Don't get me wrong, I'm happy she told me before I walked in on her moving out, but she could have given me a little more time to process this. She can't get a new apartment in a few days, right?

I sit in my truck with my head down on the steering wheel, trying to get myself together before I must face my parents.

If this is what she needs to do, I will support her, but I need to figure out a way to get leave that morning out of my mind, because I start and end my day with the memory of Poppy under me. Maybe we will be able to be friends again.

When I walk upstairs to the small hall leading to my apartment, the door is wide open. I can see my parents walking around the living room, but they haven't noticed me yet. I take a deep breath, walking through the door, and I drop my bag noisily on the ground next to the little table my mom put by the door.

My mom looks over at the door; a smile lights up her beautiful face as she runs up to me. "JAX! I missed you so much!" my mom wraps her short arms around me. "Are you here to help Poppy move to her new apartment?"

"Um," I shift on my feet, "Yeah."

My dad comes up to me, hugging me tightly, and pats my back. "It's good to see you, son. How was practice?"

"Good, Coach Harrison got mad and called it early because one of the guys did an illegal move. What furniture do we need to take?" I see a few boxes stacked by the couch.

"None, we are moving Poppy's stuff." My mom replies, carrying a box she can barely get her arms around.

I briefly debate taking the box from my mom, but I know she will gripe at me, because she is more than capable of carrying a big box. I know from experience. When I moved into my dorm freshman year, I tried to take a box twice the size of hers, and I felt like a little kid getting in trouble.

I grab one of the few boxes scattered in the living room and look around. I guess I need to take these to my dad's truck since I didn't see a moving van in the small parking lot. Something the size of a truck would have been hard to miss, and I know for a fact one wasn't out there.

"Whose car am I taking these to?" I shift the box in my arms.

My parents look at me with their eyebrows pushed together.

"Follow me." I hear Poppy say in the hallway outside my apartment.

I didn't see her outside or in the hall, so I don't know where she came from, making this whole thing more confusing. I walk across the living room while she waits for me in the hallway. She gives me a small half-smile, which doesn't meet her eyes, before she leads me to the apartment next to mine. She twists the knob, opening the door wide enough for me to go through.

"SURPRISE!" Poppy's bubbly voice rings through the apartment like she is singing.

"What the fuck?" My voice cracks.

Poppy made me think she was moving further away than right next door. She walks through the door, but I stay rooted where I am. I'm fuming, looking at her through my lashes.

"Can we talk about this after they leave?" she hisses at me; her beautiful smile disappears as she smashes her lips together, and her face flushes lightly, and she crosses her arms over her small chest.

"Where do you want these boxes?" I look around the apartment, similar to mine.

"The living room is fine." She walks to the kitchen and moves some boxes around on the counter, making herself look busy, so she doesn't have to talk to me or look at me.

I turn around, leaving her to her busy work, and walk back to my place, but before I can pick up another box, my mom grabs me by my arm, pulling me to my room, slamming the door closed.

Ugh, oh, this isn't good. My mom felt the need to shut me in a room with her, and from the way her brows are pushed together, I know she is fixing to start yelling.

"WHAT DID YOU DO?" she whirls around, scowling at me.

I rub the back of my head. I have no idea what my mother thinks I did, and I also don't know what Poppy has told her.

"What do you mean?" I try to play dumb even though that has never worked for me.

"Poppy came home crying the evening after Lewis broke up with her, but she seems like something else is making her upset, too, and when you asked where to take the boxes, I knew something was up." My mom crosses her arms.

I shrug, looking down at my mom. "I don't know. She hasn't been the same since they broke up."

My mother uncrosses her arms and puts her hands on her hips, tapping her foot on the floor. She looks away from me, and I know she isn't buying my innocent act.

"Jax, please tell me you didn't do anything stupid." This time, she removes one hand from her hips and pokes me in the chest with her pointy, wine-colored nail.

"Mom! We didn't do anything stupid." Shit! Talk about the wrong choice of words.

My mom's jaw drops as she looks up at me with wide eyes. She closes her mouth for her jaw to drop open again. She sits on my bed, her shoulders slumping forward in defeat. She rests her forehead on her palms as she grabs a fistful of her straight, dirty-blonde hair cut in what she always calls a bob.

"Please tell me you didn't sleep with her?" Her voice is so soft maybe she didn't ask what I thought she did.

I want to lie my way out of this, but I don't think I can. The way my mom asked me if I slept with Poppy was more like she was trying to convince herself I'm not stupid, but I think deep down she knows what I did. The last thing I want to do with my mom is talk about my sex life.

"Mom, I don't want to talk about this." I can't say the words to her and watch disappointment take over in her sad, pleading eyes.

"I don't care what you want right now." She stands back up, pointing at me. "Listen to me, no more. You can't have that type of relationship with her. There are too many complications with it." My mother lightly jabs me in the chest again.

"Mom, I know we can't." I look down at my mom with the corners of my mouth turned down.

Even though I know she is right, the pain in my heart stings because I let my old crush resurface, and the most selfish part of me doesn't want to bury anymore.

My mom's face softens, and she hugs me tightly. "I can't be a hundred percent sure, but I think she will take Lewis back if he tries to come back for her." My mom's hand moves to the scar I have from jumping in front of Poppy when her father tried shooting her. "You have been hurt too much for me to let this hurt you too."

"I know. You don't have to worry. I swear everything will be all right." I rub her back, trying to comfort her.

"I'm your mom, I will always worry, but I am going to try to trust you on this. I love you."

My mom pulls away from me, walks out of my room, and leaves the door open. Damn, I'm not making anyone in my life happy lately.

Once we get everything over to Poppy's new apartment. My dad turns to me. "You want to go eat somewhere?"

I'm not in the mood to go anywhere, but at the same time, going to dinner with my dad sounds a hell of a lot better than sitting at home thinking about Poppy.

"Yeah, sounds good," I mumble, grabbing my keys and wallet out of my gym bag.

"Steak sound good to you?" My father asks walking to the door.

"You know I will never turn down a good steak." I chuckle.

We get my truck, and my dad turns the music down I had blasting through my speakers when I left practice.

"How is the team dealing with Lewis's sudden departure?" My dad puts his seatbelt on.

"It's going to be a hard season. None of the second-string guys want to step into Lewis's place. They are claiming the position is not cursed." I sigh pulling out onto the main road. "Coach Harrison asked me to, but I'm struggling with the choice. I pledged my eligibility to go pro at the end of last year and I don't want switching positions my last year to jeopardize that."

Out of the corner of my eye, I see my dad tilt his body in my direction. Whenever he wants to talk to someone about something serious, he likes to face them, giving them his undivided attention.

"That is a big ask, but I think you are more than capable of switching positions."

"I don't feel like I have a choice. None of the other captains are going to step up so why should I?" I tap my fingers on the steering wheel.

"Because you're a team player as much as you are one hell of a football player." My dad nods his head. "Your teammates are great and good players, but they don't have the heart for the game like you do." My dad leans back in his seat.

I nod my head. "I see your point, but it seems like a huge risk for my senior year."

"It is a risk, but you have worked your ass off and you will continue to in this new spot. That will show scouts how dedicated and loyal you are to your team."

The truck falls quiet as I pull into the parking lot of the steakhouse. This has given me a lot to think about, and I guess the best thing I can do is to take these few days my mom is with Poppy to get my focus back on school and football again, because the next time I'm with Poppy, I am going to need to have my head on straight and my emotions in check.

CHAPTER 7

JAX

Poppy has been living next door to me for three weeks now, and I haven't seen her once, which annoys me enough to take out my frustration in football. My grades are getting better, but my mood isn't. Even though I try to erase the memory of Poppy under me by hooking up with other girls, they seem to make me want Poppy more.

I miss Poppy, and I'm ready to go over to her apartment and demand we move past what happened. I don't know if I can get over my feelings for Poppy this time, but I'm willing to try so I don't lose her entirely.

I'm working on an essay I put off for far too long at the bar in my kitchen when someone bangs on my door. I stand up from the stool, walking with long steps to see who has come over unexpectedly.

"Who the hell could this be?" I grumble under my breath, opening the door.

"Hey, man." Lewis greets cheerfully, holding up a bag of Chinese food.

Damn, he is not who I want to see, but at the same time, I am also happy to see him. He hasn't returned my texts or calls since the day he walked out of here with Poppy breaking down.

I move out of his way, letting Lewis into my apartment. I wonder if he called Poppy or if he is here to get the rest of his things.

"Hey, I wasn't expecting you." I slam the door shut, turning around, crossing my arms over my chest.

"I came back to get the rest of my things, but I had coffee with Poppy before coming over here," Lewis smirks at me.

"She doesn't live here anymore." I squint at him.

Lewis's mouth puckers a little, making his lips set in a stubborn-looking frown. "Yeah, Lilah told me some shit went down after I left, but she doesn't know exactly what happened. So, you tell me, what the fuck has been going on since I left?"

I don't care what Lilah thinks or says, because I know Poppy well enough to know she didn't tell either of them what we did.

"You are the one who left her. Did you think after all you guys have been through, leaving her like that wouldn't crush her?" I watch Lewis walk to my couch with a wide knowing grin plastered on his smug face.

He plops a plastic bag I didn't notice onto the table before sitting back on the couch, kicking his feet up like he still lives here. He stretches his arms over the back of the couch, making himself comfortable. He looks at me with a single eyebrow raised and the same smug smirk he has had since he came into my apartment. Something in the way he is looking at me makes me feel like I need to brace myself for something, because I have seen the same look on the field many times. I've never been on the receiving end, because he saves it until he is ready to mess with the other team's mind.

"Oh, she may have mentioned Poppy hasn't been acting like herself lately." Lewis smiles widely. "She said it was more than her being sad about our breakup, but Lilah said Poppy wouldn't tell her anything."

"If you recall, I didn't act like myself for a while after I broke up with Lilah. I wouldn't expect Poppy to go back to being her normal, happy self after all you guys have been through." I snap.

"You would tell me if there was more going on, right?" He raises his eyebrow, challenging me.

"Yeah." I clear my throat. "How's the new school and team? Are you ready to come back?" I chuckle softly.

He takes the food containers out of the plastic bag, holding one out to me. I take the warm food from Lewis, setting it on the table as I sit on the couch next to him, but I angle my body so I can see him.

"Exactly like I thought it would be. I'm finally on the team I want and deserve. This team is at the same level of dedication and raw talent as me, so obviously I made the right choice in leaving. However, I should have gone there after we graduated high school like I wanted to." Lewis looks at me out of the corner of his eyes. "Stop changing the subject. "So, what the fuck happened after I left?"

I look at Lewis, grinding my teeth. He can get his ass out of my house if he is going to continue to play head games with me. Something tells me he is up to something.

"I already told you I don't know what you're talking about, but if you're going to continue to be a dick, you can get the fuck out of my house." I turn my head away from Lewis, pulling my shoulders back.

"Are you going to keep lying to me?" Lewis quickly stands up, facing me with his feet shoulder-width apart, like he is ready to fight.

"I clearly have no idea what you are talking about, so why don't you spit out whatever it is you're claiming I have done. You come into my apartment accusing me of something, so either spit out what you came here to say or leave." I jaw clenches.

I stand up facing Lewis, who is also getting up with his face red and his eyes narrowed at me.

"I came back for Poppy, but that won't fucking happen now." Lewis is spitting every word as his breathing becomes heavier.

"I don't know what…" I stop when I hear Lewis growl like a damn animal.

"YOU FUCKED HER!" The veins in his neck pop out.

Before I can say anything, Lewis charges at me, but his knee collides with the coffee table, knocking it over, making the takeout lids pop off, spilling food all over my floor. He doesn't stop, and from the glaze over his eyes, I would doubt he can know what he is about to do. He moves lightning-fast, getting inches away from my face.

"Dude," I hold up my hands. If he lets me explain, he won't be so mad. "You don't understand!"

Lewis growls again, this time spewing spit everywhere as he rams his shoulder into me, as he would on the field, tackling someone on the other team. I try to push my weight on him, bracing myself for some of the impact of his weight being rammed into my stomach, but it only makes him angrier. He starts punching me in the ribs, getting all the hits in he can. When that isn't enough for him, he slams his shoulder into me again, but this time he gets lucky. I lose my footing and land on my back several inches away from the spilled food. The air is being forced from my lungs, and I begin gasping for breath. Lewis straightens up with a wide smile of satisfaction written all over his face as he looks down at me.

I groan, slowly getting to my feet, keeping my eyes on Lewis the whole time. He begins cussing at me so loudly I'm sure the people in the surrounding units can hear him, but he doesn't try to hit me this time. Lewis gets louder, not caring if the neighbors can hear him call me all the derogatory words her can think of.

Lewis has never been the type of guy to fight someone unless it's fair, but I don't think he cares right now. I won't fight him until I need to seriously defend myself. I stand there and take the venom he is spewing my way. I try not to let some of his insults affect me, because I know from firsthand experience how much hearing about the girl you love has slept with another guy, but in my case, Lilah and I weren't broken up, and I walked in on it. Sleeping with Poppy wasn't any better. This must be a bigger blow for him, because the person who slept with his ex was also supposed to be his best friend.

"We got drunk and…" I stop talking. There is nothing I can say that will take back what I did, and all it will sound like is a lame excuse. Lewis's face contorts, and a strangled groan sounds deep in his chest. "I would say I am sorry, but you've had Poppy, you wouldn't turn down a chance to be with her if you were in my shoes and let me tell you she is wild."

I know I shouldn't have said that, but Lewis has pissed me off, and he needs to get a taste of his own medicine. However, I won't stoop to his level and throw hands to deal with my anger.

Lewis pulls his fist back, punching me in the jaw. I stagger back at how much power he put into his arm. He doesn't stop, he hits me again, but I still refuse to fight back. I wanted to do the same thing to the guy Lilah was fucking behind my back, but unlike Lewis, I knew hitting him would only temporarily make me feel better. I know this is him trying to release the rage burning through him, and when he is done, he may not be as mad, but I know he will no longer have him as a best friend. If Poppy knew this was how he was handling his anger, I don't think she would forgive him. She knows firsthand what being a punching bag for someone else's emotions is like.

I hear the door behind us bang against the wall. Poppy is here, and things are fixing to go from bad to worse.

"LEWIS!" Poppy cries, but I can't see where she is, because I am too busy trying to block Lewis's punches.

Lewis is so enraged, he doesn't stop. I doubt he can hear her through the blinding rage burning through him.

"Stop this! LEWIS! STOP!" I see a flash of blonde hair to my right at the same time a punch lands on my left cheek.

Fuck, I forgot how hard Lewis can punch. I stagger back, and Poppy's hands go up. I feel her small, cold hand lightly touch my bicep.

I step back, trying to get some distance so Poppy doesn't try to get in the middle of us again. Lewis tries to land another blow on my left cheek. His swing has so much power behind it he staggers forward when his fist connects with nothing but air. He stands there glaring at me, but from his labored breathing, I know he is still fuming.

Poppy touches his shoulder, "Lewis, this is…" Poppy's words are cut off as Lewis turns around, shoving Poppy in the shoulders so hard she falls with a loud plop to the ground. He has a deep scowl wrinkling his face, staring down at her.

I doubt he can see anything behind the red-hot anger he is feeling, but damn, pushing Poppy is the last straw. If he tries to fight me again, I will fight back. I stumble to my feet, and when I can stand without swaying, I shoulder past Lewis without saying a word. I open the door. "Lewis, you need to go." I somehow manage to keep my voice calm, kicking my best friend out of my house and out of my life.

Lewis looks up at me, and I see some of the redness coloring his face turn to a lighter shade of pink. The storm leaves his glassy eyes. I can tell what he did hasn't registered yet. He is looking at me, breathing so hard his shoulders are moving up and down with each breath he takes. When he finally looks down at Poppy, who has curled into a ball, shaking from the sobs wrecking through her thin body. I watch in what feels like slow motion as Lewis's face morphs as what he did breaks through the angry fog in his mind.

"Poppy, I am so sorry." Lewis storms out of my apartment, slamming the door closed behind him.

I look around at the mess left in my living room, but I don't care about cleaning up right now. Poppy is still crumpled on the floor in a little ball, crying. The rug can be replaced, and the floor can be cleaned, but what I need to do is make sure Poppy is okay.

"Are you okay?" I crouch down to her level, speaking in a hushed tone so I don't accidentally scare her.

She looks up at me through tear-filled lashes and red, bloodshot eyes. I bend down, picking her up, and I cradle her in my arms. I take Poppy back to her place. I would have stayed here, but I know she left for more reasons than my freak-out from the morning we hooked up.

"Where are your keys?" I look at the tight leggings and crop top she is wearing; I doubt she grabbed her keys before coming to my apartment after she heard Lewis losing his mind.

"It's unlocked." Poppy lays her head on my chest, and tears instantly soak through my shirt.

I gently lay Poppy on her couch, and she turns to her side, curling into a tight ball. I grab a thick fuzzy bluish-purple blanket out of a basket near the TV console, covering Poppy's shaking body as she sobs.

I'm not ready to leave her, so I stand in front of the sofa awkwardly looking around. Poppy's apartment is feminine but not overly done, with simple design choices goes with the same ugly wall color every unit here has. I noticed Poppy chose to decorate with blues and grays here instead of the red and cream colors they did at my apartment.

"Please don't go?" Poppy faintly whispers, lightly grabbing onto my fingers as I turn away from her.

"I don't know if this is a good idea." My voice is strained as I fight with my head and heart on whether staying is the right thing to do.

"I miss you." The desperate quiver in her small voice makes leaving her harder, especially when I know she is hurting. "Jax, I miss being around you."

"Poppy…" I stop, cussing to myself.

"Jax, I miss you. I hate how I've let this go on for as long as I have." I can hear the desperation in her voice. "My body is begging me for your touch, but if I can't have it, I want my best friend back."

She has never lost me, even if we can't be together, I will always be her best friend. I've been desperate to have her back in my daily life, but we need to figure out a way to move past the best morning of my life. Which sucks, because my body still craves her, but my mom is right, being with her is not an option.

There is no way I can leave her now, even though I am frustrated at her for telling Lewis we slept together. I want to ask her why, but I don't know if the answer would help mend the distance between us. I motion for her to sit up, and when her head is up enough for me to sit down, I lean back on her couch, propping my legs up on the coffee table. Poppy lays her head on my leg and begins tracing small circles on my thigh. My body instantly begins to hum, craving more from her. I start playing with the ends of Poppy's soft blonde hair, trying to not think about the growing feeling of lust burning my stomach. Shit, I can't stop the sinful thoughts fueling the need to have Poppy again, harder to ignore.

"Why did you tell Lewis?" I fist the ends of her hair as the question I didn't want to ask slips out.

"I wanted to hurt him as much as he hurt me." Poppy sniffles. "I know I shouldn't have told him we had sex without talking to you first, but I've found out some things since then, making me see red when he texted me, asking if I would meet him for coffee before he came over to get the rest of his things. When he sat down and said he missed me and breaking up was a mistake, I couldn't stop the words coming out of my mouth." Poppy sniffles again, rubbing her nose on my pants. And I flinch at the sound of her crying.

"No, it wasn't fair to me, but I'm not mad at you. What do you mean, you found out some things hurt you?" I shift a little, which makes Poppy look up at me. "I know the way he left was awful, but did something else happen?"

"I found out he was sleeping with other people, and he said he met someone at his new college when he left. I feel so stupid, because I thought we were happy until we started fighting nonstop." Poppy tucks her hand under the blanket she is tucked in.

Wait, I didn't know Lewis met someone else. Fuck, what is it with the Jacobs siblings and cheating? Does he realize what he lost? He must have, because he tried to come crawling back for Poppy.

"When did you find this out?" I say through clenched teeth.

I want Lewis to come back so I can sucker punch him in the face. At least she's single and wasn't stepping out of their relationship to warm someone else's bed like he was. Lewis and I both lost our friendship today, but for different reasons. I have felt guilty for sleeping with Poppy for a bunch of reasons, and Lewis was one of them, but I am no longer going to regret hooking up with my best friend's ex-girlfriend.

"I had my suspicions when he first started talking about transferring colleges. However, it was confirmed when I ran into someone at a party while I was waiting in line for the restroom, and she looked freshly fucked. She had messy, rumpled-looking hair, and her makeup was smeared. She was talking about sleeping with Lewis. She didn't know who I was or if I could hear." I move some hair out of Poppy's face, and I find her cheeks pink.

"Damn! I never thought he would fuck around on you. I guess we didn't know Lewis and Lilah like we thought we did." My heart races from knowing exactly how Poppy is feeling right now. "At least you didn't know the girl he hooked up with," I say, trying to find a silver lining, but from the way she tenses, I clearly put my foot in my mouth.

"I didn't know the girl at the frat party, but the girl he is seeing at his new school, we both know her." Poppy hiccups.

"I don't know anyone who goes there." My brows scrunch together.

"Yeah, you do, do you remember the bitch you took to winter formal?" Poppy turns onto her back, looking at me with her mouth smashed into a thin line.

Wait, Lewis is seeing Lana! How the fuck did I not know she went to college in Texas? That isn't the important thing right now. How could Lewis go back to her? Lana is annoying and not a nice person. I had always wondered why Lewis would hook up with her, but I thought he stopped when he started to pursue Poppy.

"Fuck, that's messed up." I don't know what else to say, because nothing I can say will make what he did better.

"Sometimes I can't help but wonder if they were hooking up when we were together in high school. I've been second-guessing my whole relationship with him since I found out, and I hate it." Poppy kicks her feet out, stretching her short legs on the couch. "I was going to break up with him, but when he did it first, I was a little relieved, but I tried so hard to end it on good terms, but he wouldn't let me. Which is one of the reasons why I was so distraught when you came into the living room."

I laugh; she is so short her feet don't even touch the other armrest, which is fucking cute.

"I didn't even know about Lana. I'M SO PISSED! I could kick his ass for hurting you like this." I move Poppy's hair off her forehead, tucking the soft strands behind her ear.

"Jax," she gasps. "You should know violence is never the answer." I look down at Poppy's pink cheeks.

"I know." I rest my arm across Poppy's stomach.

"Why do things with us have to be so complicated?" Poppy's cheeks redden some more. "I want nothing more than to feel you on top of me again. I can't get it out of my mind. I want to do it again." With each of her words, I can picture exactly what she is talking about, and I would be lying if I said I didn't want the same thing.

"Damn," I cleared my throat. "I can't stop replaying the way you sounded and how you felt under me." I groan, feeling my chest vibrate with a groan. "Poppy, we need to consider the people who could end up hurt from us being together, especially if it doesn't work out. I don't want to risk it as much as I want to say fuck everything and make you mine now." I cough, trying to clear the lump forming in my throat. "You also need time to move on from Lewis, because I don't want to be your rebound."

"No, Jax, you could never be my rebound. Can't you feel it is hurting us more when we aren't together, and I'm not talking about sex. I know being together is complicated, and I love your family, but we need to do what we feel in our hearts." Poppy's eyes close a little, and when she's done talking, she bites her bottom lip.

Poppy suddenly sits up, turning to me as she moves a few inches away from me. I can feel the heat of her body on mine. I watch with wide eyes as she boldly swings her leg over my thighs, adjusting herself until she is comfortably straddling me.

My back straightens as Poppy rubs her hands down my chest, but I don't move an inch, other than the muscles of my chest and stomach flexing under her blazing touch. The combination of having her on top of me, the feeling of her hands rubbing my chest, and the lust pulsing through me makes my brain fog, and doing the right thing slips further away from my sex crazed mind.

The urge to touch her back intensifies quickly and grows stronger until I put my hands on her hips, holding her firmly on top of me. I know she can feel my excitement poking her, but I think it only encourages her to keep going.

Poppy smiles down at me. "Jax, I don't care who thinks us being together is wrong. Feeling this good should never be a bad thing," she whispers in my ear before playfully nipping at my earlobe.

I mean, I could try to argue with her, but I would be a fool to deny both of us what we are craving. I don't want to fuck anything up for her and my family, but damn, I feel like a horny teenager can only think with his dick with her on top of me like this. Teenage Jax would be stoked if he knew he was going to get to have sex with Jax again.

I cup her ass with my hands, giving her a gentle squeeze. She leans forward, kissing me. Fuck, her kisses are the sweetest thing in the world. Nothing will ever be better than the feeling of Poppy in my arms. She breaks the kiss long enough to yank my shirt over my head.

I chuckle. "Poppy, slow down, we have all night."

She leans back to look at me with the widest smile I have seen from her for a long time. I missed seeing her look this happy. She is glowing, and I'm so proud I am the one who is making her look more like herself again.

"Stand up," I commanded her lightly, winking at her.

Poppy leans back a little, staring at me with her bottom lip between her teeth.

If this is what she wants, we are going to do it my way. Poppy slowly stands up, looking down at me, her eyes widening, but her lip stays firmly between her teeth.

Poppy's tight leggings and crop top leave nothing to the imagination about her petite body. I said it once, and I'll say it again.

Her body was made for fucking. Damn it, I can't wait to have her bent over the couch, and if I'm lucky enough to have her a third time, I would love to press my weight on her while she is under me, like the first time we had sex. I want her in any and every way I can.

"Take your clothes off for me." I give her a devilish smile as my eyes continue to roam over her body.

Poppy hastily takes her tiny shirt off like the thin fabric is on fire, dropping the soft shirt on the floor next to our feet, but won't do. I pick her discarded crop top off the floor, standing over her. She is so tiny I am towering over her, making her look more like the doll she already resembles. She looks so appetizing in her leggings and bra, but I want her to reveal herself to me slowly.

Her eyes start watering as I pull her arms over her head. I slip the shirt down her arms, over her head, and back on. I sit down, lying back on the couch with my legs spread wide and my arms stretched across the back of the couch.

"Slowly," I say gruffly, in a simple command.

Poppy's eyes widen, her cheeks glow with the perfect shade of pink, and mischief replaces the tears and sadness in her eyes. "You're a dirty man," she bites her lip.

"You have no idea." I wink.

Poppy begins to sway to silent music playing in her head, and I know I'm in for a good show as she slowly teases me, moving her shirt up, painfully slow, revealing her lacey bra is so thin I can see her pebbled nipples on full display, begging to be freed. Once her shirt is off, she tosses it to the side. Poppy runs her fingers through her hair before she runs her hands down her small, perky boobs to the high waistband of her pants.

My eyes never leave her. She turns away from me, shimmying her hips, and I swear I'm about to bust when she bends down slowly revealing herself to me. The white lace thong she is wearing is the cherry on top.

After she frees her feet from the tight fabric, I lean forward, grabbing her by the hips. My mouth waters with the anticipation of tasting her, but I need to give her one last chance to stop.

"Are you sure you want to do this?" I practically growl at her.

We both know anytime she wants to stop, I will, because I don't ever want to do something she isn't comfortable with. She moves her cute little ass closer to me as a silent way to tell me to keep going, but I need to hear her say what she wants out loud.

"Poppy." My voice, raspy as my eyes roam over Poppy's slim body one last time. "I want to hear you say it out loud."

"Jax," she sighs. "I'm yours," her whispered plea is all I need.

I move the lace of her little underwear out of my way, and I moan as my tongue gets the first taste of her. Fuck she is the sweetest thing I have ever tasted.

I have many thoughts swarming my mind as I lie on the couch. Jax makes us a super late dinner in a pair of tight black boxer briefs, and the view makes me hungrier for Jax than the yummy-smelling food wafting through my apartment.

"Jax, can I ask you a question?" I ask, sitting up, crossing my legs.

"Only if you do it topless," he chuckles at his lame joke.

"What did you think after the first time we had sex?" I sit up, looking at him.

He pauses in front of the stove, and his shoulders tense, making the scar on his shoulder blade move. A flashback to the night my father attempted to kill me slams into my mind. Jax wouldn't have the scar if he hadn't jumped in front of the bullet sailing impossibly fast through the air toward me.

"It took me back to sixteen-year-old Jax," he laughs deeply. "I wanted to fuck you so bad back. However, I never did anything because Lewis threatened to kick anyone's ass who asked you out, so no guy in school was willing to go up against him. He was my best friend, and I didn't want to break bro code even though I liked you as much as Lewis did. After a while, I forced myself to forget about my crush on you, and I genuinely started to fall hard for Lilah."

"WAIT! What do you mean Lewis called dibs on me?" I stand up from the couch. "That's so wrong!"

"You know, he made sure no one asked you out for years while he was nothing but a jerk to you. I thought he would never make a move, and senior year, he finally grew a pair." Jax doesn't turn around as he continues to cook, but his voice drops an octave.

"What the hell?" I walk over to the bar connected to the little island of my kitchen. I put my hands on my hips. "That's messed up! So, you're telling me other guys liked me."

Jax laughs, but I'm not sure if he thinks it's funny, I'm finding this out now or if he thinks my reaction is comical to him; either way, he is laughing so hard his shoulders are shaking. "I can think of a few other guys." Jax looks over his shoulder, winking at me.

"What did you think?" I pull a stool out sitting down.

Jax turns to face me. "I wanted to have you under me for as long as I could remember, but you were always off limits."

"You can't be serious. I'm not pretty, and I can think of a million other girls who are more adventurous and confident than I am. It was always hard for me to believe Lewis wanted me, but I felt you turned on that morning, and I was like, there is no way he has a hard-on because of me." My face flames bright red.

Jax narrows his eyes. "You are not just pretty, you are sexy, but more than that, you have this glow to you."

"Wow, so can I ask you something else?"

Jax's face softens. "Yes."

"What did you feel after we had sex together for the first time?" I look down at my fingers playing with the hem of Jax's shirt I'm wearing.

Jax walks over to me, grabbing my chin with his pointer finger and thumb, moving my face until I am looking up at him, "I was ashamed, confused, hurt, and so fucking turned on, but I also regretted what I said more than anything."

Jax fixes our plates and joins me at the bar. I see I have scrambled eggs, bacon, sausage links, and toast in front of me. Breakfast is one of the few things Jax will cook, even though he is a great chef and can cook almost anything. Compliments to Roxi for teaching him the way around a kitchen. She said she didn't want her future daughter-in-law to be the only person to cook, and he needed to learn.

"I get it, I felt the same way." I bite into my toast, and the melted butter mixed with jam is exactly what I need right now. "You know, growing up, my crush was always Lewis and you, but I never thought I would have a chance with either of you. When I moved in with you and your family, I knew I had to let my crush go if I wanted to be safe. After all, you were the one who was brave enough to see past lies and call your dad for help. Looking back on it now, I don't think I could have said anything that would make you not call Shane. However, you saw me the most bruised and broken out of anyone, so I never thought you would be able to look at me as someone desirable."

"When you were looking at a picture of your mom, I looked over at you, and the last thing I was expecting was to see you bruised and hurt. I was terrified because those kinds of things were always something you read about or saw in movies, but it was never real, at least in my life. I knew you couldn't stay there, since I didn't know what to do, so I texted my dad. I told him I delivered your groceries, and something was wrong, because you were hurt." Jax pushes his eggs around his plate. "But I've always wanted you until I thought I could never have you, and even after giving up all of my hope, I still would have jumped at the chance to have you."

"Jax," I set my fork down, turning in his direction. "I know we have a lot we need to talk about, but I don't want to only hook up. I want to be with you.

Jax coughs, choking on the eggs he just forked into his mouth. "We can go as slow as you want. I want you to be mine and only mine."

"I want to be all yours, too. We need to figure out how we are going to tell Shane and Roxi." I turn back to my plate.

"Poppy, we can go as slow as you want," Jax smirks, winking at me.

"Cool, so can we go to the Halloween party together?" I take a piece of toast, smothered in butter and jam, off Jax's plate.

"As long as you wear a sexy little costume." The lopsided smirk on his face is hard to say no to.

Fine, but you get to pick out our costumes." Jax smirks, nodding his head.

I don't know what I am getting myself into, but the idea of him picking our costumes out sounds fun. I'm a little frightened since he has done something with assless chaps since he had to wear them during rush week.

"Fuck yeah, you're not going to regret this." Jax stuffs some food in his mouth.

"Keep in mind whose customer you're picking out when you're shopping," I warn.

Jax turns back to me, smiling, looking me up and down. My mouth goes dry, and warmth pools in the pit of my stomach.

"Oh, I know exactly who I am shopping for." His eyes travel over my body, leaving a trail of burning need behind. "With a body like yours, the possibilities are endless. I'm going to have my work cut out for me.

"That is not reassuring." I put my hands on my hips.

"Don't worry, Pops, I won't put you in anything too bad." Jax licks his lips. "I want to show you off but not show off everything."

I groan because he was not being very reassuring and comforting, but I guess I am going to trust him. I was the one who put Jax in charge of the costumes.

CHAPTER 8

JAX

"Jax, what the hell!" Poppy shrieks loudly from the bathroom. "I can't wear this in public!"

I knew she would freak out over the costume I chose for her, but this is her fault, because she's the one who put me in charge of choosing our costumes for the party. What Poppy doesn't know is that she only has part of her costume with her in the bathroom. I want to show her off, but I don't want her on full display for other guys to see.

"You told me to pick the costumes!" I teasingly shoot back, chuckling under my breath.

"Yeah, but I thought you would go to a Halloween store instead of putting something together, instead of making me look like it came from some low-budget internet porn." Poppy's voice rises the faster she talks.

"Pops, you could never look like a cheap pornstar. Besides, some of those costumes are more revealing than the one I have put together for you." She swings the door open so hard it bounces against the wall.

I'm completely naked, holding my underwear in one hand, when I turn around. I have the pleasure of seeing Poppy in a corset top and stockings, held in place by those sexy little silver buckles on her garter belt. My dick twitches, and I mentally remind myself we have a lot more fun planned after the party. However, I could easily convince Poppy to stay home with me to celebrate Halloween with our costumes on the bedroom floor, if you know what I mean.

"Jax, there has to be more to my costume than this." She is looking down at herself with her eyes wide and her face flushed. "I can't go out looking like this. Other guys will be checking me out, and it creeps me out thinking about it."

She twists around, looking down at herself until she finally looks up at me. A certain type of hunger instantly clouds her doe-like eyes. Poppy bites her lip, looking up at me from under her lashes, making me want to sink my own teeth into her perfect pouty lips. I watch as Poppy's eyes leave my face and slowly travel the length of my body with no shame. When she gets to my rock-hard dick, her jaw drops a little, freeing her bottom lip. Her tongue darts out of her mouth, wetting her red painted lips.

"Stop drooling. We don't have time for that." I chuckle, checking Poppy out. "Well, with you looking good, I may have to make time."

My eyes roam over her slim body before I turn around, trying to focus on getting ready so we can go to the party and get the fuck home so I can have my way with Poppy for the rest of the night. I pull the deep lilac man thong I chose, strongly considering putting some jeans on instead. I know I'm going to be more uncomfortable in this thing tonight than I was all the way through rush week, but hopefully this will be the last time I wear these things. As I am adjusting my junk in the constricting fabric of my underwear, I feel the sharp sting of teeth biting sinfully hard into my left ass cheek.

"Poppy," I growl, but not from pain; the bite didn't hurt, it only turns me on more. "Don't start something we don't have time to finish."

Poppy giggles, turning away from me. She looks at the bed and finally sees the rest of her Halloween costume. I can tell she is happier since she has more to her costume than she originally thought.

Poppy looks up at me through her lashes. "Oh, don't act like you didn't like it."

"You know I liked it, but you'll pay for that later." I walk to my bedside table and grab the little box, holding a gift I got for Poppy when I was shopping for her costume. "I have something for you."

"Jax." Her mascara-painted lashes flutter.

I can't tell whether she is nervous or excited from the little box I am holding up.

"Bend over with your hands on the bed!" I say louder than I intended, but the excitement coursing through me is getting harder to contain.

I'm so excited for the gift I got for Poppy. I grab the little vibrator I bought for her costume. I watch as Poppy slowly lowers her upper body. Once she is bent over, I move the soft fabric of her panties away from her, and I insert the vibrator in the right spot. She squirms a little, and I know she can feel the toy is now resting snuggly in the perfect position in her thong.

"Jax, that feels weird." She is whispers.

"Don't move, I promise you will like it." My raspy voice strains to get all the syllables out. "But if you don't like it, let me know, and I'll stop. We won't do anything you don't want to."

Poppy nods her head, but she doesn't say anything.

I unlock my phone and open the app I have the little vibrator synced to. Poppy squirms a little, and she looks over her shoulder at me. Her cheeks are flaming bright red, and her eyes are wide.

"Are you ready?" I ask with my eyes locked on hers.

"JAX! No, I've never done this before." She reaches between her legs, and I place a hand on her lower back.

"That's shocking considering who your ex is. If you don't like it, tell me, and we can stop." I reassure her again.

I lean over her, nipping at the pale skin on her shoulder, before turning my attention back to my phone for a second. When I think Poppy is ready, I begin moving my finger slowly around my phone screen so she can get a feel of the new sensation. She looks down at the bed, making her long hair fall, hiding her face. I move my finger a little faster, like it is dancing across the screen.

Poppy's breathing becomes labored, and she fists the bedspread. "OH!" Poppy moans loudly.

I stop moving my fingers on my screen, and Poppy sags onto the bed. I knew she would like the little gift I got for both of us if she gave it a chance. I lightly smack her ass.

"If you still want to go to the party, we need to get dressed and leave before I decide to hold you captive here." I grab my phone and walk to the side of the bed where the rest of my costume is.

The brilliant idea of the gift, as I watch Poppy's face redden, and her breathing speed up as she feels the new toy vibrating against her while she finishes getting her costume on, excites me. I grab my phone again, and this time I change the options, choosing the pulsing setting and putting the speed on one, so I can also finish getting into my costume too. I pair my man thong with white leather assless chaps, a mesh wife-beater tank, cowboy boots, and a deep lilac leopard print cowboy hat. If I were a stripper, I know for a fact I would be making bank. I don't mean to sound cocky, but I've worked my ass off for the body and muscles I have.

I can hear Poppy's breathing growing increasingly labored. After I buckle my chaps around my hips, I turn to find her bracing herself on the edge of the bed, dressed in her costume, but she hasn't been able to put her boots on yet. Her face is flushed, and her eyes are shut tight. She looks so beautiful, bent over with her mouth slightly open in a little O shape. I would give anything to drop to my knees behind her and get a taste of how sweet she is.

"Put your shoes on, I'll let you have your orgasm on my tongue," I demand a little too forcibly. However, Poppy's face lights up with excitement, and I know she wants it as much as I do.

"You're very cruel," she hisses between her teeth as she tries to straighten her back, but another shot of pleasure pulses through her, making her arch back down onto the bed. "JAX!" She moans my name, almost like she is begging for me.

Her whole body shakes, and she grabs my navy, blue sheets with white-knuckled fists. Poppy looks at me with pleading eyes. She's panting, but the way she is biting her bottom lip almost has me busting. This is the hottest thing I have ever seen, and pride swells in my chest as Poppy lets the next wave of pleasure hit her again without coming.

I can't let the sweet torture of pleasure torment her any longer, so I get on my knees behind her, moving her panting and the vibrator out of the way. Before Poppy can miss the feeling of the little vibrating bullet-shaped toy, my tongue begins lapping her up. She is so wet and hot, I know she'll get off in no time.

Poppy begins moving her hips, riding my face with no shame. I grab ahold of her hips to keep her where I want her, and I add more pressure as I swirl my tongue in the right spot has her calling out my name again.

I pull away from Poppy when she drops her head onto my bed, breathing heavily. I lick my lips, looking down at her flushed, pale skin. She looks wonderful in her post orgasm bliss, but I know I need to get us out of my apartment, or we will never make it to the party.

"Jax, can I have a taste?" She is peering up at me from under her lashes as she sits on the foot of my bed.

I can barely contain myself from the way Poppy is peering up at me with glassy, lust-filled eyes; her curls are now messy, but she still looks perfect. Since we got together, I've struggled to tell her no, and when she asks me for something so sweetly, like she is doing now, I know I can't deny her something we both want.

"You can have whatever you want." I sit next to her on the bed, and she rises slowly to her feet.

She stands there looking down at me for a moment, chewing on the side of her bottom lip.

"Do we have to take the stripper underwear off?" Her question is far more innocent than the last. She is going to make me bust before she even touches me from acting so sweet.

"If you want to do this, you do it the way you want to." I lean back on my elbows, winking at her.

"How will I know if I am doing it right?" Her voice is so soft I almost couldn't hear her.

"It's hard to fuck this up. You should know how to give head because I'm sure Lewis asked for it all the time." I mentally curse at myself for mentioning her ex.

"I was always too nervous to be around him." She looks away from me, embarrassed.

"Poppy," I say, waiting until she looks back at me before I continue talking. "Do what feels right to you." I don't want her to feel any pressure to do anything she doesn't want to do, but I would be lying if I said I wasn't thrilled to have this first with her.

She drops to her knees in front of me without saying a word. I watch as she moves her shaky hands slowly up my thighs. She stops for a second before she unbuckles the belt of my assless chaps, I feel the elastic band of my thong move from my skin. Poppy looks back up at me with one side of her bottom lip tucked in between her teeth again. When she looks back down, she hooks her other hand in the waistband of my "stripper underwear" like I have seen her do on herself. I guess she wants them completely out of our way, which is fine by me.

"Lift your hips." Her voice is shaky, barely above a whisper, but her soft command is clear.

I lift my hips a couple of inches off my bed, and she pulls the silky material of my thong down my thighs. She moves slowly, but the more she does, the less nervous she seems to be.

"Pop…" I don't get the rest of whatever it was I wanted to say out before she flicks her tongue on the tip of my rock-hard dick.

At first, I'm not sure if Poppy meant to lick me until I feel her do it again. She pulls back a few inches, licking her lips like she enjoys the taste of my skin, which only makes the pleasure of her simple movement much better for me. Poppy doesn't move, and I begin to wonder if she has changed her mind until I feel a couple of puffs of warm air hit the head of my dick before I feel her warm, wet lips wrap around me. I look down and see she is looking at me through her long lashes. A shot of pre-come shoots into her mouth. FUCK! I feel like a horny teenager getting a blow job for the first time.

She begins bobbing her head up and down in a slow, teasing motion. I want her to go faster, but I gave her control, and I intend to let her keep it. I fist the bedspread to keep my hands from moving to her hair.

She moans around me, and the vibration causes me to drop my head back, because looking down at her is too fucking much right now.

"FUCK!" I roar, making Poppy jump a little, but she doesn't stop.

She moves faster when she hears me. She begins sucking with more energy.

"Don't stop. Your hot little mouth feels like heaven!" I rasp.

She moans again as if she is trying to say something, but it is my undoing.

She keeps up her delicious torment until I am empty, milking me with her hands and mouth until she gets the last drop. I can hardly believe her when she said she hasn't ever done it before, hard to believe, because she sucked me off like a pro.

"Fuck, which was the hottest thing I have ever seen." I grab Poppy's hand, helping her off her feet, and lay her down next to me.

She kisses me lightly, but I grab the nape of her neck, deepening the kiss. Poppy wraps her arms around my neck, pressing her body closer to mine. This further proves my point about how we should skip out on this damn party and stay here to celebrate Halloween on our own.

My hands begin traveling down Poppy's back to her ass, and I know I need to stop, so I unwillingly break our embrace as her hands begin to explore my body. "We have to get going." I kiss Poppy on the forehead. "Go fix your hair and makeup. I need to get dressed." I give her perfect ass a sharp slap as she turns away from me.

The party is packed with tipsy college coeds who are talking, dancing, kissing, or playing beer pong. Poppy and I walk into the crowded party holding hands, and we immediately get some strange looks. I'm not surprised, considering everyone here knows we are best friends. The last thing I care about is what other people outside of my parents think, but I know this will make Poppy feel uneasy, at least for a little while. Over the past few weeks, I've thought a lot about how some people might react or talk about us being together, but if I let others influence my relationship, I risk losing my happiness.

When Poppy stopped talking about Lewis last week, I thought I was safe to ask her to be my girlfriend. She agreed quickly, but she also admitted she already thought she was. I told her we should tell my parents first, so they don't find out from someone else. I think the only way they would find out before we can tell them is if Macey, who is Lewis and Lilah's mom, somehow found out. We have been careful with how we act around each other in public in case Lilah is around.

I look around the living room, and the first thing I see among the sea of people is Lilah. She is sitting sideways on some guy's lap with her feet kicked out on the empty cushion next to her. She narrows her eyes. She smashes her dark red painted lips into a thin line, narrowing her eyes at Poppy and me.

"I'm going to go get us a drink." I lean close to Poppy's ear.

Poppy nods her head. I watch her walk away from me until she sits on the couch next to Lilah. I turn away from them, weaving between people who are sweating from the heat being produced by the number of people in here or by dancing. Either way, the smells hit me are like a slap in the face. Loud giggles from girls trying to get laid start to grate on my nerves. Normally, I love a crowded party, flirting, and drinking, but not tonight, because all I can do is think about getting Poppy home.

There's a line for the kegs, which allows for the perfect time to have some fun. I move to one of the walls that is facing where Poppy is still sitting. I punch in the passcode into my phone and open my new favorite app. I move my fingers around the screen as fast as I can. Poppy's head falls onto the back of the couch, and she squeezes her eyes closed. She has the cutest O-shaped lips, making me think about what she was doing with her mouth before we left. Thankfully, Lilah isn't sitting next to Poppy, so I can enjoy my view better.

"So, what's going on with you and Poppy?" Lilah's high-pitched yell rings in my ear.

"I don't see how any of your business is?" I move my fingers over the screen one more time before I lock my phone, my eyes never leaving Poppy, who is staring at the ceiling with rose colored cheeks.

"Well," she pauses, tugging at the straps of her bra top, making her boobs jiggle. "With our history and how our families are connected, I think I have a right to know what the fuck is going on between you two. Whatever you are doing with her won't only hurt a lot of people we both care about but has the potential to blow up both of your lives." She puts her hands on her hips.

"Lilah, I don't give a damn what you have to say; you lost the right to comment on my life when you were fucking cheating on me with anyone who gave you the time of day." I spit at her.

"I tried to apologize, but trust me, I regret it." Tears begin to pool in her eyes. "From my experience, I know what it feels like when your own actions ruin a lot of people's lives."

"You're right, actions do have a chance to hurt people." I push off the wall and shoulder past her, muttering under my breath, "I have to go."

Lilah catches up to me, and she grabs hold of my wrist. "Listen, Jax, it's not going to hurt Lewis; this will also hurt your family. They wanted to adopt her after they found out what her father was putting her through." I pause even though I know I shouldn't have.

I shake my head, trying to get her words out of my head. She has no right to throw my family and what Poppy went through in my face.

"Lilah, drop it." I hiss through my teeth.

I stopped coming to the parties I knew Lilah would be at, and I know now I was making the right choice. I walk away from her in a pretty shitty mood. This confirms I should have tried to convince Poppy to stay home.

"See you at Thanksgiving!" she yells at me.

I force myself to keep walking even though her words echo in my head. I knew they were invited, but I didn't think they would come. Well, not after both of their children cheated on us. I find Poppy in the same spot she was in when we got here, but her head is down, and she is scrolling on her phone.

"Poppy, can we go?" I beg, knowing I sound desperate when I get to her.

She lifts her head from her phone screen and looks behind me. I'm sure she can see why I don't want to be here. I glance behind me, and I see Lilah is still standing in the spot where I left her, with her arms crossed, scowling at us.

"Jax, take me home." She stands up, grabs my hand, and she lightly pulls me to my truck. "We have business we need to finish."

Her excitement to get me alone is a fucking turn on. I'm straining painfully against my man thong. I should've thought my costume through a little better, but I won't have to worry about for too much longer.

RED ZONE

CHAPTER 9

JAX

My mouth is dry, and my head is pounding. I didn't have a drop of alcohol last night at the party, but somehow, I still woke up feeling hungover. The nutty aroma of coffee brewing fills my nose, waking up my senses. After we left the party early last night, Poppy and I came home. We had fun exploring each other until the sun came up, but my body has a sick sense of humor and woke me up after I had fallen asleep a couple of hours ago.

The shrill sound of my phone ringing in Poppy's room gets my attention. Shit, I didn't want her to wake up yet. I had planned to make her breakfast in bed after I had some caffeine in my system. I walk out of the kitchen as the ringing stops, for it to start again.

I walk into Poppy's dark room as my phone stops ringing again. Looking at my phone, I see I have a couple of missed calls from my dad. I glance over at Poppy. Thankfully, the noise from my phone has not woken her up. My phone starts ringing again, and I answer it before the call drops.

"Jax." My dad's voice comes through the speaker loudly. "We have been trying to get a hold of you."

"I was making coffee, so I didn't hear my phone. I lie a little too easily.

I look over at Poppy, who is still sleeping next to me. She is lying on her stomach with her arms under her pillow, but her beautiful face is turned toward me. Her mouth is open a little as a small amount of drool pools around her mouth, wetting her pillowcase. She sounds so cute, snoring lightly.

"Are you and Poppy able to come over for dinner tonight?" My mom says.

I know Poppy would be thrilled to go home and have a family

dinner with the bonus of my mom's delicious cooking as much as I would, so telling my parents yes, we'll come over, is not a hard decision without talking to Poppy first.

"Yeah, I'll text you when we're on our way." I stand up from the soft mattress.

"Alright, see you later." My dad hangs up before my mom can say bye.

I don't want to think about what they could want right now, because they don't normally call this early.

Poppy stretches. "Jax," she groans my name in a sweet, raspy voice.

"Good morning." I lean down, kissing her cheek. "We are going to my parents' for dinner tonight." She turns to her side, looking up at me with a wide smile.

"Okay." I reach over, moving some of Poppy's soft blonde hair off her face.

"What do you want to do in the meantime?" "I smile, lying on my side, pulling her close to my body.

Poppy giggles, putting one of her legs over mine. I roll over onto my back, moving Poppy until she is straddling me. She blushes deeply as she looks down, locking eyes with mine. I run my hands down her legs until I get to her knees, back up to her hips. I feel goosebumps appear on her soft skin under my touch.

"Jax," Poppy sighs my name before she kisses me until I can't think clearly anymore.

I pull back, looking into Poppy's grey doll-like eyes. Sometimes I can't believe I get to be with my dream girl. She is tiny compared to me, at only five feet tall, with the prettiest pale skin I've ever seen. She has tiny freckles around her button nose. The more I look at her on top of me, her face flares from under the heat of my stare. I sit up, wrapping my arms around her slim waist. Poppy puts her arms around my neck, and I take this moment to flip her until I am comfortably lying on top of her.

I want to tell her I love her, but I know it is still too soon. Falling for Poppy is easy, and I've loved her for most of my life.

I lean down, kissing her deeply. I guess if I can't say I love you out loud, I will have to show her. Which will be easier to do than actually spitting the words out most of the time. I bring my hand down Poppy's thigh until I get to her knee. I hook one leg over my waist before I do the same with the other one.

"I hope you're ready." I lean in, kissing her neck.

"I'm ready for you," Poppy whispers.

"Pops, are you sure you're ready to tell my parents about us?" I pull into my old spot in the driveway. "I don't know why they called us here, but we can wait until Thanksgiving to tell them like we originally planned."

"I want them to hear this from us and not someone else. If we wait any longer, especially with how things went down between Lilah and you last night, we can't put this off any longer." She grabs her purse and hops out of my truck before I can say anything.

Poppy has a point. If Lilah hasn't said anything to their mother yet, it is only a matter of time before they do. I am nervous about how my parents are going to react based solely on the conversation my mother forced me into when they were helping Poppy move out, but I think they are going to need some time to get used to it.

My parents are waiting on the porch for us. I look at their tense smiles and the way my father's back straightens as he pulls his shoulders back. I can tell they want to talk to us about something important, because they are on edge. Tonight, might not be the best time to tell them Poppy and I are together.

"I'm so happy you guys are here!" my mom says, running from the front door, coming over, and hugging me tightly.

My parents take turns hugging Poppy and me. My family has always been affectionate towards each other, but for Poppy, I know that whenever she can get a warm, comfortable embrace from my parents, she treasures every moment.

"It's good to be home." I hear Poppy whisper to my mom.

Poppy loves my parents, and I know she's more nervous for this conversation than I am. Of the two of us, she has more to lose if things end badly between us. If things do end between Poppy.

"Let's go eat." Dad claps me on the back once before we follow Poppy and my mom into the house.

As soon as we walk in, I am immediately greeted by the wonderful smell of my mom's pot roast. I miss my mom's cooking as much as I miss being home, but I also enjoy being on my own. I have more freedom now, even though my parents weren't strict and I didn't have many rules growing up. Another benefit of living on my own is I get to have Poppy in my bed or her bed.

We walk into the dining room, and we sit around the table. Poppy sits across from me, and I want nothing more than to move next to her. Poppy looks at all the food spread out on the table, licking her pink, glossy lips. One of her favorite meals is my mom's pot roast, so I know she is excited. My dad picks up the first dish, putting a heaping spoonful of mashed potatoes on his plate before passing it to me.

"How's school?" My mom asks, breaking the silence.

"Good," Poppy and I say at the same time.

Out of the corner of my eye, I see my dad set down the gravy dish with more force than necessary, because some gravy spills from the side of the white China onto the table.

"What the hell is going on between you two?" my dad roars, slamming his fists into the table so hard the dishes and silverware rattle from his angry outburst.

My father's unexpected anger scares Poppy enough for her to drop the serving spoon she's holding, hard enough to crack the plate. She lowers her head, covering her ears. Poppy's narrow shoulders begin shaking as she starts quietly sobbing. I look down as Poppy is locked in terror, her glassy eyes look far away, as if she is being pulled into a memory. Poppy's biological father was an abusive piece of shit, and she shouldn't have to be crying at my parents' house in fear like this.

"Shane, I thought we were going to wait to talk to them!" my mom shrieks, making Poppy flinch.

Neither of them is paying attention to Poppy and me anymore, because they are now taking turns yelling at each other. I have never seen my parents act like this before. Every time my father yells, he keeps banging his fist on the table. Poppy is locked in place, her face is ghostly white, as she tries to fight off a panic attack. I can tell she is trapped in a living nightmare right now, but it doesn't stop her from jumping a little in her chair with every hit of my father's fist into the table.

"STOP!" I shout, scaring Poppy too. I move around my mom to Poppy's side as my parents watch me with wide eyes. "You're acting like your behavior doesn't affect anyone else. You know what yelling and loud noises do to Poppy." I give my father a pointed stare.

I carefully place my hand on Poppy's shoulder, but my gentle touch startles her so much she winces so sharply that the chair she's sitting on begins to topple over, taking her with it. I watch with wide eyes as

Poppy falls, but everything around me swirls in slow motion. I reach out to try to catch Poppy, but she hits her head on the table so hard the dishes rattle. Poppy lands on the thick rug lying on the hardwood floor before curling into a small ball, crying, but all I can hear is my heart pounding loudly in my chest.

I bend down, but I don't touch Poppy this time. "Poppy," I whisper.

Poppy looks up at me with her mascara running down her pale face. There is dark red blood staining her pale blonde hair from where she hit the dining room table. Poppy sits up, throwing her arms around me. I lift her, cradling her tiny frame in my arms. She rests her head on my chest. I can feel Poppy's warm blood and tears seeping through my t-shirt, but a ruined shirt is the last thing I care about right now.

"I'm taking Poppy to her room. When I come back downstairs, we either can talk calmly or we are going home." I adjust Poppy a little in my arms.

My father looks down quickly, but not fast enough for me not to see tears pooling in his eyes. I ignore the fact that my father is clearly regretting how he was behaving as I take Poppy to her room so I can get her cleaned up and into pajamas.

I sit her on her bed before I walk to her closet to get her some soft, silky pajamas out of her dresser, and I go grab a wet washcloth from the bathroom. I sit next to her, and I press a warm rag on her head where she is bleeding. Poppy hisses, trying to move her head away from me. I'm sure she is hurting like hell. I look at her head, and I sigh at some relief I feel, because her gash isn't bad enough to require stitches, but still doesn't replace all my worry. Poppy has more than her fair share of head injuries in the past.

"It's all going to be okay?" I eventually say to Poppy.

Poppy doesn't say anything, but I can't help but notice she looks anywhere but at me.

Once the bleeding has stopped, I stand up. Poppy needs some food and water, but I stop. Poppy grabs my hand, and when I look back at her, the tears flowing down my face break my heart.

"Where are you going?" Poppy looks up at me under wet lashes as her bottom lip quivers.

"I am going to get you some water and food. After you get something on your stomach, I will give you some ibuprofen." I smile weakly, trying to keep my anger in check. "I can help you change into your pajamas when I get back if you would like." I wink; we both know if I had a choice, pajamas are always optional, but I am not trying to make any dirty jokes right now.

Poppy nods, lying back on her pillow. She closes her eyes. Before I leave her room, I turn the light off. I'm sure the lights are hurting her eyes, but she will never admit how much pain she is.

I walk downstairs grumbling under my breath about how pissed I am about Poppy being hurt, because my dad lost control of his anger and scared the shit out of her. I can't believe how my parents were acting, especially my dad. I've never seen him lose his cool like that. I walk into the kitchen, and I open the refrigerator. I can still hear my parents arguing, but at least they aren't yelling at each other now.

"I thought we agreed we were going to let them come to us about whatever is changing between them." My mother demands lightly.

"Roxi, I don't know what happened. I saw them looking at each other, and I snapped." My father mutters. "But you know exactly what is going on between them." The way my father's voice drips with anger shocks me.

"I get that, but we only know what Lilah told Macey, and that's not much." I hear some scraping noises, almost like my mom is eating or something. "We don't even know if what she said is true. Couldn't there be more between them than hooking up?"

"Yeah, but why would they walk into a party holding hands if nothing is going on?" My father groans. "Don't you think it is weird Jax wouldn't tell Lilah what is going on between them?"

My mother hums. "Hmm, not. I think Jax was right not to answer any of the questions Lilah was asking. She lost any right to know what is going on in our son's life when she cheated on him, and they broke up."

"I guess you're right, but why wouldn't they tell us?" I hear a chair scrape on the floor.

I walk to the doorway to the dining room and watch as my dad picks up Poppy's chair, pushing it back under the table. I know my father is beating himself up for how he acted, and even though I am so mad at him, he doesn't need to punish himself.

I walk into the dining room and watch as my mom turns to me. She has a plate of mashed potatoes, carrots, and a roll in one of her hands.

"I came to make Poppy something to eat so she can take some medicine." I rub the back of my neck.

My smashes her lips in a thin line, looking away from me. I think she knows I was listening to them. "I was going to bring you guys something to eat. Can I help you take them upstairs?"

I nod my head. I don't think Poppy wants to see my mom, but I don't want to make my mom feel worse about everything that has happened tonight.

"Um. Yeah, that would be great." I reach my hand out, taking one of the plates full of warm food.

"Thank you." That's all she says before we walk upstairs in awkward silence.

We get to Poppy's room, and my mom hands me the other plate. "I'll give you guys some space, but please let me or your father know if either of you needs anything. We feel bad, and we'll apologize after she gets some rest."

I nod my head, lifting the left side of my mouth in a crooked grin. "Thanks."

I walk into Poppy's room, which is dimly lit from the hallway. She is still lying back on her pillows in her regular clothes. The closer I get to her, the more the shadows cast on her face make her look exhausted.

"Pops, my mom made us some food." Poppy opens her eyes. I set our plates on her desk. "Let's get you in your pajamas before you eat."

"Okay," Poppy says weakly as she opens her glassy pink eyes filled with pain.

She lifts her arms, and I pull her shirt over her head. I take her tiny lacey bra off. I can't help but look at her soft skin and her small, perky breasts. I blindly reach for her pajama top, refusing to take my eyes off her body. I put on the soft bedspread. She takes this opportunity to take off her jeans and her pajama bottoms. I help put her arms in the top, and I slowly button it up, watching her smooth and slim body disappear under the red fabric.

"We should probably take you to the doctor to get your head checked out in the morning," I say, getting our plates, and I join Poppy in her bed.

"Yeah, you're probably right." Poppy takes her plate, laying it on her lap.

We talk quietly as I eat and Poppy pushes her food around on her plate. She has only eaten a few bites, but she is yawning, and her eyelids are starting to droop from exhaustion.

"Here." I grab her plate, putting it on her desk with mine, and I hand her some medicine. "Take this. I'm going to put our dishes up."

I kiss her cheek, "Jax, can you stay with me until I fall asleep?"

I put our plates back down and climb back in bed. Poppy turns onto her side, and I scoop her up in my arms. We lay there listening to the tick of the clock on her bedside table. Poppy's breathing slowly becomes heavy. I wait a few more minutes before I slip out of Poppy's bed, tucking her in, and I walk down the stairs.

I put our dishes in the sink. I need to go find my parents to talk to them about what happened, but for the first time in my life, I feel like I can talk to my parents.

"Ugh!" I groan, turning away from the sink.

I walk out of the kitchen to the living room. My parents are not hard to find. They are cuddled together on the couch.

"Hey," I say, sitting in the overstuffed armchair Poppy likes to sit in.

"How is she?" my father asks, sitting up on the couch more.

"I'm sure she is hurting more than she wants me to see. I looked at her head, and it doesn't look like she'll need stitches, but I still want to take her to the doctor tomorrow." I lean back in the chair.

"I need to apologize." My dad starts to stand up, but my mom puts her hand on his knee.

"No, let her rest. Jax can take care of her tonight." My mom has a sad smile on her beautiful face.

I can see the worry on both of my parents' faces, but there is more sadness than concern in my mom's watery eyes. I can tell she wants to say something. We all do, but no one knows where to start.

My dad clears his throat. "Were you going to tell us you guys were seeing each other?" My father questions me in a stern but soft tone.

He sounds angry, but he is keeping control of his anger and actions this time. Maybe this conversation won't be as bad as I anticipated.

"Yes, we were going to tell you at dinner, but you started going crazy. I don't understand how you both knew." My hands ball into fists on my lap.

"Macey told us. I guess Lilah went to her crying about what she saw, and you wouldn't tell her anything." My father says, grabbing my mom's hand.

My blood begins to boil at the mention of my ex's name. That family needs to mind their own business. I bet Macey came over here trying to get the information out of my mom, but it backfired since she doesn't know anything.

"Jax, we love Poppy, but being with her complicates everything," my mom begins crying. "I mean, we were her guardians and had she not aged out of the system, we would have adopted her."

"Sort of, she was never officially adopted, so there is nothing legal keeping us from being with each other." I lean forward, propping my elbows on my knees.

"We're not talking about legal issues." My father's back straightens, and I can tell this is uncomfortable for him. "Son, Poppy is like a daughter to us, and she has far more to lose than you do. I don't think you should take this further with her unless you're intending to marry her."

"Marriage? We haven't been together long enough to even think about that. We just started dating." I feel my face scrunch up.

I'm not ready to think about marriage. I always thought I wouldn't meet my future wife until I was out of college. Even with Lilah, we didn't want to consider marriage until we were established in our own careers.

"We don't want to see either of you get hurt again." My mom leans forward and pats my knee. "We love both of you more than anything."

"Mom, it's too soon to think about that, but things have happened so fast." My back straightens, and I watch as my parents exchange a glance with their lips pressed into a thin line and their brows scrunched together. "We love you too, and we hate we didn't get to tell you the way we wanted to."

"So, I was right when I talked to you while we were helping Poppy move out." My mom gasps. "How could you lie to me? We don't hide things from each other in this family."

Shit, my mom is the one getting worked up this time. She crosses her arms over her chest, huffing at me. Her cheeks turn a light shade of pink, and her eyes narrow at me as if she is waiting for me to make a move before she attacks me with her claws. I don't like it when my parents are upset with me, but I always feel worse when I let my mom down.

"No, we hooked up once before that. We didn't start dating until three weeks or so later." I cross my arms mimicking her.

"Why couldn't you have told us?" My mom whines. "We shouldn't have had to hear about it from Macey." My mom sags into the couch with her arms still crossed as if she gives up on trying to be angry at me.

"Mom, we wanted to tell you guys in person. It was not fair for Macey to tell you guys, because she doesn't know shit about what is going on between Poppy and me. I swear we never meant to hurt anyone." There is a lot my parents don't know. "The truth is, I've had feelings for Poppy since middle school. Yeah, it started as a crush, but when Lewis called dibs…"

My dad stands up red in the face. "Damn it, Jax, she isn't a trophy someone can call dibs on." The veins in my dad's neck are starting to pop out, but at least he isn't yelling.

"Dad, I let my best friend have the girl we both wanted. Lewis had liked Poppy since we were in youth football, and she would cheer for us on the sidelines." I smile at the memory. "He heard someone in the locker room in like seventh grade talking about asking Poppy to a dance, and he flipped." I shake my head. "I didn't know until that moment he liked Poppy still, because I thought he was mad at her for dropping their friendship when her mom died. I told myself I can put my crush for her aside for my best friend. I eventually started to move on, and I started dating Lilah, but when she cheated on me..." I swallow hard. "That fucking crushed me. I loved Lilah, but the way I feel for Poppy is not something I can describe because it's so new, but I don't want to stop being with her because things can get complicated."

"How do we know this isn't about sex?" My dad asks with his eyes narrowed at me.

I shrug. "I don't think it's something you need to know. I think all matters is we are happy together."

I'm not telling my parents I can have sex with anyone. They don't need to know sex is easy to get; it's the feeling Poppy makes me feel is hard to find words for.

My mom has tears in her eyes, but she has a huge smile on her face. "We do want that."

"We also don't want either of you to get hurt, but if it's what you want, we support you. try to remember she is always going to be a part of this family, whether you guys work out or not," my dad says while my mom nods in agreement.

"I know, and I wouldn't want it any other way. Good night." I get up out of the chair, and I hug my parents before I go to Poppy's room to check on her.

I stand in her doorway thinking about what my parents said, and I know being with Poppy is right, but I probably shouldn't push my luck with my parents. I don't want to leave Poppy alone when she is hurt, so I crawl into bed with Poppy anyway. She is still on her side, curled in a ball. I scoop her up to be my little spoon. She snuggles closer to me, and I can't help but think she fits perfectly in my arms.

"How did it go?" she asks in a raspy voice filled with sleep and lusty need.

"Everything is going to be okay." I kiss her head, and I hold her until she is snoring lightly several minutes later.

I lay awake for about two hours when the door to Poppy's room opens, and my mom tiptoes in. She has a bottle of aspirin in her hand. She hasn't noticed me yet, but I don't think she'll tell me to leave.

"How's our girl?" My mom moves some hair off Poppy's forehead.

"She's worried you guys are mad at her, but she'll be alright." I move some hair from Poppy's face so my mom can see her better.

"We were mad when Macey told us, but I'm more worried about her than anything else right now." My mom looks down at me. "We never wanted to make her feel unsafe here."

"She knows both of you love her. You guys can work it out tomorrow." I lay my head back down on my pillow.

"But we made her feel unsafe, and it is the last thing we ever wanted to do." My mom's bottom lip begins to quiver.

"Dad could have handled his anger better, but if Macey hadn't opened her mouth and let us tell you how we wanted to, I think things would have gone a little smoother."

"Yeah, you're probably right, but it doesn't change how concerned we are about what could happen if this ends badly." My mom's eyes pierce into mine.

She is right, but if we all think this relationship is doomed from the beginning, isn't it the same as telling us they don't believe we can make it work?

"Mom, we are happy, and we want to be together." I look down at Poppy, who is still asleep. "Can you guys give it some time to see if you can see if Poppy and I being together is not a trainwreck?"

My mom gasps. "That's not what we think."

Poppy shifts, snuggling closer to me. "That is not what we think."

"That's how it felt, but it also terrifies Poppy to disappoint both of you. The anger and saying how wrong for Poppy and I being together shows us how disappointed you guys are."

"I'm sorry, I can honestly say for your dad and me, we don't disapprove, we don't want anyone to get hurt." My mom sighs. "I wish you could believe us when we told you we are going to support both of you if this is what you want."

I nod. "Yeah, I do believe you."

My mom leans down, kissing Poppy's forehead before she leans over and almost falls on top of her, trying to kiss my cheek. I get up on my elbow and lean over Poppy, trying not to wake her up so my mom can kiss me good night. Despite how bad tonight was, I would love nothing more than to be the kind of parents mine are one day, and if I have Poppy by my side, I might be.

"Good night. I love you." My mom shuts the door, leaving me with nothing but angry thoughts.

I'm pissed Macey couldn't mind her own business, and I'm also mad at Lilah for spewing what I'm sure are lies to her mother. People need to mind their own damn business. I would like to work out my frustrations in the gym, but I don't want to leave Poppy. I put my face in her neck, and her sweet perfume calms me enough to let go of some of the anger racing through me.

CHAPTER 10

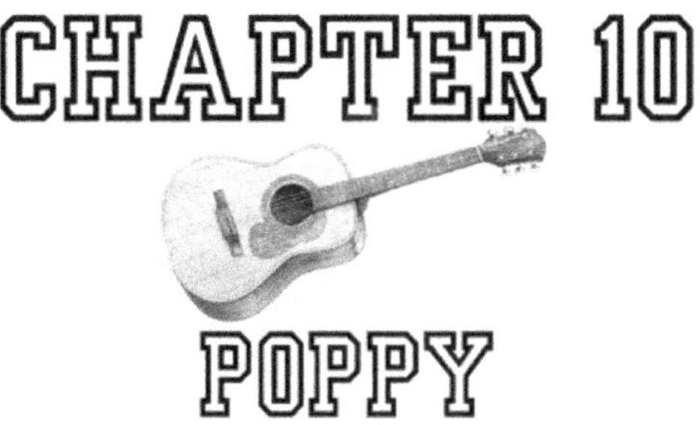

POPPY

To say last night was a disaster would be an understatement. I wish I could say this was the first time I freaked out at the table during supper at the Taylors' house, but I can confidently say last night was the first time I got hurt. I don't know what happened other than when Shane started banging his fists on the table, I felt like I was pulled back to when I was sixteen or seventeen and my dad was yelling at me for something he thought I did wrong. It would start with angry looks but soon escalate into yelling and fists pounding on the table. Sometimes that was all, but most of the time, dishes went flying and so did my father's fists. On calmer nights or nights when he didn't come home, I wasn't allowed much for dinner, if any at all. Many times, I sneaked food, but it was never enough to avoid being caught or to ease the hunger pains clawing at my stomach. Living with my father felt like tiptoeing through a minefield.

So, when I moved in with Jax's family senior year, I was starving and extremely nervous, but more than anything, I was terrified of them finding out everything I've been through and what would happen next. Everything felt so uncertain; the safety I eventually found would be taken away from me. But like I was saying, my first dinner here was a disaster. Shane had tried to include me in a conversation while I was trying to sneak a small bite of the best pot roast I had ever had. I freaked out in front of everyone, including Lewis, who was there for dinner too. I dropped my fork on my plate and broke their fancy dishes. They all were so good about the whole situation, but they did send Jax and Lewis to the kitchen so I could eat without feeling self-conscious. They had told me I could eat whatever I want and if I wanted something different, they had no problem making me whatever I wanted. I felt seen without feeling judged for the first time. They made me feel safe, which made living there with them feel more like home than it did when I lived with my father.

I push those ugly thoughts away, pulling on my socks. I'm waiting for Jax in the living room, so we can leave. I don't like reliving those dark times, but there are some memories I can't stop. I hope Shane knows it wasn't him I feared, but the nightmares forever locked in my mind.

"Poppy, can we talk before you leave?" I jump at Shane's unexpected voice coming from the stairs.

"Of course." I sit up, looking at him.

I lean over again to put on my shoes. I can hear Roxi close behind Shane, which is not surprising; they both want to make sure I am okay after last night. I sit up and watch as they both sit close to each other on the couch. Shane leans back while Roxi sits on the edge.

"We want to apologize for how we acted at dinner last night. Yesterday." Roxi sighs. "I had lunch with Macey, and she was demanding to know why Lilah was so upset. I honestly had no idea what she was talking about." Tears pool in Roxi's eyes as her voice cracks from the emotions overtaking her. "She accused me of lying to her."

Shane puts his hand on Roxi's knee. "Lilah said you guys were…" Shane shifts in his seat, clearing his throat. "She said you were sleeping together to get back at her and Lewis for breaking up with you."

"No, we aren't doing that. I mean, we both made mistakes, but cheating or vengeance is not something Jax and I had thought of or talked about." I begin nervously rubbing the hem of my shirt between my fingers. "Lewis did break up with me, but I was going to break up with him, too. I was still heartbroken about our relationship ending, but after I found out what he had been doing, I couldn't stay with him any longer."

Roxi and Shane look at each other with their eyebrows knit together. I never told Lewis I knew he was cheating on me, so he may not know I found out how unfaithful he has been.

"Honey, what are you talking about?" Roxi scoots up a little more on the edge of the couch, which I didn't think was possible without her falling onto the floor.

This time, I clear my throat and square my shoulders. I never planned to tell them, because I didn't want them to feel like they had to pick sides since they are friends with Lewis's mom and dad.

"Well…" I look over my shoulder. Jax must be upstairs still. "I have found out he has been sleeping around during our whole relationship."

They both gasp. I know this is a lot and surprising.

Tears well in my eyes at the sting of having to tell them something I hate to think about. I thought Lewis was my dream guy, but I guess his unfaithfulness was a blessing in disguise, because I found who I want to be with in Jax.

"We are sorry you had to go through that, but we don't have to talk about it if you don't want to," Roxi says, putting a hand on my knee.

"Thanks," I mumble, tucking some hair behind my ear.

"We want to apologize for last night. The last thing we want to do is frighten you and make you feel unsafe." Shane sits up on the couch.

"You do not have…"

Shane interrupts me. "Yes, we do." I watch him sit on the edge of the couch like Roxi, but he takes hold of her hand. "We overreacted, but most of all, I let my anger control the situation when I knew better. The way we acted was not acceptable."

"I'm okay. I promise. It was a bad night, but you have every right to be angry with us. I wanted to tell you in person about how things between Jax and me have changed." I begin playing with the hem of my shirt.

They both nod their head, but I wish they would tell me everything is going to be okay.

"We have a couple of other things we need to talk to you about." Roxi glances at Shane.

Shane clears his throat. "First, we need to discuss your relationship with Jax." I want to say something, but I need to let them say their peace before I say mine. Either way this conversation goes, I will not change my mind about being with Jax. "We don't want either of you to get hurt, or anything to be awkward between you two if it doesn't work out. However, you both are adults now, and if this is what you want, we will support you."

"Poppy, we want you to know, no matter what happens between you two, you will always have a home here." Roxi tears up.

They glance at each other, and I get a sick feeling in the pit of my stomach. They have more they would like to talk to me about. I take this as a victory of them being okay with Jax and me, but I was right when I said I wanted to be the one to tell them. I am livid with Lilah and Macey for putting their nose in my business.

"We didn't invite you guys over to talk about your relationship, but there is something else we do need to talk to you about," Shane says, looking at me with his brows pushed together.

Roxi wipes her palms on her sweater dress before grabbing a hold of Shane's hand, squeezing like she is trying to get her courage from him. "Since you didn't want anything from your father's estate or his belongings, we had everything put up for sale. Well, they have finally sold everything, but they found some things you may want to keep. Most of it is small things like jewelry and other trinkets that would have been sentimental to your mom, and a few things of your father's would be worth holding onto, like family heirlooms. There are some letters your mom wrote you as she was dying; they have some specific instructions on them; you'll understand when you read the labels on the envelopes." Roxi hands me a decorative box about the size of a standard shoe box. "The money from the sales has been deposited into a savings account. Shane will get you all the information sometime in the next week."

The box is beautiful with watercolor poppies and gold foil highlighting the beautiful flowers. There is a gold metal label frame on the front of the box. Inside the frame is a piece of cream cardstock with my name written in elegant black script.

"Um, thanks." I rub my hand across the lid.

"Poppy." Roxi clears her throat. "There is one letter in particular you need to read first." She pulls out an envelope tucked between Shane and her on the couch.

Shane gently pulls the envelope from Roxi's grasp, and she looks at me with a small frown. "It's going to be okay," Shane whispers to Roxi before he leans over, kissing her temple.

"Your mom told Macey and me about this project and why she was doing it. I forgot about them until the lawyers gave them to us. I grab the envelope from Shane, and I see my name written on the white paper in the same script as the box, but this one is in red ink. "You already had some of those moments, so you can read those letters when you're ready, but this first one has some information in it I know will be hard for you to read, but know we are here for you, and it is okay to lean on Jax. He will be able to love you through it."

I look at the letter, back at Roxi and Shane. My brain feels like it is going to explode. I don't know how to process all of this, especially since neither of them would go into details about what is in these letters. I feel a little blindsided because I have been doing so well at trying to forgive my dad for all he did to me in therapy, but something in the pit of my stomach flips, making me think something bad is about to happen. He somehow has the power to hurt me even from his grave.

"What Roxi is trying to say is if you need anything, we are here." Shane puts his hand on Roxi's bouncing knee.

I want to say something, but I'm at a loss for words, and the sound of Jax's footsteps is a welcome distraction. "Hey, are you ready?" Jax asks.

"Um," I clear my throat, looking back at Jax. "Yeah. I have some homework I need to finish."

I stuff the envelope into the box and stand up, hugging Roxi and Shane, before I follow Jax out to his truck. I put the box on the floorboard of the back seat, trying to erase it from my mind as long as I can.

I sit through the long drive in silence, trying to process what happened and what I want to say. Thankfully, Jax doesn't try to ask me what's wrong or about the box, even though I know he wants to from the number of times I catch him glancing at me out of the corner of his eye.

"Let's go to the doctor before we leave town. You're not looking too well." Jax says stopping at a stop sign.

I lay my head on the cold window, and the cooling sensation feels good on the gash and bruise I got from banging my head into the table. All I do is nod my head and close my eyes, letting sleep overtake me.

"What's in the box?" Jax asks while he pulls into the empty parking space next to my car.

"Jack's estate is finally closed. Shane and Roxi said these are some things from my mom and Jack, like family heirlooms and little sentimental trinkets they thought I might want one day." I swallow hard. "My mother also wrote me a bunch of letters before she passed away. The real reason your parents wanted me to come over to dinner last night."

"Shit, "Jax curses under his breath. "Are you okay?" He turns his body in my direction.

"I'm excited I get to have some more of my mom's things, but I am nervous about what the heck could be in this letter. Your parents said there is going to be information is going to be tough to read." I take a deep breath, trying to calm my building nerves. "I can't help but think once I read these letters, something in my world is going to change."

"Poppy, you don't have to read them if you don't want to. Maybe we can watch a movie or something to get your mind off everything for a little while?" Jax looks me in the eye with a sad crooked smile.

"I want to be alone for a little bit. I'll call you later, and we can do something for dinner." I quickly kiss Jax on the cheek before I climb out of his truck with tears pooling in my eyes.

Jax stays in his truck with his mouth open wide. I think he wants to say something, but he doesn't. I grab the box containing my parents' things out of the back seat. I slam the door closed before I run across the parking lot, before Jax can see I am breaking into what feels like a million pieces. I was doing so well until I started talking to Jax about the box I got this morning.

With each step up to my apartment, my head begins to throb more as the tears blur my vision, making finding my keys difficult. I drop the box, and the contents spill all over the hallway. I frantically start shoving things back in the box when a big hand holds out a letter. I know hand doesn't belong to Jax, because I had spent the last couple of years holding it. I grab the envelope from Lewis and stuff it back into the box while I scramble to pick up everything else.

"What the hell are you doing here?" My voice cracks as I stand up, looking around to make sure I picked everything up.

"Are you hurt? What's going on? Where's Jax?" Lewis asks, looking at me, back down the hallway.

"That's none of your business!" I quickly shove my key in the doorknob, letting myself into my house, slamming the door right in Lewis's face.

Why is he here? The last time I saw him, he was fighting with Jax, and he pushed me onto the floor. I put my purse down on the bar and grab my phone from the side pocket. I wonder if Jax is still in the parking lot. I call him, and like normal, he picks up before the second ring can stop. I need him to get Lewis to leave. I can't handle him being here right now.

"Pops." Jax greets simply, but the fact is his voice is scratchy hurts, because I know he is hesitating with answering the phone.

"Ugh," I walk through my living room quickly, making my way to my bedroom. "Lewis is up here." Jax curses under his breath. "Can you get him to leave?"

"I'm on my way up," Jax says before he hangs up on me, but I don't mind because other than thank you, I don't have anything else to say.

I sit down on the floor at the foot of my bed and place the box in front of me, tossing my phone over my head onto my bed. I look at the box while I try to wipe sweat off my palms on my pants, before I slowly lift the lid like something might jump out at me if I move any faster. I sort everything in neat little piles. I can tell which things are from my mother and which ones belonged to my father. Jack has only a few things in here, and I would like nothing more than to get rid of them, but if strangers thought they were worth hanging onto, maybe I should.

I don't want to deny my mother's dying wishes by not reading these letters, but I don't want to feel the grief I tucked away to protect myself during the years of my father's cruelty.

I lay down on my side, curling my knees to my chest, and I let myself cry, allowing the hurt and pain of the past to wash over me. The rug over the carpet makes it soft enough I don't feel like I need to move, but it's still not all comfortable. I know I could curl up on my bed in my comfortable blankets but is what I used to do after my father would punish me. However, the last thing I want is to be reminded of how broken I felt back when I am breaking now.

I faintly hear the front door of my apartment close with a soft thud. I know Jax has come here to tell me Lewis is gone. I can hear his footsteps get closer to my room, and I brace myself for him to walk in, seeing me like this.

"Poppy?" I hear him call out in a gentle tone.

I don't respond to him because I don't have to. Jax is the type of guy who will always come looking for me. He has all his parents' best traits wrapped up in a perfect package, and if I weren't such a mess, I would be more than happy for him to be with me right now.

A few seconds later, my door slowly opens, and Jax pokes his head in with a goofy look on his face before saying, "Lewis is gone." The silly look would normally make me laugh, but the devastation has my heart in a tight hold has me crying a little bit harder.

Jax's face falls as he opens the door a little wider. "Pops," He steps into the room, closing the door softly behind him. He picks me up off the floor, carrying me to my bed. He positions us to where we are face to face. I loop my leg over his, and he wraps me in his safe and warm arms.

"Poppy, what can I do?" Jax's normally smooth humor, laced in his deep voice, is replaced with a raspiness of emotions I've never heard from him before.

I wrap my arms around Jax's neck, pulling myself closer to him until I can bury my face in his neck. "I'm all right. I need you." I sob.

"It's okay, I'm here."

At Jax's words, tears flow freely down my face and onto Jax's skin. He rubs my back, letting me cry until I'm completely raw and my throat and eyes burn from the overwhelming emotions, and it becomes a little easier to bear.

I cough, trying to clear my throat. "I know."

I don't know how to tell him what I need from him when I don't even know myself. His arms are comforting, but it doesn't take away the fear clawing in my heart at the thought of what could be in these letters.

Eventually, Jax's deep snoring fills the room I have grown to love, almost lulling me to sleep. My heavy eyes snap open as I jolt. My body or mind won't let me fall asleep as the visual of the letter keeps popping into my head.

I ease myself out of the comfort of Jax's arms and my warm bed. I crouch down looking for the letter with my name in red ink on the front. I shut Jax in my room and quickly grab a fluffy blanket out of a chocolate brown wicker basket by the faux fireplace and walk out to the balcony for some extra privacy. There's a slight chill in the air, but thankfully, the sky is clear tonight. You never know what to expect with Oklahoma weather but tonight isn't as cold as it has been this last week. I can see the full moon and stars tonight, which is surprising with all the light pollution we have here.

I look at my name written in red ink for a long moment, thinking this handwriting looks exactly like my father's. I tentatively rip the envelope open and unfold the thick, expensive piece of paper my mom wrote on. The sight of my name written out in my mom's elegant penmanship makes me feel a little woozy. The color of the ink and paper blur together as bile rises to my throat, but I manage to swallow it down. I can get through this. My mom wouldn't write me something to hurt me, right?

To my sweet Poppy,

Seeing my mom's handwriting brings tears to my eyes. I miss her so much. Some days, the memories I have of her are too much because they are mixed up with the dark memories of my father.

I can't tell you how much it pains me, knowing I am going to be leaving you so early in life. The agony I feel with you here on earth without me is almost too much to bear, but I gather strength and comfort knowing you are going to have the best father taking wonderful care of you.

Yeah, right. If only you knew how he treated me. I want to rip this letter into shreds, but I also want to know more about my mom, and this will give me a piece of her I've been searching for. The bad thing is I don't even know the answers I'm searching for. I sigh, setting the letter down, looking up at the night sky as tears pool in my eyes. I pick the letter up, and the letters blur from the tears in my eyes. I wipe my eyes with the back of my free hand. The words appear, and my mom's handwriting calls to me.

I have decided to write you a bunch of letters. I don't remember exactly where I got this idea from, but when I learned about it, I knew I had to do the same for you. On the envelopes, there is a brief description of when I want you to read the letters. I hope I can make you laugh, give you some answers to questions you may have, and maybe some advice through my written words, since I can't be there. I'm sure you would want to ask why I wanted you to have this one on your fourteenth birthday.

What is she talking about? This letter is labeled with my name. This keeps getting weirder. I did think the label on this one was weird, with how different it was from the others,

Well, Poppy, I have a secret I need to tell you, one I want you to know.

Oh, boy, a secret. I don't know whether I want to know or if I can handle this. I've heard some secrets are better left with the dead, and I think this one is probably true.

I hope you're not surprised when I tell you I wasn't perfect. I have made some huge mistakes, but there is one thing I need to share with you. However, I refuse to regret this one, because it gave me you. I know this has the potential for you to look at me differently, but one day you may want to know this.

How important can one secret be, especially if it has the potential to change how I see her? If this is serious, doesn't it have the power to blow up my life? These are more questions to go with all the ones I already have.

A lot of things happened the year I got pregnant, some good and some not. One of my biggest dreams was to be a mom and to have a beautiful daughter named Poppy. I've told you part of the story, anyway, I had to go to my great aunt's house the year I got pregnant. Your dad came to visit me often, but while there, I had reconnected with a childhood friend. His name is Graham Bradley. We were childhood best friends, a lot like how you, Lewis, and Jax are. During my time at my great aunt's house, I had an affair with Graham, and he is your biological father. I have included what information I have about him on a sticky note on the back of this letter.

My stomach turns, and I feel like I am going to throw up. I'm not sure what to do or think with this information and is not the end of the letter. What else does she have to tell me that's so bad?

I am so sorry I am not here to tell you about this in person, but I thought in case anything happened with your dad, you would have a chance to have another family, because I know life is short and can be taken from you before you are ready to hear this. If you could ever be ready for this kind of thing. I want you to have a happy life filled with love, Happiness, and so much success, but I know I am still with you, and I love you more than anything.

My tiny flower, I love and miss you tremendously!
♡ -Mom

I crumble the letter in my hand when I see the nickname she gave me, Lewis would call me. I used to love when they called me that, but now those two little words hurt my heart more than anything else in the whole world.

How the hell can she leave this kind of bomb in a letter so casually?

I was right, this letter did have the potential to blow my world up, because it feels like everything around me is coming crumbling down, and I don't know what to do.

I don't know how to process what I read. What does my mother mean? Jack wasn't my biological father. How could it happen, and how sure is she that I am Graham Bradley's daughter? I know she said she had an affair, but if my dad went to visit her, isn't there still a chance he is my biological father? And if all of this is true, did Jack know?

I wonder if I had had these letters sooner; maybe my life could have changed for the better, but instead, I had to live through a nightmare. My face heats as anger surges through my blood. I endured so much at the hands of Jack when maybe I didn't have to.

I push away from the little table and grab the lighter for the candle we keep outside to keep mosquitoes at bay. I start to light the letter on fire, but blow it out before the flames can burn away my mother's words. Maybe one day I'll have the courage to find my biological father. I pick up the envelope and set it on fire. Watching the white paper with my name in red ink burn is oddly comforting in a sick way. After the paper turns to ashes, I go back to bed to the safety I feel when I'm with Jax.

"Where did you go?" Jax grumbles as I hug him from behind, making him my little spoon.

"I needed some air, so I sat on the balcony for a little while." I kiss the back of his head.

"I would have come with you. Why do you smell like smoke?" Jax's voice is muffled by his pillow.

"I know, but I needed to burn the past alone." I kiss the back of his head before I bury my face in his warm neck, breathing in his rich woodsy scent.

There isn't much I can take comfort in right now, but holding the man I am falling hard for makes the room spinning around us feel a little less big, cold, and lonely. I blink as more tears fall down my cheeks, soaking into Jax's skin.

I can't help but wonder if Jack knew about me not being his biological daughter. I hiccup as a sob breaks through me. Jax turns onto his back, pulling me into his arms.

"Cry all you want. I'm here for you." Jax rubs his hand down my back. "I can listen whenever you are ready to talk."

I open my mouth to say something, but I begin crying harder.

"Shh, you don't have to talk now." Jax tightens his hold around me, making me feel warm and safe when the world feels anything but right now.

The blurry room spins, and I feel lightheaded. I'm not sure if it is from the emotional overload or the fact that I hit my head. I snuggle into Jax some more, and I take comfort in knowing I'm not alone.

CHAPTER 11

POPPY

I've been searching on social media, and everywhere else I can think of to look people up online for a week to find this Graham guy my mother claimed is my biological father. I haven't found anything, and honestly, I feel more defeated as each day passes without learning anything about him. I never realized how difficult tracking someone down with only a first and last name is, especially since the address I have for him belongs to someone else.

With all this extra stress, I had three extra emergency therapy sessions this week. They have helped me think things through, and I have decided it is time to lean on my family for help. Don't get me wrong, I am still mad and hurt, I am now finding this out, but I think about everything I've been through, and I'm left with what seems like a thousand more questions I know I won't get the answers to. My therapist told me my feelings are valid, but I need to get to the root cause of why I am feeling this way, because there is more to this than the discovery of me having a different biological father than I originally thought. I feel like I am going to spiral into what I would guess is about another thousand questions.

I have distanced myself from everyone this past week. I missed out on one of Jax's games, and I have been ignoring his calls. I don't know how to tell him someone I thought was my dad, someone who hurt me and caused me so much pain, was not my biological father. How do you tell someone who had parents that has done nothing but loved hi unconditionally? Jax knows how my dad was, but he doesn't know the worst of what I've been through an I will never tell him. I don't want to poison him with that, because he already has scars from my father.

The wind whips around me, and I shiver as my hair and dress fly up a little. I am standing outside of Shane's office, trying to get enough courage to walk in, so I can ask for his help tracking this man down. I want him to know I want to know who they are, but they are my family. I would like to at least meet them, but they may not even want to do that. My phone vibrates in the pocket of my jeans. I know this is probably Jax calling me again, but if I hear his voice, I know I will break down in tears. I know he is worried about me, but if I hear his voice, I will fall apart.

I open the door before I chicken out and walk to the receptionist. I have never seen this one before, so I'm guessing she is either a temp or a new hire. I know his last lady retired a few weeks ago, but I can't remember if he had been able to find a replacement or not.

"I'm here to see Shane Taylor." I stop in front of her desk.

"Do you have an appointment?" she asks, not even looking up from her laptop.

"No…"

Her eyes look up at me. "You will have to make an appointment before you can see him."

"Oh, I don't need an appointment. If you page back and let him know Po…"

She stands up from her chair with her face turning red. "I said, come back when you have an appointment." She tips her head forward, looking at me from under her long lashes, which are clumped together with thick black mascara.

The phone rings, and she looks away from me, sitting in her chair before greeting the person on the phone with a cheery and fake "Shane Taylor's office." I'm sure she practiced in the mirror for a couple of hours.

The girl puts the phone receiver down and glares at me. I know for a fact that if she looked at the list of people to be patched in or to send back with no appointment, I would be one of the top names on there.

I could easily call or text Shane, I am here, but I want to mess with the rude lady some, so I call her instead.

"Hello, Shane Taylor's office, how can I help you?" she says in a sugary sweet tone, practically giving me a cavity with how sweet and fake she sounds.

"Yes, this is Poppy Monroe. I need to speak to Shane." I watch as she begins typing things into the computer with her long, pointed nails.

She glances over at me, and I start moving my mouth like I am talking to someone. "Yes, I see you are considered an urgent contact. If you will hold for a second, I will patch you through."

At that moment, Shane opens the door to his office. The girl whirls around in her office chair, she stands, adjusting her short and a little too tight black skirt.

"Poppy, I'm happy to see you." Shane comes over, hugging me.

"Thank you. I'm sorry for dropping by, but I need to talk to you about something." I hug Shane back, struggling to hold back tears.

"Of course." Shane wraps his arm over my shoulder, leading me toward his office. "Poppy, this is my new receptionist, Olivia." I watch as her eyes widen when she realizes what she has done. "Olivia, if Poppy ever calls or comes in, please notify me immediately. She is family and a top priority of mine."

"Yes, sir," she squeaks before I walk into Shane's office.

Once the door is shut, I go sit in one of the chairs across from Shane's desk. "Roxi should be here any minute," I say, looking around at some new photos Shane or Roxi had put up.

Every time I see myself in their family pictures hung proudly for their business partners to see, I always feel so honored. I think this was part of the reason I was surprised by the surprisingly unwelcoming greeting from the receptionist, because there are pictures of me out there, too.

"Poppy, is everything okay?" Shane looks at me with his brows furrowed.

I sit there until the door opens and Roxi walks in, oozing confidence. I wish to be like her one day, because she knows how to command a room when she walks in. She once told me it took her years to learn how to be so one with herself, and having a man who only sees you in a room full of people helps with self-esteem.

"Poppy, you look lovely as always." Roxi kisses my cheek.

"Thanks," I reply, even though I know Roxi is lying, because I didn't put any effort into my appearance today. "Um, I want to talk to you guys about something."

I don't miss the way they look at each other. Shane's brows knit together, and his lips mash together. Roxi's eyes widen, and she squares her shoulders.

"Okay, do you want to go to our house so we can talk. Maybe Jax can come over for dinner?" Whenever Roxi talks about Jax, her face lights up with a wide smile full of love.

"Um, no." Roxi's smile falls. "I actually asked Jax to meet at Jim's Onion Burgers and BBQ Shack."

"Onion burgers do sound good, but what do you need help with first?" Shane asks, looking more confused.

"I want to talk to the people who handled my father's estate. I would like more information on where these letters were uncovered."

"That should be easy enough," Shane says, picking his phone up from his desk.

"Well, I was hoping I could now." I bite my lip, hoping he says yes.

Shane scrolls through his phone and writes a number on a bright green sticky note. "Thank you, I'll explain when Jax is with us."

I follow Shane and Roxi out of his office, and I walk to my car in the small parking lot. Once I'm safely inside my car, I dial the number I got from Shane.

"Hello, Busy B's Estate Sale and Realty, how may I help you?" a chipper, squeaky voice greets me.

"Yes, my name is Poppy Monroe, and you settled my father's estate. I have a quick question about some things you guys sent to my former guardians." I drum my fingers nervously on my steering wheel. I hope she can't hear how nervous I am.

"Yes, I was the one who found those items. How may I help you?" The person sings way too cheerfully.

"Oh, thank you for getting me these things. I was wondering if you could tell me where you found the letters, but more specifically, the one that had my name written in red."

"Oh, everything in the box was already in there. I found it tucked under some papers in a cabinet in the downstairs office, but the letter with the red ink was hidden in the top drawer of the desk." The lady still sounds chipper. "However, there was another envelope in the drawer with your name on it, but it was written like the other letters in the same black, elegant writing with your name and captioned with something about fourteen years old. You should be able to find one in the box, too."

I clear my throat. "Oh, um, thanks."

So, my thoughts this last week were confirmed. There is a big chance Jack opened the letter, which would mean he could have known I wasn't biologically his all this time. My mind swims, and my stomach dips. If he knew and still hurt me as he did, which makes him worse than the monster I thought he was. The parking lot around me begins to spin, and blank spots appear in my vision. I don't want to believe Jack is capable of doing something so awful, but he is, since he was able to hit and punish me for all those years, and he never even apologized for it.

My parents are easy enough to spot in a burger place. Poppy asked me to meet her. I pull out the two empty chairs at the table, and I sit down. "Hey, what are you doing here?"

"Poppy came by the office and asked us to join you guys." My mom smiles at me. "She is making a phone call; she will be joining us, but it has been a while." My mom looks at my dad. "Should we call and see if she is okay?"

The waitress comes up and asks us what we would like to drink, and naturally, my father orders a sweet tea with half lemonade for Poppy and himself. My mom orders water with lemon, and I get a sweet tea.

"Did she say what she wanted to talk to us about?" I ask when the waitress walks away.

"No, she said she will explain everything when we are all together."

The bell over the door rings, and Poppy walks in with a halo of light around her, making her look like she is glowing. She walks to us, and I notice she is turning the heads of the people at the other tables around us. She doesn't know how beautiful she is, which is one of the many things I love most about her, because I am the one who gets to show and tell her.

"Sorry, I'm late. My phone call lasted longer than I thought it would." Poppy sits at the table, looking frazzled with her windblown hair. "I want to start by saying how sorry I am for not getting back to you guys sooner. I needed some time alone this past week to process what was in the letter my mom wrote to me."

"We are happy you are finally reaching out." I place my hand on Poppy's bouncing knee. "We're just worried about you."

"Well, I could use some advice right now." Poppy takes a couple of small sips of her tea. "I found out something shocking in the letter, and I don't know what to do with this new information. I had some extra therapy sessions, and one thing she kept saying was to lean on my loved ones." Poppy reaches into her purse, pulling out a crumpled paper that looks to be burnt in one corner. "I may have started to burn the letter so I could be the only person to know this secret, but I don't think I want to be the only one to have this information anymore."

I watch as Poppy hands the paper to my parents, and let me say, the whole time they are reading, their mouths open more as their eyes flicker across the page and to Poppy. What could be in the letter has shocked my parents speechless? I feel like I sit there for a long time before they give the letter back to Poppy, but she hands the burned paper to me.

I take the paper out of her shaking hand. I begin scanning the letter with the familiar nickname her mom has always called Poppy since the day she was born until she died. I scan the letter before I read it. I know this isn't long, but the contents written to Poppy have me reading more than once. There is no way I am reading this right, because this says Jack wasn't Poppy's biological father.

"Poppy." My father clears his throat, breaking the silence. "We had no idea about any of this."

"Apparently, no one other than my mom did. I think Jack knew, but I have no proof. I tried looking up the guy my mother said was my dad, but I couldn't find him on any social media sites." Poppy says as the waitress brings us our food, but I'm no longer hungry.

I can't be frustrated at Poppy for shutting me out anymore, especially after learning what she did. I don't know how she will be able to move past this information, but it proves how strong and resilient Poppy is.

I push a few pieces of my fried okra and curly fries over, squirting a heaping amount of ketchup on the wax paper lining the basket my food is in. Poppy takes the ketchup from me, and she squirts some on her wax paper and more into a cup of mayonnaise she asked for, so she can mix them to dip her fries into.

"Sorry, I think we are a little shocked by this new bit of information." My mom finally says.

"I get it." Poppy giggles softly. "I am still reeling from all of this, too." Poppy looks up at me. "I was furious the last two days, because of the news. I kept thinking if I knew about this guy, maybe I wouldn't have been subjected to Jack's torture."

"We don't know that." My mom frowns. "Jack may not have been your father genetically, but he was in every other way…" My mom trails off.

"In every other way that counts." My dad finishes for my mom. "But he also put you through is not something a father should ever be due to their child."

"I know. I called the company, because it was the only letter written in red ink and not in my mom's typical nice script, but it also wasn't sealed like the others." Poppy dips a curly fry in her ketchup and mayo mixture.

"What are you thinking?" I stop dipping a few fries in ketchup to turn my full attention to Poppy.

"Well, I know this is going to sound crazy, but I think Jack found the letters or knew about them. He read the first one and found out my mom had an affair, and he took his anger and grief out on me."

"Why?" my father asks before taking a large bite of his onion burger.

"I called the lady who handled my father's estate and asked about where they found the letters. She said this one was in a drawer of Jack's desk she even described the envelope. I would show you, but I let it burn."

"That doesn't mean he read it," I say, picking up my burger.

"I know." Poppy looks down at her mostly untouched food. "I would like to know why he hurt me so much."

My parents look up at Poppy with their eyes wide. "Honey…" My mom starts, but she stops looking at my father.

"It's okay, I know I won't ever get those kinds of answers." Poppy picks apart a curly fry. "I would like to see if we can maybe find this guy. He may have some stories about my mom I've never heard. She did say they were childhood friends." Poppy picks up her burger with only cheese and tomato on it and takes a bite of her greasy cheeseburger.

"What if he doesn't want anything to do with you?" My father asks the question I wasn't brave enough to say out loud.

"That's fine, or it will be. It would be nice for both of us to know we both exist. Right?" Poppy says between bites of food.

I know if finding him goes wrong, she will be crushed, but maybe she will let us be there for this time.

My father wipes his mouth. "I'll talk to my lawyers and see if they can help in any way."

"Thank you." Poppy relaxes a little, and she puts her hand on my thigh.

They start making plans about talking to the lawyers while I am still trying to process all this information thrown at us. The check comes, and my father pays for it before hugging us goodbye. I wait until Poppy is in her car and she pulls away before I speed to her apartment with thoughts bombarding me about how Poppy has been dealing with this life-changing news for the last week on her own.

The restaurant is about halfway between my parents' home and ours, but I had to stop for gas. After I got back on the highway, I may have broken a law or two to get home quickly.

Poppy is leaning against her car, waiting for me as I park my truck. Her hair is blowing in the wind, and I know she has to be cold, because she is wearing a dress. I climb out of my truck and before I can shut my door, Poppy wraps her arms around my waist.

"I'm sorry for shutting you out this last week." Poppy moves her hands under my shirt.

I turn around, lightly cupping Poppy's chin, moving her face to look at me. "I didn't like it, but I can understand why you did, especially after hearing what you found out."

"Thanks." Poppy bites down on her bottom lip.

"I want to be there for you and help you through all the curve balls life throws at you, but I can't if you push me away." Poppy wraps her fingers around the wrist of my hand that still has a hold of her chin. "No matter what happens between us, I will always be there for you."

"I know, I'm sorry," Poppy whispers.

"Let's go inside, and if you're up for it, maybe I can help you find something on this man, but if you would rather do something that requires no clothes, who am I to say no?" I kiss Poppy's forehead as she breaks out in a fit of giggles.

CHAPTER 12

JAX

I run down the field, cradling the ball in my right arm, trying to protect the ball as someone runs down the right sideline. I glance over my shoulder and push off with my left leg, moving my body to the right in time to avoid getting tackled. I begin running toward the end zone again, pushing with my legs to gain more speed. I push harder, wondering how I managed to miss the last tackle, when a large force slams into me.

Where the hell is Walsh? He is supposed to be protecting me downfield, and he let some big guy sack me in my blind spot. I jump to my feet and look at the player who tackled me. He runs backwards to his team with a big shit, eating grin plastered on his round, chubby face. I jog back toward my team as Walsh appears on my right side.

"Where were you?" I ask as he holds his fist out to give me a fist bump.

"Damn it, they kept getting in my way and messing with me," he grumbles. "These guys came to play."

"Shit, they came to play dirty." I shake my head.

Walsh snorts as we get in the huddle. I received a few slaps either on my helmet or pads from my teammates, silently telling me I am doing a good job.

"If we play this one right, we will either score or keep the ball away from them long enough for the clock to time out," Zeke grunts.

We all nod, bouncing on the balls of our feet, ready to go back on the field. This time, I am going to fake getting the ball, so they come after me. They will expect that, which is fine by me, because when Lewis left, they gave me his spot, so this play I get to run my old position. Our second-string said he didn't want to be the one to step into Lewis Jacobs' place, and it is bad luck. So, I'm stuck until we can find the right man for the job, but the odds are highly unlikely this season.

The whistle blows, and the fake out goes like planned. Soon, the ball makes its way back to me. I manage to run the ball until I see Zeke open, near the end zone. I pull my arm back, and the ball goes sailing through the air. The crowd goes still and completely silent, almost like they are holding their breath too, but Zeke is ready. The ball is flying in a perfect spiral. Zeke jumps, catching the ball. He lands on his feet like a cat, running a few feet, and getting the touchdown in time for the buzzer to ring.

The crowd goes wild, whooping and hollering in their cheers for a good game. We won the game. My teammates all start gathering in the center of the field, and Walsh calls out our victory chant. There is nothing like feeling the adrenaline of a game, the euphoria of the win, pumping through your blood. One of my favorite feelings I get from playing football; it comes right after the way I feel with Poppy being in my arms. I scan the crowd, my eyes automatically searching for Poppy's, because there is no one I would rather share this moment, this win, than with her.

"JAX! STOP!" Poppy giggles while I kiss down her neck as she tries to unlock the door to my apartment.

I nip the part of Poppy's neck connecting to her shoulder paint with perfect little freckles. Every time my lips touch her soft skin, goosebumps rise, and she gasps.

"Are you sure you want me to stop, because your body is telling me otherwise?" I begin kissing her soft skin again.

Poppy pushes the door open, tripping over her feet, and we tumble into my apartment, landing on the floor with a hard thud. I know the fall must have hurt her, because there was a loud thud and the floor shook under my weight. We hit the floor hard, and I curse under my breath. I landed on top of Poppy. I feel her wiggle under me, turning onto her back, and she looks up at me through her lashes with her mouth spread into a huge smile, showing me all her pearly white teeth, lighting up her beautiful face. I want to ask her if she is okay, but my concern disappears when she squeezes my ass.

"Jax." Poppy sighs. "I love feeling the weight of you on top of me.

It makes me feel safe." Poppy blinks a few times.

"Pops," the sound of her phone ringing stops the dirty comment.

"Wow, perfect timing." I groan instead.

This phone call better be important, otherwise I won't be happy about being cock blocked.

"Hold that thought." Poppy squirms under me again. I stand up, helping her to her feet.

The call drops, starts ringing again. Poppy grabs her little purse, and she quickly gets her phone as the ringing stops again. She looks at me before walking to the couch and sitting down. She calls whoever is trying to get a hold of her, but I already know it's my parents.

I sit next to her as she puts the phone on speaker and places it on the coffee table. I move her hair off her neck as the phone continues to ring. I lean in close, inhaling her sweet vanilla scent. I am so close to her soft, creamy skin when my lips dart out to wet my drying lips, and I accidentally lick her.

"Jax, what are you doing?" Poppy sighs.

I kiss her neck lightly. "What does it look like?"

Poppy leans back into me, the ringing stops, and is replaced by my father's calm voice, and the lustful heat flowing through my body vanishes like a bucket of ice water is being dumped on me.

"Poppy, do you have a moment to talk?" My father's voice fills the room.

"Sorry, I missed your call. We got home from Jax's game." Poppy begins playing with the hem of the jersey she is wearing.

"You're fine. How was the game?" Shane asks.

There is a distinct whooshing sound in the background of the phone; I would bet my dad is driving.

"Really good. They fought hard and won." Poppy shifts, pulling away from me. She looks at me with her wide eyes, making the little tattoo of our school logo dance as she smiles so big I can see all her perfect white teeth.

"That's good. We are sorry we couldn't make it to the game, but we are so proud of you." My mom's voice rings through the speaker.

"It's alright, there is always the next one." I shrug even though they can't see me.

I would have loved for my parents to come. Poppy has someone to sit with when they do, but when they called me this morning and told me what was going on, I knew they couldn't miss this urgent meeting. I don't take the support I get from my parents and Poppy for granted, because I know it is more than some of the guys on my team get from their families.

"We will see you in a couple of minutes." My dad hangs up.

Poppy looks at me with her eyebrows scrunched together and her mouth dropped a little. Neither of us was expecting a surprise visit from my parents today.

Poppy jumps when a knock on my door breaks the quietness that has spread through her apartment. I kiss Poppy on the side of the head. I let my parents in. When I open the door, my mom hugs me before she breezes past me straight to Poppy, hugging her tightly. My dad walks in, barely saying hi, but I can't help but notice he has a folder clutched tightly in his left hand.

My parents walk to the dining room table, sitting down. Poppy and I look at each other with an eyebrow raised before we join them. I kind of know why my parents might be here, but I don't know exactly what happened with their meetings with the lawyers this morning. Poppy is looking at my parents as she starts playing with the hem of her jersey again. Her knee begins to bounce, and I place my hand on her thigh, causing her to jump a little.

"We sat down with our lawyers, and they said they hadn't found anyone by the name of Graham Bradley who could be connected to your mom." My dad says, putting the folder on the table.

"I mean, it has only been a week since they started looking, so there is still hope. Right?" Poppy looks at my dad, but she puts her hand on mine.

Shane looks at me and back at Poppy. "There are two people by the name Graham Bradley who live in this state, one is living closer to the panhandle, and the other is not in the right age range." My dad clears his throat, shifting a little in his seat. "However, we have the name of someone who knew another man by that name, and they agreed to meet with me, but she is only willing to meet with Jax and me."

"So, what does this mean?" I ask my dad.

"It means one of two things. He could live out of state, or he has passed away. I don't know why she doesn't want to talk to Poppy, but the best chance of us getting any information is for Poppy not to come with us." My dad looks away from Poppy. I can tell this is not the news he wanted to give her.

Poppy's grip on my hand tightens at my dad's words.

"Well," My mom says, "I thought, while you go with your dad to meet this woman, I could do something fun with Poppy, like go shopping or get our nails done."

"That's fine." Poppy looks down at the table, but there is an unmistakable shake in her small voice. "Um, if you will excuse me for a moment."

I know Poppy is disappointed she can't go with us, but I know she will have a great time with my mom. Those two love doing girly shit together, and if anyone can get Poppy's mind off things, it's my mom. She is the perfect person for the job.

Poppy stands up from the table so fast her chair gets caught on the rug and falls to the floor with a deafening thud. "Let me get ready really quick," Poppy says, running out of my apartment with tears in her eyes.

My mom stands up, but I stop her. "Let me go talk to her. I know she is anxious to get some answers, and I'm sure she is a little hurt this woman doesn't want to meet her."

I walk out of my apartment and straight to Poppy's. I find her pacing in her room at the foot of her bed with her arms crossed. She turns, and her head snaps in my direction.

"Pops, I know this is hard…" She walks to me, putting her arms around me, and squeezing me tightly.

I put my hands on her back, rubbing up and down, trying to calm the storm brewing inside of her.

"Jax, that was so vague. How am I supposed to relax while getting my nails done and shopping with Roxi when I won't be able to stop thinking about whoever this lady is?" She cries into my shirt. "What if I'm related to her or she knows who my biological father is?"

I grab Poppy by the shoulders, moving her back enough for me to see her sad face hiding under the glitter and school logo tattoo on her cheek. Poppy hiccups as she tries to hold back more tears from falling down her face. I hold my arms open wide for her, and she immediately rushes into them, burying her face into my shirt again.

"I will text you updates when I can…" I trail off when I realize I promised something difficult for me to keep.

I never want to tell Poppy or make a promise I can't keep. I don't want my word not to mean something.

"You promise?" Poppy's question is hard to answer because there are some things I won't tell her over a text.

"Yes, but there are some things you shouldn't find out over texts." I rub her back again. "If you don't hear everything from me, it's because I need to tell you in person, but I will let you know what I can.”

Poppy sighs. “I know,” she whispers, looking up at me with glassy eyes.

I look at Poppy with her sad eyes, and all I want to do is curl up on the couch and watch a movie until we slowly forget what we are watching and get lost in each other.

“When my parents are gone, I plan on picking up where we left off when we got home.” I kiss my way down Poppy’s neck, nibbling softly.

“We can be quick.” Poppy giggles.

“Quick will never be enough for me. When I have you under me, I will take my time.” I reluctantly pull away from the warmth of Poppy’s neck.

Her pink cheeks turn a dark shade as the flaming blush creeps down her neck. I love it when she blushes, and it’s a good thing for me she does often.

“JAX! It is time to go!” My father hollers from the door.

“I’ll text you when I can.” I kiss Poppy before meeting my dad in the hall.

“How’s Poppy?” My dad turns, leading me down the hallway to the parking lot.

“She is nervous, but I think spending time with mom while we meet up with this lady is going to be good for her.”

My father nods. “I know, but there are some things I don’t want to tell her until we have dinner with this woman. I’ll tell you more about it in the truck.”

My father doesn’t say anything else, so I continue to follow him. Poppy was right, my father is keeping a tight lid on something, but from the sounds of it, he is not telling her everything to protect her or not make her worry more.

My dad unlocks the door, and I climb into my father’s truck. “Where are we going?” I ask.

My dad holds his phone out to me with an address on it.

“We are meeting her at a diner where she works.” I put the phone in its holder. “So, from the two names left, we were able to connect Poppy’s mom to this town. We can’t get any information on where he is. The name we got is of a Wynona Bradley, and all we can get is that this is his mother.” My dad backs out and starts driving toward the highway. “Our lawyer thinks talking to her first is a good start.”

“So, if this is the right guy, this would be Poppy’s biological grandma?"

"That's what the lawyers told me. They say the other man is not in the right age group, and from what they can see, he doesn't have any ties in this area of Oklahoma." My dad looks over his shoulder to merge into the next lane.

"Why didn't you tell Poppy all of this?" I readjusted the strap of my seatbelt, rubbing against my neck.

"Well, this is where it gets complicated. As I said, they couldn't find any information on him, so they are thinking he may have passed away."

"Shit." I curse under my breath. "Couldn't they look at death records?"

"Yeah, I think it would discourage Poppy from looking to see if she has any other family." My father shakes his head. "Besides, if this is Poppy's grandma, she may want to know her granddaughter. I would like to at least try to come home with something other than bad news if I can."

I look out the window as my dad drives us further away from home. I hope Poppy was serious when she said she won't push me away, because if this is a lot for me to take in, I can only imagine how she is going to react.

We pull into a small parking lot that has several cars parked in front of a diner. This place is a hole-in-the-wall restaurant. I hope the food is better than this place looks, because it looks like you can get food poisoning faster than you can finish your meal.

"Do you think the food here is safe to eat?" I break the silence lingering in the truck.

My dad chuckles. "There's only one way to find out."

We walk in, and we are immediately greeted by a "Seat Yourself" sign, but the problem is, we don't know what the person we are meeting here looks like. We stand there looking around when an older lady in the last booth along the windows looks at us and waves her hands in the air.

"Dad." I lightly hit my father on the shoulder with the back of my hand. "I think the lady over there is trying to get our attention."

As we walk to her, she stands up wearing the same uniform the other waitresses are wearing. "Are you Mr. Taylor?" she asks in a kind but loud voice.

"Yes, I'm guessing you're Mrs. Bradley."

"That was my mother-in-law. Please call me Wynona." I cram into the same side as my dad. "We can move to a table if would make you more comfortable."

"That would be great, my son is a big guy." My dad holds his hand out to help Wynona out of her side of the booth.

We move to the table closest to us. I pull the menu from the holder on the table and scan their massive list of food. Maybe the safest thing to order is a burger, because those are hard to screw up.

A waitress comes and greets us all cheerfully. "What can I get you guys to drink?"

My father holds his hand out to Wynona, and she orders a cup of coffee while my father and I order sweet tea. The waitress nods, walking away.

"So, your lawyers called me, saying something about how my son Graham might have a daughter, but they can't locate him," Wynona says, cutting straight to the point of this meeting.

I shift in my seat, and my father clears his throat. "Yes, that is correct."

"Okay, but my son never had a daughter. He did have two sons, though." She narrows her eyes at us.

I can tell this lady is feisty. She talks with so much emotion, and her hands fly all over the place. When Poppy is excited about something, she talks animatedly like this.

I look at my dad. "I'm sure he didn't know about her. My girlfriend's mother wrote her a letter before she passed and put down the name Graham Bradley as being her biological father."

My dad nods his head. "Yes, Ellenor, also said in the letter she knew him from when she was little and ran into him while she was here taking care of her great aunt while she was dying."

"Ellenor!" Wynona's wrinkled face scrunches up, making her look older. "Was her last name Cooper?"

I have no idea what her mom's maiden name is. She was always Ellenor Monroe to me. If Cooper was her last name, we must be getting closer to finding Poppy's biological dad.

"Yes..." My dad glances at me out of the corner of his eye.

Her eyebrows shoot up as she gasps. "I lost my son and his wife in a car accident many years ago, but there are some secrets I've held onto…" Wynona trails off as a glass of tea is being placed on the table in front of me.

"Are you ready to order?" the waitress asks cheerfully.

We all nod, trying to process the information she dropped on us, taking turns ordering quickly so we can get back to our conversation.

Wynona clutches her coffee cup with one hand, bringing her other hand, and places her palm flat on her chest. Her once raised eyebrows scrunch again.

"I'm so sorry to hear that." My father takes a sip of his tea.

"I remember this young girl whose name was Ellenor Cooper. She would come over every summer and spend two months with her great aunt, a few doors down from mine. My son befriended her quickly, and she would spend as much time at my house as they would at her aunt's. Ellenor had this magnetic energy to her, and you couldn't help but love her, and my son was no exception." Wynona tips her cup back, taking a sip of her coffee.

The way she's talking, I swear she is describing Poppy.

"That was one of the many things I liked about Ellenor. She was so charismatic, and you couldn't help but laugh when she was around." My father pulls out two envelopes from his pocket, taking out some pictures.

The top one is of Poppy's mom holding Poppy in the hospital the day Poppy was born. My father slides the pictures to Wynona, who gasps loudly at the sight of Poppy's mom.

"This is her." Wynona picks up the square picture with shaky hands. Her thumb rubs the corner where the date is.

"These are all copies; you may keep them if you would like to." My father unfolds a paper. "This is also a copy of the letter Poppy got from her mom."

We sit watching her as she reads the letter. Her eyes move quickly left to right as she scans the words. We sit in silence while we wait patiently for her to absorb this information, as we had to do a week ago.

"I know my son had an affair with her around this time. They were both going through things in their own marriages and brought them together. I'm not trying to justify what they did." She says her eyes drift back to the picture of Poppy and her mom.

"If you don't mind me asking, how did you know this was going on?" My father asks as the waitress begins placing our food in front of us.

Wynona looks down at her chicken-fried steak. "One night, I had to go pick up my son at a bar after he had a few too many drinks. He was talking about Ellenor and how he still loved her. Before I dropped him off at home, he asked me if he should confess to his wife about having an affair." She sighs, picking up a couple of her fries. "I told him he has to do whatever will make him happy, but living with a kind of secret can be hard."

"That was probably a difficult situation for him to be in." My dad places his hand on top of hers.

"Yeah, it was, but I am not sure Ellenor's daughter could be Graham's. His wife had gotten pregnant around the same time. He wouldn't have gone his whole life without being in her life if he knew," Wynona argues, "if she is my granddaughter, I would be thrilled, but how can we know for sure?"

My dad takes another photo out of the folder and hands it to Wynona. "This is a current photo of her."

"She is beautiful like her mom." I see her lightly touch the photo where Poppy's eyes are. "She looks happy, but there is so much sadness in her eyes. My oldest grandson has the same look, too. He lost his spark after his parents died, but his wife has given some of it back."

"Poppy has had some challenges growing up. I don't know if you know this, but Ellenor passed from breast cancer when Poppy was about ten years old…" My dad stops hesitating to say more about the darkness Poppy had in her life.

Wynona gasps, "I had no idea. That poor girl."

"Would you be comfortable doing a DNA test to see if there are any genetic links between you two?" I look at my father, and he nods, agreeing to my idea.

"That would be fine, but what good would this be for anyone if we investigated this now. She has a father…" Wynona stops talking and looks at us as my father and I exchange a side-eyed glance. "What?"

"I won't go into any details because this isn't my story to tell, but my son, Jax." My father waves his hand in my direction. "He's Poppy's boyfriend. She came to live with us during her senior year because her home life was not safe."

Wynona's eyes tear up, and her bottom lip quivers. She pushes her plate of untouched food away from her, looking down. "If she was Graham's daughter, I would have taken her in, too. She would have known so much love." Her voice is shaking from all the emotions surging through her. "I took my grandsons in, and she would have had her brothers growing up."

"We have no doubt you would have been a wonderful grandmother to her." My father scoots a little closer to her, holding her hand as he lets who might be Poppy's grandma cry.

I feel awkward sitting here while this lady processes the huge amount of information we've given her. I kind of hope she is Poppy's grandma, because she seems capable of showing Poppy a different kind of love than my family or I can give her.

She looks up at my father with red eyes. "What do we do now? If she is my granddaughter, I want to get to know her and be a part of her life if she will have me."

"Well, I think we should do a DNA test to confirm she is your granddaughter. There will be some markers to tell us if you are her paternal grandparent." My dad looks at her, searching her eyes and face.

I did the same thing when we got here. I've been trying to find any connection, at least in physical looks, tying her to Poppy.

"When do we go?" She looks at me.

"I can take you anytime I'm not in class or at practice." I offer.

"Oh, what sport do you play?" She looks at me. "If I were to guess, I'd say you play football. My oldest grandson used to play in high school, and you have a similar build to him."

I laugh. "Yeah, I play for college. I am hoping to go pro one day."

"Well, I am off work for the day if you want to go now." Wynona offers.

"That is fine with us," I say a little too fast. I probably should have let my dad answer.

"Yeah, let me make a call to my lawyers and see where they suggest we go while Jax takes care of the bill." My dad takes his wallet out, placing some cash on the table for a tip before walking outside to make his call.

While I wait in the short line to pay, I text Poppy with a vague update. I know she is probably worrying herself sick over what is happening, but if I can give her some peace to enjoy herself with my father I am going to try.

Jax: Everything is going well, but I don't have time to talk. I'll see you when I get home.

My phone vibrates, and I look at it.

Poppy: I can't wait to hear everything.

Poppy sends me a cute little picture of herself in a dressing room in a pair of tight black jeans, a deep blue sweater, a black sweater on top, and a pair of black leather boots. She looks damn good, and I am proud she is my girlfriend.

"Jax?" Poppy asks, lying on my chest, drawing circles on my bare skin.

I move Poppy's hair off her shoulder. "Yeah?"

"Do you think she could be my grandma?" Poppy turns her face, accidentally digging her chin into my chest as she looks at me.

"I think there is a good possibility." I rub my hand down Poppy's arm, making Poppy shiver from my touch. "She recognized your mom from a picture my dad gave her."

"I wish I could have been there, but we should get those test results back in a couple of days, so I may need to find a way to distract myself to keep from thinking about it all the time." Poppy pulls her bottom lip between her teeth.

I roll Poppy over on my bed, pulling Poppy with me. I shift until I'm hovering over her with my arms propping me up.

"I can think of plenty of ways to distract you." I lean down, nipping her lightly on the shoulder.

I press my weight onto Poppy, trapping her under me with her arms pressed to her side. I kiss my way from her shoulder to her neck, leaving a sloppy wet trail of kisses behind as I make my way to her soft, pouty lips. I kiss Poppy until her nails blissfully bite into the skin in my back, and I can feel her quake under as lust begins to fill us.

I pull back a few inches and watch as Poppy becomes undone with a fit of giggles filling the room as mischief begins to light up her eyes. She squirms under me, freeing her arms, which were trapped at her side. I feel her small hands move over my shoulders, and she cups the back of my neck, looking up at me with this sweet, innocent, and somehow devilishly naughty all at the same time.

"Then you'd better get to work," she bites down on her bottom lip.

"Yes, ma'am." I lean down, kissing her neck. "As much as I love this silky little nightgown on you, I think it would look better off of you."

She lifts her arms above her head, waiting patiently for me to strip her bare for me. She is always so eager to please me, as much as I am busting at the seams to rock her whole world.

I put my arms around her waist, turning onto my back, causing Poppy to roll with me. She sits up, and I watch with a huge grin while I wait for her to straddle me. She moves like she can read my mind, throwing one leg over my waist. She always does this little wiggle with her hips when she tries to straddle me from her legs, begging almost too short to touch the bed from how short she is. I find the move extremely cute and a major fucking turn on. If I'm being honest, Poppy can do anything, and I would find it cute.

I move my hands behind my head, and I look up at the prettiest girl I have ever seen. Poppy shifts above me as she moves the bottom of her nightgown over her hips. I watch with wide eyes, trying my damnedest not to blink as Poppy reveals her creamy white stomach up to her small but perky tits. My hands twitch with the need to reach out and touch her. She pulls her nightgown over her head so fast her hair falls over her shoulders, hiding parts of her body from me. I take my hands out from under my head long enough to move Poppy's hair from her chest. I trace my hands down her arms until I grab onto her slim hips.

"You know, you're the one who is supposed to be distracting me." She laughs, winking at me.

"Well, you've done a damn good job at distracting me." I reach up and lightly pinch one of Poppy's pebbled nipples.

"If you keep up that sweet torment, I will not be able to think of anything or see anything but stars in my eyes."

"That sounds like a challenge I'm up for." I sit up, looping my arm around Poppy's slender waist again, but this time I scoot until my back is resting on the headboard.

Poppy puts her hands on my shoulders and shifts, making herself more comfortable before she looks at me. "I can feel how up for it you are," she bites her lip, trying but failing to stifle giggles, making her whole body shake.

I lean forward, resting my forehead on hers. I move my hands to her hips, holding her to me. I love the feel of Poppy on top of me. I am a lucky man.

Poppy continues to laugh as I feel the tips of her fingers slowly dip into the waistband of my navy boxer briefs. She brings her head down, kissing my chest, leaving a little wet spot where her lips were. I wish they could stain my sink like tattoos. God, I am falling more in love with Poppy, and I don't ever want to stop.

CHAPTER 13

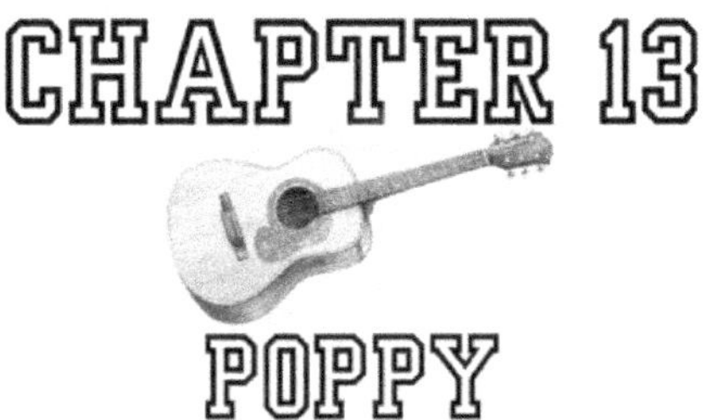

POPPY

The crowd around me is screaming and cheering, not caring that they are damaging their vocal cords. Jax's name is being chanted as he races past large men in pads with the football safely tucked in the crook of his arm. He looks so powerful as he makes his way across the field. I sometimes feel like I am transported back in time when I was a little girl, and I would watch Lewis and Jax play youth football. I was their personal cheerleader. I also think about when I would come for Lewis, and I think about our relationship.

I had always thought Lewis would be my one and only but was never the case. After I found out he was cheating on me, something in me changed. I still love him, I think I always will, but I lost all respect and trust I had for him. I can't be in a relationship with someone when those two super important things are being shattered beyond repair.

When we were sophomores in high school, I tried hard to forget about my crush on Jax. I was attracted to his silly and playful personality, but I always thought I wouldn't have a chance with him. I moved in with his family during my senior year, and I started to get closer to him and Lewis. I began to feel again for Lewis. I buried my crush on Jax so I would not have to leave the first place where I had felt safe since I was a little girl.

I stand up, snapping out of my depressing thoughts to join the man next to me, shouting for Jax to run! "Go, Jax!" I screech.

When I got ready before the game, I wanted to look extra cute for my boyfriend by wearing a pair of jeans and one of his extremely large jerseys is hidden under a puffer jacket in the perfect color of cream. When Jax gets me home after the party tonight, he will peel me out of my clothes like he does most nights. I know he will like the surprise waiting for him, but until, I am more than happy to look good on his arm.

Jax makes a touchdown, and I jump up and down screaming until my throat is sore. He cleared most of the field due to his impressive speed and his powerful, long legs. I watch as Jax checks for one of his teammates, and in lightning speed, his arm pulls back, throwing the ball to what you would think is an empty spot on the field. Chance somehow swoops in, catching the ball, running the short distance to the end zone, and making the winning touchdown.

The crowd goes wild! You can hear some boos from the opposite team's fans, but our cheers soon drown them out. The band begins playing the fight song, and the cheerleaders start dancing to the music. People around me hug or high-five someone, but my eyes are locked on the field. Jax is facing the stands, and he is looking right in my direction. He blows me a kiss, and when I return it, he runs back to his teammates. I never know if he can see me in the sea of people, but he knows where my tickets are, so I like to pretend he can.

"I wonder if Jax is going to be at the party later." I hear someone behind yell over the crowd.

"Probably, but doesn't he have a girlfriend?" I am assuming whoever replied to her is her friend.

"Yeah, but you know her ex fucked around behind her back, so I may have a shot." She giggles.

I turn around and see one of the girls who used to live on my floor when I stayed in the dorms. I am not surprised this is coming from her, because Lewis fooled around with her, too. This confirms how you sometimes will never truly know someone.

"Everyone knew he got around." The other girl shakes her head. "I don't know how she never found out, but I don't think you have a chance with Jax."

The girl who wants a piece of my boyfriend stomps her foot. "Why not?"

"His ex cheated on him. He was devastated until he got with his new girlfriend. I do not think he would want to hurt someone else like that." She shrugs, glancing over to the field.

The two girls finally leave the stadium, but I can still hear one of them talking about how she is still going to try to get Jax in bed even though he has a girlfriend. I don't have a lot of friends, and this is part of the reason why.

I wait in the stadium for the crowd to thin out before I go wait for Jax by the tunnel with the other players' girlfriends. I never understood why they were always distant around me when I was with Lewis, but I'm with Jax now, and they have accepted me into the little circle of friends they made. There is a lot about the time I was with Lewis that I don't understand, and the more I think about it, the worse I feel. He has tried calling me several times since I saw him after I got the box of things from Roxi and Shane, but I don't answer any of them. He has even left voicemails unopened. I don't know whether he wants to know what's wrong or if he wants to get back together but finding out how unfaithful he was ruined any chance of that.

I walk into the tunnel and see a couple of clouds of smoke from the girls who vape, and I hear soft whispering from some of the others. This group is cliquey. The upperclassmen's girlfriends tend to stick to their group, while the underclassmen stay away from the others. I've heard there is a major difference between one group being the wives of the players and the other girlfriends. I'm guessing I didn't fall into either of those categories when I was with Lewis, but I fall into the wives since I'm with Jax.

"Poppy," Katerina, Zeke's girlfriend and one of the girls in the wives' group, says, getting my attention. "I heard what those bitches said. Don't worry about it. Jax is not a fucking moron like Lewis." She pulls a long drag off her vape.

I shrug. "I know, but it still sucks to hear."

Katerina sucks some spit between her teeth. "Yeah, but we never thought Lewis was good enough for you."

Lidia, Walsh's girlfriend, nods her head in agreement. "That is why we never talked to you when you were with Lewis." She stands in front of Katerina. "Jax is a far better match for someone like you, but we have always wondered why you always went to dinner with Jax and his parents and not with Lewis's after the games."

I blush. I haven't had to explain this complicated part of our relationship yet, but I knew at some point I would have to. "Well, I moved in with his family my senior year." I lean on the wall next to Katerina.

"Oh, scandalous," Lidia laughs, "So they are like parent figures to you?"

"Yeah, Jax and his family took me in when we were in high school, but I was never adopted or anything." I know my face must be a deep shade of red right now.

"Besides, it's no one's business," Jax says, making all of us jump as he enters the tunnel.

I know why he is so quick to jump to my defense. I find it sweet because he doesn't want people to judge me or say something rude about that part of our past. I've learned people get extremely uncomfortable when they find out I think of his family as mine even before we got together, but when I tell them way in as few details as possible, they get embarrassed.

"Sorry, it's not like how it sounds." Katerina smiles weakly. "We like Poppy with you way more than when she was with Lewis."

"They were comforting me after I had to hear a girl talk to her friend about her plans to fuck you at the party later." I shrug away from the wall I was leaning on with Katerina. "The rest was girl talk." I lean up on my toes, puckering my lips.

Jax leans down, meeting me halfway. I feel his large hand lightly rest on the small of my back, pulling me flush against him. The way Jax kisses me makes me weak in the knees, and I see stars in my eyes.

Jax pulls a couple of inches away from me, breaking our kiss. "Are you ready to get out of here?" His warm, minty breath fans over my face.

"You have no idea." Jax releases me from his comforting embrace, but before I can miss the feel of his warmth, he grabs hold of my hand. "Bye, girls, see you at the party."

They say something along the lines of see you there or bye, but I'm not paying too much attention because Jax is leaning close to my ear as we walk to his truck, whispering all the naughty things he wants to do to me when we get home. I know anyone who passes us is wondering why my face is deep red, but with each word he says, the more I don't care what others might be thinking.

When we get in Jax's truck, he turns to me, but I climb into the passenger seat. "Where would you like to eat?"

"I want some chicken strips and fries." I put my seatbelt on.

Jax closes my door and jogs around the truck. I don't know how he has so much energy after playing a hard game, but her does.

I know where he is going to go. Most of the time, we go to Chicks after a game. I get the chicken strips and fries while Jax gets the wings and onion rings.

I watch as he climbs into the truck too and buckles his seatbelt.

"How is getting it delivered today?" Jax slowly backs out of his parking space.

"Yeah, maybe we can watch a movie?" I put my phone in Jax's center console, looking out the window.

Jax drives the short distance to our apartments with his hand on my thigh, singing country music, but I can't help but worry about the test results. We were supposed to get them a day or two ago, but nothing.

"Poppy, you, okay?" Jax asks as he pulls into the parking lot of our apartment.

"Yeah, I'm ready to get these test results back, but more than that, I want to know if everything is going to be okay."

Jax parks turns to me, giving me his full attention. "If it's not okay, then we will face whatever happens together."

"Do you think she will want anything to do with me if the results show she is my biological grandma?"

"It would be her loss if she doesn't." Jax puts his hand on my knee.

I unbuckle my seatbelt, get on my knees, lean over the center console, and I loop my arms around Jax's neck, hugging him as tightly as the space will allow me to. "Thank you."

My phone starts ringing, and I reluctantly pull away with a heavy sigh. I would bet Shane and Roxi are calling like they normally do after a game when they can't go. I would love it if they're calling to tell me they finally got the results from the DNA test back.

"Hey dad," Jax says, answering my phone. "We just got home from my game."

"How was the game?" I hear Roxi's question fill the cab of the truck.

We both know they watched the football game on TV. "Oh! The game was so good. Jax played his heart out."

"We agree. We are so proud of you, honey." Roxi gushes over her son winning.

"Thanks, guys." Jax, always being the humble guy he is, has a cute shade of pink covering his tan cheeks. Finally, it is his turn to blush instead of me.

He clears his throat. "Have you heard any updates about when the test results are going to be in?" He asks, changing the subject.

"Well, we called the labs, and since Poppy is no longer a minor, they emailed them to her two days ago." Shane's voice deepens, and I can tell he is not happy about the miscommunication on where the results were being sent.

"Wait! You mean to tell me I've had the results all this time?" I shriek, reaching for my phone out of Jax's hand.

"Yes, do you want us to be with you when you read them?" Roxi, being the rockstar she is, always wants to make sure we have all the support we need.

My hands begin to shake, rattling my phone, making the screen look blurry. "I, um." My voice sounds strange, almost like it is underwater. "I don't think I can wait any longer now I know I have the answers in my hands."

"Poppy." Jax takes my phone from me. "Let me see."

I wish there wasn't a console between us, because I could use a tight hug from Jax. I am grateful to have him and his family here with me, even if Shane and Roxi are here through the phone.

Tears begin streaming down my face. "Jax, I don't think I can look. Will you do it for me?" I whisper into the silent truck.

I can barely feel Jax's large, warm hand squeeze my thigh as I try to focus on pushing my next breath through my lungs. "Of course."

The air in the truck begins to thicken as I choke back a sob. I faintly hear Jax tell his parents he will call them back. He climbs out of his truck and jogs around to the passenger side. I watch with wide watery eyes as he opens my door and scoops me into his arms.

"Where are we going?" I hiccup, wrapping my arms around Jax's neck as he cradles me to his chest.

"I'm taking us to your apartment so I can hold you through whatever this email says." Jax presses a kiss to my temple.

My heart skips at Jax's words. He made me swoon so hard I feel a little dizzy from the emotions swirling too fast through me, practically giving me whiplash. "Thank you."

I can hear Jax's even breathing and his heart thumping steadily as he carries me up the stairs to my apartment. His soft coat brushes against my cheek, being soaked from my tears. Jax sets me to my feet in front of my door while I fish my keys out of my purse. I hand my keys to Jax, and he unlocks the door. I hope I am ready for this.

"Whatever happens, I'm here." My back tenses, and I feel like he confirmed part of my biggest fear.

We sit on the couch, Jax covers us with a periwinkle blue knit throw blanket as the sound of his phone rings three times before Shane's voice pierces through my apartment. "Hello."

"I'm as ready as I am going to be." I whimper.

Jax puts his arm around me, holding me close to his strong body.

Jax pulls up the email and clears his throat. "By order of blah blah blah…" Jax mumbles some things like my name and Wynona Bradley. "This DNA shows genetic similarities in what could be from a paternal grandparent." Jax goes on to explain the lab circled all the similar genetic markings I have to her, concluding biologically she is my grandma.

The question now is, what do we do with information? I know Shane will contact her, but part of me wants to even though I know she doesn't want contact with me until she knows the results, which isn't even guaranteed.

TAYLOR
12
END ZONE

Poppy squirms under me with a light sheen of sweat covering her pale skin, begging me for mercy as I pin her arms above her head. Nothing in this world feels better than being skin to skin with Poppy.

I pump my hips faster and harder as she climaxes, screaming my name, "JAX!" in a hoarse voice as the pleasure becomes too much for her.

Watching her fall apart under me is enough to send me over the edge, and once we are both still and breathless, I turn onto my back, pulling Poppy to my chest.

I can feel her heart thumping rapidly in her chest as our sweat mixes. There is nothing better than coming home from an away game pumped full of adrenaline from kicking ass on the field to a naked Poppy waiting for me in my bed.

Poppy lays her head on my chest, not letting the fact that I am sweaty bother her as she starts to draw circles on my chest. I move the hair falling over her back off her skin, and I rub my hand down her back.

"Jax, I want to go home early for Thanksgiving." Poppy props herself up on her elbow. "I know we are all going to your game, but I was on the phone with Shane, and he said Wynona would like to meet me." Poppy swallows hard.

Listening to Poppy talk about my family after sex is a mood killer, but I didn't give her a chance to say much of anything other than hi when I walked through my bedroom door before I practically pounced on her.

"Only if you are one hundred percent sure, you are ready." I move some of the hair sticking to the sweat on Poppy's forehead off her doll-like face.

"I want to meet her, but I'm also nervous about it." Poppy props herself up on her elbow, looking at me. "What if she takes one look at me and wants nothing to do with me?"

The fear in Poppy's eyes is easy to see. I hate how much she is tormenting herself over this. She had no control over any of these past decisions, and now she does, I want to make sure this is something she wants.

"It is her loss if she doesn't want to get to know you." I begin rubbing my hand down her back."

"You're my boyfriend." She stops tracing shapes on my skin. "You have to say that."

I shake my head. "I might be a little biased, but you know I don't say anything I don't want to."

I don't want to tell Poppy I am nervous about her getting close to these people. I do not want to see her hurt, and this has the potential to do that. However, I do think anyone who chooses to not to have Poppy in their lives after seeing how great she is is their loss.

"Thank you." Poppy leans up, kissing my cheek.

"When are we going to meet her?" I stop rubbing Poppy's back, resting my hand on her hip.

"Umm, Roxi called me this morning, asking me if I was ready to meet my new grandma." Poppy snuggles into my chest, drawing lazy circles on my bare skin.

"Well, if you're sure this is what you want, let's do it." I yawn as Poppy relaxes into my sore body from the game, making me tired.

"Jax, I need to tell you something," Poppy whispers.

"You can tell me anything." I run my hand up her back, feeling her shiver from my touch.

"I did something yesterday I probably shouldn't have." Poppy's hand moves down my stomach as she draws circles on my skin. "I got her address from the DNA test results, and I went over there. I never got out of my car, and I don't think anyone saw me." Poppy clears her throat. "I don't know if my bio dad was her only child, but she was with two guys. One was around our age or a couple of years older, and the other was still older, but I couldn't pinpoint by how much. Is it bad I'm hoping they are my brothers?"

"They may be your cousins. You can ask if you have any aunts or uncles." I relax a little.

"I would love that too." Poppy yawns.

I'm bummed about going to him early for Thanksgiving, because I had planned to take Poppy away for a romantic night, but I can another time. I know we haven't been together that long, but I want to tell her I love her. However, I want her to have everything she wants, and I know she wants a family more than anything.

I listen to Poppy's breathing grow heavy until little snores fill the room. "I love you," I whisper, even though I know she can't hear me.

Poppy is in her bathroom at my parents' house, smearing sparkly pink gloss on her already perfect lips when the doorbell rings, making her jump. I walk behind her, caging her with my arms on each side of the counter.

"They're here," she whispers, staring at me in the mirror.

Her mouth gapes open and he breathing begins to pick up. She is more nervous than she was when we got here this morning. I guess Wynona wanted to cancel this morning when one of her grandsons insisted on coming with her since the drive was a couple of hours. However, after talking to my mom, she agreed to come with the extra guest. She doesn't know whether he is her cousin or brother, and the anticipation of finding out is driving her crazy.

Before I can say anything, my mom's sweet voice fills the room. "Poppy, Jax, are you guys ready?" My mother peeks into the bathroom, but I guess she is checking to see if the coast is clear, and she's not walking in on Poppy and me in a compromising position.

Poppy leans into me. "I'm as ready as I am going to be," she pulls away from me as my mom nods, leaving the room.

I chuckle hard, making my shoulder shake at my mom. She may be grinning like crazy, but she is still nervous about our relationship even though she claims she has fully accepted Poppy and me as a couple. Getting my parents' seal of approval means a lot to me, and I know it does to Poppy too.

"Do we need a code word in case you want to leave?" I lean down kissing her cheek.

Poppy giggles, grabbing my hand. She leads me out of her room and to the stairs. Sometimes Poppy says walking down the stairs together reminds her of the first night she came to live here. I had come to her room to take her to dinner, and I can still remember the frightened look on her face.

A deep booming voice saying, "Nice to meet you," distracts me from my memory.

We step into the living room, and I see everyone shaking hands with everyone until Wynona looks over my mom's shoulder, gasping.

"Hello," Poppy's sweet voice stops everyone in the room. "You must be Wynona."

"Yes." The little old lady comes forward with tears filling her eyes. "You look like Ellenor." She hugs Poppy tightly. I can see Wynona's lips moving.

She is saying something only Poppy can hear.

Poppy's shoulders start shaking, and I know she is silently crying, holding onto her grandma for the first time. It's not until I look away from Poppy and Wynona embracing that I notice her grandson is looking at them with his eyebrows pushed together.

"Grams, are you okay?" Wynona pulls back a little and reaches her hand back never letting go of Poppy's hand.

Poppy reaches for me, and I grab her free hand.

"Otis…" She holds her hand out for him and moves the other until she is holding one of Poppy's hands. "I have someone special I want you to meet."

"Grams?" I can hear the confusion in his deep voice.

"There are some things I learned not too long ago, and I want you to promise me right now you will keep an open mind." Her brows are set in a stubborn line, wrinkling her face more.

The other stranger in the room is a beautiful girl. She comes over to the guy named Otis, grabbing his hand. "Grams, what's going on?"

"Otis, I would like to introduce you to Poppy. This is my first time meeting her, but I knew her mom when she would come visit her great aunt down the street from me. She and your father were childhood friends turned sweethearts until she stopped coming to town sometime in high school," she says, never taking her eyes off Otis, watching him closely.

His eyebrows scrunch a lot like I've seen Poppy do when she is confused, but from a little bit of information, Wynona says, shifts the energy in the air from nervousness to a thick tension, making everyone in the room tense. I know she is saying Poppy, and this man named Otis is her brother.

"Nice to meet you." Otis holds his hand out to Poppy.

Poppy lets go of me and reaches out with a trembling hand.

"Nice to meet you, too." Her voice shakes.

Wynona clears her throat. "Otis, this is my granddaughter and your little sister."

Something in the air shifts again, and Otis drops Poppy's hand like she is on fire. "WHAT ARE YOU TALKING ABOUT?" he yells so loud that Poppy drops to her knees, covering her ears.

"I'm sorry, I'm sorry, I'm sorry." Poppy keeps repeating as she curls into a protective ball at our feet, protecting herself from an invisible blow from her she has grown accustomed to.

Wynona, Otis, and the mystery girl all freeze, looking down at Poppy with their jaws dropped and eyes wide with horror not knowing what to do or say.

"Pops," I whisper, crouching down on the balls of my feet.

I keep my hands on my knees, but I know she can feel my body heat radiating from me with how close I am to her. Poppy stays curled up, repeating "I'm sorry."

"What happened?" Grams asks, looking at my parents. "Is Poppy going to be okay?"

I don't blame him for triggering Poppy like this, because none of them have any idea what she has lived through. However, irritation bubbles in the pit of my stomach.

"Let's go to the dining room. They will join us in a little bit." My mom's soft words let me know she is leaving me to comfort Poppy.

"Pops, we're alone now," I whisper again when everyone else is out of the room.

She sits up, looking at me with mascara staining her blotchy cheeks. She looks so sad and broken. I want to pick her up and hold her until she is happy again.

"Jax, I don't know what happened? His voice startled me, and I was instantly taken back to living in my father's house with him yelling at me, and his hand raised, ready to strike me across the cheek." Poppy wraps her arms around me, and I scoop her up, carrying her to her room.

She looks toward the library where the piano is. I know her emotions are surging through her at an overwhelming rate. I feel Poppy's finger on the back of my neck like she is playing the piano. Music is her escape and helps calm her, no matter what she is doing, because she gets so lost in what she is doing, all the harsh realities she has lived through disappear. Poppy lays her head on my shoulder, sighing.

"Let's go clean your face, and when you're ready, we can go back down to dinner." I adjust her a little in my arms.

Poppy hiccups, nodding her head. "Okay."

"Have I told you how proud I am of you? I know your classes have been kicking your ass lately, but you will make a great music teacher. Even though I still think you should try to put yourself out there and become a songwriter."

"Thank you." She lifts her head a little. "I looked into this one contest for songwriters, but I have to send in a video of me playing an original song with lyrics."

I set Poppy down on the bathroom counter. "Which song were you thinking of sending in?"

Poppy's cheeks flame bright red as she looks up at me as I wet a rag. She turns the water on and washes her face. "I've never played this one for you, but I would like to when it's completed."

I lightly press the washcloth to Poppy's face slowing cleaning the smeared makeup. "Whenever you want to. I love listening to you play and sing."

Poppy opens her mouth but shakes her head. "I think I'm ready to try this again. Hopefully I won't freak out this time."

I finish cleaning her face, and she turns around looking at herself. I hear her mumble to herself, asking if she will ever be normal.

We walk hand in hand down the stairs. We can hear Wynona telling Otis the ending of how she found out Poppy is her granddaughter. I stop when I feel a slight tug on my arm. Poppy has stopped in her tracks, looking at the dining room with huge eyes.

"I'm not mad at you or this girl. I'm pissed because Dad had cheated on Mom. Did Dad even know about this, and when were you planning on telling us, we have a sister?" At least he isn't screaming now, but I can tell he is not happy.

"Us?" Poppy gasps. "I never thought about how all of this could affect them. I was so concerned about having more family."

"Otis, don't talk to your Grams like that," The girl who came with them says.

"Sorry, Vi," Otis mutters.

"No, I don't think he knew about Poppy, but I will tell you now so you can try to get this through that thick skull of yours, but I want her in my life. I love you and your brother, but I have enough love to give to her, too." Wynona clears her throat. "I was going to tell you next Friday."

At this point, Poppy begins walking again, and I watch as she squares her shoulders and walks into the dining room. I follow her, and I can feel everyone's eyes on us as we sit down.

"She has the same color eyes as you, Wells." The nameless girl I only know as Vi whispers to Otis.

He presses his lips into a thin line as Poppy takes the seat next to my mom and across from her grandma.

"I'm Poppy." Poppy extends her hand out to Otis.

This is her small way of trying introductions again, but what she doesn't realize is how brave she is.

"I'm Otis, and this is my wife, Violet." Otis grunts, but he sticks his hand out after he waves toward his partner.

Wow, what are the chances of each of them being named after flowers?

"It's nice to meet you. I want to apologize for freaking out back there." Poppy is, of course, trying to dismiss her own feelings by making them more comfortable about what happened.

Both of my parents open their mouths to tell her not to be sorry, but I shake my head at them as I sit in the chair next to Poppy. I don't think this is the time to tell her she has nothing to apologize for, because she'll look at everyone with big puppy dog eyes, and tell them how sorry she is anyway.

Wynona clears her throat as we start making our plates. "If you don't mind me asking, what happened back there to make you react in such a way?"

My jaw drops as everyone in the room freezes. Dishes are put on the table, and I watch as the color drains from Poppy's face.

"Oh, um, I had a bad upbringing after my mom passed away." Poppy looks down, and I watch as she begins knotting her fingers together.

"You still had what you thought was your dad. I lost both of my parents at the same time, so what about your upbringing could be that bad?" Otis asks, scooping up some mashed potatoes onto his fork.

"Let's talk about something else. This is hardly a topic to have at dinner." My mom is trying to politely move the conversation to something else while trying to save some of Poppy's privacy.

"I'm sure it's not, but now I know I have a long-lost sister, I need to know she isn't connecting with Grams to use her," Otis says, putting his fork down on the table a little too hard, making not only Poppy jump, but also his wife, too.

I feel my face heat. Poppy would never use anyone for anything. She lived through hell for many years because she didn't want to inconvenience others. I ball my hands into white-knuckled fists and open my mouth.

"I guess now is as good a time as any to tell them. I mean, I did freak out after Otis's yelling triggered me." Poppy clears her throat and pushes her plate away. I know after she tells her story, she isn't going to want to eat anymore. "After my mom passed away from breast cancer, I was, of course, living with my widowed father, Jack." Poppy looks off in the distance behind Wynona's shoulder. I know she is zoning out as she is being taken back to a time she wishes she could forget forever. "Things changed so fast, and my father began to get angry. At ten years old, I've never seen someone get so angry before." Poppy shivers. "It started with yelling and belittling me, but nothing lasted long. He started drinking two days after my mom's death. Things went drastically downhill from there because he was too busy drowning his grief and anger in whiskey to see what a monster he was becoming. Dishes and anything made of glass were constantly thrown in his drunken rage." Poppy's voice begins to shake as tears fall from her eyes.

"Oh my." Wynona gasp.

Otis looks over at Wynona, and he places a hand on her shoulder. She reaches up, grabbing his hand as tears fill hers and Violet's eyes.

"Nothing extinguished my father's anger, not the whiskey, or even when he started using me as his punching bag." Poppy takes a deep breath. "If it wasn't for Jax finding out what happened to me our senior year of high school and…" Poppy stops, taking a quick sip of water. "Shane and Roxi taking me in, I don't think I would be alive right now."

Grams and Violet are crying, but Otis's jaw is ticking. He looks like he is ready to kill someone. "Where is he now?" he says through his teeth.

Poppy's back straightens, and she looks at my dad, at me. She doesn't want to tell this part. Poppy hates to tell people he isn't alive anymore.

My father clears his throat. "Ugh, he is no longer alive."

I can see the shock and confusion on everyone's face. When my mom said this wasn't the conversation to have at dinner, she wasn't lying.

"Oh, my." Wynona clutches her chest. "You poor thing. I wish I had known about you sooner so I could have taken you in."

Poppy gives her grandma a sad smile. "Thank you. Roxi and Shane have done so much for me. I don't know how I'll ever repay them for the love and patience they show me. Jax saved my life in more ways than I would like to admit. I know I'm safe with them." As Poppy subtly hints about the shooting, I rub my shoulder where my scar is.

"Well, we still need to tell Wells, my youngest grandson. He should handle the news of having a sister better than Otis did." Grams smiles.

"I think we need time to adjust to all of this before we start changing all of our lives," Otis says with a slight high pitch to his voice.

"Well, I'm not getting any younger, and it would be wrong to keep Wells in the dark now, since you know. I am going to spend as much time getting to know my granddaughter as I can."

I must say I like this woman's spunk, and she is not letting her grandson dictate what she wants.

"I know, but…"

Wynona cuts him off. "Otis Bradley! You listen to me right now. I will not allow you to tell me who I can and cannot spend my time with. I would love for you to get to know your sister, but I'm leaving the choice to you. She is my son's only daughter and my only granddaughter. Do you understand?"

I watch as Poppy gets up from the table with shaky hands and tears pooling in her eyes as Wynona continues to talk to her grandson. My parents and I sit there not knowing what to do. I hear the piano, and I know all of this is becoming too much for Poppy.

"Excuse me," I say, pushing my chair back.

I stop when I see my dad shake his head and hold up a finger. He is about to say something, but Otis opens his big mouth again. "Well, it's not polite for her to leave the table blare music through the whole house." Otis crosses his arms.

"Otis, I know this is a lot for you, but it sounds like she has been through a lot. Maybe try to get to know her before you write her off." His wife places a hand on his bicep.

"Come on, I want to show you something," My mom says as a song, I've never heard Poppy play before, echoes in the dining room.

Everyone gets up and pushes in their chairs, forgetting about the amazing meal on the table. I'm sure my mom spent a lot of time planning and making everything. This evening hasn't gone like I would have liked it to, but even this isn't the worst dinner we've had here.

We silently follow my mom to the library. Poppy is easy to spot at the piano. Her eyes are closed and her mouth open slightly. She looks like she is releasing all the emotions she was trying to hold back into the beautiful song she is playing. I love watching and listening to Poppy play the piano. She puts everything she has in her music. Poppy is always beautiful, but when she is playing the piano or guitar, something in her changes, and this stunning woman appears, making her look like a beautiful painting.

I hear another small gasp come from Wynona, making Violet walk to her. She loops her arm in Wynona's. They stand there watching Poppy finish one song and go straight into a song I know she wrote for my mom. Otis sits down in the overstuffed chair faces the piano. He doesn't look so mad anymore, but I can tell he is still not happy. I don't blame the guy, because this is a lot to take in. Besides, I don't think I would do much better if I were in his shoes.

Poppy opens her eyes as she plays the last few notes of my mom's song. Her cheeks flame red, and her mouth presses into a thin line. I can tell she wasn't expecting everyone to come in here and watch her.

"You play beautifully," Violet says.

"I have never heard that song. What is it?" Wynona asks, walking to the front of the piano, standing directly in front of Poppy.

"Oh, um…" Poppy looks down. I'm sure she is either fiddling with the hem of her shirt or her fingers.

"Poppy is a wonderful musician. She wrote those songs." I say, puffing my chest like the proud boyfriend I am.

"I'm sorry, I left the table the way I did. I got anxious, and playing helps calm me," She mumbles, embarrassed.

"Let me reheat the food, and we can get back to the meal." My mom starts to turn away from the group.

"Let me help, and we can eat sooner. Your food smells delicious, and frankly, I'm starving." Violet says, laughing.

I know my mom wants to decline her invitation to help, but arguing with her generosity would be rude, too. "Thank you." My mom smiles kindly.

My dad and I slip out of the door unnoticed to give them some privacy. Things are going to be changing quickly, and I know this will be a lot for Poppy, but she is going to experience a new kind of love I'm sure will change her life for the better.

CHAPTER 15

JAX

Frat parties in Texas are pretty much the same here as they are back home. Too many people crammed in a house with plenty of beer and liquor to go around. The girls here even look the same, but none of them interests me, because the girl I want is waiting for me back home.

"Good game!" I hear Lewis's familiar voice shout at me over the music. "I didn't know you took over my spot on the team."

We kicked some major ass on the field today. Let me tell you, his new team fought hard, and they didn't make this victory an easy one. He said he finally found a team he thought was worthy of him, and I want to laugh in his face, because if it was the case, they should have won. Besides, if you look at the stats for this season, you can see my team has won more games than they have.

"Thanks, you guys didn't make it easy." I chuckle half-heartedly. "I didn't have much choice. No one else wanted it; they claimed it's cursed now."

"Yeah, the last thing my guys wanted was to lose to my old team on our field." Lewis looks at me, crossing his arms. "How's Poppy?"

"OMG!" I hear a shrill screech on my left. "JAX! What are you doing here?" I look over and see Lana weaving through the crowd.

She is wearing a tight jean skirt and a tiny tank top, leaving nothing to the imagination. I give her another once over when she is closer, and I see her stomach is a little round, but the rest of her is still slim. She almost looks pregnant. Lana is still a knockout, but damn, her voice still sounds like nails on a chalkboard to me.

"Oh, I came here to celebrate the win with some of my teammates." I look between Lewis and her as she wraps her arm around Lewis's waist.

"Nice, Lewis, I'm going to head home. My feet are killing me, and

I am craving pizza and ice cream." Lana leans up, and Otis bends down, meeting her the rest of the way.

Man, Lewis does look happy, but in my opinion, I think he downgraded from Poppy.

Lewis places a hand on Lana's belly. "I'll be home a little later. I'd like to catch up with Jax."

"Okay, see you, Jax." Lana walks away with her hips swaying side to side.

"How's Poppy?" Lewis asks again.

I shrug, looking away from Lewis and the scowl he is giving me. "She is doing well."

I don't plan on telling him the big changes happening with Poppy. The last thing she needs right now is for him to appear in her life again, because I think he will try to insert himself back in her life.

"That's all you're going to say. I know things haven't been all rainbows and sunshine in the dramatic life of Poppy Monroe." Lewis moves until I am looking at him. He has his arms crossed over his chest and a single eyebrow raised.

"No, it hasn't, but it is not for me to tell. Do you want to tell me when you knocked up, Lana?" I mimic Lewis's raised eyebrow at him.

"You wouldn't like anything I have to say, and I don't want to fight with you right now." Lewis sighs. "I want to catch up with my friend and see how Poppy is doing."

"Sorry, man, I guess I'm not over how we left things the last time we saw each other." I relax a little, but I'm still pissed at him, because his little answer confirms he was cheating on Poppy more than I thought or knew about.

"I get it. I'm not either, but I had time to think about it." Lewis turns, giving me his full attention. "Do you want to grab a bite to eat?"

"I could go for a burger." I raise one of my shoulders. "I'm sure you've already found the best ones around here."

"You know it." Lewis chuckles, almost reminding me of my old friend.

I wouldn't mind hearing him out. Lewis is a lot of things, but he was a damn good friend, and I don't want to forget him with all the drama we've had lately.

"Cool, I know you probably had a lift, so I can drive." Lewis shoves his hands in his jeans' pockets, pushing past a couple of girls who had their eyes on us and a distinct flirtatious smile.

I know for a fact if we stayed there long enough, they would have found the courage to talk to us, but leaving with Lewis is better than having to let them down easy, because the only one I want to be buried inside is Poppy.

My phone rings as I weave through the crowd.

"Lewis, I need to answer this." Lewis nods, but he keeps walking to his Jeep. "Hey mom," I cheerfully greet.

She doesn't respond right away, but I can hear some heavy breathing. "Jax. When are you coming home?"

"Um, I'll be home early in the afternoon tomorrow?" The hairs on the back of my neck stand up, making me feel like something has happened.

Lewis glances over at me with his brows pushed, but he doesn't say anything.

"I don't have much time, but if you can make it home tonight, it would be better." My mom says so fast that her words sound like they are running together.

"Is Poppy going to be okay?" I look out the window so Lewis can't see my face. I wish I weren't trapped in Lewis's car right now.

"We can talk about it when you get home." She uses her mom voice, the one telling me not to ask her again.

"Okay, I'll call you when I figure something out." I hang up with a heavy sigh.

As I wait for my coach to answer the phone, Lewis glances at me, asking. "What's up?"

"Um, I don't know just yet." The ringing on my phone silences.

"Taylor, is everything alright?" The gravelly voice of my coach drones in my ear.

"I'm not sure. My mom called and said there is a family emergency, and I need to come home tonight if I can."

I listen as my coach tells me to be careful and to let him know if there is anything he or the team can do to help.

"Jax, I can drive you home if you need a lift." Lewis offers, catching me off guard. "I don't have practice tomorrow."

I doubt letting Lewis give me a ride home is the right thing to do. I don't know what is waiting for me back there, and the last thing I want is for him to insert himself in whatever is waiting for me at home, because he lost the right when he walked out of our lives.

"Ugh, yeah, that would be great." I still say against my better judgment, because this is still better than wasting time finding another way back to Oklahoma.

I text my dad I managed to get a ride home, but I leave out how at first.

Jax: I got a ride home. Do I need to go home or to the apartments?

My dad doesn't waste any time replying to me with a short message.

Dad: Tell them thank you and come to the house.
Jax: I'll tell Lewis thank you, and I will use the card to pay for the gas.

"Thanks again. I truly appreciate it." I put my phone in my pocket.

Lewis's car still smells the same. He has always liked the black tree-shaped air freshener.

"Of course, you are my best friend, and I would do anything to help you out." Lewis glances at me before scowling at the road in front of us. "Plus, I've been a shitty friend, and I want to help."

"Come on, man, neither of us has been the greatest of friends to each other since we came to college. I mean, I did get with Poppy not long after you guys broke up." I look at Lewis out of the corner of my eye in enough time to see his hands tighten on the steering wheel.

"Yeah, but you are better for Poppy. I think you figured out quickly enough when you saw Lana." There is a flatness to Lewis's tone, almost like he regrets admitting out loud or maybe he regrets fucking around behind Poppy's back. "I fucked up when I cheated on Poppy and look at me now. A woman I have only liked for sex is pregnant, claiming the baby is mine. I fucking hate it. Both of our parents are pressuring me into marrying her."

"Yeah, it sucks. Poppy said she knew you were cheating on her." Lewis cusses under his breath. "So, Lana is having your baby?"

Lewis sighs. "She swears it's mine, but I won't know for sure until the baby is born and we can do a paternity test."

"I'm sorry, man, this has got to be stressful for you. Can I ask you a question?" I finally look at him, because I want to see his face when I ask him this.

"Sure," he glances at me before turning his attention back to the road.

"How long have you been cheating on Poppy?" I grab onto the door handle to keep from punching him as he drives, because I know his answer is going to piss me off.

"Shit," Lewis curses under his breath. "I've been hooking up with Lana since high school, but I guess if we are going there. I've also slept with several others throughout my whole relationship with Poppy. It won't make what I did any better, but in high school, Lana agreed to leave Poppy alone if we continued to hook up."

Lewis is a damn fool. Poppy is worth the world and more. If Lewis was unfaithful in his relationship with Poppy, he shouldn't have blown up the way he did when he found out I had hooked up with Poppy. I wonder if it's because he knew I was giving it to her better.

"So, how are things with you and Poppy?" I can tell from Lewis's profile he isn't angry when he asks, but from his slightly raised tone, he isn't exactly happy either.

"We're really good. Things haven't been easy, but being with her is." I fidget with my seatbelt.

"Jax, I meant what I said. You are better for her than I ever was. I loved her, but not in the right way. It was never the way she needed me to love her, because I always had too many secrets." Lewis shakes his head.

I kind of feel bad for the guy. To be fair, a lot of this was his choice, but I can see how much he regrets what he did.

"Poppy and I are really doing well. We haven't been together long, but I am falling hard for her." I shrug still, trying not to give too much away, which is difficult because there was a time when Lewis and I would talk like this all the time. "She could be the one."

Lewis shakes his head, chuckling deep within his chest. This laugh isn't lighthearted or one filled with humor. This one is a little darker, filled with what I think is arrogance and anger. "No shit, but you've had feelings for her as long as I have." Lewis's mouth tips up in a cocky smirk at the same time his brows furrow. "How do your parents feel about it?"

I sigh. I would like to move on with this conversation, because as much as I know, Lewis is doing a nice thing by giving me a ride home. There is still this nagging feeling in the back of my mind that he is fishing for something.

"They weren't happy about it at first, but they are supportive about it now." I look out the passenger window.

Lewis nods, but otherwise, he doesn't say anything. I continue to look out the window until I see my parents' house. The last half of the ride was awkward, but at least we never fought. I don't think either of us knew what to say.

"I don't know what is going on, but I'm not going to force myself into your business. We want you to know if you need anything, you can reach out." Lewis pulls into my driveway, parking next to my dad's truck.

I half smile, still looking out the window. "Thanks."

I step out of Lewis's Jeep, walking to the door. I hesitate for a few minutes before I unlock the door; going into my parents' house is almost eerily quiet.

"MOM! DAD!" I shout, letting them know I am home.

Leaving the music building at school to go home, so I call Jax is bittersweet, but my time slot was over. I'm excited to talk to Jax and congratulate him on his game, but I almost had the perfect audition video to submit for the songwriting competition Jax has been encouraging me to enter since I told him about it. I know I can play at home, but the acoustics in the music room are so much better, especially for a recording.

"Hey, are you Poppy Monroe?" I hear a shrill yell from behind me as the doors to the building shut behind me, with the lock clicking has the hairs on the back of my neck to stand.

The last time I was accosted like this, my dad was going to kidnap my ex-boyfriend and me. That night was awful and ended with Jax jumping in front of a bullet for me. So anytime I get this sickening feeling telling me to run.

"Um..." I try to take a step back.

"DON'T WALK AWAY FROM ME!" The voice wails so loud it echoes into the dark.

I look over my shoulder, confused, "Violet?" I ask, even though I know who this is.

She laughs so loud and deeply, goosebumps, crawling all over my arms. Something feels off, which is confirmed when I turn around, facing her. The look in her eye is something I have often seen in my father's, but I saw it more when he was drunk than when he was sober.

She keeps laughing, but her eyes narrow at me. "You actually think I'm Violet?" She laughs louder this time. "I'm guessing she didn't tell you she has a twin sister?"

"Um, no she…" I trail off as whoever this is steps toward me.

"I'm not surprised; she doesn't like to tell people about me for some reason. My name is Nova. If you were smart, you would leave my sister and her family alone." Her upper lip curls, making her look even more menacing.

"I," I stutter.

I found out I have two brothers and a grandma. I want more than anything to get to know them. How do I know these aren't empty threats?

"I don't care if you see the good-for-nothing husband of hers while you can, but I have plans for my sister, and I know he will get in the way like he always does. I would watch out, or you are going to end up hurt too." She balls her fists and stomps her foot. "Don't make me have this chat with you again, I won't be as nice." She warns, backing away.

I make a mad dash to my car, but I have a feeling she would bust my windows out and drag me out of my car by my hair to make her point crystal clear. Why do people have to keep approaching me like this in parking lots?

I open the door, and as soon as I feel my seat under me, I pull the door closed, locking it three times to make sure I am safe. Tears pool in my eyes. I find my phone in my backpack, and the first person I call isn't Jax or Shane, but Otis. He needs to know his wife has lost her mind.

The phone rings several times before an exhausted-sounding Otis says, "Hello," followed by a little kid screaming.

"Otis," I hiccup as the emotions I was trying to suppress spill out of me.

"Poppy?" My brother's voice is deep and raspy, but concern is laced in his normally booming voice.

I hate calling him in tears like this, because we aren't close yet, but after the disastrous dinner, he has reached out a couple of times to talk to me.

"Otis, I don't know how to say this, but I think your wife snapped."

"What are you talking about? She is currently bathing Hawk," he curses under his breath. "One second, let me get somewhere a little quieter."

Hawk is my adorable nephew and the spitting image of his father, while his twin sister, Harley, is a mini carbon copy of her mom, Violet. I haven't gotten to meet them yet, but I've seen pictures, and they are so cute.

"No, she cornered me at school a few minutes ago. It was extremely weird." I look around the empty parking lot. "She kept telling me to stay away from her."

"FUCK!" Otis roars so loudly I need to pull the phone from my ear. "VIOLET! WE HAVE A PROBLEM!" Even though he is still yelling, it isn't as loud this time. I think he pulled the phone from his pocket. "Poppy, where are you?"

"Oh, I'm in my car at school. I was leaving the music building when Violet surprised me."

"Poppy, I am so sorry." I hear Violet's voice fill the phone. "That was not me. I didn't think I had to warn you, but is my twin sister, Nova." I hear Otis cuss under his breath again. "Is Jax home? I think you need to go somewhere safe."

"No, he is at an away game in Texas." I begin chewing on my thumbnail.

"Call Shane and see if he can meet you at the closest police station. Unfortunately, we are going to have to put another restraining order on my sister. Send Otis a pin at whatever police department you guys go to, and we will meet you there."

"Okay." Dial tone sounds in my ear before I can say anything else.

I immediately call Shane, and he says to meet him at the police station closer to his home, and he'll let Otis and Violet know where to go.

The drive to the police station is closest to Shane and Roxi feels like a lifetime, but they are waiting in the parking lot for me when I get there. I get out of my car and climb into the backseat of Shane's car while we wait for Otis and Violet to get here.

"Poppy, are you okay?" Roxi asks, turning in the passenger seat to get a better look at me.

"Yeah, sneak up on me as she did, and the look in her eyes reminds me so much of Jack, especially the night of the winter formal." I feel my bottom lip quiver.

Lights flash across us, and we see a white SUV park next to my Mini. Violet wastes no time hopping out and opening the back door. We climb out of Shane's truck in silence. Shane, Roxi, and I go on the sidewalk and wait for them as they get their twins out of the back seat.

Violet walks up to us first. "I'm so sorry this is happening." Violet gives me a sad smile.

I know my face is probably a splotchy mess because I cried the whole way here. "This isn't your fault. I'm glad it wasn't you."

"No," Violet laughs, but I can tell it's not from humor, because this is the type of laugh I do when I am trying to lighten the mood whenever I must talk about Jack. "But she at least had the sense to not to lay a hand on you."

We walk into the police station, and the fluorescent lights burn my aching eyes. I want to ask her what she meant, but I stop short as soon as I hear Shane saying we would like to make a report and ask for the same detectives who were assigned to father's case.

We are told to go have a seat, and someone will be with us soon, but no one anticipated us to wait for over an hour before Detective Scotts walks into the waiting room with his partner, Detective Whitman.

"Mr. Taylor, I was told you wish to file charges against someone?" Detective Scotts is friendly, and his tone is even, but he had said the last time I saw him, it would be great not to have to see me again, because it would mean something is wrong.

Violet clears her throat. "Ugh, yes, we wish to press charges on my sister. She threatened Poppy tonight, and I know for a fact she may try more than verbally scaring her."

Both detectives exchange a glance, and they look back at us with sadness in their eyes.

"Let me go grab the paperwork, and we can get you home. We are so sorry you are having to deal with this after everything you've been through." Detective Whitman gives me a half smile with sadness clouding her eyes.

I'm slightly annoyed and veering on the edge of anger, because the last thing I want is for people to pity me. All I want is to be in Jax's warm and safe arms right now.

I am quiet unless someone speaks directly to me, but when they said they would be in contact with us if they need anything else, I stand, knowing the routine with them a little too well. They are ending the meeting, and I am grateful.

I hold my hand out, shaking theirs. "Thank you for all your help," I say before rushing out of the same police station I sat in many times when it came to making statements for Jack when they couldn't go to the Taylors' house.

This is all too overwhelming, but more than anything, I am having trouble dealing with the emotions and memories all of this is bringing up.

"Don't worry, Jax is on his way home now," Roxi says, putting her arm around me.

"Can you drive my car back to the house?" I ask, laying my head on her shoulder.

"Yes, Shane will go get pizza before he comes home. Otis, do you guys want to come over for pizza?" Roxi asks.

"IZA! The twins shout in their way of saying pizza.

Everyone laughs as they manage to break the heavy feelings we are having right now, but thankfully, I have so many people in my life now, and when Jax comes home, I know he will be able to melt all my anxiety away with a simple hug.

CHAPTER 16

JAX

Poppy is standing at the foot of my bed in nothing but a lacey bra and matching panties. Her hair falls past her shoulders in loose waves with a slight blush on her cheeks. Even though she is getting dressed, I still find what she is doing to be sexy, because Poppy looks as good in clothes as she does out of them.

"Pops, you look good enough to eat." I look up and down her delicate body with a wolfish grin.

"You want a taste?" Poppy asks as her blush deepens, creeping down her cheeks to her small boobs.

I hum low in my chest and let my eyes roam over Poppy's slim body again. "You have no idea how much."

Poppy's sweet blush somehow deepens more, and I watch as she begins to shiver with desire, anticipation, or a combination of both. Either way, I'm more than pleased with the reaction she is having to my sinful words.

I scoot to the foot of my bed until I am a couple of inches from Poppy. She watches me with wide eyes as I put my large hands on her narrow hips. I can smell the sweet scent of her vanilla soap, making my mouth water.

I run my hands up her stomach, and I can feel her trembling under my soft touch. "Jax." Poppy sighs my name as her head falls back. "I'm yours."

At her sweet words, I grab her in my arms, spinning us around, and I lightly lay her on my bed. I glance at the clock; I look down at Poppy. Her hair fans out around her, highlighting how angelic and innocent she looks, even though I know she is far from innocent.

"Should we give your toy another tries this evening?" I wink, grinning down at me.

"WHAT?" Poppy's wide eyes almost pop out of their sockets. "No!"

"It would be so hot." I nip the sensitive skin on her shoulder.

"It would only be hot if you were there watching and controlling the toy." Poppy's hand lightly brushes past my shoulders until her fingers lace behind my neck. "But you can have me however you want right now and again when I get home in a couple of hours."

A small ding kind of kills the moment, interrupting the plans I had for Poppy and me. She stretches under me, grabbing her phone off the nightstand.

I watch her bottom lip jut out in a sad little pout. Whatever she is reading is not good news.

"Is everything okay?" I ask before kissing Poppy's neck.

"Oh, yeah." Poppy sighs. "Harley is sick, so Otis was wondering if we could reschedule." Poppy reaches over, putting her phone back on her nightstand.

When she looks back at me, I can tell she is trying to blink back some tears. I bet she is sad, because she was looking forward to spending time with Otis and Wells.

"Well, now you're free, can I take you out tonight?" I ask.

She looks up at me with wide eyes and a huge smile. "Can we go to dinner and karaoke?"

She knows I'm not going to tell her no. My goal is to make her feel better about her canceled plans, and I am going to start now. "Deal, but first I need to have my appetizer." I wink at Poppy before I begin kissing my way down her neck.

My hands move to Poppy's hips. She lifts a little, reaching up behind her back, and she unclasps her bra, slowly, almost painfully slow, she slips the straps down her arms, revealing herself to me.

"I thought I was the main course?" She asks.

"Pops, you're so much more than." I look up at her from under my lashes. "You're my whole world."

"Poppy!" I yell, but I wake up in an unfamiliar room hooked up to beeping machines connected to me by tubes.

I try to sit up, but pain shoots through my whole body. I have no idea where I am or how I ended up here. I feel like I'm in some horror movie where my killer is hooking me up to God knows what, just to keep me alive and miserable.

I look around, but everything is so blurry I can barely make out the white walls of a hospital room. I feel around blindly for the button, alerting the nurses I need something, when last night's memories slam into my mind like a freight train.

My heart begins pounding harder as I picture Lewis on top of Jack as he points a gun at Poppy in the parking lot of our school. Homecoming is supposed to consist of having a good time and dancing with your hot date. However, I was walking around the parking lot desperately looking for Lewis and Poppy.

At the thought of Poppy, I begin to worry about whether she is okay or not. I frantically feel around the bed with tears streaming down my face. I won't be able to forgive myself if I wasn't able to get to her in time.

A couple of minutes go by, and I still can't locate that damn remote. I begin running my hands all over the guard rails, and every button I touch I push. A beeping sound from one of the machines I am hooked on speed increases. I'm sure the annoying sound is coming from a heart monitor, but I don't care about it right now. I really need someone to tell me Poppy is okay.

There is a light knock on the glass door, and someone walks into the horribly lit room.

"Oh, good. You're finally awake," a small feminine voice says.

"Is..." I try to talk, but my throat burns from being so dry.

"Let me take your vitals and get the doctor in here. You had a tube down your throat, so your throat might be a little sore. It is probably best if you don't talk right now." The nurse grabs the thing to take my blood pressure, and all I remember before the doctor walks in.

The doctor washes his hands, and he looks over at me. My eyelids begin to feel heavy as the room starts to go dark. "Jax, if you want to see your parents, try to fight the exhaustion if you feel like you can. You've been unconscious for a little while now."

"How long..." I ask, looking between the doctor and the nurse.

"Well..." the doctor hesitates. "You've been unconscious for a little over two months."

Over two months. No, that can't be right. The beeping of my heart monitor speeds up as black spots darken my vision and cool sweat drips down my temples.

"Jax, you need to calm down." I faintly hear the raised voice of the

nurse over the ringing in my ears.

"Sorry," I apologize with a scratchy voice that shouldn't belong to me.

"Get him some ice cubes to chew on," the doctor instructs the nurse. "We will have to slowly give liquids and solids, so we don't upset your stomach.

After the nurse and doctor leave me in the plain room with a glass wall and door, I wait what feels like a lifetime before my parents walk into my room. They said before I can have any more visitors, they need to move me to a regular room, but I wonder if my parents will sneak Poppy back here.

I lay back on my bed, and darkness overtakes me before the nurse can get me ice.

A flash of white light blinds me, and I wake up in the hospital again. The doctor said I gave them a good scare because I was out for two days.

My mom walks in with a duffel bag, and my father is trailing behind her.

She smiles at me, sitting on the edge of my bed, grabbing my hand. "Honey," she says to me, even though she glances back at my dad. "We need to talk to you about something before we can allow Poppy to come visit you."

Okay..." I swallow hard, wincing from my sore throat, as my parents sit around me. "Is Poppy okay?"

"Oh, yes," my mother says.

My father clears his throat, joining us, but he sits on the other side of me. "We need to discuss if she should continue to live with us or not." My parents exchange an undecipherable look.

"What do you mean?" I ask, feeling my heart thumping hard in my chest.

My mom places her hand on mine. "So much has happened since Poppy moved in." My mom's eyes begin to water. "We almost lost you because of it."

"None of this was her fault, and she didn't ask me to jump in front of a bullet for her. She can't go anywhere." My voice starts to rise, and the beeping on my heart monitor picks up. "She is safe with us."

"Jax, what's all this about?" my mom cries, waving her arms in the air.

I sigh, "I love Poppy, and I want her to have the best life. Having parents like you and living in a happy home."

"YOU LOVE HER!" my parents yell at the same time.

How can I play this off as a sister type of love? The last thing they need to think is that I have feelings for Poppy.

"I don't mean it like. She is like a sister to me; besides, I have feelings for Lilah." I clear my throat. "Is Poppy okay? Did she get hurt?"

"Jax…" My dad pauses, rubbing the back of his neck. "She is okay. All she had was another concussion and some significant bruising. She has appointments to check for swelling and other things."

"Why?" I look at my dad.

My mom sighs. "Well, as you know, we don't know how many concussions and head traumas she has had, so there is always the risk for brain damage."

"But is she okay?" I look between my parents.

How can she be okay if they suspect brain damage?

"Yes, she has had some headaches, migraines, and other symptoms the doctors are concerned about. There is a chance she is going to have those types of symptoms and more for the rest of her life." My dad purses his lips. "Son, if you're sure you still want Poppy to live with us then she will still be welcomed. We didn't know how you would feel since her dad was the one responsible for you being in here."

"Poppy didn't ask for any of this, and she needs people who won't give up on her when shit hits the fan. I am going to be a person for her." I look down at the tube stuck in my arm; the tape is going to hurt like a bitch when we pull it off my arm hair.

They both nod their head and when I think this conversation is over, my dad checks his phone. "We are fixing to go talk to Poppy, and when we are done, she can come visit, but Jax may be upset and crying. She has been blaming herself for you being in here, and before we came in here, we got a call that might upset her. It requires her father's lawyers and ours to be here."

"What are you talking about?" My brows scrunch together.

"Honey," my mom squeezes my hand. "Poppy's father was found in his motel room yesterday morning from an apparent overdose."

"Shit," I curse under my breath. "I'll be waiting here."

My parents laugh a little at my lame joke as they go tell Poppy the man that was supposed to love and protect her is dead. I don't know how she is going to take the news, but I will be here if she wants me to.

I look around the room, and the sound of beeping lulls me to sleep.

I faintly hear the door open, and I feel a soft feather-like pressure on my head. I think someone kissed my forehead, but I never saw who it could be. A pretty light shines in the distance, and I want to reach out and touch it, but I don't, because a loud beeping and bright lights blind me. I feel like I am floating as a gust of wind blows around me. I faintly hear my name, and my body jolts a couple of times before I slowly lower back onto my hospital bed as the light dims.

The next time I open my eyes, I see my mom sitting next to me, crying.

"What happened?" My body hurts almost like I was run over by a truck.

Tears fill my dad's eyes. "While we were talking to Poppy, your heart stopped, and you had to be resuscitated. You were out for a little while. Poppy is going to be here any moment, but we can't stay."

As if on cue, there is a loud knock, and Lewis walks in. "Hey, man."

"Hey," I say, looking behind him. "Where's Poppy?"

"She is nervous about seeing you," Lewis says, giving me a small half smile. "It is really fucking good to see you awake right now."

"Poppy, come in here. I could use a good hug." My voice booms through the room.

Poppy walks in with her normally creamy pale skin looking whiter than the ugly hospital walls. She trips over her own damn feet before she hugs me tightly, but not enough to hurt me. "I'm so sorry. I never wanted you to get hurt." I can feel Poppy's tears soaking the shoulder of my hospital gown.

"What do you mean? I've never been better. This isn't your fault, don't blame yourself for what someone else chose to do."

I see my parents smile at me. I know they are proud of what I said. They sit, and we talk for a few minutes, but the nurse comes in and tells everyone they must leave. My mom says she can't wait until I'm in a normal room so she can stay with me.

Poppy is the last one to hug me, and I hold on to her for a few extra minutes. "Everything we've been through, all the pain and heartache, only made us stronger. This year has been hard, but I would do it all again, because nothing in this world feels better than saving Poppy."

"Jax," Poppy cries again. "I love you." She pulls back, kissing my cheek.

I sit up in bed as the sound of Poppy saying she loves me echoes in my ears. I know she probably didn't mean like she was in love with me, but I hope one day, when we're ready, she will tell me she loves me for real.

"Jax," Poppy's sleep-filled voice filters through the words I want to hear from her.

I open my eyes and see a curtain of blonde hair hanging like curtains around my face before I see Poppy's gorgeous face. I reach up, cupping her face, slowly caressing her cheek with my thumb.

"I'm okay. It was only a dream." Poppy lowers herself onto me with her head resting on my bare chest over my thundering heart.

"I'm here if you want to talk," she whispers into the darkness of my room.

"I know." Poppy hooks her leg over mine, holding me to her as tight as she can.

I shake my head, whispering, "No."

I don't like to talk to her about my nightmares, and she never pushes me to. I think she understands because she also has nightmares of her own. She is locked still and silent when she has them, but she still wakes me up every time she has one. Watching her lie there, her face scrunched up as she sleeps through some of the most awful moments in life, is truly heartbreaking.

Poppy's hands begin moving up my stomach to my chest, and over my shoulders. I feel her move on top of me.

"Well, how do you feel about a distraction?" Poppy is now hovering over me again, but this time she is straddling me.

"Depends." I move my hands to her narrow hips.

"On what?" Poppy's smile lights up her face.

"What kind of distraction are you talking about?" I smile with one side of my mouth tipped up.

"Well," Poppy leans down. "Some of this." Poppy leans down, kissing the side of my mouth. "And some of this." Her hand digs into my chest. "Maybe some of this." Poppy wiggles her lips.

She is driving me crazy in all the best ways. "I'm liking what I'm seeing and feeling so far. "What else do you have in mind?"

Poppy sits up, taking my shirt off, making her hair fall around her. I look at her like this forever and never get tired of the view.

She slowly moves her hands up her body until. I watch with wide eyes, refusing to blink so I don't miss a thing as her hands travel up her chest and she moves her hair. I lick my dry lips. If this is my reward for waking up from a nightmare, I will have one every night.

"Pops, you're killing me." I groan, making her smile.

"So that means I'm doing a great job at distracting you." She winks at me.

"You're doing so much more." I sit up, wrapping my arms around Poppy.

I cup her chin, holding her still as I slowly bring my lips to hers. I kiss her until she is clinging onto me for dear life. I can feel her breathing speed up and her heart rate thundering.

"Jax, make time stop," Poppy says.

"That's a tall order, but I'm up for the job." I chuckle before I kiss her again.

CHAPTER 17

POPPY

Jax parks next to the curb of the cutest craftsman-style home I have ever seen. There are already a lot of cars here, but I know for a fact we aren't late.

"POPPY! JAX!" I hear Grams holler from the porch. She is wearing the cutest pink apron with a white ruffle trim I've ever seen. "Come on in! Dinner is about ready!" She smiles.

Jax grabs my hand, and I instantly feel a little less nervous than I was when we pulled into the neighborhood. I walk slowly, dragging my feet up the sidewalk. I still feel like I should have brought something to contribute to the meal, even though Grams told me not to.

We step onto the porch, and I see the perfect rocking chairs ever. Violet is sitting in one of them with Hawk on her lap. She has a children's book held up in her hand, reading to him, and changing her voice with each character. She expressively reads, making me want to sit on the floor in front of her to find out what happens next.

I sit next to Violet as she finishes reading the book. Hawk climbs off her lap and runs out onto the yard, where he begins to run in circles on the grass. The screen door next to us bangs closed, and I jump from the sudden loud noise.

"Harley, don't let the door slam!" Otis hollers from somewhere in the house.

"Sorry, I get jumpy around loud, unexpected noises if I don't have a full-blown panic attack." I smile weakly, looking down at my lap.

"Don't apologize, but can I ask you a question?" Violet shifts, crossing her legs.

"Of course." I shrug, because I don't have anything to hide.

"How are you able to talk about what you've been through so

easily? You have so many internal scars." Violet pulls her bottom lip into her mouth, chewing nervously.

The thing Violet doesn't know is I do have physical scars on me. I have small ones on my lips from the many times my mouth got in trouble when I was in trouble. I have a tiny, faint scar on my cheek that I can easily cover with makeup. I have scars in my hairline that I can hide with my bangs, and many from gashes I got on my head, but they are all hidden in my hair. I wish was all I have, but I do have some other parts of my body from other injuries I acquired throughout the years of my father's abuse, but I won't tell her about them. The physical scars are still not as bad as the emotional and mental scars I carry with me every day. Therapy helps, but nothing will ever make the ghost of my father's transgressions disappear.

"I ask because it sounds like you have been through similar situations as me, but you seem so put together, and you seem like you do not let what you've been through hold you back."

I look down at my lap. I know her sister is dangerous, but I didn't know Violet's sister ever hurt her.

"I mean, I have triggers. It's not surprising since I lived in constant terror from when I was ten to when I moved with Jax's family at 17, but therapy is a big help. I've done some support groups for children who were in an abusive home. They helped, but those sessions also made me depressed." I glance at Violet, and I can see she has her whole body turned in my direction, giving me her full attention. "Listening to what other people had to live through was…" I shake my head. "Well, it brought back a lot of memories I suppressed."

"I have nightmares, and Otis wants me to talk to someone about it, but I don't know how to find the right person."

"For me, I don't want to be in a small room with a man talking about all the things I went through when I lived with Jack, but you have to set up the first appointment and keep looking until you find the right therapist." I don't tell her that my safety almost cost Jax's life, and I spend a lot of time talking about it during my sessions. "I have nightmares too, but I'm good at hiding them. I had to learn how when I lived with Jack, or I would have been punished."

"Okay, I will try that." Violet's cheeks are pink. I think she is a little embarrassed to ask me for advice.

"You can always call me; we can meet up and talk or sit in silence. Whatever you need." I light the side of my mouth.

"Dinner is ready!" Wells yells so loudly I jump again, but this time tears well up in my eyes as black spots appear in my vision as I try to fight an awful memory of my father yelling at me.

"Poppy," Violet whispers, but I stay locked where I am, bracing myself for the impending slap I know will never come.

The door slams closed next to me two more times, and I wince like I've been slapped hard across the face.

"Poppy," Jax's voice cuts through the sound of glass breaking from the memory I am trying to fight off. "You're safe."

I blink a few times until I can see the worry overtaking Jax's handsome face. "Why can't he stop haunting me?" I ask, leaning into Jax, hugging him tightly.

Jax doesn't say anything, but he holds me until my breathing is calm. I straighten back up and glance in the window behind me. The house is quiet except for the sound of my niece and nephew asking if they can eat.

Jax helps me up, and I smooth my hair down. "You look great," he says, kissing my forehead.

Wells looks down with red cheeks and his brows pushed together. "I'm so sorry."

"It's not your fault." I grab my glass of water with shaking hands, spilling some on the table.

Otis is watching me with his brows furrowed. "Is there anything we can do to help not trigger you?"

I purse my lips. Jax, Shane, Roxi, and anyone else who was with me since I left my father's house would know my triggers already. I love that he is asking me, because this means he cares enough about me to not set me off. However, having to say them out loud to a room full of people is embarrassing, even though I know I have nothing to be ashamed of.

"Ugh, like yelling, slamming doors, breaking glass, and loud noises, especially when they are unexpected, are one of my biggest triggers." I glance around the table, and Grams's mouth is slightly parted with tears in her eyes. "Um, food and mealtimes can sometimes cause an anxiety attack."

I give them enough to paint a nasty, ugly picture no one wants to ever have in their heads. I wish so much all of ended with yelling, doors slammed, and broken dishes, but sadly, my father went beyond. I know I hinted I have food issues, but they don't know exactly how. The only people I know are my therapist and, unfortunately, Jax, because he has seen me at my worst when it comes to my food insecurities.

No one likes to hear about these things, especially when it comes to types of eating disorders. My therapist said mine came from the need to survive, because any chance I got to sneak food, I would binge eat. I still have those same fears of wondering when I am going to eat, so I will get out of bed and sit on the kitchen floor, eating whatever I can until I feel like I am going to throw up. I remember the first time Jax caught me gorging myself. I had been living with the Taylors for about a week after my dad agreed to let me leave. I was sitting on the floor with food laid out in front of me like a picnic, and he came in. I was crying, and I kept asking him not to hit me. Jax sat down and told me to hand him the ice cream. I didn't eat anymore once he joined me, but he ate two sandwiches and finished the last bit of the ice cream before we went back to bed.

I feel Jax squeeze my thigh, trying to comfort me, but I can feel the bubbles of an anxiety attack still burning at my chest. I try picking up my glass again, only to spill some more water onto the table. I curse under my breath and look down at my lap. I am messing up the whole evening.

Jax lightly squeezes my thigh, letting me know everything is okay. "So, what games do you guys play after dinner?" Jax asks, changing the subject, so some of the pressure is off me.

"Oh, we play a variety. Mainly cards, because is the easiest with large groups like this." Grams smiles but narrows her eyes at her grandsons. "They like to let me win. I try to tell them I am old, and my heart won't give out if I lose a game or two." Grams lets out a full belly laugh, making the rest of the room laugh too.

Light conversation flows as we all begin to eat, but my nervousness doesn't go away. I don't eat too much, and I know everyone is trying to give me extra time to eat more, but I push my plate away from me. I know when we leave, my stomach will be grumbling at me for picking at my food, but knowing Jax, he will stop somewhere for me.

Otis and Wells clear the table while Grams grabs a deck of cards.

I have a hard time keeping up with the directions Grams is telling us, but it's fine. I am probably going to lose anyway. I've never been good at any kind of games, but I still have fun, because I do. We play two games; I lose each time, while Grams and Jax each win a game. They do these dinners weekly, and I am always invited, so maybe Jax and I can go every other week or so.

I've had family dinners at the Taylors' house, and those are my favorite memories. I never thought I would have a bigger family the one I got with Jax, Shane, and Roxi, but I did, and now I don't want to lose them.

Jax hands me a greasy bag containing a loaded burger, fries, chicken strips, and onion rings. My mouth waters as he pulls away from the Chicks drive thru window. I watch out the window as he pulls into a parking spot.

A smile splits my face in half as I know what we are fixing to do. I was so nervous after freaking out and spilling water at dinner, I didn't eat much, but thankfully, Jax knows me well enough to know I am still hungry.

Jax puts his truck in park and turns the ignition off. Is he thinking what I hope he is thinking?

"Are we having a tailgate picnic?" I ask Jax, but he is already unbuckling his seatbelt.

"Is that okay?" Jax looks at me with a silly, lopsided smile and a single eyebrow raised.

He knows I love it when he smiles at me. I unbuckle my seatbelt, and I open my door.

"Are you kidding? We haven't done this since the summer before we started college." I look over my shoulder at him, smiling so big my cheeks hurt.

We jump out of Jax's truck and into the dimly lit parking lot. I am giggling like a girl on a first date. Jax balances our drinks awkwardly in one of his large hands as he pulls the handle, lowering his tailgate. I set the bag down, and I put my hands down on the rough lining of the tailgate, so I can push myself up, but I pause when I feel Jax's large hand on my ass as he tries to help push me up.

"Trying to cop a feel?" I look back at him, and he is checking me out with zero shame.

"Any chance I can get." Jax chuckles, winking at me.

I watch as he pulls himself up onto the tailgate. I can see the muscles under his shirt flex, and I watch with my mouth slightly open as Jax sits on the tailgate in one swift, graceful movement. He made the look so easy, but with how tall he is, he can get up on the tailgate of his lifted truck; it is not trouble for him.

I turn to face him, bending one leg in while the other dangles in the air off the tailgate. Jax takes our food out of the greasy paper bag and flattens it to make a makeshift tray. He opens the plastic silverware he asked for and cuts the burger in half while I split up the four-piece chicken strips between us, two for him and two for me. Jax and I have been sharing food like this since freshman year of college. I know Lewis and Lilah would get annoyed when we did this around them. Sometimes Lilah would grumble under her breath about me not being his girlfriend. Lewis would pick a fight with me about something stupid later. Thankfully, now we can share our food without their attitudes.

I lick my lips as Jax hands me one half of the burger. I take a large bite, moaning as the greasy food coats the inside of my mouth. Jax opens a mini thing of barbecue sauce and begins dipping two fries in the dark red sauce.

"Jax?" I ask, popping a mini onion ring into my mouth. "Do you remember the first time we had a tailgate picnic?"

"I remember them all. Why?" Jax takes a large drink of his pop, but what he doesn't know is how much he made me swoon in one simple comment.

"I was thinking about how beautiful that day was. The sun was so bright, warming my skin, and the pretty wildflowers among the tall, unruly grass were dancing in the light breeze, making the hot day unbearable, but what I remember most is that we were both having an awful morning. You took me on a picnic to try to cheer both of us up."

"Yeah, Lewis and I got into a fight because I had asked Lilah out even though he wasn't happy about it. He started a fight with you because you said you wouldn't pick sides." Jax sticks half of a chicken strip in his mouth.

I nod my head, picking up a chicken tender and tearing a piece off. I take off the top bun and put the piece of chicken inside. I eat the last bite of my burger and eat the delicious combo in one bite, nearly stuffing my mouth.

Jax laughs at me, but he picks up his burger and takes a bite.

After I finally swallow the large bite, I say, "You know, back then I thought picnic dates like this would be so romantic. I had always wished Lewis would take me on one, but when we got to college, going on dates with him became so rare unless it was to go to a party."

Jax looks at me with his eyes slightly narrowed. "Are you saying you wanted to do this with Lewis?"

"Not at all. I was so mad at him for trying to put me in the middle of his anger at you I was contemplating breaking up with him." I look down, blushing. "I'm saying, something you did to cheer both of us up meant a lot to me, and I liked it so much I wouldn't have minded it being a date."

"What?" Jax asks, his eyes widen, and his eyebrows shoot up. "You thought about breaking up with him?"

"Yeah, I thought about breaking up with him. When I was sitting on your tailgate, eating tacos, and laughing with you, I kept thinking about how Lewis never did anything this sweet for me. I wanted Lewis to be the one to find me, so I didn't have to live with you. I wanted the day to be more than what it was." I look down at my half-eaten food, pushing the smashed bag closer to Jax, silently letting him know I am done eating.

"Yeah, things were so complicated at times. You know, sometimes I can't believe the girl I had the biggest crush on ended up living with me, but I secretly got a kick out of it." Jax chuckles, but there is no humor in his voice. "Every time Lewis had to leave, I was the one who got to be with you."

"Do you ever regret the day you came to my house to drop my groceries off and you found me hurt?" I look at him from under my lashes.

I have wanted to ask him this for so long, but each time I try, I chickened out. I will never regret the choice of letting him come inside Jack's house, because look at where I am now.

"I will never regret getting you help. Finding you bruised and broken was like getting sucker punched in the heart. I couldn't understand how anyone would be able to hurt someone like you, especially you. I knew I wouldn't be able to live with myself if I left you there without doing something, and all I could think to do was call my dad." Jax takes our empty food wrappers and stuffs them in the bag. "Besides, it all worked out in the end, because I got the girl in the end." Jax winks at me before hopping off the tailgate of his truck.

I turn around and sit on the tailgate as Jax jogs to the trash can, throwing the bag and empty cups away. I'm happy he doesn't regret saving me, but it is funny how we both crushed on each other, but he never made a move out of respect for his friend. I watch Jax walk back to me, and my eyes travel the length of his tall, strong body.

"You have no shame." Jax laughs.

He stands in front of me, looking down at me with a crooked smile.

A shiver runs through my body. Jax puts his hands on my knees, gently moving my legs apart, giving him more room to step closer to me. He cups my chin with his hands, kissing me deeply, making the stars in the sky double.

I sigh as Jax pulls away from me. "Let's go home."

With the help of the best boyfriend a girl could ask for, my feet gently touch the pavement of the parking lot, and we drive home singing terribly at the top of our lungs. Moments like these with Jax are the ones I live for, and I hope no matter where life takes us, they never stop.

CHAPTER 18

JAX

Poppy is sitting on my balcony playing her guitar, looking sexy as hell in my sweatpants and hoodie. My clothes are way too big for her, and when she walks, she has to hold my pants up to keep them from falling. She is working hard on her songs for the competition she has coming up. I'm so proud of her for going after something terrifying her. She is the most talented musician I have ever met, and I am not saying that as her boyfriend.

"Pops, I am leaving for the gym!" I say loudly, walking into the bright sun, which practically blinds me.

I blink away spots begin to appear. Poppy stops playing her guitar, chuckling under her breath. The cool air whips through my clothes, making me shiver. I know Poppy is cold, but I don't think she cares right now.

"Are we still going to have dinner together?" Poppy looks up at me.

"Yeah, I can make you whatever you want." I lean down, kissing her forehead. "Don't stay out here to long. I don't want you getting sick."

Some days, the last thing I want to do is leave Poppy, and today is one of them. I like winter, but sadly, we mostly get temperatures between the 40s and 50s each day, with cold snaps and little to no snow during the winter. What Oklahoma usually gets is ice and sleet.

I'm walking down the hallway to go to the parking lot when I pass by Violet. She has her head down, looking at her phone not paying attention to anything going on around her.

"Hey, are you here to see Poppy?" I ask.

Violet stops walking, looking at me over her shoulder. She smiles, but something about her seems different from the few times I have seen her.

"Oh, hey, is Poppy home?" She asks, looking me up and down almost like she is checking me out.

"Ugh, no. She is at my place." I point behind me.

"Thanks." She walks away with her hips swaying.

Something seems off with Violet and this whole situation, but I don't have the time to question what is going on, because I will be late for team workouts. I get in my truck and back out of the parking lot, still thinking something is not right. For a moment, Violet and another woman who looks like her pop into my head.

"SHIT!" I curse out loud as soon as I remember Violet has a twin sister who is not exactly the nicest person, and I may have led her to Poppy.

I should have realized this sooner. Violet has never been to either of our apartments, so I doubt she knows where we live. However, her sister knew where Poppy was the night she cornered her outside of the music building, so I wouldn't put it past her to know where we live, too.

I make a U-turn back into the parking lot of my apartment building. I know I'm going to be late to the team at the gym, but I don't care right now. I'll take whatever consequences I get from the coaches later.

Once I park, and I turn my truck off, I jump out of my truck, leaving the door wide open, running at top speed to my apartment. I stop for a split second when I see the door to my apartment cracked. I can feel my blood begin to pump through my body, my hair on my arms sticks up, and small beads of sweat begin to drop down the back of my neck.

"POPPY!" I yell, stopping in my living room.

She is sitting on the couch with her legs crossed under her, facing Violet. They are laughing at something was said before I came crashing into the room.

"Hey, I thought you had to go to the gym?" Poppy asks, looking at me.

"I do, but I forgot my wallet." Violet narrows her eyes at me as I walk past them, but she doesn't say anything. "Don't forget to text me what you want me to pick up for dinner before I come home later."

I hear Poppy tell her she'll be right back. I don't have to suspect anything anymore by the look I receive from Violet's twin sister. Poppy follows close behind me, pushing lightly on my back.

Once we are in my room with the door shut, Poppy turns around, grabbing her wallet. "Here, put this in your pocket so it looks like you came home to get something when you came back. When you leave, call Otis first, because if this is Violet, we have nothing to worry about, but if not, we need to call the police." Poppy whispers, walking out of the room.

Poppy looks up at me through her lashes, bouncing from one foot to the other. I know she is nervous and can tell the person out there is not Violet.

"Okay." I kiss her on the top of her head. "I should go."

I walk quickly through the living room. "Have fun," I say, forcing a smile before I close the door behind me.

I go down the hall and start walking down the stairs, before I call Otis.

"Hey," is his easy greeting.

"Hey, I'm checking to see if the woman in my living room is Violet or Nova."

"Violet is out back pushing the kids on the swings," Otis says before cursing under his breath. "Call your parents, and I'll call the detectives. Whatever you do, don't leave her alone with Poppy." The call dies, leaving the sound of the annoying beeping in my ear.

I text Walsh to let him know there is a family emergency, and I will not be able to make it to the gym as I turn back and walk down the hall. I unlock the door to Poppy's apartment and let myself in. I need to be close by in case she needs me.

I pull up my dad's number and wait while it rings a few times before going straight to voicemail. "Shit!" I curse calling my mom. Thankfully, she answers on the first ring.

"How's my boy?" my mom answers cheerfully.

"Mom, Violet's sister is at my apartment. I think she might be up to something." I run my free hand through my hair.

"Why did your dad not call me?" my mom asks with her voice cracking. "You need to be taking care of Poppy and not calling everyone!"

I know this phone call reminds her of all the calls she received about Poppy's father showing up when I was a senior in high school. My mom has grown to love Poppy like a daughter since the time she first moved in with us, which is not surprising, because if anyone gets to know Poppy, they immediately fall in love with her.

"He didn't answer his phone," I say slowly, like something is wrong with him not answering the phone. There is a long pause on the other end of the phone. "Mom, are you there?"

My mother sighs, "I will call him, but I will also head to his office, and we will be at your apartments as soon as we can. Please keep me informed on what is going on."

As soon as the phone call ends, I hear a loud, almost evil laugh coming from my apartment, making me jump. I drop my keys and phone. Chills creep down my spine, causing goosebumps to pimple on the back of my neck and arms. I have heard similar creepy laughs come from Poppy's father, but this one is different. I don't know how to describe it, but hers isn't angry like Jack's was, but more like she has no emotions in her laugh, almost like one from a scary movie laugh.

I pull open the door, and I hear another scream come from my apartment. I try to push the door open, but it won't budge. Someone locked the door after I left, because I know for a fact, I wasn't the one who did it. Even when I walked out the second time. I pat the pockets of my gym shorts, but I come up empty.

"SHIT!" I curse loudly; my keys might be somewhere in Poppy's living room.

I jog back to Poppy's apartment, and my phone rings. I find my phone and keys on the floor where I dropped them when I heard Poppy scream.

"We dropped the twins off with Grams, and we will be there soon," Otis says.

"Okay, something is going on. I can hear Poppy screaming." I grab my keys walking back to my apartment.

I shove my key into the lock, and once I hear the click, I push again, but the chain lock on the door stops me from coming in.

"Let me in!" I try to say in a calm voice, but I can hear the desperation I am feeling come cracking through me.

"Leave or I will hurt her!" I hear Nova's muffled growl.

"I can't do that!" I say, ramming the door with my shoulder. "Just know I already contacted Violet and the police!"

"You think I care! My sister needs to pay for everything she took away from me!" Nova shrieks before laughing, sending chills down my spine.

"Jax, go!" I can tell from the shakiness of Poppy's scream she is crying.

"I'm not going to leave you!" I run into the door again, but the chain doesn't break. I think if I run into my door one or two more times, I should be able to break in.

I straighten up and look at the gap in the door. I try to think of this as football practice, and I need to move the dummies down the field. I widen my stance to be shoulder-width apart and bend my knees as I raise onto the balls of my feet. I bawl my hands, filling the adrenaline pump through my body as I look at the door through narrowed eyes. This would feel a lot better if I were on the field in my shoulder pads and helmet. However, standing like this brings me back to the night I pushed Poppy out of the way of the gun her father had pointed at her in the parking lot of our winter formal during high school.

A sudden rush of dread fills me as sweat dampens my skin. I don't know this girl well, but I have learned anyone can be capable of anything if they want to, and Nova is clearly choosing violence from the screams coming from inside my apartment.

I push with one foot, the other, and before I know it, my shoulder hits the wooden door painfully. I hope I didn't injure myself, but if I did, saving Poppy is worth all the pain and more. The chain finally gives out, and I stumble into the room. And let me tell you, I was not prepared for the sight in front of me. Poppy is lying on her back, and Nova is on top of her. I freeze watching like a deer stuck in headlights, as Poppy tries to twist and turn on the floor, trying to wiggle free from being held down. Nova looks back at me with wild, bloodshot eyes.

Nova's lips pull back from her teeth, almost like a dog warning you to back off right before they attack. "I told you not to come in here!" she spits.

I freeze, and I put my hands up to show I'm not here to hurt her. I don't know what she is capable of, but if she can go to someone else's home and attack them, I wouldn't be wrong to assume she would do whatever she thinks is right in moment, with no afterthought or care of the consequences.

Nova slowly stands up, getting off Poppy. "I don't know what it is about my sister and the people she chooses to have in her life. No one listens or does as I tell them to." Nova steps over Poppy, taking a step closer to me. "I've been trying to convince your girlfriend here to leave Violet alone. She is my sister, and neither of you can take her from me."

I raise my eyebrow. I have no idea what she is talking about. My eyes leave her as I watch Poppy scramble to her feet. She tries to run around Nova, but she gets in the way, blocking Poppy from being able to come to me.

"Nova, why don't we wait for Violet to get here, then you guys can work this out?" I suggest holding my hands up, trying to show her I mean no harm.

Nova's face falls and tears begin to fall fast down her cheeks. "She doesn't care what happens to me. All she cares about is her husband and her two little brats."

"NOVA!" I hear a familiar voice behind me. "They have nothing to do with this!" I turn around to find Violet barely inside my living room.

"Oh, the perfect sister is here. Have you talked to Mom since you faked your death?" Nova laughs, making the hair on my arms stand.

"Let Poppy through. You're breaking the protective order against you. I will not stop the police from throwing you in jail, this time." Violet moves around me and stops beside the side table next to my couch.

For the first time since I broke into my own apartment, I see something other than a wild look on Nova's face. The redness in her face pales to a pink color, and her eyes widen as she pushes her red painted lips into a thin line, but I still can't pinpoint what emotions are surfacing.

Nova begins shaking her head. "In the contract you signed with Alastair, you can't put me in jail if you want to keep the money."

"True, but I made him add the contract is only valid if you guys are married. Since you are divorced, I can do what I want."

"You wouldn't actually let me go to prison, right?" Nova's voice is small and barely audible, but I can hear the slight hint of fear.

"I am so tired of all this drama. You are making it hard to be around you to the point I don't care if you are locked behind bars or checked back into a hospital." Poppy moves slowly around Nova as Violet talks. "You haven't been the Nova I love in a long time, and you know this. I don't want things to get bad enough next time I need to be away from you; I can't fake my death."

Poppy finally comes to my side, wrapping her arms around me and burying her face in my shirt.

"Can you take Poppy to her apartment? I think Violet can get her to leave if they don't have an audience." Otis whispers, but his shoulders are still tense.

"Of course," I say as Poppy's sniffles turn into hiccups.

Before Poppy and I can leave, a loud knock on the door makes everyone turn their attention away from Nova. A high-pitched wail has us turning away from my parents and the detective who came in.

My eyes widen when I look back. Nova is standing behind Violet, but what I wasn't expecting to see is Nova has her arm around Violet's throat, holding her twin sister tightly to her body.

Violet's back is arched from the chokehold her sister has her in. I take a step back, but Poppy grabs my hand. I lead us to Poppy's quiet apartment, flopping down on the couch like a bunch of bricks are weighing me down. This has been more exhausting than my team workout would have been.

"Jax, what's going on?" Poppy asks as she begins pacing in front of me.

My head falls onto the back of the couch. "Honestly, I have no idea."

Poppy is grumbling under her breath, walking a little faster. I know she is trying to work through everything is happening, but I know she is also struggling with what she should do, and we can't help in this situation. There is a high-pitched scream coming from the hallway, followed by something I would describe as a banging from someone kicking a wall.

I open the door to investigate the noises. I watch as both detectives are dragging Nova down the hallway, literally kicking, and screaming. I bite my lip to stifle a laugh threatening to form.

"That was dramatic," Poppy whispers. I look down to see Poppy is standing under me, watching the show Nova is putting on.

"That would be my sister for you." Violet's normally smooth voice comes out shaky. "Poppy, are you okay? Did Nova hurt you?"

Poppy tenses at question. I know Nova probably got a few hits in, but nothing compares to what she has been through with her Jack, not by far.

"I…" Poppy stutters. "I'm okay. She only got a couple of good hits in before Jax busted his door down to get to me."

My mom hugs Poppy by her side, smoothing down her hair.

"Let's go into Poppy's apartment, and we can order some dinner." My dad says, trying to get us out of the hall and out of view from the other neighbors who have opened their doors to see what the big commotion is.

Otis, my dad, and I pull over a kitchen chair so we can all sit in the living room comfortably.

When we all sit down, Poppy looks around the room at everyone is here. "So, what do we do now?"

"You are going to have to go down to the station and file a report, but first, you need to decide if you want to press charges on Nova or not." Violet's voice is small, and I can barely hear her.

We sit in silence some more, and I look at Poppy. She has tears in her eyes, and I know she is torn on what she should do. Even though Nova is a stranger to us, she isn't to Violet, and Poppy doesn't want to hurt her, because she is Otis's wife,

"Why do things have to be so complicated?" Poppy murmurs.

"I don't know," I whisper back, putting my hand on Poppy's knee, which is bouncing from the nerves are rattling through her.

Violet begins talking about the options we have, but I tune her out. I hate this happened. I was leaving this morning to go to the gym, and somehow, with all the drama happened, the day slipped away. We are waiting for Chinese takeout to be delivered, meaning I won't be able to take Poppy out for our date as I promised.

Tomorrow I will take Poppy to the field where we had our first truck picnic, as Poppy calls them, and I will tell her I love her. I fucking hope nothing gets in the way of me telling this wonderful, caring, and sinfully beautiful woman how I feel.

CHAPTER 19

JAX

The sun is blinding me through the windshield of my truck, but I don't care, because I have Poppy next to me. Her head is propped against the cold window. The sun is lighting her pretty heart-shaped face, making her freckles pop on her beautiful, pale skin.

She had fallen asleep about twenty minutes into our drive. A late '90s or early 2000s country song softly plays through the cab of my truck. So far, this has been a perfect drive, minus the potholes come with Oklahoma roads.

I keep thinking back to the day my mom told me I should figure out whether I want to spend the rest of my life with Poppy or not, and the easy answer is yes. I always wanted a love like my parents have, and with this wonderful, breathtaking woman next to me, I think I have found it. I pull off the gravel road onto an opening in the fence; my truck barely fits through. I find the perfect spot in the field. I don't want to face the road, and even though all the grass is yellow, and no more wildflowers are growing, because the cold weather has moved in, I know Poppy will love this date no matter what.

I quietly get out of my truck, trying hard to close the door without waking Poppy up. I want to get everything set up before she sees what I have been planning. I look through the tinted window and see Poppy hasn't moved. I open the back door of my truck and begin setting up the picnic. I think she is going to be surprised, but happy. She mentioned not too long ago how she has always wished for a date like this. I make the bed of my truck as warm and cozy as I can with several thick, fluffy blankets and pillows, so I can sneak into my truck without Poppy seeing them. Luckily for me, Poppy didn't look in the backseat, or I would have been in trouble. Even if she figured out what we are doing today she would have been bouncing with excitement either way.

I pull the ice chest out of my truck slowly; this sucker is fucking heavy, and I would still like to let Poppy sleep as long as I can. She was up late working on schoolwork since she spends most of her normal waking hours practicing for her songwriting contest coming up.

I lift the ice chest into the bed of my truck, adjusting the pillows and blankets a little until I can't stall anymore, and I let my nerves get the best of me. I walk to the passenger door and knock on the window until Poppy's head pops up. She rubs her eyes, stretching as her mouth opens wide, yawning, but I can only think of what I would like to do to her mouth right now. I adjust my growing erection in my jeans before I open the door, putting my hand on her thigh.

"Jax?" Poppy's raspy, sleep-filled voice causes my dick to harden more.

"Are you ready for your surprise?" I hold my hand out for Poppy to take.

She looks over my shoulder, and a wide smile splits her face in two. "YES!" Poppy takes my hand, hopping out of my truck, and she wraps her arms around me, burying her face into my thick coat.

I wrap my arms around her small body, hugging her shivering body close to me. "Poppy, are you sure you don't want to go home? It's cold outside." I clear my throat. "Maybe I should have planned something wasn't outside."

Poppy pulls back from me. The way she raises her eyebrows, looks at me with her enormous eyes wide open, shaking her head. "Absolutely not! Are you kidding? I told you I wanted this to be a date, and I will be upset at you if you take this away from me now."

I laugh at her reaction because she is so cute when she is being stubborn. I follow Poppy to the back of my truck. Poppy stops long enough to take in what she sees, whirling around, hugging me tightly.

"JAX!" she gasps, "This is so amazing!"

I lean down and kiss her deeply. Poppy grabs the back of my jacket to steady herself. She's the kind of girl who loves to show her affection in any way she can, whether through physical touch, words, or gifts. However, if Poppy writes a song about you, in my opinion, her favorite way to express love is through music, and I desperately want to inspire her to write one about me, but I won't tell her. Poppy uses to show how she feels about someone, and I don't want her to feel pressured to write about me.

I move until I am a couple of inches from Poppy's face. "I love you," I whisper, even though we are alone in a field.

The cold wind whips around us, but my heart stops when Poppy tenses in my arms. Poppy looks up at me with glassy eyes. My heart begins pounding in my chest, bracing myself for her to say she doesn't love me.

"I love you, too," Poppy whispers.

I lean in, kissing Poppy deeper and more passionately than I did before. My body sags, relieved at her own quiet declaration of love. Poppy loops her hands around my neck. I feel one of her arms resting on my shoulder, and her other hand fists my hair.

Poppy pulls back a little, gasping for air. Her stunning pale face is a deep shade of pink, and her lips are parted enough I could easily close the small space between us, kissing her again, but I don't.

"Let's eat," I say, even though I am no longer hungry for the food I packed us, but I'm a man starving for his girlfriend's touch.

"Oh…" Poppy clears her throat. "Yes." Poppy puts her hands on the tailgate of my truck, and I help lift her but putting my hands on her hips.

I watch Poppy crawl to the back of the truck, leaning against one on the pillows I brought to help make sitting in the back more comfortable.

I climb up in one swift move, and I move quickly to Poppy's side. Once we are both settled, I grab a blanket, covering us to keep us warm, even though I have plenty of other ways to create heat if needed.

I lick my dry lips, looking down at how cute Poppy looks bundled up. I shake my head, trying to clear the lust-filled thoughts making me dizzy. I lean over, pulling the ice chest a little closer to us, and I start pulling out food, handing Poppy her favorite peanut butter and strawberry jelly sandwich.

"Thank you for doing this. I didn't know how much I needed a day in the middle of nowhere with you." Poppy takes a bite of her jelly sandwich, humming happily, making my dick twitch.

She loves peanut butter so much she will eat almost anything with it. She once joked if she had to live on a deserted island and was only allowed to bring one kind of food, she would bring peanut butter. Poppy looks at me dead in the eyes, taking another bite of her food, moaning once again. This amazing woman is driving me mad, and I think she is enjoying it.

"Poppy," I warn in a deep raspy voice.

Poppy looks at me from under her lashes. "What?" she asks before taking another bite of her sandwich, moaning, but this time her eyes flutter.

Poppy knows exactly what she is doing. She is still looking up at me under her lashes as I lean down, kissing her again. Poppy's lips don't taste like fresh minty toothpaste or gum; instead, I taste the sweetness of the bright red jelly and saltiness from the sticky peanut butter of Poppy's sandwich. Poppy doesn't pull back, but I can feel her move her hands had her sandwich, so I am guessing she is putting it down. She shifts again, and before I know what she is doing, she is straddling my lap, grabbing onto my coat, and deepening our kiss.

I slowly move my hands up her legs, making her shiver. I don't know whether she is trembling from the cold outside or it's because she is turned on. I think this woman is going to be the death of me, and I will die a happy man. The repeating thought of knowing being with Poppy is wrong, but like she has said before, "if feeling this good is wrong, then I don't want to be right."

As if she is reading my mind, Poppy whispers, "Jax, I want you."

"It's too cold out here," I warn in a raspy voice.

"You know what they say? Body heat is the best way to stay warm." Poppy smirks, saying what I was thinking earlier.

Poppy shuffles until she is sitting on my lap, straddling me.

I grab Poppy's small ass, squeezing firmly before I move my hands to the fly of her jeans. I slowly pop the little metal button on her jeans before I unzip the long zipper of her pants. I brush my finger on Poppy's soft skin right above the hem of her panties.

Poppy leans her forehead on mine. "Jax, I love you," she sighs.

With those sweet words, I slip my hand into Poppy's silky underwear, and right as I spread her a part, inserting two fingers inside her, I kiss her cheek. "I love you too."

Poppy grabs onto my coat, throwing her head back. "You make me feel so good."

I chuckle, lowering my mouth to Poppy's neck. "I'm fixing to make you feel so much better."

I move my hand, pumping my fingers inside of her, making her gasp. Her jeans are tight and restricting my movements, but Poppy doesn't seem to bother her; in fact, which seems to only fuel her hunger for more.

I kiss her neck where her pulse point is, and I can feel her heart thumping wildly as her pleasure climbs. Being able to make Poppy flush, light sweat dot her skin, her breath speeds up, and her gasp is one of the best feelings of my life.

Poppy and I are walking into her apartment after a great afternoon of making love under the cloudy blue sky, surrounded by tall dry grass. We got halfway home when it started snowing, but the cold didn't bother us as we kept each other warm.

"Jax, I had the best day." Poppy takes her coat off, hanging it on the hook in the entryway.

Poppy turns around, looking at me with a smile splitting her face in two. I love seeing her this happy, especially after she has been so stressed the past few days with everything going on with her sister-in-law's sister tormenting her to get close to Violet. We know nothing other than Nova is highly possessive of Violet, but still, the question of what she will do to keep Violet to herself doesn't escape me.

"I did too." I lean down, kissing Poppy on the forehead.

"For the first time, I wish we didn't have to go to dinner in a little bit," Poppy says, turning away from me.

I laugh as she walks through the living room, shedding her clothes all the way to her room. I follow her, knowing we don't have time for anything other than to get ready, but I can't resist the chance to see Poppy naked.

"Where are we going for dinner?" Poppy asks when I sit on the edge of my bed.

"I think we are going to the Mexican restaurant down the road," I say as my eyes roam down Poppy's back.

She is in a white lacey bra and matching bra thong. My hands twitch and my mouth waters at the beautiful sight of Poppy's pale skin, which I know is so soft to the touch. Images fill my dirty mind as a loud knock interrupts my train of thought. I stand kissing Poppy on her bare shoulder, and I walk to the living room.

The knocking continues as I keep walking with long strides to the door. My eyebrows scrunch together; this is not how my parents typically knock on the door. Whoever is here is not pounding on the door, but the rapid taps make me feel like they are in a hurry or something. I open the door to find Grams standing in the hallway with her fist raised, ready to knock again.

"Oh, good, you're here," she says, walking past me without waiting for me to invite her in.

"Is everything okay?" I ask, stretching out every syllable, watching as this spunky old lady, whom I've grown pretty fond of, sets her purse on the coffee table and sits down.

"Oh, yes. I was supposed to stay at Otis's house while I get my kitchen repaired after a little fire, but Harley has come down with a fever." Grams sits on the couch.

"Oh! You had a fire? Are you okay?" Poppy asks from the hallway.

"Oh, yes, I am fine," Grams waves her hand dismissing Poppy's concern. "The fire broke out this morning. It's not bad; some singed drywall needs to be replaced. Let me tell you, my house stinks to high heavens." She chuckles.

"You can stay here," Poppy says, sitting next to her grandma on the couch as someone else knocks on the door.

I walk over, opening the door, and I am not surprised when I see my parents standing in the hallway hand in hand. They both have easy smiles, but my mom's mouth stretches into a huge grin. I move out of the way, and my parents come in as Grams continues rattling on about how she just walked away from her eggs and sausage for one minute.

"Wynona, if you need anything, please let us know." My mom says, sitting on the couch next to Poppy.

"Thank you, did I come on a bad night?" she asks, looking around the room.

"No, not at all. We were going to dinner." My dad shrugs off his coat. "We would love for you to join us."

"Oh, I can't intrude more than I already am." Grams, huffs. "I was the one who showed up unannounced."

I can tell she is not happy about the possibility of ruining our plans with the way her eyebrows furrow and her lips press together in a stubborn line.

"You are definitely not intruding. I would love to have you with us." Poppy says, looking at Grams with a wide, but hopeful smile.

I can tell she wants to get to know Wynona as much as she can, and this, to her, is the perfect opportunity.

"Oh, if you're sure I'm not being a bother, then I would love to join you guys for dinner." Grams grabs her purse and stands up.

"Wynona, I hope you like Mexican food." My dad laughs.

"Oh, yes, but I hope you guys are prepared to see me devour some chips, salsa, queso, and tortillas."

"It can't be worse than watching Jax stuff his face the whole time we are there," my mom laughs at her joke.

I can't help but join in on her laughter, because it's true. I will demolish my own basket of chips with refills and tortillas before cleaning my plate of chimichangas. I would probably go as far as licking the plate, but that only embarrass my mom and Poppy, then finish off my meal with a sopaipilla.

We climb into my truck, and Poppy is talking to Grams about a game I have in two days, and she asks if she would like to go, and how she would love to invite Otis and Wells too. I like having people come and support me, but looking into the crowded stands and seeing Poppy in the same seat she is in every game makes my blood pump with additional adrenaline. Don't get me wrong, more times than not, I can't see her in the crowd, but since she sits in the same seat, I know where she is. I swear I can feel her eyes burn into me, feeding the fire burning in my veins. However, the best feeling is after we get home and we celebrate my hard work on the field, win, or lose.

I park next to my parents and open the door for Poppy. Grams climbs out of my truck, still talking about something I have managed to tune out.

She turns to the restaurant and inhales deeply through her nose, taking in the mouthwatering smell of the Mexican food finds its way outside. "Geeze Louise, I can't wait to get in there." Grams rubs her palms together, licking her lips.

She gets as excited about good food as Poppy does. I would imagine all her family is good eaters. Poppy's brothers are large, but like Poppy, Grams is small, but with more curves than her granddaughter.

We walk in, and Grams puts her arm in mine. "I'm happy you came to dinner with us. I know Poppy is thrilled to have you staying with her for a while."

"I was going to go to Wells's house, because it is closer to work, but I thought I would see if I could stay here. I want to spend as much time with her as I can before I leave this beautiful world." Grams smiles. "However, if I am going to intrude, I do have other options."

"Absolutely not. I have a guest room with your name on it." Poppy smiles widely.

Our name is called, and once we are seated, someone immediately brings chips, queso, salsa, and tortillas to our table. Just like Grams promised, she dives right in, eating and talking with so much enthusiasm about the fire, and how she is lucky Otis had started his own contracting business straight out of college, so he can take care of fixing her house.

Our meal goes by fast, as Grams is the only one talking, but to be fair, none of us can get a word in. I don't mind, though, because the way she talks about her grandkids, including Poppy, is with so much love you want to sit and watch her face light up.

"Oh, I will need to go to the store after dinner. I need to pick up some groceries and get you some juice." Grams scoops up a large amount of salsa on her chip, shoving it into her mouth before standing up from the table.

"I have some fruit and juice at home, but if you need anything else, we can make a list, and I can pick it up tomorrow after class," Poppy says, her face turning pink.

We climb in the truck as Poppy and Grams talk. When I was hugging my mom bye she whispered in my ear, "Let them have this time. They both need it." I would be lying if I didn't say I wasn't a little frustrated, because some of my time is being taken away from Poppy, but I would feel like a major dick if I to this away from both of them.

When we get back home, they go to Poppy's apartment, and I go to mine. I flop on the couch and watch whatever comes on, but it is so boring, I begin scrolling on social media. I keep doom scrolling, but stop when I see a post Lewis is tagged in. Lana posted a side picture of her pregnant belly with Lewis standing behind her. Her hands are resting on her baby bump, and Lewis's hands are on hers. The caption reads *Lewis Jacobs is going to be the best daddy to our little guy and soon the best husband.* I'm not surprised they are engaged. I mean, he has been fucking her since high school, but I somehow think this has been a big part of Lana's plan. Trap him before he goes pro.

I sigh, wondering if Poppy has seen the post. I stand up, grabbing my gym bag. I need to blow off some steam, and since Poppy isn't here for me to bury myself in, then sweating while lifting heavy weights has to do the job.

TOUCHDOWN

CHAPTER 20

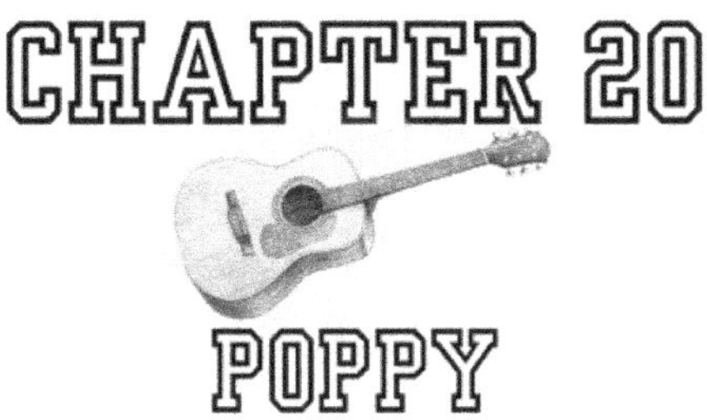

POPPY

"Poppy!" Otis yells over the roar of the crowd. "I'm going to get a beer. Would you like anything?"

I pull my wallet out, but he shakes his head. "I would like water and some popcorn." I never take my eyes off the field as someone tries to make an illegal tackle on Jax. "RUN!" I scream at the top of my lungs.

"I got it." I glance to my side. Otis asks everyone else if they want something, and Wells walks sideways out of the bleachers, past Shane and Roxi.

I put my wallet back in my pocket and turn my attention back to the field where my sexy boyfriend zooms down the field with the ball tucked in his arm. He runs a few feet before a player from the other team tackles him. I stand on my tippy toes trying to see over the tall man in front of me, because I can barely see what is happening on the field through his big head.

"Jax, get up!" I scream through my teeth as tears sting my eyes.

He continues to lie there for a few minutes as he waits for one of the trainers to come over and check him out. Anytime he gets tackled, fear grips my heart, and I have to stop myself from running onto the field while I wait to see if he gets up.

A few long minutes later, Jax stands up, and a rush of air I didn't know I was holding pushes past my pursed lips.

"He's okay." I hear Roxi gasp.

A whistle blows, and the team huddles. The thing I hate most about football is the tackling, but as long as Jax is okay, I will continue to grin and bear it. The team lines up, and I watch as Jax looks into the stands. I wave and blow him a kiss, like a few other girls around me are doing, but I know he only sees me. He crouches down, gets into position, and the referee blows the whistle, signaling the start of the next play.

The other team gets the ball and tries to run, but Jax is fast and tackles the player a couple of feet from their end zone, effectively blocking his opponents from making a touchdown.

Wells and Otis return from the concession stand, and Wells hands a water bottle and a box of popcorn as they squeeze past me. "What did we miss?"

"Jax blocked a touchdown." I stuff a few pieces of popcorn in my mouth.

"He's a hell of a player," Otis says, clearly listening to what I was telling Wells.

"Yes, he…" I stop talking and turn back to the game as another shrill whistle blows.

I watch as the ball gets thrown into the air. Jax runs with all his might to get the pass, but as the ball begins to descend, a player on the other team tackles Jax in an illegal move. I faintly hear the man in front of me grumble something about how the other team is playing fucking dirty and one of our guys is going to get hurt, but everything around me seems to be still, and the crowd goes silent minus a few deep boos coming from angry fans.

I watch Jax lift off the ground from the force. The sight in front of me feels like it is moving in slow motion. The crowd grows quiet, and when Jax lands hard on his left shoulder, I can hear the impact of his shoulder pad hitting the turf. The coaches and trainers run onto the field, and I watch with tears spilling down my face as the trainer waves over one of the emergency responders. They run onto the field with a gurney, and my heart kicks into overdrive.

I move past my family and walk to the railing separating me from the field. The crowd is silent as the people surrounding Jax make sure he is okay.

"WALSH!" I scream and he turns at the sound of my voice. "Is he okay?" I ask as I feel a hand touch my back.

I look out of the corner of my eye at Roxi. She has tears in her eyes too. I turn my attention back to the sidelines as Walsh is patting a few guys on the shoulder before they jog over to me.

"Hey, can you help me get her over the railing?" Walsh asks someone behind me.

I look behind me as Roxi whispers. "Tell me how my boy is." As the rest of my family joins us.

Three sets of hands belonging to Shane, Wells, and Otis lift me in the air. They lift me like I weigh nothing, and I feel Walsh and the other guys grab me, before I am sat down on the ground. I run onto the field as Jax is being lifted onto a stretcher.

I ran onto the field with tears filling my eyes. One of the security guards with a round stomach blocks me a few feet away from Jax.

"Ma'am, you need to go back to the stands, or I will have to escort you out of the arena," he grunts, making his beer belly bounce.

"No. I can't, he is my boyfriend!" I start yelling out Jax's name, crying harder.

One of the coaches hears me, and his face morphs into a thin line and a deep red neck as a vein in his forehead pops out. The guard grabs my arm with his sweaty, chubby hand painfully hard. My vision begins to blacken as the man's face transforms into my father's. Oh, God, please don't let me have a panic attack on this football field in front of hundreds of people.

"Ma'am, you need to calm down and go sit back down." I faintly hear him say, but all I can hear is the loud panting my father would do right before yelling in my face with his breath reeking of whiskey and mint.

I flinch as my body begins to shake so hard my teeth begin to rattle. I suck in a deep breath, but instead of a calming exhale, I begin screaming at the top of my lungs.

"Sir, let her go." I hear the deep, familiar voice of Coach Harrison. "This is the injured player's girlfriend. She will be riding with him to the hospital."

I feel the man's grip loosen on my arms. Coach Harrison puts his arm around me, but he doesn't touch me. I feel like this is his way to not only comfort me but also act as a shield.

"Is Jax…" I hiccup around a sob. "Is he going to be okay?" I ask Coach Harrison as we get closer to the ambulance.

"I'm not going to lie to you, because you will see when you get in the ambulance, but Jax is unconscious." I suck in a shaky breath. One paramedic climbs in the back with Jax and the other begins to close the back doors. "Hold on, she is his girlfriend and will be riding with him."

The guy stops as we jog the short distance. I look into the brightly lit ambulance compartment. Jax is lying on the stretcher completely still and his eyes are closed. He is hooked up to a small machine. All I can feel is my heart pounding hard in my chest.

"Ugh, which hospital are we going to?" I ask the paramedic who is grabbing something off a shelf with a door on it.

I unlock my phone and look up the hospital as notification after notification fills my phone so fast my head begins to spin. I send the name of the hospital Jax is getting transported to Shane as the paramedic begins to put a needle in the crook of Jax's arm, hooking him up to a tube and a bag full of clear liquid.

"Can I hold his hand?" I hiccup.

"Yes," the guy says in a serious voice, almost like I broke his concentration. "You should also talk to him," he adds in a less serious, almost calm tone.

I nod my head. "Jax, it's me, Poppy. I'm here." I grab his hand as I fly off the seat as an ambulance goes over a bump or pothole. "I love you! We are going to be at the hospital soon, but in the meantime, you are in great care."

The ambulance jolts again, but the guy working on Jax doesn't stop. I need to try to remember to send this guy and the female driver something for all they are doing to get Jax to the hospital quickly. I slide on the bench to the right a little as the ambulance speeds up. I would guess they are getting on the highway.

The girl on my side of the ambulance finally says something. "Sorry, this can be a bumpy ride sometimes." I had almost forgotten she was here until she said something. I watch as she leans over me to Jax's head. She has a little thing in one hand and with the other she opens one of his eyes, shining what I now know is a flashlight in his eye.

"Good pupil reaction on the left side," she says before repeating the same thing on Jax's right eye. "Delayed reaction on the right side. Possible concussion," she says as the guy writes on a clipboard.

"He landed on his right shoulder, and he was wearing a helmet," I mumble.

"Yes, a concussion is a traumatic brain injury. He can still get one even with a helmet if the force is great enough…" I tune her out as she keeps on explaining what a concussion is and how people can get them.

What she doesn't know is I've had more than my fair share of concussions, so I'm too familiar with the head trauma department. I have permanent brain damage, which results in many different things, ranging from ringing in my ears, migraines, and blurred vision. I try to hide when I am feeling bad, but Jax can always tell.

The ambulance comes to a screeching stop, and the man who has been working on Jax continues what he is doing when the doors fly open. The other woman who was with us in the ambulance immediately starts talking to someone outside the ambulance I cannot see. Jax begins to get wheeled out of the ambulance, and that's when things begin to move at lightning speed. People in scrubs begin to push Jax through the automatic doors, still talking. I have to jog to keep up with them, but none of them are paying attention to me. They are all focused on Jax, and I couldn't be more grateful for.

"Where are you guys taking him?" I ask everyone, hoping one of them will answer me.

"Miss..." A petite woman in scrubs stops walking next to the gurney and faces me. "We are going to examine him, so I will take you to a waiting room. Are you a relative?"

"Oh, well..." I stammer, "That's complicated, but I'm his girlfriend."

"I'm sorry, but we can only pass medical information to his family." She gives me a sad look.

"Can you tell me anything? I have no idea where we are, even at." Tears pool in my eyes.

The nurse leads the way to a small waiting room is close to the door we originally came through. I go and sit in a chair on the far side of the room, pulling my phone out of my pocket as it stops vibrating.

I see I have several missed calls from Shane and Roxi. I call Shane back since this is the last missed call I have.

"Poppy, how is he?" Shane's voice is strained and thick, like he is trying not to cry.

I start to ugly cry at the worry in his voice. "He was unconscious the whole way here. We are at the emergency entrance." I hope he can hear me through my sobs.

Someone much bigger than me walks quickly past the door to the waiting room. "OTIS!" I say loudly, hoping he heard me.

I walk fast, and once I am through the door, I collide with something that feels like a brick wall.

"SHIT! Poppy, are you okay?" Otis asks, catching me before I fall onto my ass.

"Yeah, where are Roxi and Shane?" I ask, sniffling into Otis's shirt.

"Wait here?" Otis walks me to a chair, and I sit down, biting my thumbnail. "I'll go get them."

The last time I was in the hospital was when Jax jumped in front of a bullet for me. My knee begins to bounce as footsteps echo from the hallway into the room. Normally, hearing footsteps would send me into a panic attack, but not this time. I know those footsteps belong to my family, and they are here, worried sick for Jax. I need to be strong for them.

"Poppy!" Roxi cries out, jogging over to me.

I meet her halfway, and we collide in a painful hug, but I don't think either of us cares right now. We hold onto each other, letting all of our emotions pour out and into each other. Each of us is hurting for the man who is here, and to make it all feel worse, we don't know what is happening with him. I feel another set of arms circle us, and the sweet but musky scent of Shane's expensive cologne fills my nose.

"All I know is…" we all pull away from each other and sit in the chairs behind me. "Jax was unconscious the whole way here. His left eye was dilating normally, but there was a delay in his right pupil. They didn't say anything other than trying to teach me what a concussion is and how people can get them."

Roxi falls into a fit of giggles. "I'm sorry, I am, but you've probably had more concussions than everyone in this room combined."

"That's true. I should have been the one giving the lessons on head trauma." I smile weakly.

I pull my knees up to my chin, resting my head on my legs, laughing at Roxi's momentary fit of hysterics and my lame joke, but I know for a fact Jax would have appreciated them. I wrap my arms around my shins and close my eyes, replaying the other day when Jax told me he loved me for the first time.

He surprised me with the most romantic date ever. It was a cold day, almost too cold to have a tailgate picnic, but he had made the back of his truck comfy and warm with pillows and blankets. When he woke me up, I didn't know where we were, but I didn't care. All I knew in the moment I would go anywhere with him. However, when he whispered those three little words to me, I was shocked. The world around us melted away, and all I saw was him. The chilly air warmed around us for a moment before I whispered the I love you.

"Violet." Grams says, breaking the silence had fallen over the waiting room. "How did you get here so fast?"

I look up to see Otis grabbing some pizza boxes out of her arms.

"As soon as Otis called me, I asked Freya to watch the kids until her mom could come over. She will be here soon." She hands Wells one of the two plastic bags she has on her arms. "I figured everyone would need some food, and I picked up some pizza." `

"How did you get here so fast?" Otis asks, kissing Violet on the forehead.

"Family needed us, so we don't need to talk about how many traffic laws I broke right now?" Violet says with a small laugh.

"Oh, thank you so much." Roxi immediately gets up to help, but Grams shakes her head.

"You let us feed you." Grams chuckles, "We will take care of you so you can be ready for Jax." She pats Roxi on the shoulder.

I rest my head back on my knees. My stomach is twisting in knots, and the idea of food makes me feel sick. Grams makes a plate with a slice of cheese and pepperoni pizza and two garlic knots with some sauce on the side.

"Here you go." She holds the plate out to me.

"Grams, I'm not hungry." I tilt my head up enough to see her.

"Well, I'm sure you're worried sick, but Jax wouldn't want you to starve." She pushed the plate closer to me.

I grab the food, and I take a tiny bite of a garlic knot, fully aware of all the eyes on me, which makes me not want to eat. I pick up the slice of pepperoni pizza and take the smallest nibble I can. The greasy chunk of food hits my stomach hard. Even though I don't want to, I take another small bite, but this one is slightly bigger than the first one.

"Taylor." A tall doctor in a pair of dark green scrubs and a white lab coat with short dark hair pushed to the side of his tan face says, walking into the waiting room.

"That's us," Shane says, walking over to the doctor.

"I'm Doctor Kline. I have examined Jax, and he will be okay. He has a concussion, and he dislocated his right shoulder." I breathe a sigh of relief, and the doctor's eyes slide to mine. "We are going to keep him overnight to monitor his head trauma. Only family is allowed in the room right now, because he needs rest, but he is asking for someone we think is named Poppy."

"That is his girlfriend, but she is family. They are all family." Roxi waves to everyone in the room.

Doctor Kline nods, but leaves after telling Shane what room Jax is in.

"We're going to head home, but text or call us if you need anything," Otis says, coming over, hugging me.

I hug everyone, bye, and watch as they start cleaning up the dinner Violet so kindly brought for everyone. I wave before walking into the hallway with Shane and Roxi. With each step, the walk to see Jax seems to take longer. You know in horror movies when they make a hall look like it is stretching, well, exactly how this feels right now.

Roxi grabs my hand and gently pulls, drawing my attention. "Poppy, Jax is going to be okay."

My heart skips, because I should be the one reassuring her. We get to the door, and I have a flashback of the last time Jax was in the hospital. Shane knocks once before opening the door. Roxi walks in holding onto Shane's hand, but I stay in the doorway like my feet are cemented onto the floor.

The room is dimly lit, but the privacy curtain is pulled back, so I can see Jax in bed with his eyes closed. He is so still, and his face is relaxed. I walk until I am standing at the foot of the bed. Roxi sits on the side of Jax's hospital bed, and Shane sits in the chair behind his wife, looking at his son, hurt and in a hospital bed for the second time in his life.

Jack never looked at me with a once of love after my mom died, but he never looked as if he cared anytime I was hurt. More times than I can count, I should have gone to the hospital after Jack was done taking his anger out on me, but I was never allowed, because it would tarnish his spotless reputation as the widow who was left with a daughter image. Don't get me wrong, his reputation was trashed as soon as Jax found me, but for his own doings, not mine.

"Poppy?" Jax whispers with a scratchy throat.

Roxi moves and sits on Shane's lap. I quickly take her place on the mattress. "I'm here and so are your parents."

Jax doesn't open his eyes, but the hand next to me turns. I am terrified I'm going to hurt him more if I touch him, after all, this is the shoulder he fell on. The doctor said he dislocated it, but he is lucky.

"Poppy…" Jax groans in pain.

"I'm here," I say, but I still don't grab his hand.

I watch as Jax slowly flexes his fingers. I carefully lay my hand on his, and his fingers curl, holding me there. I look at his handsome face; his eyes are still closed, but he has a lazy half smile on his face as his breathing slows. I look over my shoulder at Shane and Roxi.

"I think he was waiting for you before he let the medicine kick in," comes from the door in a sweet voice. "He would drift asleep only to wake up again before saying Poppy. All the nurses thought he was asking for a flower."

Roxi chuckles under her breath, probably not to wake Jax, who is snoring now. "No, that would be his girlfriend."

She nods her head. "We are working on getting him into a regular room and out of the ICU," the nurse says, walking back out the glass door. "We don't have any beds available, but when we do, he will be the first one up."

"Poppy, we need to go to Jax's place and get some things for him. Is there anything we can get for you?" Roxi says, cutting through my thoughts of who is going to stay with him tonight.

I wanted to stay the night, but I also didn't want to overstep because I'm his girlfriend now. I know Roxi wants more than anything to stay with Jax, but we both know we can't stay in the room since he is in the ICU.

"An overnight bag is fine with me. I begin fiddling with the hem of the sheet covering Jax. "Could you stay with me in the waiting room until we are allowed to come back to see him. I don't want to be alone right now."

I watch as Roxi and Shane's bodies physically relax as their shoulders slump and the lines in their foreheads smooth. I can tell I made the right choice. I may not have a kid of my own, but I know they aren't ready to give up certain parts of being his parents yet.

"Of course, we'll be back soon." Roxi kisses the top of my head.

I sigh when they walk out of the glass door, lying back on the bed, and resting my head on Jax's pillow. "You scared me today," I whisper to him. "When you didn't move, and they signaled for the EMTs, I knew you were seriously hurt. I have never been so terrified in my life, and I think it should say a lot since I spent most of my teen years terrified for my own life. However, the fear of someone you love getting hurt is different. I don't know how to explain it."

I know he is not going to answer back, but his snores are comforting because that means he is going to be okay. I close my eyes and let the sound of the machines beeping soothe me. I'm going to lie here until someone comes and kicks me out. Jax's fingers loosen around my hold as his snores become deeper. Whatever medicine they have him on must have him feeling good.

Something tickles my cheek, and I try to swat it away, but whatever is attacking me comes back. I groan and put my arm over my face. I

don't know what time it is, but I'm not ready to wake up. I was having the best dream. Jax and I were at another tailgate picnic. The field had wildflowers blooming and waving in the wind. His cocky smile fades, and the sight of him getting tackled and flipping in the air plays in my mind, reminding me where I am.

"Jax," I gasp, but I don't want to open my eyes, because I don't want it to be true.

"Poppy, wake up." Jax's familiar and comforting raspy voice fills the room.

Am I still in Jax's room? How did no one kick me out of here by now?

My stomach drops as I feel a feather-light touch trace over the edge of my bottom lip. I blink open my eyes slowly, trying to adjust to the harsh fluorescent hospital lights greeting me. I slowly sit up and look over at Jax. He has the rolling tray with questionably looking scrambled eggs on a plate, along with some other breakfast food. I've spent enough time in the hospital to know their food is edible, bland.

"How long have you been awake?" I ask, sitting up and looking around the unfamiliar room.

"I woke up when they started moving my bed, so I would say about four hours." Jax glances at the clock, nodding. "I think they needed the space in the ICU for a car accident or something. At least, that is what I got from listening to the people as they moved me here."

"Why didn't they wake me?" I look around, seeing if I can find my phone so I can update Shane and Roxi on which room we are in. "I need to…" Jax touches my arm, stopping me from getting out of the bed.

"I asked them not to wake you." I look back at Jax with wide eyes. "I called my parents. They know what room I'm in, and they are bringing us some better food."

"Yeah, they said they were going to come back last night." I relax and lean back on the bed.

Jax shakes his head. "My dad told me a nurse wouldn't let them stay, because of the time, but they should be here any minute."

"Oh, so how do you feel? Do you need anything?" I start to stand up, but Jax stops me again.

"I need you right next to me." Jax grins at me with a crooked smile as a knock on the door echoes through the small room.

"Good news." Roxi breezes into the room in a flash of bright pink from the dress she has on. "Jax is going to be released in a few hours."

Shane comes in carrying two small overnight bags, but he doesn't say anything. Roxi leans over me, kissing Jax on the head.

"What did you bring for breakfast? It smells good." Jax chuckles. Of course, he is thinking of food right now.

"Oh, all of your favorites. We have thick slices of French toast, eggs, bacon, sausage, grits, and hashbrowns." Roxi starts unloading the food containers out of a tote bag and makes Jax's plate first with big heaping spoonfuls of the eggs, grits, and hash browns.

This is pretty typical of Roxi. If she knows you are sick or had a bad day, she will make all of your favorite foods. I make my plate, leaving out the grits. I can't get past the texture of them. Roxi hands me a little pack of peanut butter and a banana for my French toast. She always thinks of everything.

We eat, talk, and laugh through breakfast. Everyone is starting to relax some since we learned Jax is getting to go home, and after I get freshened up, Shane and Roxi step out so I can help Jax get cleaned up and changed.

"You need one of those sexy little nurse costumes for when you take care of me after I go home." Jax wiggles his eyebrows at me.

"I'll see what I can do." I wink at Jax, making him laugh so hard I have to brace myself as I lean over trying to breathe through a fit of giggles.

I lean over Jax and kiss his left shoulder before I help him get his shirt on. This man makes me laugh more than anyone I have ever known. One of the things I have always liked about Jax is his carefree spirit and his humor.

"I'm ready to go home and lie in bed with you and watch some movies." Jax yawns.

A light knock on the door interrupts us, and a tall nurse with a killer figure walks in, but I have to give Jax his props, because he didn't even check her out. Although I'm sure she doesn't need to have Jax ogling her to feel good about herself. She oozes confidence.

"Well, the good news is you can go home, but you will have to take it easy for a couple of weeks. Tomorrow, call your primary doctor and set up a follow-up appointment next week to check on your shoulder and concussion." She says, reading the clipboard she got off the bed. "Mind if I take your blood pressure and temperature?" she asks, putting some hand sanitizer on her hands.

I watch as the nurse fusses over Jax, smiling and laughing at all of his jokes. I glare at her, and when Jax notices, he just laughs.

Shane and Roxi come into my room after the nurse leaves and begin helping Jax with his papers. I do a grocery order to be dropped off later for Jax's favorite dinner. I am going to surprise him and Grams with a delicious meal and watch a movie.

CHAPTER 21

JAX

One thing I hate is feeling like a bedridden person and not being able to do much. However, one thing making the injury feel worse is I'm going to miss Poppy's competition. She has been running on double time, taking care of me and practicing. When I went to the doctor yesterday, I asked if I was cleared to fly, and she said no, because I'm still having headaches and blurred vision from my concussion. Thankfully, my mom and Grams are going with her. They are turning the trip into the ultimate girls' weekend, but the sting of having to miss out on this huge moment in Poppy's life doesn't hurt any less. I'm seriously hoping Poppy is not disappointed that I am not able to go with her.

I told them to call me with any update, no matter how small they think it is. Poppy said, "Fine, but if she wins the contest, she wants me to throw a costume party, and I have to wear my assless chaps. What she doesn't know is we're having a party regardless, because what she is doing is huge and needs to be celebrated. However, I know with her talent and the songs she's prepared, they would be fools not to choose her, and I know I'm biased, so my opinion doesn't count.

I lean back on the couch, closing my eyes as my head begins to pound. My dad should be here anytime. My dad, Wells, and Otis are meeting at my apartment to watch the game today. We will video call with my mom, so we can watch Poppy's performance. My phone starts ringing, and I sit up, looking at who is calling me, with Walsh's name flashing on the screen.

"Hey man…" I rub the back of my head as my vision begins to blur.

"Jax," he responds with a loud thudding sound behind him, making my headache intensify. "I have everything ready to go, but there's a problem with the flyers." Walsh keeps talking like I care about anything coming from his big mouth.

"Walsh, where the hell are you? The sounds in the background are killing my head." I lean back on the couch again as I begin to get dizzy.

"Sorry, I'm at the frat house, and they are having a beer pong contest this. I'll step out real fast." I wait as the whooshing sound slowly goes away. "Like I was saying, I snuck into the library and printed the flyers, and my dumb ass spelled costume wrong. Who knew there was an e at the end."

I'm honestly not surprised. My brothers like to party, and they will start early in the day if they can.

I snort, trying to stop myself from laughing. "Everyone, but why were you doing paper flyers instead of posting about the party?"

"Well, I was trying to keep it small as you asked." Walsh groans.

I can't be mad at him, because that is what I told him to do. Even when we plan birthday parties, and we don't want a large turnout, people find out, and we are packed anyway.

"Just spread the word. The only thing people need to know is they don't get in without a costume," is what I am trying to say, but my words begin to slur, and it comes out garbled and sounding weird to my own ears.

"You good? You don't sound so good." Walsh asks.

"Yeah, my head is killing me, but my dad should be here soon." I sigh.

"Got it, man. Let me know if you need anything." Walsh says, hanging up without waiting for a response.

I'm not too worried. I don't care if I'm the only one in costume, because all my attention will be on Poppy and trying not to bust out of the thong I'll be wearing to notice anything else. However, I did think about wearing jeans. A loud knock on my door interrupts my thoughts. With a heavy groan, I get to my feet and shuffle to the door.

I open the door, and the smell of all of their colognes hits me at once, making me feel even more disoriented. The three of them begin to double.

"Jax, you're not looking too good." My dad says, stepping close to me.

"I'm fine." I know he is not convinced since I slurred my words.

"You're anything but fine. I think we need to go get you checked out," Otis says.

"That's a good idea." My dad, looping his arm around my back, Otis comes to my other side to help my father.

I wobble on my feet. I am thankful to have the support. I feel so unbalanced, and black spots are appearing in my blurry surroundings. I am a little worried I might pass out.

"Fine, but I don't want Poppy to know until after her contest." I put my arm around Otis's shoulder. "I don't want to risk her being distracted or her deciding to back out to come home early."

My dad sighs, shaking his head, clearly not happy about me wanting to hide this from Poppy for a little while, but I know he will respect my decision. "Alright, but I'm telling your mom."

I roll my eyes, making me dizzier. "Fine."

"Okay, but I will not make any promises your mom will not tell Poppy." His grip around my waist tightens.

I groan and complain about the dumb ass who tackled me in an illegal move as we slowly go down the stairs. I mean, I would be with Poppy, cheering her on in person if I didn't get injured by the careless move I got injured from.

"How is Wynona enjoying being in Nashville?" My dad asks to change the subject as soon as we get in his SUV.

"She is loving it. We've received so many pictures; we had to tell her to stop. As you can imagine, it didn't go over well with Grams. So, I told her she can tell us all about it over dinner when she comes home." Otis laughs at Wells, interrupting him. "She is loving her first trip with Poppy. She wanted to take us to Nashville when we were younger, but she never got the chance." Otis continues to laugh.

I lean my head against the cold window. This fucking sucks. I was looking forward to beer and a game with my dad. I close my eyes as the building passing me makes my stomach turn.

I can hear my dad talk to Otis about his businesses, and the next thing I know is my dad is yelling my name, trying to wake me, but the weird thing is I don't feel like I am asleep, but at the same time, I don't feel awake. I feel heavy. When I try to open my eyes, they stay closed. The fog in my head thickens, ringing in my ears deafens me, but not enough for my dad's worried voice to cut through.

I finally lift my heavy head, and I am shocked to see two guys in scrubs outside of our SUV with a wheelchair staring at me with my dad next to them.

"Violet, the kids will be okay with Freya until I get home. Just get Nova settled at the clinic and stay as long as you need." Otis says on the phone in the backseat with Wells.

I don't want to be rude, listening in on his conversation, but I can't help myself, even though my father keeps saying, "Jax," and snapping his fingers at me, trying to get my attention. I'm still drawn to the drama happening in Otis's life right now.

"If the psychiatrist thinks you should stay, stay. I know you're tired of living like you have to look over your shoulder and try to anticipate her next move." Otis sighs heavily, getting out of the SUV.

"Jax," the nurse says this time.

I finally accept my dad's hand out of the truck as Otis comes back into earshot, and I can hear more of his private conversation.

"No, but if you have to stay with her for a little while so we're not constantly worrying about the safety of our family, I think you should." We walk through glass doors, and heat instantly blasts in my face. "I know, but we've talked about this, and you agreed; if we could get her to go, you would do whatever you need to so she can get the help she needs, and from the sounds of it, I think you do." The conversation quiets as my dad and I go through another door.

"So, what brought you in today?" the older male nurse, I would say is about my father's age, pushing my wheelchair, asks.

"I have a concussion, but I've been getting more headaches and blind spots in my vision." I prop my elbow on the arm of the wheelchair, putting my aching head in my palm.

"He has been slurring his words, too," my father chimes in.

"Okay, we will get you checked out." The wheelchair stops moving in a small waiting room. "I'll get your intake forms to fill out."

Otis and Wells find us several minutes later, and they begin watching the game on the TV while I sit in the wheelchair with my head down. The bright fluorescent lights in here suck. Whoever decided these lights were a good thing never sat in a room full of them with a head injury.

A curvy nurse about my mom's age comes out of a locked door calling my name. "TAYLOR!" I look at my dad, and he nods.

I barely lift my head from my hand, but my dad waves to her.

"I hear you're having some symptoms after a concussion. Let's go back and see what's going on." She grabs the handle on my wheelchair. I was expecting her to struggle to push me, but she moved us down the hallway at a faster speed than the man who was pushing me to the waiting room did. I look down as nausea rolls in my stomach from the lights and the speed we are going.

I hope this exam goes by fast and they let me go home instead of making me stay the night. The last thing I want to do is be cooped up here without Poppy to keep me company.

Driving home with my dad, griping about how we should go get a second opinion, because the doctor said I need more rest, didn't help my headache, but I convinced him I would go home with him this weekend. Thankfully, I fell asleep on the way home, and I didn't have to hear him anymore.

I'm now lying on the giant U-shaped couch in the den with the game playing while my dad gets the pizza and drinks for us. He could have gotten the food on the way here, but he wanted me to rest, even though I could in the car.

I need to text Poppy since I haven't heard any updates from her all day. I fumble to get my phone out of my pocket, but when I look at my screen, I blink away more black spots. This shit is getting old.

Jax: How is the competition going?

I know I won't get a response anytime soon, but I still send an encouraging text, too.

Jax: Kick ass! I can't wait to celebrate with you! Love you.

I hear my dad before I see him. "He's fine. I got home with pizza." My dad gives me a weak smile as he sets the box on the ottoman and cracks the top off two beers, handing me one. "No, I can take care of Jax until you guys get back. Poppy…" My father sighs into the phone. "Jax wants you to do your competition and…" he stops talking.

I open the lid, chuckling under my breath, and put a couple of large slices of supreme pizza on a paper plate, lying back down on the couch. I told them not to tell her until after she went on, so now they have to reap the consequences.

"I promise I'll keep you guys in the loop." My dad playfully rolls his eyes. "Break a leg out there. Jax and I will be watching you on a video chat."

He hangs up, looking at me as I shove half of my slice of pizza in my mouth. I shrug, and he grabs two slices of pizza and a couple of wings before turning to the big screen on the wall. My father is part of the reason sports and football are a huge part of my life. Unlike him, I want to go pro before settling down with a family, but the more I'm with Poppy, my dream is evolving, but still somewhat the same.

"She is fixing to get on stage. They are going to video call us. Do you still know how to get it on the screen?" My dad hands me his phone as my mom's name begins flashing on the screen.

I turn off the game and set up a video cast, and before I know it, a dark stage barely visible from the dim lights. A spotlight hits the center of the stage, revealing a stool and a mic stand.

I turn up the volume, and I can hear my mom whisper. "Can you guys hear me?"

"Yes!" I shout back, I'm excited to watch Poppy perform on a real stage for the first time.

A strange sensation hits me, and my mood instantly plummets, and the phone begins to slip out of my hands. I can't be there for Poppy and support her as she follows her dreams. She comes to all my games, and her first big event, I can't come to. I'm sure the heavy fog clouding my brain is also from my concussion.

"Jax, are you okay?" My father asks, scooting closer to me.

"Yeah, I'm mad I can't be there with her." I look at the screen on the wall as the lights change on the stage.

"She knows you're watching," Wynona whispers from her seat next to my mom.

"Poppy Monroe!" an invisible announcer calls out.

I watch as Poppy walks out on stage with her guitar hanging on her back by the custom guitar strap with bright red poppies embroidered on it. She looks incredible in her little black dress and black boots. Her hair sparkles in the spotlight, highlighting her beauty.

The band behind her starts playing, and she smiles. She begins singing, and her voice rings out through the crowd. In one fluid movement, her sparkly red guitar is moved to the front of her, and she begins playing. She looks so comfortable and confident on stage. I know music is what Poppy wants to do, and watching her look so free proves it.

This is a whole new type of confidence oozing from Poppy, and I know I'm not the only one being mesmerized by her right now.

"She looks amazing up there." My mom's voice is thick with awe.

"She is a natural," my dad comments.

I don't say anything. I can't, because watching Poppy sing and play her guitar for a crowd is the best thing I have ever seen. The lyrics and the melody to the song, thumping through our speakers makes me tap my toes. I don't know how the other contestants did, I don't care, but I can tell you I think Poppy should win.

The way Poppy moves her body is sensual without even trying. The way she moves her hips to the beat and the light in her eyes as she sings her heart out is a major turn on. If I hadn't already fallen in love with her, I would right now by watching her. Poppy plays the last note, and the lights dim. The crowd in the bar goes wild. Poppy beams at the crowd before bowing and walking off stage.

"We will call back when they announce the winner," My mom says before cutting the call before either of us can reply.

I feel around the couch for my phone, only to find it in the crack of the couch.

Jax: You were fucking amazing! I'm so proud of you!

I lay my phone on the cushion next to me, and I grab my forgotten pizza.

"Dad, she was so good." I know I have a big, silly smile on my face, but I can't help how fucking proud I am of her.

I look over at my dad and see the same smile he gives me after a game, no matter if our team wins or loses.

I eat the rest of my pizza and grab some more when dad's phone rings again. My dad answers the call and hands me the phone after a quick hello. I connect the video call back to the big screen and watch as the stage replaces the game. This time, the stage is completely lit. You can see the color of the medium stain on the wood. I see Poppy in a line of people. You can also hear the rumbling of the people in the crowd who are having low conversations as they wait for the winner to be announced.

I glance at everyone on stage, and all of their shoulders are square, and their back is straight. They look nervous, but not Poppy; she looks radiant as she stands out from the others around her. Her shoulders are back, but not from nerves. She looks confident, calm, and ready to hear the results.

A tall woman in a nice pantsuit and heels walks on stage. "Excuse me," she says in a deep southern twang.

The audience quiets down, and I hear my mom whisper, "Here we go."

"The judges and I were impressed by the talent we have seen on this stage tonight. As you know, the winning song will be picked up by our label to be a songwriter. One of our recording artists will record the song." The crowd cheers, whooping, and hollering. "Now let's get to it. The winner is…" I don't know why people pause so long when announcing the winners. I find the wait to be annoying. "Poppy Monroe."

The crowd roars, and the others on the stage either hug Poppy or shake her hand. The people in the crowd start standing up, and I look away as the video on the screen shakes as she cheers for Poppy. I stand on my feet, hugging my dad.

My head is swimming, and the room spins, as I clumsily collapse onto the couch. I text Poppy even though my screen is blurry.

Jax: I am so proud of you! I can't wait to celebrate with you. Love you.

I set my phone down, kick out my feet, and lie down on the couch. The game has started again, and we are in the final quarter. Our team is up by 30 points, and the crowd is going wild. This would have been one hell of a game to go to, but I am happy I got to watch Poppy perform, even if it was over on a phone shared to a big screen. I can't wait for the party to celebrate. Poppy won and is going to get a contract to be a professional songwriter. Her dreams are coming true and I know one day I will be playing pro ball too.

CHAPTER 22

POPPY

A ding signals through the cabin of the airplane, and the sign to fasten your seatbelt lights up. "Attention passengers…" the captain says. "We are preparing for landing. Please fasten your seat belts and thank you for trusting us with your travels."

I put my tray up, and I buckle my seatbelt, with shaky hands, because I'm still reeling and feeling the high of winning a life-changing experience. I can't believe I won the whole contest. I was so freaking nervous on stage in front of so many strangers. There is something about singing your own songs to people is thrilling and terrifying all at the same time.

A lot happened quickly after the contest. I had to attend a few meetings, and I even met the artist who will record my song. I'm so excited for who it is and hear them sing my lyrics. They asked if I wanted to move here yet, and they offered to help me find a place to live, but I'm not ready to leave my family. Still, with technology, I can write songs and play them for the label from anywhere in the world.

The line of people getting off the plane is long and makes me feel anxious. I am so ready to see Jax, Shane, and my brothers. We are going out to eat, because everyone wants to celebrate me. I still can't believe how much my life has changed since I was a terrified seventeen-year-old girl, leaving her home to go to another. Jax, Shane, and Roxi changed my life, and it keeps getting better.

"Even though I had more fun with you two ladies than a barrel full of monkeys, I am ready to get home and see how Otis is doing on the remodel of my kitchen." Grams chuckles.

Roxi begins talking about the remodel and the pictures Otis sent her last night. You can tell she'll be able to move back home soon, and part of me doesn't want her to go.

I walk through the crowded airport with my head in the clouds. Reality and the airport around me escape me until I run into someone and my purse falls to the floor. Thankfully, my stuff doesn't spill all over the place.

"Sorry," I mumble under my breath.

"Poppy?" Lewis's familiar voice has me standing up.

"What…" I stutter, "Are you doing here?" I pick up my purse, turning around with no intention of hearing what he has to say, but I stop dead in my tracks when someone else I know walks up to us with her hips swaying and her perfect curls bouncing around her head.

"Oh, look who it is…" Lana's face turns red under her cheeks, colored with a bright pink blush. "Poppy Monroe."

"Lana." I greet, squaring my shoulders when I see her swollen, clearly pregnant belly.

She must have seen me looking at her stomach, because she put her hand on her baby bump, giving me a full toothy smile like she did when she cheered. "Lewis is going to be a great daddy."

My stomach drops. I knew he had been with her while we were together but seeing them together hurts more than I would like it to. One day, I wanted to be the person who was going to marry Lewis Jacobs and live happily ever after with him. However, I have a better man in my life now. One who isn't going to cheat on me and hurt me.

"Are you going on a trip?" Lewis asks, looking behind me where Roxi and Grams are waiting for me.

"Poppy!" Grams shouts, walking over to us. "Who are your friends?" She sticks out her hand for them to shake, but they stare at her like she has lost her mind.

I adjust my purse on my shoulder I had forgotten about. "Oh, this is Lewis, he is my ex-boyfriend, and this is his girlfriend, Lana."

They both shake Grams's hand even though Lewis's shoulders are tense and his eyebrows are furrowed, while Lana huffs, shifting on her swollen feet.

"It's so nice to meet you. I am Poppy's grandma, Wynona. We'd better go. Jax and Shane are waiting for us out front. Oh, Roxi and I also invited your brothers to dinner." Grams says this, knowing they can hear.

"Grandma and brothers? Poppy, what the hell is she talking about? Your grandparents died a long time ago." Lewis asks, putting his hand on my shoulder.

I turn around, and when I see the hard slant in his eyes, anger boils in my blood.

"Yeah, some things happened after we broke up, but you don't get the right to know now." I cross my arms over my chest, shrugging his hand off of me.

I walk away from Lewis and Lana feeling stronger, even though I'm a little sad she is pregnant. I don't care about them being together, but seeing how much she is showing, it feels like a slap in the face, even though I know they have been sleeping together since high school.

We walk out of the main entrance, and the first thing I see is Jax holding up a sign reading, *congrats rockstar*. I hear Lewis mutter under his breath, wondering what the sign means, but I don't pay any attention. I go straight to Jax and throw my arms around his neck. As soon as his strong arms wrap around me, I am hit with warmth spreading through my chest, and I know I'm finally back home, safe and loved.

"I am so fucking proud of you!" Jax says, before kissing me breathless.

When we pull apart, and I hug Shane, who excitedly yells, "Congratulations. We are so proud of you!" My ears ring, but I can't stop looking over Shane's shoulder at Lewis, who is staring over here with his normal pouty lips pressed into a thin line and his eyebrows scrunched together, making his forehead wrinkled.

He is handsome, but after learning who he is as a person, I don't find him attractive anymore.

"Thank you." I pull back with glassy eyes.

"We can't wait to hear about the contest," Shane says, helping Jax with our bags.

"Oh, I was so nervous playing my music for such a big crowd." I feel my cheeks flame red from the attention I am getting. "But it was a thrill at the same time."

"You couldn't even tell you were nervous," Roxi said, getting in the passenger seat. "You looked like you've lived your whole life on a stage."

"I did in my dreams." We laugh as Shane turns his SUV on and country music plays softly through the speakers.

As soon as we get in the car, Grams begins singing to the music on the radio, and I'm not surprised she has a good voice, even if she is slightly off-key. She doesn't care who can hear her sing terribly, but I've learned that Grams doesn't bother herself with what others think of her.

I laugh under my breath, thinking about how I could hear her screaming at the top of her lungs, "That's my granddaughter!" while I was singing.

The drive to the restaurant doesn't take long. This is a central location, so meeting here wasn't a problem, although Otis and Wells said they would drive anywhere for me. Shane and Roxi will have to take Grams, Jax, and me home since Shane picked up Jax last night, because he couldn't drive. So, they will be spending the night at his apartment tonight.

When Roxi told me he was getting dizzy and slurring his speech, and he had to go to the hospital, I was so mad when we got back to the hotel. I did calm down, because I need to be patient with him, like he was with me. The last couple of times I had concussions, I tried so hard to hide my symptoms too, so I can understand what he is going through.

We pull into a little Italian restaurant, and the smell of garlic takes over my senses. My stomach growls and my mouth waters at the thought of pasta and breadsticks.

We walk into the restaurant, which is decorated in creams, terracotta, and sage green. The colors and the atmosphere here are calm and elegant. This place is fancy, and I'm sure expensive, which won't bother Shane and Roxi one bit. I thought inviting Wells and Otis was Grams's idea, but I was wrong. Roxi had asked Shane to ask them when they went to the football game they never made it to.

Otis walks in with Harley and Hawk first, then Wells, followed by Freya. Violet isn't able to come since she is still at the therapy center with Nova, but she did call me to tell me congratulations.

Once we are all here, Shane goes to the hostess to get us in line for a table.

"How is Violet doing?" Grams asks, hugging Otis.

He clears his throat. "She's stressed, but trying to stay in good spirits. Apparently, these new doctors are making it difficult for Nova, and she has thrown a few tantrums, at least is how Violet described them. We have talked about going to another facility, but we don't know if Violet can convince Nova to go."

"What are they saying is wrong with Nova?" Freya leans down, picking Harley up and putting her on her lap. "I know Violet wants to get her an official diagnosis, so Nova can be treated properly.

"They want to see if Nova has an attachment disorder of some sort."

Otis clears his throat. "But they also want to look into bipolar disorder or schizophrenia."

"Those are all treatable, right?" Freya asks.

"Well, the thing is, Violet doesn't want to keep Nova hospitalized or institutionalized, but they keep trying to persuade Violet into keeping Nova at either of those places, which is what is best for her right now. I guess the doctors keep saying she has to learn to live on the right kind of medications and do the right therapies to live a semi-normal life." Otis picks Hawk up on the bench next to Grams.

"How is that best for Nova?" I speak up, genuinely curious.

"That's the thing, without a proper diagnosis, we can't be sure what the right thing to do is. Violet goes to all the therapy sessions, and Nova is actually opening up to her…" Otis clears his throat.

"Taylor!" The hostess announces our party's table is ready.

"We can talk about this later." Otis clears his throat, but his shoulders stay tense. "Tonight is about Poppy."

Jax grabs my hand when we sit down at the round table in the middle of the restaurant. Once we are all seated and our drinks are ordered, Grams and Roxi jump right into telling them about the weekend.

I am happy, and my heart is full of excitement, and the love I feel from everyone at this table. I do miss Violet. She is my sister-in-law, but she has some healing to do with Nova. I hope they can get Nova the help she needs, because I know Violet would like her sister in her life.

As soon as they are done filling everyone in on the weekend, and we talk about the meeting with the record label, Otis goes back to talking about Violet and Nova. The good news is, Violet or Nova doesn't have to agree to going to a hospital or anything yet, but in the end, it will depend on the diagnosis and how Nova does with therapy and treatment. However, if she continues taking her medicine and doing well in therapy, she may have a full, healthy life. Maybe there is some hope for her after all.

I was a little unsure because the day Nova came to my house, she wanted to scare me away from Violet. I could tell there was a void in her eyes. I've seen the exact same look in my father's eyes when he was too drunk and angry to know what he was doing to me, at least I like to think he didn't know he was a monster. Even though he was sober for a lot of what he did too. I don't know all they've been through, but Nova is lucky to have a sister who is fighting to find out what is wrong with her.

"Pops, are you ready?" Jax asks, getting my attention.

"Yes, let's go home." We say our goodbyes to Otis, Wells, and the kids.

I look out the window past Jax, because I am sitting in the middle seat, thinking about how happy and lucky.

About a mile from the apartments, Jax leans close to me and whispers into my ear. "I can't wait to show you how proud of you I am after everyone goes to sleep and I can sneak to your apartment like we are teenagers."

I feel my cheeks burn at his unspoken promise, because I know what they mean. I am thankful the car is dark to hide the redness of my cheeks from everyone sees how turned on Jax made me from only his words.

CHAPTER 23

JAX

Leaving the doctor today was great. I got all clear to play again, so the first thing I do is head to campus. Team workout starts in thirty minutes, and I'll get there in enough time to get my gym clothes on if I don't make any stops. My phone rings, and I answer without looking at the caller ID.

"Hello," I say, tapping my fingers on the steering wheel to the music playing in my head.

"Hey," Poppy's sweet voice fills the cabin of my truck. "What did the doctor say?"

"I got the all clear to play again." I slow down at a stoplight. "I'm on my way to the gym now."

"That's great. I have some homework I need to do, so I will meet you at home after." She sounds like she is asking a question with the way she stretches the words "so" and "after."

Poppy and I haven't talked since I found out the record label she signed with wants her to move to Tennessee or California. I'm not mad at her because she never said yes, but she also never said no. I am confused why she doesn't want to talk to me about it.

All I want is for her to be happy, and if she wants to move, I will fly out at any chance I can. Distance isn't going to keep us apart, because I won't allow it to.

"Yeah, I'll see you at home after," I grunt.

I need to let this misplaced hurt and anger go, because the last thing I want to do is for Poppy to think I don't support her.

"Jax, I'm not going anywhere. I am happy here with you." I can hear the sadness in her voice.

"I know, but I don't want to hold you back." I sigh. "Can we talk about this at home? I will bring home some takeout. After we talk, we can make a pillow pallet on the floor and watch movies."

If we have a date night at home, cuddling on the floor on soft blankets and pillows is one of Poppy's favorite things, but for me, the best part is when we forget about the movie and get lost in each other.

"Jax," Poppy gasps. "That sounds wonderful. Can we have fajitas and margaritas?"

"Sounds good to me. I am at the gym." I say parking in one of the few empty spots. "I'll see you in a few hours. Love you."

"I love you too," Poppy says before she ends the call.

I grab my gym bag off the back seat and walk through the chilly parking lot. I open the glass door, and I can instantly hear a bunch of grown college men gossiping like little schoolgirls. One thing about guys, they let on about how they can't stand gossip, but in reality, most of them love some good tea as much as women do.

"Taylor, what are you doing here?" Coach Harrison barks behind Chance as he spots him on some weights.

"Got my doctor's note saying I'm good to come back." I hold up my release forms.

"Alright, get changed." I stop by his office, placing the papers on his desk, lyre I go change into my gym clothes really fast.

The locker room is pretty cleared out. There are a few freshmen still here horsing around, but I mostly ignore them as I change into some gym shorts and a t-shirt.

"Taylor, work with Benny today." Coach Harrison commands when I step out of the locker room.

I resist rolling my eyes. There is nothing worse than working with Benny. He is the team's trainer and can be brutal to whichever player he is working with, especially if they are back from an injury.

"Alright, Taylor. Are you ready to hate me?" Benny comes up behind me, clapping me hard on the back.

He is a big guy, but other than the grueling workouts, he is a great person. He is often referred to as the team's bodyguard because he often looks like a bouncer at a club. I walk over to the bench and sit down.

"Alright, let's get you in shape for this week's game." Benny hands me two large hand weights. "You've been out for a while, so tell me if your shoulder or head hurts. Don't play down anything so you can get back on the field faster." Benny stands behind me with his arms crossed, but he as a gentle smile tugging on his lips.

"Sounds good to me." I adjust my position on the bench and look up into the mirror to get a full view of my stance to make sure I am doing my work out to my full potential.

As I am walking down the hallway to my apartment with steaming hot Mexican food, I can hear the sound of Poppy playing the piano. The familiar tone to the song, she finally told me she wrote for me after the first night we slept together, and I had put my damn foot in my mouth, vibrates through the door. I stand there listening to the song, which has some sensual, happy, and sad all at the same time. She says she has lyrics for the song, but she isn't ready for me to listen to them. I know they will say exactly how she felt at the time, and when she is ready, she will sing them to me.

I unlock the door, and Poppy stops playing. She has learned to listen to everything in the background, even over the beautiful loud music Poppy is playing. She had to learn to listen and anticipate her father's arrival home, because she never knew which dad she was getting when he came home from work or the bar, and she wanted to avoid the risk of setting him off. The last time she was at her father's home, and she didn't hear the door over the piano, was the day my heart broke for the first time, because she told me she couldn't walk for two days after he was done punishing her. She said, thankfully, it was during summertime.

Well, there was the day I saved her. I saw what Poppy was having to live through, and I could imagine how she was able to keep a scary secret from everyone so well.

I finally push the door open to find Poppy standing in the middle of the living room, looking so cute and sweet enough to eat in a red silky nightie with white lace trim. This is a new one, trust me, I have memorized how sexy she looks in all of her little night gowns.

"Fuck, you are beautiful." I walk with long, deliberate steps until I can lean down, kissing her on the cheek.

I can feel her cheek warm under my kiss, knowing I put a little blush to her cheek makes my dick swell a little in the sweatpants I changed into before leaving the gym.

"Thank you. How was the workout?" Poppy grabs one of the bags, and I follow her into my apartment.

"I worked with Benny, so I'm pretty sore," I say, looking around my living room.

Poppy had set up the living room for the movie we are going to watch after we talk, but damn, she looks so good, and since I haven't been able to touch her since before my concussion, I don't know if we will even get to watch much of the movie.

"During the movie, I can give you a massage if you would like?" Poppy looks up at me from under her lashes.

I lean down, chuckling softly until my lips meet her bare shoulder, nipping her soft, pale skin as my free hand grabs Poppy's slender hip. "I know something you can massage."

Poppy lightly hits me on my chest with the back of her hand, giggling as she grabs the other bag from me and starts setting the food out on the coffee table. I kick off my sneakers and sit down on the floor. Poppy is still standing up, leaning over the table, and I get the perfect view up her little nightgown. She has on a matching thong. I put my hand on the back of her knee, and I move my hand slowly up her thigh. I feel goosebumps erupt all over her skin.

"Jax," Poppy sighs before she playfully smacks my hand away. "Save those roaming hands for the movie. I am starving."

Poppy sits down next to me, but I want to feel her body against mine. I move until my back is on the couch before swinging my leg over Poppy's head. I scoot up until she is sitting between my legs, and her back is on my chest. She continues to open the containers of the food before she hands me a fork. Poppy dips a chip in salsa and puts some in her mouth, crunching loudly. As she chews, she moans quietly under her breath, and she gives a little wiggle happy dance.

She leans back, looking up at me through her lashes. "This is so good. Thank you for thinking of this. Are you ready to talk?"

"I want to know what you're thinking." I grab a tortilla out of the foil package.

"I don't plan on moving. However, I wasn't going to make this huge decision without talking to you first. Would living in Tennessee and getting to work face-to-face with celebrities be fun and exciting? Yes, but one of my favorite things to do every day is coming home to you, and I can't imagine being in another state." Poppy takes another bite of food. "Sometimes the distance between our apartments feels too far, and you are right next door."

"I don't want you to resent me later on if you don't go because of me." I set my food on the table.

"I won't, but Jax, you're not the only reason I'm not ready to make the move." Poppy turns in my lap, facing me.

What she says finally clicks. I'm a jerk for making this all about me. She finally has the family she has always wanted, and she is not ready to leave them. Even though we would come back to visit often I know for her it wouldn't feel the same.

"Moving won't change anything, and you will still get to see them a lot." I kiss the top of her head, and her soft hair tickles my nose.

"I know, but I am just now getting to know them." She looks down. "I'm not ready yet. Maybe we can talk about it when we graduate."

I don't tell her I don't know where I'll be, but I think she knows that too. If I get drafted to a pro team, I could be away from Nashville or California.

"Whatever you choose to do, I will support you and be your biggest cheerleader." Poppy turns around, swinging her leg over me.

She puts her forehead on mine. "Does it come with the skirt and pompoms?"

"Only for you."

Poppy shifts until she is fully straddling my lap, causing her nightgown to move up her thighs, bunching at her hips, showing me more of her perfect thighs.

"How did I get so lucky?" Poppy leans in, kissing me on my jaw.

"I don't know, but I think it's time for both of us to get lucky." I wink.

Poppy giggles as her cold hands move under my shirt and onto my stomach. My muscles twitch from her soft touch, and I inhale sharply. "Fuck, your hands are cold."

Poppy doesn't stop moving her hands up my body. Her freezing fingers brush against my nipples, and I groan from the perfect torture of her touch and the coldness her hands bring. She looks up at me through her lashes like an innocent lamb about to be devoured by a lion.

I wait, letting Poppy remove my shirt before I move my hands to her knees, sliding my hands under the lacey hem of Poppy's nightgown. Poppy looks into my eyes as hers sparkles with playful mischief. I move my hands slowly up her narrow hips over her tiny thong. I feel Poppy shiver and her goosebumps multiply as I move my hands lightly over her rib cage.

"Jax..." Poppy mumbles, her head falling back.

Her long hair brushes against my sweatpants. Poppy's hands and arms raise above her head, allowing me to easily slip her nightgown over her head. I look at her, memorizing all the details of her in her thong.

Fuck, she is so beautiful, but I can't look at her anymore without feeling her soft skin. I lean in, pressing my lips to her collarbone.

"Jax," she sighs again.

"What do you want?" I ask even though I know the answer.

"I want…" she trails off when I hook my thumbs in the side of her panties.

"Poppy, tell me what you want," I repeat myself.

She lifts her hips, telling me silently to strip her until she is completely bare in front of me.

"I want…" she gasps when my hands touch her knees. "I want all of you."

I nip at the pale skin on her shoulder. "You already have me."

CHAPTER 24

JAX

Tonight is the costume party I promised to throw for Poppy if she won the contest. She gave me full control over what her costume is, which is probably a mistake on her end. I put her in what I want to see, but I think she secretly likes it.

"JAX! This one is worse than what you put together for Halloween." Poppy says as the bathroom door swings open, hitting the dresser. "What is with you making me look like I stepped out of an early 2000's music video?"

This time, I'm as fully clothed, well, as much as my costume will allow me to, but not much, considering my outfit consists of white assless chaps, a red man thong, a red feather boa, and a white cowboy hat that has a fake plastic tiara on it. Every time I wear this costume, I am reminded just how uncomfortable it is, but seeing Poppy's smile and sweet blush take over her beautiful face is well worth the several hours of torture I'll be enduring.

"Well, I thought a cowgirl would be fitting since I plan on taking you on the ride of your life after the party." I smile at Poppy, allowing my eyes to roam over her body, which causes her blush to spread down her neck and chest.

"Well, that is a little disappointing. I wanted to ride a cowboy later." Poppy beams at me.

She is proud of her dirty joke and rightfully so. She can come up with some good jokes when she's not trying.

I chuckle. "You do it every day."

Poppy stops mid-step, looking over at me with her mouth gaping open. I reach out and wrap my hand around her small wrist. I lightly pull her to me.

"Jax," she leans down, kissing me.

"It's true. I love you." I say pulling back, looking up at her. "We won't ever get to the party if we keep this up."

Poppy nods. "You're probably right."

Poppy adjusts the straps on her triangle bikini top, and my eyes stay glued to her every move. Poppy looks gorgeous in her costume, and I can't wait to show her off at the party. The funny thing about Poppy wanting a costume party she's not exactly a party girl. In fact, Poppy has always hated going to parties, especially with Lewis.

I know the last party we went to together wasn't great, because I left in a bad mood, because of Lilah. Poppy hated parties since the first one she went to, but before Lewis and she broke up, she overheard two girls talking about Lewis cheating on her. I never told Poppy I knew he was sleeping with Lana in high school, and it makes me feel like an asshole. I know I need to tell her, but it wasn't confirmed until I saw Lana going down on Lewis at a field party one night in our senior year; my suspicions were confirmed.

"Jax, are you okay?" Poppy asks, putting her freezing hands on my cheeks, getting my attention.

"Yeah, I'm thinking of Lewis," I admit, even though I know how much bringing his name up will hurt her.

Poppy's smile vanishes, and I see the hurt in her eyes at the mention of my old best friend's name. "I'm sorry."

"Don't be. It's not your fault we aren't friends anymore, but I'm the one who should be apologizing to you."

Poppy sits on the bed next to me, grabbing my hand. "You don't have anything to apologize for." Her eyebrows scrunch together.

"Yeah, I do." I sigh, "I saw Lana blowing Lewis at a field party in high school." I look down at her, and she grabs my hand. "I should have told you back then."

"I already knew about it. I was hiding in a stall in the restroom with a headache from one of my concussions. Lana and her big mouth were bragging about what she and Lewis had gotten up to in his Jeep. She said you were walking away when she resurfaced from sucking Lewis off. She was hoping you were going to tell me so I would break up with Lewis." Poppy presses her lips into a thin line. "That is why I was never comfortable going down on Lewis. I didn't want my mouth where hers was."

"I didn't know this." I shift a little to get a better look at Poppy. "But you deserve to be treated like a second thought."

"I know, but I didn't tell anyone, not even Lewis. I thought maybe he would be faithful when we got to college." She grimaces so hard the bed shakes. "I was so out of it and wrapped up in trying to stay away from my father at the time; what he did and how he betrayed me didn't hurt as much as it should have."

"I get it, but it's still shitty." I put my arm around her.

"Oh, you're not wrong, because when everything was over, and I was able to process what he had done, I never fully trusted him again. I also thought I could handle him cheating on me, because he wasn't hitting me or yelling at me. Looking back on it, I realize I was wrong, because it hurts just as much." Poppy lays her head on my shoulder. "Jax, can we talk about this later and go to the party?"

"Fuck yeah." I stand up, grabbing Poppy's hand, pulling her to the door.

"Do you want to have some more fun tonight?" Poppy asks, grabbing the little toy I bought her for the Halloween party, off the nightstand.

"Bend over," my simple command makes her shiver, but she listens to me by bending over the side of the bed.

This is going to be one hell of a night. My girl looks hot as fuck, and I plan on celebrating her in so many different ways throughout the night.

Jax looks delicious in his assless chaps. He has a perfect ass, and I want to sink my teeth in his skin. My motivation for the party wasn't to celebrate me winning the contest, but to get him in his assless chaps again. I know if I asked him to, he would model them for me, but I selfishly want to rub in the other girl's face how sinfully sexy my boyfriend is while he celebrates with me. Even though he will be on full display and all of them will be checking him out, I know his eyes will only be on me.

Jax makes me feel sexy and powerful. Even though he put me in the most revealing outfit I've ever been in. I don't feel insecure like I thought I would. When you have a man like Jax looking at you like you are his world, you feel like you can do about anything. including wearing assless chaps with a little string bikini. Even though I am still trying to forget how exposed I am right now.

We walk into the party, and all eyes are on us as the guys from the frat yell congratulations. Walsh hands me a cup and from the looks of the liquid, he gave me red wine.

"Drink up and dance your ass off, because you deserve it, rock star." Walsh chuckles as Jax pulls my arm toward the living room, where people are dancing.

A huge grin plasters my face as Jax stops with people all around us. He pulls me close to his body, rocking his hips against me. His hands roam my exposed skin, leaving a trail of fiery passion and lust in their wake. Before our drinks can empty, a new one is placed in mine or Jax's hands. Jax's fraternity brothers are taking care of us tonight because Jax asked them to make sure I have one hell of a celebration.

Time blurs, and all I can think about is Jax's body on mine as we dance time away. I hiccup as Walsh put my third cup of wine in my hand.

"Want to go play beer pong?" I blurt out without thinking whether playing against Jax is a good idea or not.

Jax looks at me with his eyebrows raised and the corner of his mouth tipped up in a half smile. "You hate beer pong."

I sway a little, but not from dancing; the wine is making my head swim. "I want to make a little bet." I tease, biting my lip.

Jax looks at me with a wide grin, narrowing eyes. "What are you wagering?" he moves close to me, and I can feel his hot breath fan over my neck.

"Well, if you win, we go somewhere quiet, and you can do whatever you want to me, but..." I hiccup. "If I win, I get to do whatever I want to you."

Jax spins me around until my back is pressed firmly to his chest. He brushes my hair from my shoulder, and I feel a hint of his warm breath on my already hot skin. Jax's arms come around me, and I see he has his phone out and the screen unlocked.

"You know I could distract you," Jax says, moving his fingers over the app controlling the little vibrator in my bikini bottoms.

My head falls back, and I sigh. Jax continues to move his fingers over the screen of his phone. The sensations are a little too much for me in the hot room and the wine buzzing through my blood. I have to bite my lip to keep from moaning loudly over the music.

The vibrations stop, and I stay where I am until my breath evens out. I'm left wanting, no craving, so much more from Jax's torturous teasing.

"Even if I lose, I still win." I turn back in Jax's arms. "I mean, no matter the outcome, there is a happy ending."

"You're on," Jax says, lacing his fingers in mine.

He leads me around the mass of college students grinding on each other to the dining room, where Walsh is playing beer pong with one of the guys from the school's baseball team. I have seen him many times, but for some reason, I can never remember his name.

"Can we have next?" Jax asks, watching as Walsh's ball hits the rim of a red cup before bouncing on the table.

"UGH!" he groans loudly. "Yeah."

I watch as the drunk baseball player sinks his ball into the cup, leaving Walsh with one left. A loud growl rips through Walsh before he picks up the cup of beer, downing it in two large gulps. The other guy aims to line up the shot he wants to take. I can tell he is trying hard to concentrate through his drunken state. He licks his lips and squints his eyes, flicking his wrist without tossing the ball.

The longer he takes, the more Walsh fidgets, growing increasingly aggravated. The guy teases Walsh once more before the little ball sinks into the red cup, making him drink the warm beer from his last cup. Walsh downs his warm drink, wiping the drops around his mouth with the back of his hand. They move around the table, meeting in the middle, and Walsh claps some money into his opponent's hand. Now I understand why he was getting so frustrated at losing. I don't know how much he lost, but from the way he is walking away cursing loudly, it must have been a lot.

Jax lines up the cups, but I noticed he didn't put as much beer in our cups as people normally do. We are playing six-cup beer pong versus the normal twelve-cup beer pong the fraternity usually plays.

"Pops, you can go first," Jax says smugly, smiling at me with a huge lopsided grin.

I grab a ping pong ball and toss it toward his triangle of cups. The white plastic sphere bounces on the rims twice before falling into the corner cup on my left. Jax tips his cup in my direction before putting the beer to his mouth and setting the plastic cup back on the table with an audible plink of plastic on the wooden table. I shoot again, and this time my ball lands on the table next to the front cup.

I watch as Jax takes a shot. The ball makes a splashing sound as it lands on the beer without even hitting the rim of the red plastic cup. I'm not going to be surprised when Jax wins.

Jax shoots again, and the ball bounces on the rim of a cup before dropping into the cup diagonal to the one he got before. He shoots three more times, and each time the ping pong ball lands in a cup, leaving the cup at the point open. He flicks his wrist lazily, and the ball flies past me.

I scowl at him, putting my hands on my hips.

"What?" he shrugs, acting innocent.

I narrow my eyes at him. I think he is trying to lose the game. I square my shoulders and shimmy a little, acting like I'm warming up before I shoot the ball, landing the ball in the nasty beer, making Jax drink again. I get to go two more times with success before my third ball bounces on the table inches from the cup. I have three cups, which makes me wonder how Jax plans to miss until I win.

Jax lifts his hand, and someone calls his name as he releases the ball. I watch the little plastic ping pong ball fly by the lone cup in front of me. Well, maybe I'll be able to win after all. I take advantage of him trying to see who said his name, and I lean over, dropping a ball in his cup. I know I'm cheating, but I doubt he will care since he wants to lose.

"Ahem." I cough, getting Jax's attention, pointing to the cup with a ball in it.

Jax picks up the cup and drinks with a smile stretched on his face, making the beer dribble down his chin. I don't know whether I gave myself a disadvantage or not by putting a ball in the front cup. I shoot again, making another shot only for it to sail past all the cups.

Jax looks at both of the cups in front of him. I'm doing better than I thought, but I know I would have lost miserably had Jax decided not to miss those two throws.

Jax's eyes look me up and down. "Damn, I chose a damn good costume for you." Jax growls.

I boldly trace the front of my bikini top as Jax tosses his ball, making him miss, but I can tell he doesn't care by the way his glazed eyes lock on my hands. His tongue darts out of his mouth, wetting his lips. I wish he were kissing my body right now instead of across the beer pong table.

A crowd starts to form around us, and I can tell some of the frat guys want to take our place while others are enjoying the show of Jax actually throwing a game for once. I make two more shots and miss my third one, leaving us both with one cup. I left myself with the hardest cup to get so he might as well end this game for both of us.

Jax cocks one side of his mouth up while he raises his eyebrows, challenging me. He tosses the ball, and one of the onlookers catches it, looking at Jax like he has lost his mind. I'm sure he doesn't understand why Jax would throw away the game like this, but he doesn't know our bet, and if he did, he would probably high-five Jax.

I take another shot, missing again.

"How about we call it a draw, and we both lose?" Jax raises his eyebrow, daring me to challenge him.

"A tie is fine with me, considering you were missing those throws on purpose." I mimic him by raising my eyebrow too.

Jax struts around the table, grabbing my hand, pulling me toward the backyard. "I have a surprise for you."

I can easily tell some people left while we were playing beer pong, but there are still a lot of people outside, and my eyes land on Lewis. He is off to the side with his arm around someone who is not Lana. I would ask him what he is doing here, but Lilah is also next to them, sitting on some guy's lap. I don't like them being here, but I'm not going to be the one to kick them out.

"ATTENTION! PARTY GOERS!" Walsh yells into a megaphone. "THIS ISN'T YOUR TYPICAL PARTY! THIS IS A CELEBRATION."

Jax and his teammates line up in front of one of those inflatable movie screens. Walsh hands the megaphone to Jax, and he comes to me, pulling lightly on my wrist, positioning me until I am in front of everyone. My face heats as I feel all these eyes gawking at me in my string bikini and assless chaps.

"For those of you who don't know who this insanely beautiful woman is, let me introduce you!" Jax waves his hand down my body. "This is my extremely talented girlfriend, Poppy!"

I see a few girls roll their eyes, shoulders slump, or cross their arms over their chests, pursing their lips together as they glare at me. They are not happy to hear Jax is not available to hook up with tonight. I bite my lip to hold in the laughter bubbling in my throat at their jealous reactions.

"Jax?" I look away from the people for a second to see a huge smile on my boyfriend's face.

I look back at the sea of people in the crowd, and my eyes stop at Lewis again. His face is red, like he is holding his breath. I would bet he is fuming mad at the declaration Jax made. I look at Lilah again, who is glaring at Jax, before I turn my attention back to her brother.

The screen lights up, taking my attention away from my ex-boyfriend. I see the dimly lit stage, glowing from the stage I played on for the songwriting contest. My name is announced through large speakers. They are going to play this for the whole party to see! I watch in amazement at myself, but when someone whistles, a sense of dumb struck horror and embarrassment surges through me.

The video cuts to black, and the audience whoops and hollers. The screen lights up, and the lady who announced the winner comes on. The crowd shushes, waiting to see the next part, but I feel a pair of eyes burning into me.

Lewis is looking at me, and I can see the bewilderment on his face as Walsh and one of the other guys lift me onto their shoulders. While everyone chants my name, I look back at two people who used to be important to me. Lilah is chewing on her bottom lip, still scowling at Jax. I think she might be jealous, but if she hadn't cheated on him and ruined her relationship, maybe they would still be together. My heart pounds in my chest thinking they could still be together had he not walked in on her with another guy.

I'm pulled off their shoulders and into Jax's arms. "Let's get out of here. We have to fulfill the bet we made earlier."

"Lead the way." I giggle.

CHAPTER 25

JAX

I fall into bed with a heavy sigh. Poppy thought volunteering to babysit the twins today while Otis goes to family therapy with Violet and Nova would be fun. I never knew kids were so exhausting. Even though it's only six in the evening and we haven't even had dinner, I could probably crash for the night.

"I know Nova has to level out first, but I still can't believe they are going to release her to live with Violet and Otis," Poppy says around her toothbrush.

"Yeah, Otis didn't say much about how he's feeling, but you can see the worry etched in his face," I say, turning to my side, watching Poppy through the bathroom door. "What do you think?"

"Well," Poppy spits out some toothpaste, then rinses her mouth out before she continues. "I don't know Nova well, and the only interaction I've had is the couple of times she cornered me." She comes into the bedroom, looking down at me with her hands on her slim waist. "So, I don't think I get to have an opinion, but if Violet and Otis think this is a good idea, then we should support them."

I lean up, grabbing Poppy's hand, pulling her into my bed. "Good point." I pull on Poppy's hand again, and this time she falls into bed next to me. "Did you have a good day with Hawk and Harley?"

Poppy smiles from ear to ear. "They are so cute! I love being an aunt. I'm a little sad I didn't get to see them as babies, but I can at least be thankful I get to have them in my life." Poppy lays her forehead on mine. "You know, I've always wanted a big family and to have siblings. I never would have thought in a million worlds it would happen. I mean, what are the odds I got everything I've wished for since my mom passed away? Well, except for my mom to be alive."

I brush some of Poppy's soft, wavy hair off her shoulder. "I would say pretty slim, but after everything you went through you deserve the whole world and more."

Poppy moves until she is straddling my waist. She looks down at me with a small smile.

"Grams goes home tomorrow." Tears well in her eyes as she changes the subject.

"I know you're not ready…" A loud knock on the door interrupts me.

Poppy jumps from the unexpected sound of the loud banging noise. I sit up. wrapping my arms around her slender waist.

"I'll get it!" Grams hollers.

The familiar sound of Grams shuffling fills the quiet room.

I groan, letting go of my beautiful girlfriend. "I'll go see who it is."

I get out of bed and open the bedroom door before I hear yelling from the direction of the front door. Lewis angrily screams Poppy's name. Poppy walks around me, moving fast to the living room.

"Who are you?" Lewis slurs.

Great, he has been drinking. Lewis isn't normally an angry drunk, but he can be if he starts drinking in a foul mood.

Grams begins poking Lewis in the chest. "Who are you to come here yelling at my granddaughter like that?"

Lewis sways, looking down at Grams, blinking. I would guess he is trying to blink the drunken blur from his eyes, but he is failing miserably. "Who are you?" he grunts.

Poppy and I move like we are one. Walking past the couch, stopping right behind Grams, who now has her hands on her hips.

"I'll tell you who I am, if you tell me who you are?" Her eyebrows scrunch, making her wrinkles on her face more prominent.

I try not to laugh at Grams's tone. I can tell she means business, but she isn't going to let Lewis push her around.

"Well…" Lewis stumbles to the side a little. "I am Poppy's boy, I mean ex-boyfriend."

Grams chuckles under her breath. "Then you don't have any right coming over here acting like an angry, drunken fool now do you?" Grams's thick southern accent gets stronger as she talks to Lewis.

He stands there swaying, glaring down at Wynona for what I think is at least ten minutes.

"Lewis, I think you should go," Poppy speaks up for the first time since Lewis came barging in.

"Why didn't you tell me about the contest?" Lewis slurs and stumbles a little.

"You aren't in our lives anymore," Poppy whispers.

I can hear the hurt in her voice as much as I can see the pain contorting Lewis's face. I feel bad for Lewis, but at the same time, I don't, because he showed up here uninvited. He did a lot of things I would say are unforgivable to me, but those were his choices. Now he has to live with the consequences.

"I'm…" Lewis turns around, leaving without even shutting the door behind him.

"Wait here." I kiss the top of Poppy's head. "I'll go check on him."

I jog down the stairs and to the parking lot to find Lewis sitting in his Jeep. As I get closer, I can see his head is down, resting on his steering wheel. Maybe if I leave, he will go sleep off the alcohol here, but I can't go back to my apartment with him here drunk like this, because if he drives home and something happens, I will feel responsible.

I knock on the window. "Lewis," I yell loudly.

Lewis doesn't move, so I knock again. This time, he raises his head, looking out the window with glassy eyes, but with the window tint, I can't tell whether he is crying or has a drunken gaze. He stares at me, squinting his eyes like he is trying to see me.

"Can I take you somewhere?" I offer loudly, knowing he can hear me, but I don't know if he can understand me.

Lewis nods, opening the door. "Can you take me to my parents?"

"Yeah, I'll see if Poppy can follow." I pull my phone out of my pocket.

I watch him aggressively open his door, almost falling to the pavement. Lewis stumbles around his Jeep and into the passenger seat. He sits down with a huff, not bothering to close the door. If there wasn't so much tension between us, I would probably laugh.

"Hey," Poppy answers on the fourth ring.

"Hey. Lewis can't drive. Can you follow me to his parents' house?"

"Ugh, yeah," she sounds unsure.

"Grams can come." I offer. "You will need to drive my truck, though."

I know how much she hates driving my truck, but I know she will say yes so she can spend some more time with Wynona.

"Sure…" Poppy trails off, still sounding unsure.

"Thanks, man," Lewis mutters under his breath.

I get flashbacks of the last time I was in the car with Lewis since our friendship ended. He was driving me home from Texas to Oklahoma after my mother called me about a family emergency.

"Just let me know if you are going to barf so I can pull over." I don't care if he does, we are in his Jeep, but I would rather not have the smell of whatever he ate in drank stunk in here the whole way to his parents' house.

Poppy comes out with Wynona, and I wait until Poppy is situated in my truck and I see the headlights come on before I back out of the parking space to take my old best friend home.

"I'm sorry for coming over unannounced, but I was so confused at the airport when I saw Poppy there with Roxi and some lady who keeps claiming to be her grandmother. At the party with the video, I wanted to know what's going on and if she is okay." Lewis hiccups. "I didn't mean to come over this drunk, but I was a couple of miles away and the closer I got, the angrier I became. I thought if I went to the bar to have a few drinks, I might be able to cool off."

I adjust my grip on the steering wheel. I'm not sure what I should say, but maybe if I tell him some things about what has been going on, he will leave us alone.

"Well, to simplify everything, Poppy entered a songwriting contest, and she won. I threw the party to celebrate her winning." I drum my fingers on the steering wheel nervously. "After Halloween, Poppy found out Jack wasn't her biological father…"

"Shit, and she found out so soon after everything I put her through." Lewis's voice is raised a little, but he isn't yelling as he interrupts me.

"Yeah, so she is her grandma, and she has two older brothers." I shrug a little.

"Wow, I've missed so much not being in your lives." Lewis lays his head on the window.

"Yeah, what's going on with you? Are you excited to be a dad?" I ask, but I'm met with his snores, which suits me fine.

I zoom through the interstate trying to get Lewis to his house as fast as I can, but not lose Poppy, who is still following me.

A long couple of hours later, I pull into his driveway with him still passed out on the passenger window. My shoulder relaxes a little, and I release the steering wheel with sore fingers from how hard my grip was. Poppy pulls my truck in behind me as I begin shaking Lewis.

"Hey, you're home." I continue shaking him.

"UGH! Leave me alone," he groans, slapping my hand away.

"Whatever you say." I get out of his Jeep, slamming the door.

I turn to see Poppy walking across the lawn toward her childhood home. I didn't think about her childhood home being next door to Lewis's parents' house when I asked her to follow me. As far as I know, she hasn't been over there since she moved in with my parents. I know she's gone to Lewis's parents' home a few times while they were together, but he always said she refused to look over there. She stops at the edge of the lawn, looking back at me. I hear a car door shut, and I turn around to see Wynona climb out of my truck.

"Is she okay?" Grams asks, stopping next to me.

"I don't know. This was her childhood home." I say, turning my attention back to Poppy.

Grams gasps, putting her hand on her heart. I know Poppy has confided in her a little about what she has been through while Grams has been staying with her, but I don't know if she knows the worst of it. I don't think anyone does other than her now since Jack has passed away.

Poppy starts walking again, slowly with short, hesitant steps. She has her hands down at her sides, but her fingers are rubbing the hem of her shirt poking out of the bottom of her coat. She is trying to calm the raging emotions surging through her, but I don't think anything other than leaving would help.

"Should we go with her?" Grams's voice is so low I could barely hear her over the wind.

I shake my head. I think this is something she needs to do on her own, but I don't want to say those words out loud in case I'm wrong. I watch as Poppy pulls her coat tighter around her. She continues walking, not looking back. Even though she is taking small, deliberate steps, slowly getting closer to a home she felt trapped in for so many years, I find what she is doing to be brave.

A flash of headlights shines over Poppy, making her freeze. She doesn't move as the car slowly pulls into the driveway. I don't know what I should do or how to help Poppy, because there is no telling what is going on through her head right now. The car stops in front of the garage door long enough for it to open and the person can pull inside.

I take long strides, walking quickly to Poppy with Grams close on my heels. I don't know if this person saw her, but I would like to get Poppy out of this situation if I can. I reach out, and touch Poppy's trembling shoulder.

"Pops, we should go." I move around her, finding her eyes wide and her mouth slightly open.

"Poppy, are you okay?" Grams chimes in, moving to my left.

Poppy blinks several times, breathing hard as she tries to pull her coat tighter around her. Moments like these, I want to pull her into my arms and tell her I'm here and nothing can ever hurt her again, but I know nothing will help her right now.

"Excuse me," a soft, feminine voice breaks through the darkness around us. "May I help you?" The sound of heels clacking on the pavement closer to us makes Poppy jump and scream so loud it echoes into the night.

"Sorry, this is my granddaughter's childhood home. We dropped a friend of the family off next door, and she wanted to take a little look at her old house." Grams shakes the woman's hand.

"Oh," the woman shifts on her heels before she gasps loudly, making Poppy wince. "Are you Poppy?"

"Um, yes?" Poppy looks at me out of the corner of her eye.

"Well, we renovated the attic for our kids to have a place to hang out, and the contractor found a little box tucked away, hidden in a little cubby hole. I asked the neighbors about it, and all they would tell me was the girl who lived here was named Poppy, but they got weird when I asked about her parents and how to contact them." The woman takes a few steps back. "I think you would love to have this box. Would you like to come in while I grab it out of the office?"

"Thanks, but we can wait here..." I say at the same time Poppy nods her head.

I don't know if this will be a good idea, but I won't tell Poppy she shouldn't go in there. She has bad memories here, but she also doesn't know who this lady is. However, if this is something she feels she needs to do, I'll support her and help her through whatever she happens after we leave.

"Come on, I didn't change much. The house was so beautiful, I would have hated to see all the charm be taken out for more modern touches." The kind woman giggles.

We follow the woman through the garage and to the living room, where Poppy gasps. She is looking right at the piano her mother taught her to play on, and she was playing it the same day I found her hurt. I think out of everything in the house, she may have the most emotional attachment to it.

"Poppy, are you okay?" Grams whispers, grabbing her hand.

I don't think the lady heard Grams, because she smiles ear to ear. "I love the piano. Isn't it beautiful? We saw it when we toured the house, and funny enough, they were doing an estate sale. I told my husband I wanted the house and the piano. I am the luckiest lady ever, because he made both of my dreams come true." The lady keeps rambling on, not noticing the shocked look on Poppy's face. "I've been taking lessons, and I think I'm getting pretty good at it."

Poppy walks over to the piano, and with a shaky hand, she puts the fallboard down. "My mom taught me to play on this piano." Her voice trembles as hard as her hands.

"Oh, what a fond memory to have. I bet you had the best life here. Make yourself comfortable, I'll be back in a moment." The lady walks through what I know is the office door, not knowing she put her foot in her mouth.

"She didn't look into the past owners too well," Poppy mutters under her breath, walking to me, and grabbing my hand.

"Pops…" I trail off when I hear the same sound of heels clacking on the floor.

"We'll talk about this when we get home," she hisses under her breath.

"Here it is. We didn't go through it, but the box is labeled with your name." The lady walks back into the living room. "As a mom, I would think this is something another mother hid for her daughter to find one day, so I couldn't throw it in the trash. I put it in the cabinet in the office for safekeeping, in case you showed up one day." She hands Poppy the box.

Poppy doesn't lift the lid; she doesn't even look at the box.

"I'm so happy you showed up tonight. Would you like to see the rest of the house or your old room? I sometimes wonder what my childhood room looks like now with new people living there."

I know she isn't trying to intentionally hurt Poppy by asking these questions, because she doesn't know the horrific things have happened to Poppy here, and maybe not knowing is for the best.

Poppy looks back at Grams and me, clearing her throat. "Can you guys give us a moment?"

I nod, but Grams says, "sure dear, we will be right outside. Take your time."

I walk with Grams to the door, and right before I close the door, I hear the lady ask when she moved in here with her mom and dad.

"Do you think she is going to be okay?" Grams asks again.

"Ugh, yes. I don't have…" The door opens, and Poppy walks out holding the box.

"Again, thank you for showing up. I am even happier to have given you the box now." I look up at the lady at her words, and I see her eyes are glassy and tears well up above her bottom lashes. "I hope you have a good night." She closes the door quietly behind her.

We walk back to my truck in complete silence. I look at Lewis's jeep and see him still hunched against his passenger door. I would leave him there, but it is too cold to sleep in the car. Even though we aren't friends, I don't want him getting sick from freezing in his car all night.

I tap on the window, and Lewis jerks up.

"What!?" he slurs with a scrunched, angry face, making him look like a bulldog.

"You're home. Go inside, it's too cold to stay in your Jeep!" I leave him there, drunkenly cussing me out.

I climb into my truck and buckle my seatbelt. Poppy grabs my hand, and a calmness flows through me. I was tense waiting for Poppy while she talked to the lady who now owns her childhood home, even though I tried to play it cool. I know I failed miserably. I want her to do whatever will make her happy.

Silence falls in the darkness of the cab. We begin to leave town, and the only noise we can hear is Poppy quietly sobbing. I know Wynona, and I are both itching to ask her what she talked to the woman about, but neither of us wants to push Poppy to talk; she will when she is ready, and until then, I will drive us back home, watching the streetlights dance across my windshield.

CHAPTER 26

POPPY

I can feel Jax's eyes burning into me as I get ready for the game.

"You're going to be late." I chastise him, looking at him through the mirror.

He lies down on his side with his head propped on his hand. "I've got time."

I adjust my bra strap as I turn to face Jax. I'm only wearing my jeans and bra. I love when Jax watches me get dressed as much as I love feeling his gaze on me when I take my clothes off. Jax's eyes begin taking in every inch of my body, leaving a trail of blazing heat wherever he looks. He has this way of making me feel powerful and sexy with one single glance.

"Whatever you say." I giggle, grabbing my jersey with Jax's number and last name on the back. "Should I put a hoodie on under the jersey?"

Jax sits up, grabbing my belt loops with his pointer fingers, pulling me between his long legs. His hand travels up my stomach over the cups of my bra and stops at my shoulders.

"You can put on whatever you want, but it will not stop me from peeling every last layer of clothing off of you later tonight." Jax leans in, kissing my belly button, and I feel my knees grow weak.

"Jax," I sigh at his promise.

He knows what he does to me, and I think he feeds off of it. Jax's hands move from my shoulder down my arms.

"Yes, wear the hoodie, because you'll be freezing otherwise," Jax says, grabbing the jersey from my hand.

All I can do is nod my head. I'm unable to form words as my arms are being gently lifted above my head. Jax grabs the black hoodie with our school's logo on it, pulling the sweatshirt, followed by the jersey on me. I swallow hard as soft fabric brushes against my sensitive skin. My body heats as a deep chuckle rumbles in Jax's chest. I never knew how hot and sensual getting dressed by Jax would be.

Jax stands up, pulling me tightly into his arms. I feel safe and warm wrapped in his tight embrace. He leans down, making his hot breath fan down on me.

"Now I have to go," he says, kissing me until I'm breathless.

When he walks out of my room, I sit on my bed trying to catch my breath. I'm excited to watch Jax on the field, but I am nervous. My whole family is coming to the game today, and we are tailgating first, but Violet had asked if Nova could come too.

Jax and I said it's fine, but I'm also nervous, because I don't want her to get jealous or she gets triggered by something and she snaps. I slip on a pair of fluffy socks to help keep my feet warm as I slip on some little black leather ankle boots.

I walk into the bathroom, and I put on the little tattoo I got with the school's logo on one cheek and Jax's number on the other. I dig through my makeup bag and pull out the perfect gold highlight and dust it on my cheeks and the tip of my nose, before putting some glitter on too. I put on the perfect shape of red lipstick and topped it off with some lip gloss, matching the glitter perfectly, as someone knocks on the door.

I give myself one last glance in the full-length mirror in my room before rushing to open the door.

Grams greets me first, "Poppy, you look so darling." She squeezes me tightly.

"Yes, I love your little Storm Hawks logo tattoos," Freya says, hugging me next.

"Oh, I have extra for anyone who would like some." My cheeks heat at all the attention I'm getting.

Nova clears her throat. She looks different from the last time I saw her, but she still looks good; I would venture to say better this time. "I would like that."

"Do we have time?" I ask Shane, trying to find Shane among the people in my entryway.

"Of course," he says behind Roxi, looking at his watch.

"Cool, we'll be right back."

I help Nova, Violet, Freya, and even Roxi put on the little tattoos in their cheeks. I don't have any more with Jax's number, but they look cute either way. Nova and Violet are looking through my makeup, and they find the eye black I had from the last game. Getting ready for a game with the girls is fun.

"Do you mind?" Violet asks, holding up the little stick of face glitter.

"Go for it." I smile, looking for the other glitter. "I have some other colors somewhere.

"This one goes well with the tattoos," Nova says, taking the glitter from Violet and helping her put it on.

I can't help but think how normal Nova seems right now, so maybe therapy and her meds are helping. We walk back to the living room, and all the men compliment us, and Grams chuckles, making a joke about if she were younger, but she started mumbling toward the end.

I shiver, pulling my coat tightly closed as the cold wind whips around me in the parking lot. The sky is white, almost like there might be snow. It is going to be a cold game today, but with the number of people crowded in the stands, I'm hoping I won't freeze the whole game. I slip my mittens and beanie on as I wait for Shane to unlock the SUV.

Roxi bounces in her seat, singing as we drive the short distance to the stadium, and finding parking wasn't easy. However, her infectious giddiness made the situation a lot easier. We hop out of the SUV, looking around the parking lot for the rest of our group, but they are easy to find in the next row to our left.

"I heard there are going to be some new food trucks." I loop my arms with Roxi's.

"How are we going to choose what to eat then?" We walk fast through the parking lot.

I laugh at Roxi. She is a major foodie and loves to try new things. "How about we narrow it down to at least two different trucks, then split our orders?"

"I've taught you well." Roxi and I laugh so hard you can see puffs of air clouding in front of our faces.

"RUN!" I'm shouting with Otis on my left, screaming with me, but he adds a few select words in his encouraging rage.

Someone tackles Walsh from the left, but he jumps right up,

charging down the field to catch up with Jax, who has the ball. Jax is running, but he fakes right and goes left, missing a tackle for himself. My heart is pounding. These guys are working hard, and the other team is playing aggressively and not making it easy for them.

"GO! GO! GO!" I begin bouncing on the balls of my feet the closer Jax gets to the endzone.

Jax swerves right, missing another tackle. Another big guy comes to his left to attempt another tackle, but Walsh digs in, tackling the player, leaving a few feet to the end zone for Jax to get his touchdown.

"Yeah!" We hoop and holler, hugging the person next to us.

They may have time for one more play, but our team is winning by more than twenty points. They huddle around talking until the whistle blows.

They line up, and the crowd stills, almost like everyone is holding their breath. Suddenly, there is movement on the field, and the ball is in the other team's hands. The crowd is going wild, but Chance tackles someone before they can get more than a couple of yards down the field. I didn't even see him coming.

They get in formation, and this time, Jax gets the ball. He takes off running toward our endzone only to be tackled. I stand on my tippy toes trying to get a better look over the tall man in front of me. I can barely see Jax roll onto his feet. Giving two thumbs up in my direction to let me know he's okay. I release the breath I was holding and watch as they try to make another touchdown, but the other team gets the ball, charging to their endzone before the whistle sounds.

Even though the other team got the last touchdown, they still didn't win. Our side of the stadium erupts in a deafening roar, but you can't understand what anyone is shouting. Otis and Shane wait with me for the crowd to clear while everyone else in our group tries to get in line for the restroom.

"How have things been since you won the contest?" Otis asks.

"Oh, they've been good. I'm a little busier, but nothing too bad. I have a movie interested in one of my songs, which is exciting. I'll fly to California for a weekend in a couple of weeks to meet with the producer, director, and the film's composer."

"Wow," Otis's eyebrows shoot up. "So, my sister is going to be famous?" he chuckles.

"I wouldn't go that far, but it's a little scary to think I could be," I trail off, walking up the steps to leave. "This song doesn't have any lyrics yet, and they are thinking of bringing in a couple of writers and maybe a producer for me to work with."

"Isn't that a good thing?" Shane asks from my left side.

"Yeah, I think so. It would definitely be good to have some more connections, right?"

"Yeah, with any career, you want to have the right kind of people around you. I would say this is a huge step in your career." Otis puts his arm over my shoulder. "I'm proud to be your big brother."

Warmth sweeps through my heart at Otis's words. I didn't know what kind of relationship we would have, especially after the first time we met, but surprisingly, we are extremely close. Wells and I get along, and we talk, but I still feel like there's a distance between him and me.

I clear my throat. "Thanks. I love having big brothers." We round a corner, and a girl around my age runs into me.

"Sorry…" she mutters before running away.

I wonder what she had so upset. We continue walking, and Shane gets in front of me as two deep voices are shouting at each other, echoing through the cement walkway. They sound angry, and from the slurring, you can tell they are drunk.

"Come on, let's get out of here," Shane says, grabbing my hand and pulling me away from the arguing men.

I follow close behind Shane with Otis blocking me on my right. They become more tense as the men's yelling gets louder and more aggressive, almost to the point where punches might be thrown. We round the corner, and we can still hear the faint echoes of the men's angry roars.

"Wow, I'm glad we won, but I would never get in a fight with someone else, no matter what the outcome of the game is." I shake my head, completely baffled by the outrageous display of toxic masculinity those guys are showing.

"I would have in high school, but only if someone came at me first." Otis laughs with a deep, serious tone. "I was angry for a long time after my parents died. I would never start fights, but I would make sure I was the one to finish them."

I understand being angry after a parent dies. I was devastated by my mom for dying and furious at her for leaving me with a monster. I had learned I needed to let go of my anger for me and no one else. I learned I couldn't forgive her until I was free from the torment and pain I was in for years after her death. Some days are bad, and I feel like I can't breathe from how much I am missing her, while other days are a constant reminder of all the bad things someone, who was supposed to be my father, treated me. Sometimes my father sounded like those men who were fighting back there, and others, he was way more frightening.

We walk until I can feel the freezing cold air from outside blow through some open doors. I'll have to round about half of the stadium outside to get to the tunnels where I'm meeting Jax, but thankfully, Shane called Roxi and told her they were walking with me.

"We all have a little anger in us. Some more than others, but I have learned, especially after what Poppy has been through, it's how we handle our big emotions." Shane's hushed voice rings loud in my ears. "Jack was grieving and furious when his wife died, so he turned to liquor and violence to cope. Poppy lived through something no one should, because of how he handled himself after her mom died."

"That's a good point. The Navy taught me a lot about controlling my anger, and even though I wasn't deployed for long, I didn't leave in one piece, and I was still dealing with my own grief from my parents' deaths. I'll always remember the lessons and control the Navy taught to me, but it took me finding Violet to understand them." Otis doesn't smile; in fact, his mouth is mashed into a thin line. "She calms the rage burning inside of me."

"I didn't know you were in the Navy." My eyes widen, and my cold, dry lips part.

"Yeah, I was medically discharged on my first mission. I was angry and kept people at arm's length, refusing to let anyone close until I met Violet."

"How did you and Violet meet?" I slow my pace a little because something tells me this might be a good story.

A wide, lopsided smile spreads over Otis's face. "Grams had roped me into helping Wells move into his dorm his first year at college, and the first time I saw her, we literally ran into each other. She fell for me." We all laugh at his little joke. "I didn't expect to see her again since I was so busy, but she had hit on me, and I didn't want to be the fool who turned down the prettiest girl he had ever laid eyes on. A few short hours later, I learned it wasn't her…"

"NO!" I interrupt Otis. "Please tell me you didn't hook up with Nova."

Otis shakes his head. "Unfortunately, I did. I thought I lost any chance with Violet, but somehow, she was able to look past it."

A giggle bursts through me. "At least you came to your senses and only slept with Nova once.”

Otis shoves his hands in his pockets. “There was a party where Nova pretended to be Violet, and you know…” he trails off, grimacing.

“Violet is a remarkable woman to be able to look past something like that.” Shane chuckles.

We finally reach the tunnel where the other girlfriends are waiting. A couple of them are huddled together trying to keep warm, while two of them are vaping, and the rest are playing on their phones.

“Thanks for walking me here. We’ll see you at the restaurant.” I hug Shane and Otis before finding a spot not too close to the ones vaping.

“Monroe!” Walsh greets me by my last name when he steps into the tunnel. “Jax got called into the coach’s office.”

“Okay, no worries.” I cross my arms over my chest, tucking my hands under my arms to keep them warm.

“Alright. See you later.” Walsh lightly pushes me in the arm, making me lose my balance as he and his girlfriend, Lidia, pass me.

“Yeah, you kicked ass on the field. Thanks for keeping Jax safe.” I lean back against the wall.

“Just doing my job!” Walsh’s voice echoes through the tunnel even as he disappears.

I play on my phone while I wait for Jax. My social feeds are mostly filled with the news, and fans of our team are celebrating our win.

“Pops!” I hear Jax’s booming voice echo in the tunnel, making me jump.

“CONGRATULATIONS!” I cheer, running to him, throwing myself into his arms.

Of course, Jax catches me effortlessly. I wrap my legs around his waist, caging him to me. Once I’m stable and I know I’m not going to fall, I grab Jax’s face, kissing him deeply. I feel Jax’s hands grab a little tighter on my butt. My head begins to spin, and my breath feels like it is being pulled from my lungs, but damn, I don’t want to break this world-shattering moment. My hands move from Jax’s face, and I wrap my arms around his neck, holding onto him anyway I can.

“Damn, Poppy,” Jax whispers, pulling back from me a little, but he doesn’t put me down. “That is one hell of a congratulations.”

Jax kisses me again. “Thank you. It was one hell of a game.” I loosen my legs around him as he sets me gently to my feet. “You’ll never guess what Coach Harrison wanted to talk to me about.”

"I have a guess, but I would rather you tell me." I grab Jax's hand as we slowly walk out of the tunnel into the freezing wind.

Jax lets go of my hand, and I would be offended, but before I can object, he puts his big arm over my shoulder, pulling me closer to his warm side.

"He wants to start training me for the NFL. He said there are a few teams interested in me for next year."

"JAX! This is amazing news." I squeeze Jax tightly around his waist.

"This has been my goal for so long, and when I put my eligibility, I specifically said I wanted to graduate college first, and I think it's all happening." Jax leans down, kissing the top of my head. "I mean, I'm not in, but my coach wouldn't ask me to train with him if he didn't think I could make it."

The crowd is mostly cleared out, but several people are still gathered around the front of the stadium talking.

"I knew you would get to this point. Watching you on the field is not only hot, but Jax, you are so talented. Your strength and speed are truly amazing. You were born to do this."

"Thanks." Jax smiles down at me.

Jax leads me to his truck, which is not far. He got here early enough, but a lot of times our school will save parking spots for the football players. I am glad we are getting to have this moment alone together before we go meet our families at the restaurant for an early dinner.

"Jax, I meant what I said. I love watching you play football. I know this is the path you were destined to take." Jax opens the truck door for me.

"Whatever path I go on won't mean anything to me without you there." Jax leans down, kissing me softly on my cheek.

I climb into the truck, watching as Jax jogs around to the driver's side. He gets in, and the wind whips around the cab of the already cold truck, making me shiver. Jax slams the door closed, cranking the engine to life. The soft, familiar hum of 90's country plays through the speakers; the song playing over the radio takes me back to the summer after we graduated high school.

Lewis and I had gotten into a fight because I kept telling him to go to whatever college he wanted. Lewis tried to claim I didn't want to be with him, while I wanted him to follow his dreams. We fought about where he went to college until we broke up, but after a particularly bad fight with Lewis, Jax took me back roading to cheer me up. We got shakes, and we were singing songs with the windows down until the sun set. Both of us laughed and sang so much our voices were hoarse by the time we got back home. I remember feeling so light and free in his truck, and sometimes when life's drama gets to be too much, Jax is the only one who can make me feel better.

Jax pulls into the parking lot of the crowded Italian restaurant. I'm guessing other people from the game want Italian food to carbo-load after a high-energy game, too. We get out of the truck, and like when we left the stadium together, Jax pulls me close to his side, and I instantly am blocked from most of the freezing wind whirling around us.

The air smells crisp and earthy with an almost clean aroma I always notice right before it snows. I would be shocked if we actually got snow, because Oklahoma gets more ice or sleet than anything.

"Man, I'm ready for some carbs." Jax inhales deeply as he opens the door, savoring the smell of garlic, oregano, and other Italian spices.

We find Otis easily, because he is taller than most of the other people in the small waiting area.

"Excuse me," I say, trying to weave around an elderly couple.

I lose Jax in the sea of people as I begin to get pushed further away from where I saw Otis.

"Poppy!" I faintly hear Jax's holler for me over the talking people.

"JAX!" I shriek when I feel a sharp pain on top of my foot.

I think a woman stepped on my foot with her high heels. Tears well in my eyes from the throbbing pain shooting up my leg, but more than anything, I want to find Jax or one of my family members, where I know I will be safe.

"POPPY!" I hear Otis's booming voice yell over the crowd.

The small waiting area goes quiet and still. The number of people in here should be over capacity. I get pushed again by an elderly man in a knit sweater, and I bump into a lady in our school shirt with Taylor and Jax's number 12 on the back.

"WATCH IT!" she squeals, whirling around to face me. "Who do you think you are?" She puts her finger in my face when she dramatically spits the word "you" at me.

"I'm sorr…" I begin to stutter.

"Poppy, there you are!" Jax says loudly over the crowd. "Are you okay?"

The woman looks behind me at the sound of Jax's deep voice, and I watch as her eyes widen and her cheeks turn pink. "You're Jax

Taylor."

"Yes, if you will excuse my girlfriend and me, we have to get back to our families," Jax says politely, even though his eyebrows are furrowed together.

The lady nods as Jax turns me around, leading me back to our group. There aren't as many people here as there was the first time we tried to walk across the small waiting area, so getting to our group was a lot easier.

Everyone hugs me like they didn't spend a few hours with me. I'm not complaining, I find their affection nice, but sometimes overwhelming. It took me a long time to get used to people showing me any kind of positive attention again after going so long with nothing but aggression and hatred. Lewis helped me, but at the end, when everything was a fight, finding the good affection between both of us felt impossible.

"Taylor!" The hostess calls out, letting us know our table is ready.

We follow the hostess to a large table in the center of the room. Thankfully, Shane and Roxi thought ahead and got reservations for everyone. I sit down next to Jax, but I am surprised when Nova sits on my other side. She smiles at me but doesn't say anything.

"That was a crazy game," Wells comments as we all give our drink orders.

"I know, we had similar scores and wins as the other team throughout the season, but we worked hard, and it paid off today," Jax says, putting his hand on my thigh.

Jax doesn't mention anything about the meeting he had with his coach, but I can tell the possibility of him going pro hasn't set in, because he is still on edge. I know Jax is going to do great, but he needs to believe it, too. The way he presents himself on and off the field is absolutely amazing. I'm having a great time at dinner, but more than anything, I can't wait to go home after we show up at the party for a little bit and have my own celebration with Jax.

CHAPTER 27

JAX

The workout I went through was intense. But the burn in my body doesn't bother me; in fact, it makes me feel more alive in some ways. I'm still feeling high from winning the championship game last week. If I were single, I would be reaping the benefits of all the girls throwing themselves at me, but I am happily taken. Still, it doesn't stop the girls from coming to me and trying their hardest to get me alone. Hell, some even hit on me in front of Poppy.

Earlier this week, Poppy joked she doesn't blame them for trying to get with me, because I'm one fine piece of ass. Should I feel objectified? Probably, but do I? Hell no, because she said she trusts me and she knows I would never do anything to hurt her. Besides, we both know what it feels like to be cheated on, and I never want to be the person to cause her heart to break.

I pull into the parking lot of my apartment, and I park my car next to a shiny, expensive car. There are several students here who can afford this car, but I know none of them has this car with the sparkly license plate frame and matching steering wheel cover. Plus, there's no student sticker in the window. This is Nova's car. I recognize it from the last time she was here.

Maybe she came with Violet, but Poppy isn't here, so I'm not sure exactly what to think or do. Should I call Violet or Otis before I let Nova know I've seen her? I sigh, walking to her car, and I'm not surprised when I see the driver's seat empty.

I grab my gym bag and walk through the cold parking lot to the hall where my apartment is. Nova is sitting on the floor with her back pressed against Poppy's door with her knees pulled up to her chest, her forehead resting on her knees, and her arms hugging her legs. I can't see her face, but her hair is down and knotted in a huge mess.

"Nova?" When she hears my voice, she lifts her mascara-stained face off her knees. "Are you okay?"

"Sorry, I don't mean to impose. This was the first place I could think of, because I would be safe here until Violet and Otis could come get me." She hiccups from her crying. "I promise I'm only here to wait for my sister."

"Come on, you can wait at my apartment. Poppy won't be home for a few more hours." I walk past her, unlocking my door.

Nova is wearing a velvet sweat suit. She stands up, dusting off her butt, and pushes her knotted hair behind her ears.

"Thanks, I really didn't know where else I could go." She tucks her messy hair behind her ear.

I watch as she walks to my couch. She slips her shoes off and curls up on the couch as she did in the hallway.

"No problem. Have you talked to Violet?" I put my gym bag on the kitchen counter.

I walk to the fridge and get two bottles of water.

"No, I keep getting her voicemail every time I call." Nova's voice is muffled, but I can still understand her.

"Let me make you something to eat while I try to get a hold of someone. The controller is on the coffee table if you want to watch TV." I place Nova's water bottle on the coffee table before I go back to the kitchen counter, and I get my phone out of my gym bag. I see a couple of missed texts from Poppy and one from Otis.

Poppy: Hey, I need you to call me ASAP
Poppy: Something happened with Nova.

I can easily tell something is off with her, but I can't exactly tell you what it is. Sure, the times I've seen Nova, she didn't look all the way there in the eyes, but with her appearance and clothes, she looked as perfect as she could. She had on expensive clothes and a bag, which I'm sure is made of real leather. Even though her tracksuit isn't expensive, Nova doesn't look like a girl who enjoys athleisure.

Otis: Call me if you see Nova.

This is a good reminder to check my phone more often.

I call Otis, and he doesn't answer. I hang up and try again as I open the fridge and pull out the hamburger meat I put in there this morning, but the meat is still frozen, so I will have to figure out another way to make myself look busy.

"I don't have much. Does pizza sound good?" I ask while I try calling Otis again.

Nova doesn't say anything, which is a little concerning. I glance into the living room, and she hasn't moved. I walk quietly to the balcony, and I open the door.

"Hey, can I call you back? Nova is missing from the facility." Otis says on the third ring.

"Yeah, she is here." Otis cusses under his breath. "She is crying on my couch."

"Violet and I are on our way. We don't know anything other than one of the nurses called and told us Nova is missing. They think she will show up here."

"She didn't say much other than she didn't know where else to go while she waited for you." I look through the window, and Nova still hasn't moved. "She looks like she has been crying a lot, and she looks disheveled."

"Hey, Jax, this is Violet. She sometimes makes herself look like she is a mess." Violet sighs, "Keep an eye on her. I'm texting Poppy not to go to your apartment until we know what is going on."

I hear a beeping sound in the background. I would be willing to bet they are getting in the car.

"I won't. I'm going to order us pizza and try to keep her distracted."

"Thanks," they say at the same time before the line goes dead.

I walk back inside, and I open the app for the pizza place Poppy, and I like. I ordered my favorite pizza, but I have no clue what she would like. "Nova, what kind of toppings do you like on your pizza?" I ask while sitting in the chair next to the couch.

"Did you get a hold of anyone?" Nova raises her head, looking at me with her face stained with mascara.

"No, I left a message for them to call me, but I didn't tell them you were here." I lie without a second thought.

"I like veggie pizza and add pineapple." Nova lays her head back down, but I don't miss the giant smile showing her perfect white teeth.

Something is definitely wrong, but I don't know what to do to prevent this whole situation from getting worse.

"I'm going to do some homework while we wait for Violet or Otis to get back to you, but the pizza should be here in thirty to forty-five minutes." I clear my throat around the lie I made.

Before I can move, Nova slowly lifts her head off her knees, lowers her legs, and crosses them. She turns her body toward me, shoulders pushed back and chest out. My stomach tightens, and my mouth suddenly goes dry. Nova's creepy smile stretches her face, causing her eyes to widen unnaturally, making her look even more terrifying. She could be a killer in a slasher movie, and people would be scared shitless.

"I can distract you." Nova begins to unzip her velvet sweatshirt.

I clear my throat and shift in my seat uncomfortably. "I'm good." I shake my head.

Nova continues to unzip her jacket, showing hints of a lacey bra underneath. Fuck! I don't know how I'm going to get out of this and keep her distracted long enough for Otis and Violet to get here.

"Come on, I bet you've never been with someone like me." Nova scoots a little closer in my direction on the couch.

The wild look in her eyes sparkles as she starts to push her jacket off her shoulders. I stand up, walking to the kitchen. I know I shouldn't put my back to her, but it's a hell of a lot better than looking at her while she is in nothing but her pants and her bra.

"I'm sure, but I'm in a relationship, and I won't do anything to hurt Poppy." I grab onto the edge of the kitchen counter.

"Come on, I can keep a secret," Nova whines a little.

A knock on the door saves me from having to reply. I know it's not the pizza, because I never finished the order.

I open the door, and I'm greeted by a man whom I've never seen before, but something about him is familiar. There is also a woman behind him in an expensive coat, and an overwhelming floral perfume fills my doorway. I wonder if this is Violet and Nova's parents, because of the resemblance between Violet and Nova, and this lady is wild.

"Are you Jax Taylor? I am Adam Willard, and this is my ex-wife, Elizabeth. My daughter Violet called and told me I need to get here with their mother." The man seems less than thrilled to be here or he is trying to mask his emotions, because his voice is pretty monotonous.

"Yes, please come in." I step out of their way.

The woman nods, walking past me, and somehow her already pungent perfume gets stronger and burns my nose. I don't know how much of the bottle she drowned in, but I'm sure it cost more than the already expensive stuff my mother wears.

"Nova, you're not supposed to be here!" The woman sits down next to her daughter.

With them both next to each other, you can tell how much they look alike. They have the same dark auburn hair and the same expensive taste in clothes. There is another knock on the door. I answer it, finding Otis and Violet in the hallway. Each one has one of their kids in their arms. They must have sped over here, or more time has passed than I thought.

I move out of their way, but Otis grabs Harley out of Violet's arms. "Can I go watch them in Poppy's apartment?" Otis asks.

"I can watch them if you would like to stay with Violet." I offer, moving into the hallway.

Violet visibly relaxes a little, but you can still see the tension in her shoulders. You can tell this is the last thing she wants to be dealing with right now, and I don't blame her. I would do anything to get out of the extremely weird and potentially dangerous situation that is happening in my apartment. Including watching their twins.

"That would be great." Otis nods his head.

"Let me get my keys." I turn around quickly.

"Nova, why did you come here?" Violet asks with a slightly raised voice.

"Well…" Nova begins zipping up her sweatshirt. "I was trying to get your attention, and I thought maybe he would want to fool around, but he turned me down. In fact, he wouldn't even look at me. Is he even straight?"

I grab the stuff off the bar, and I quickly leave my apartment, not waiting to hear anything else.

"I thought this place was going to do her some good. Violet was so positive about everything. She kept saying she was starting to see her real sister again. I don't know what version of Nova is in your living room right now, because I haven't seen a good Nova since I've met her." Otis says as he helps me get the kids settled in Poppy's apartment.

"She seemed normal last week at dinner after the game." I get two sippy cups out of the counter, Poppy, and my mom bought when we babysat.

"Water, milk, or juice?" I ask Otis as I open the refrigerator.

"Water is fine. If you need anything, come get me."

Otis leaves, and I finish placing the order for pizza. I got a couple of kinds if they wanted some after calming Nova down, and a cheese for the two toddlers. I put my phone in my pocket for it to start ringing.

"Hey, sorry I didn't call you. Things have been crazy, and I'm watching Hawk and Harley while Otis and Violet deal with Nova."

Harley squeals, laughing, scaring Hawk and me. I laugh as Hawk's bottom lip begins to pout, but he doesn't cry.

"You're fine, I figured things were crazy. I pulled into the parking lot and was wondering if I could sneak into my apartment."

"Yeah, you are safe to sneak up here right now."

Poppy breathes out. "Thank goodness. My last class got canceled, so I didn't know whether I should go to the library or if I could come home. I'll be up in a few minutes." The line goes dead, and the kids start moving around Poppy's apartment.

I go to the shelf with the toys Poppy bought when she babysat the twins and put them on the floor for them. They begin to play and talk, which sounds more like gibberish than actual words. Poppy comes in saying hi to the kids before she comes over to me. I wrap my arms around her slim waist.

"Do you know why she showed up here?" Poppy lays her head on my shoulder.

"Nova." I shrug. "She said she needed a safe and warm place to wait for Violet and Otis to come get her, and this was the first place could think of."

"You know this whole situation is crazy." Poppy opens her mouth to say something else, but a knock at the door interrupts her.

I get the pizza, tipping the delivery driver heavily. I set the boxes down and wait for this pizza to cool down before putting plates on the living room table for Hawk and Harley. I join Poppy back at the table, and she has already taken a bite of her chicken, pepperoni, and Italian sausage pizza, moaning at the greasy food.

"Watch yourself. You know what those sounds do to me, and I can't do anything right now with the two munchkins a few feet away."

"Sorry," Poppy giggles, but I know she is anything but sorry.

"Violet's parents are here." I move Poppy's long, soft hair off her shoulder, changing the subject.

Poppy puts her slice of pizza down, giving me her full attention. "Oh! What are they like?"

"I don't know. I only saw them for a few minutes before Violet and Otis showed up, but they were wearing expensive clothes. Which answers my question on how Violet was able to fund Otis's construction company when they got married, while still in college."

I know I sound judgmental, but I'm not. I'm curious about their family. After all we've heard about what Nova has done, I can't help but think she should have gotten in some serious trouble. I guess what they say about having money is true. You can buy your way out of some things with enough money.

Otis comes to get the kids about an hour or so later. He told us Nova didn't feel safe at the therapy group without Violet there. She left in the middle of the night, going as far as breaking into the office, her car keys locked in. They kept asking her what she was so frightened of, but she refused to say anything. They finally got her to agree to go back if Violet found somewhere to stay nearby.

"Can we stay home tonight?" Poppy asks, lying on her couch.

I would be a fool to say no. After all, the excitement and drama I do think we should have a night at home to do nothing and relax, but if our night ends with us in each other's arms with no clothes on, who am I to complain.

"Abso-fucking-lutely." I climb on the couch lying behind Poppy.

She hands me the controller, and I begin searching for something to watch. Maybe we should start a new series since we finished one a couple of nights ago.

"It was good to see Hawk and Harley today, but I wish it wasn't, because there was drama with Nova," Poppy murmurs, snuggling into my chest.

"I know, it's like they can't catch a break." I agree.

"Since meeting them and finding out Violet has a twin, I've thought about what it would be like to have a twin." My skin begins to burn more under the lazy shapes Poppy is drawing on my chest.

"What do you mean?" I stop watching the movies I'm scrolling past as I look down at Poppy's perfect profile.

"Well, I think they would have some unique bond, right? After Violet told us the doctors think Nova has some kind of attachment disorder, I thought maybe this kind of disorder is rare, but I've looked into it, and the things I found out gave me chills." Poppy shivers.

"I've never thought about it. What you are saying makes sense, but we don't know every single thing they've been through." I kiss Poppy's temple.

She turns her head, looking at me. "Yeah, I don't think I want to know everything they've been through."

"I couldn't agree more." I start flipping through the movies again. "What do you want to watch?"

Poppy doesn't answer me, but I can feel her eyes burning into my face. I look down at her. Poppy is biting her bottom lip. Her hands move down my stomach, and I feel her cold fingers brush against my skin.

"Jax, what will happen when you do get drafted into the NFL?" Poppy's hushed voice sounds far away.

I was hoping I didn't have to answer this for a little while longer.

"Honestly, I don't know, but what I do know is. It doesn't matter where I get drafted; nothing is going to change between us. We'll decide what is best for us, together." Poppy smiles, leaning up on her elbows, peppering small wet kisses on my neck to my jaw.

"Have I told you how much I love you?" she asks between kisses.

"Yes, but you can show me too." I smile, pulling Poppy as close to me as our bodies will allow.

The tiny couch under me is uncomfortable, but I easily forget about my discomfort when I feel Poppy move my shirt up enough for her soft, freezing cold hands to move up my stomach to my chest.

She shifts until she is straddling my hips. "Well, let me go ahead and show you."

Somehow, the girl I already love more than my next breath makes me fall deeper for her.

"Then I am all yours." I wrap my large hands around Poppy's slim waist.

"Just the way I like you." Poppy giggles.

I feel Poppy start to pull my shirt up higher. I shiver when the cool air swirls around us and touches my warm skin. After my shirt is tossed to the side, I watch with my eyes wide open, refusing to blink, so I don't miss a thing as Poppy slowly, almost like she is trying to torture me, takes her shirt off. She is wearing a cute little light blue bra with this crisscross-looking thing in the front, making her small chest somehow look a little bigger. The first time I saw Poppy in this sexy little contraption, I was a little annoyed to find out it didn't clasp as I thought, but the bra goes on and off like a shirt.

My palms twitch, begging to reach out and touch her silky-smooth skin, but I'm a man of my word. I told her she can show me how much she loves me, and I'm ready to take whatever she gives me.

CHAPTER 28

JAX

The bar is buzzing tonight. There are a lot of people, and I'm wondering how many of them are here to perform for open mic night or came to watch. Poppy is going to get to perform four songs, and of course, she is doing all originals.

The guy on the stage now has an acoustic guitar, and he is pretty good. He is singing a pretty popular country song, but I think it fits his voice nicely. Welsh and his girlfriend, Lidia, are at the bar ordering all of us beer. I check my phone to see if Otis, Violet, Wells, and Freya are able to come. There is still no response, but with all they have going on, and Poppy deciding this morning to sign up, we aren't expecting them to come. `

The chair next to me scrapes on the floor so loud I can hear it over the music. I look up from my phone to find the girl I hooked up with the night I caught Lilah cheating on me sitting in the chair smiling.

"Hey, remember me?" She asks, leaning in close.

Her flowery perfume is making my head spin with how strong it is.

"Yeah…" I rub the back of my head, leaning back, trying to put some distance between us.

"You left before I could get your number." She leans closer to me. Clearly, she isn't getting the hint.

I'm so tempted to move seats. "Sorry, I had to be at practice early." I lie a little too easily.

"I know," she giggles, but it sounds more like an evil cackle. "Want to buy me a drink?"

"Sorry, I'm here with my girlfriend," I say as Walsh and Lidia come to the table.

"Oh… sorry." The girl gets up with her face turning red.

"What was that about?" Walsh asks, handing me a mug full of

foamy beer.

I chuckle under my breath. "Well, the night I caught Lilah fucking another man, I came here and shitfaced. Next thing I knew, I ended up going to her apartment." I shake my head. "She thought she was going to get a second night with me."

Walsh throws his head back, roaring with laughter.

The guy stops singing his song, and he transitions into a slower country number. This one is older, but still well-known to any good country music fan.

"He's pretty good," Lidia says, successfully changing the subject.

"Yeah, he isn't making my ears bleed." I take a drink of my beer.

"Do you know when Poppy goes on?" Walsh leans back in his chair, putting his arm around Lidia.

I shake my head. I have no idea when she is going up, but I know for damn sure she is going to know how proud I am of her. I've never told her, but sometimes during a game I can hear her yelling for me, which only pushes me to play harder.

The guy ends his song, walking off the stage. A girl around my age wearing distressed blue jeans with a black tee tucked in brings out a guitar stand and the acoustic guitar I got custom-painted with poppies, and a matching red strap with her name embroidered on it in white thread onto the stage.

"Poppy is going up," I say to Lidia and Walsh.

The girl steps up to the microphone. "I'm pleased to announce our next performer is going to be playing four original songs for us. Give a big hand to Poppy Monroe."

I stand up, clapping and whistling. "Hey man," I feel a hand on my shoulder.

I glance behind me, finding Wells with his arm around Freya. I can't ever remember whether they are married or not, but if I had to guess, I would say they are engaged.

"You made it," I say, pulling a chair from another table up for one of them.

"Yeah, sorry, we almost missed it. Otis is bummed, but he took the kids out to spend some time with Violet and Nova." He smashes his lips into a thin line.

My eyebrows raise, but I know now is not the time to talk about what he just said. Poppy walks up to the microphone with her cherry red electric guitar sparkling under the stage lights.

"Good evening." Poppy smiles, her eyes sweep across the

audience, stopping when she sees me.

I sit there held captive by this newfound confidence in Poppy. This was the same confidence oozing from her in the video from the contest, but seeing it in person is so much better, not to mention sexy as hell. Poppy begins moving to the beat of the music as she plays her guitar. No wonder she won, because I don't want to take my eyes off her. I chuckle at Wells, who mutters something like damn, Poppy is good, or can you believe she's my sister. I don't know for sure, because the bar is beginning to slip away, and all I can see is Poppy.

Shit, I wanted to record this, but I noticed Lidia is already doing it.

"Hey, can you send me those?" She nods, but Walsh points to the stage.

Poppy's little black skirt is sparkling in the lights, but damn, her short legs look so good. I can't help but picture them wrapped around my waist while she is wearing nothing, but her tiny skirt bunched up around her slim waist.

"WOOOO!" I hoot and holler when she finishes her first song.

I have heard Poppy play the last song many times but watching her perform it like this is something else. Poppy changes her guitars out, and I immediately recognize the opening to the song. She told me she wrote about the first time we hooked up. It is sexy, but there is a sadness in the way she is singing. I know I hurt her with what I said, but I think we moved past it, plus she wrote a damn good song out of it.

Poppy moves on to another song with her acoustic guitar, and this one I've never heard before. The lyrics she is singing are of a hungry, burning passion, and the desperate need to feel the touch of someone.

She sings the line, "your touch ignites my world brighter than a million suns."

I hope like hell she is singing about me and not Lewis, but I know if I ever ask, I may not like the answer.

Poppy continues singing, and my mood lifts when she sings another line, "the love we've made under the stars, in a field of wildflowers is only ours." It takes me back to the day I told her I love her, but I'm not going to mention how all the wildflowers were dead.

The song ends, and I would give anything to hear more. Poppy switches back to her electric guitar. She plays the beginning chords to the song she wrote the summer after our freshman year of college. She told me has never had so much fun, and the summer she was the most carefree and at home with herself. Funny enough, looking back on it now, Lewis was gone a lot visiting family and traveling. Poppy and I spent the majority of the time with each other.

Poppy finishes singing, and the crowded bar erupts with applause, but I don't want this to end.

"THAT'S MY SISTER!" Wells yells over the crowd.

Poppy's radiant smile splits across her face. She moves her guitar, so it hangs off her back before she bows. When Poppy straightens up, she grabs her other guitar and exits the stage.

"I'll be back; I'm going to see if Poppy needs some help."

I weave around the tables, to the hall leading to the bathrooms, and the door from the little stage the bar has. I stop at the entrance of the hall, because the girl from earlier comes out of the men's restroom, fixing her top. She spots me, coming over. Her once neat and smooth curls are now messy, almost like someone ran their hands through them.

"You sure you don't want to ditch your little girlfriend to come have a good time with me?" She runs the tip of her long nail down my shirt.

I move around the girl I'm regretting hooking up with more and more. I'm too much of a gentleman to tell her she got some.

The door to the stage opens, and Poppy comes out with her guitar cases in her hands.

"Let me help you." I grab both of her guitar cases once she is completely out of the door.

I lean down, kissing the top of Poppy's head. "You were unbelievable. I can't wait to watch you perform again."

Poppy's cheeks turn a sweet shade of pink. "Thanks, who is that?"

I turn around, looking to see who Poppy is talking about, but I already know. "She's the girl I hooked up with after I walked in on Lilah cheating on me," I say, turning my attention back to my jealous girlfriend.

Poppy's jealousy is cute. She doesn't get possessive over me often, but when she does, she gets a little sassy.

"Oh, her?" She scrunches her nose, and the tips of her mouth turn down.

"Yeah, it seems to be biting me in the ass now." I follow Poppy past the girl, fully aware of the holes she is burning through Poppy and me right now.

"Can we go eat? I'm starving, and bar food isn't going to cut it." Poppy scrunches her nose.

"Yeah, we can go anywhere you want." I lift the guitar cases over the tables, following Poppy to our table.

Poppy squeals, running to Wells. He leans down, hugging her. I hang back for a minute, letting her have some time with her brother. Wells has been more hesitant about having a relationship with Poppy, but maybe this is the turning point in their relationship.

"So, you're going to let your girlfriend hang all over another guy?" the girl behind me says.

"I don't think it is any of your business, but he is her brother." I walk away from her.

"You guys want to go to dinner with us?" Poppy is asking everyone.

I would love to have Poppy to myself, but I told her this was her night, and she can have whatever she wants. Besides, I will have her alone later tonight.

Everyone agrees, and we leave the bar as a girl and guy duo take the stage singing loudly, off-key, and with a drunken slur. I'm glad we aren't staying to witness the train wreck of a performance.

"I'm so happy you guys were able to make it, but I'm not going to lie, seeing you guys walk in made me a little nervous," Poppy says to Wells.

"Why would you be nervous? You kicked some major ass in there." Freya says, smiling widely.

"Well, playing in front of new people isn't scary. Playing for people I care about is nerve-racking, but in a good way." Poppy's cheeks turn pink.

The night sky is peppered with a few stars, and the moon is full, making every exhale visible in the crisp winter air. Poppy shivers, and if I didn't have my hands full with her guitars, I would pull her close to my side. Poppy is talking with everyone while I put her guitars up.

I will let Poppy talk with Wells and Freya all she wants, but it is fucking freezing out here, so I hope she doesn't want to stay out here long, especially since she is in a tiny skirt. When I step next to Poppy, her arm goes around my waist, and I pull her close to my side. She lays her head on my rib cage.

"We'll see you at the restaurant?" Poppy waves.

"Yes." Wells nods.

We get in the truck and as I wait for the cab to warm up a little Poppy looks out into the dark parking lot. "I'm glad they were able to come. I don't get to talk or spend much time with Wells, and I want to get to know him more."

I don't have to say anything, because I know she doesn't need me to. All I do is back out of the parking spot, grabbing Poppy's hand as I drive to the restaurant in a comfortable silence.

I watch Poppy, who is drunk from drinking pina coladas at dinner, trying to unlock the door to her apartment as she giggles loudly. I would be worried about her waking up the neighbors, but most of them are probably at a party right now, one of the good things about these apartments. Most of them, at least in this building, are college students.

"JAX! Why isn't the door opening?" Poppy says a little too loudly.

I lean Poppy's guitars against the wall, looking at what Poppy is doing. She is trying to unlock her door with the key to my apartment. I grab the keys from her. When I get the door open, Poppy walks in, shrugging her coat off, tossing it on the couch, but she misses by a lot. I grab her guitars off the wall and put them next to the piano before shutting the door. I turn around, taking my own coat off as Poppy is shedding the rest of her clothes, throwing them around the living room.

I chuckle under my breath. "If you want to get me naked, all you have to do is ask."

Poppy stops fiddling with the zipper of her skirt at my words. Maybe I will get what I want, which is Poppy under me or on top of me with nothing but her skirt on.

Poppy sways, looking up at me with pink cheeks, but her blush doesn't stop there as it creeps down her neck and over her chest. "What?" she hiccups.

I grab her wrist and pull her next to me. "Let's go have some fun."

Poppy steps up to me until I can feel her chest press against me. "No one else is here. We could have fun anywhere?"

"I will take you anywhere and everywhere?" I let go of Poppy's wrist and move my hands down her back, stopping at her hips.

Wrapping her fingers around the waistband of my jeans, Poppy's cold fingers make me shiver. "I want you now."

I lift Poppy into my arms, and she wraps her legs around me and I take her to her bedroom.

CHAPTER 29

JAX

"SPRING BREAK!" Poppy yells as we climb into my truck.

"I'm ready to have my girl all to myself." I smile, looking in my blind spots to see if I can back out.

I've never brought a girl to my family's lake house without my parents going, but my dad surprised my mom with her dream trip to Grease. They are going to try to go to Italy while over there, because my mom wants to go on a wine tour. I asked her if there is such a thing, and she said if not, she'll make her own.

Poppy bursts out into a fit of giggles. "Jax, you have me all to yourself all the time."

"Yeah, but not in the middle of nowhere, where no one can hear you screaming out my name, begging me to let you come." I climb into my truck, shutting the door. "Maybe if you're lucky, I'll let you come more than once."

"JAX!" Poppy gasps.

"Exactly, but louder." I chuckle at my joke as Poppy's face turns deep red.

Poppy doesn't say anything. She leans forward, pairing her phone to my truck, turning on the music. Probably a smart thing to do on her end, because she knows I can make more dirty jokes.

"We still need to stop by the store?" Poppy asks, turning down the volume. "Do you want to stop now or go to the one Roxi and I always go to?"

"I haven't thought about it. This is my first time going without my parents. Maybe we can go to the general store. My mom seems to love it."

I merge onto the highway following the directions even though I know how to get there.

Poppy starts giggling. "She likes this place, because they have really good fudge in the bakery, and she will eat it while shopping, so she doesn't have to share with you or Shane."

"Really?" I chuckle.

My mom would always wait so she could go shopping there before buying groceries. She never let anyone go with her until Poppy moved in with us.

"I get the peanut butter swirl brownie." Poppy looks out the window, smiling.

"I'll buy you a brownie and whatever else you want." I reach over the console, grabbing Poppy's hand.

"I would love that," Poppy whispers over the music.

Before long, she is singing to the playlist she put on while I drive us. I sing along too, not as well as Poppy. She is happy, and the weight of the world she normally carries around with her has lifted.

Cars zoom past, and one even cuts me off, but I try not to let them dampen my mood. After about an hour, Poppy falls asleep. Every time we go to the lake house, I am reminded of the first time Poppy came here. Poppy fell in love with the house and loved playing her guitar around a campfire for everyone. Her preferred instrument to play is the piano, but everyone loves listening to her play her guitar as much.

Some jerk slams on their brakes in front of me, but I can't blame them as we get stuck in standstill traffic. Hopefully, we can get to the general store before they close.

"Pops, wake up," I say, pulling into a parking place of the general store after sitting in traffic for an extra hour due to a wreck.

"Are we there?" She mumbles, not lifting her head from the window.

I laugh, "Yeah. Come on, you got to show me this brownie you told me about."

"You'll probably love their chocolate chip cookies." Poppy takes her seat belt off, and we hop out of the truck at the same time.

"I'll have to get one. What do you want to do for dinner tonight?" I look at the little general store.

Poppy looks up at me, shielding her eyes with her right hand.

"Do you want to do something different? We normally do pizza on our first night here."

Usually, on our first night at the lake, my mom will get pizza on her way to the house from getting groceries. She always claims she doesn't want to cook after traveling, but I know it is because she loves their pizza.

"We can get pizza, or if you want to try something new, we can." I put my keys in my pocket as we enter through automatic glass doors.

"Okay, we can think about it while we shop." Poppy grabs a basket.

I follow her through the store as she makes her way to the bakery area. I can smell fresh-baked bread and cinnamon rolls. If their treats are as good as their store smells, I won't be disappointed. Poppy puts her face a few inches from the glass case displaying the desserts. She has a major sweet tooth and loves anything with peanut butter and chocolate.

"Can I get two chocolate chip cookies and two peanut butter swirl brownies?" I ask the lady behind the counter.

She straightens back up, and her arm brushes mine. Electric heat spreads through me at her innocent touch.

"Thank you." She leans up on the balls of her feet.

I lean down, kissing her cheek. Poppy is so sweet; she is the best girlfriend ever. I'm so happy we both decided to bulldoze past the complications standing in our way to be together.

"Can we still sit on the dock and watch the sunset?" Poppy asks, pushing the cart, grabbing things off the shelf from the list we made before we left.

"We can do whatever you want." I grab a big bag of charcoal off the bottom shelf, shoving the dusty bag on the rack on the bottom of the buggy.

I look at Poppy, and her cheeks are pink. She is not thinking about food anymore, because her lip's part and she is breathing heavier. I will be a gentleman right now and not ask her what she is thinking, but as soon as we are alone, I'll ask her for the details of the dirty thought running through her mind.

We walk through the small general store, going aisle by aisle until Poppy leads us to a register.

Poppy starts chatting with the worker as she waits for the total. I look at the selection of candies and magazines around us and I understand the impulse, because I want to buy something, but I won't.

When we get to the truck, Poppy stands there talking about what kind of pizza she wants, telling me we need to try their garlic bites.

Even with her food insecurities, she got from her dad controlling when she would get to eat, she's still considered a foodie, because she is down to try almost anything.

I chuckle under my breath at her excitement, but as I'm getting the last thing in the truck, Poppy gasps, "Jax."

"What?" I ask, looking around, but when I don't see anything, trying to figure out what I may have missed.

"I have the best idea, but it will require us to go to the liquor store." Poppy gets in the truck after putting the cart away, but she doesn't elaborate on what her idea is.

I drive across the street to the liquor store, and Poppy tells me to wait in the car. I don't know what she is up to, but I have learned a long time ago not to question her.

I'm drumming my fingers on my steering wheel, singing the song on the radio, when Poppy finally leaves with a paper bag cradled in her arms as she walks in an almost skipping way, making her hair bounce. I don't know what she bought, but she has a wide smile on her face.

An elderly man with salt and pepper hair follows her with a large case of beer. Who does Poppy think is going to drink all of this? I don't plan on drinking the whole break, because I am conditioning for the NFL.

After they load everything up, we go to the pizza place and order our food. Maybe I should have ordered our dinner while Poppy was in the liquor store after all, I do know what we want.

"Are you going to tell me what your idea is?" I ask while sitting down at a table.

Poppy shakes her head. "No, where is the fun in that?"

I laugh, "Well, is there anything I can do to help?"

"Of course you can. After dinner and the sun sets, you can get a fire going."

Is she thinking what I'm hoping she is? The first night she came here, we snuck down to the fire pit and sat around telling ghost stories. We snuck a beer for me, and a little wine for her. I'm not going to ask her any other questions, because I know I want this to be a surprise.

Once we get the pizza, we drive home. I tell Poppy I will unload the truck if she takes the dust covers off the couch. She quickly agreed before rolling the window down and singing to the music. Her long hair flies around her, making her giggle.

I pull into the driveway, and when I step onto the gravel, I inhale deeply. I miss the smell of this place. We walk in, and the sun shines through the windows,

"I've missed this place," Poppy says, walking to her room with her suitcase.

I quickly wrap my arms around her waist. "Where do you think you're going?" I ask, burying my face in Poppy's vanilla and flowery-scented hair. "You get to sleep in my room with me."

Poppy turns in my arms, wrapping me in hers. She looks up at me from under her lashes, but I can't miss the blush creeping down her neck to her chest and disappearing under her little sundress.

"Okay," she whispers right before I bend down, kissing her until we are both breathless, and I want more.

"Why don't you grab us a drink and go out to the dock. I'll get the paper plates, pizza, and meet you there." I loosen my hold on Poppy.

She walks away from me, and I wheel her suitcase into my room. I'm happy Poppy is going to be in here with me, because I sleep better with her in my arms.

I walk into the kitchen, grab plates, and the treats we bought from the general store, putting them on the pizza box after I put all the groceries away. I carry them outside where Poppy is waiting for me at the edge of the dock with her feet kicking in the water, even though the water is probably still cold.

"It feels so good to be back," Poppy says with her face pointed to the sky and her head tilted back. "I remember the first time I came here. I was so scared, but I felt so free. I have no ties or memories of Jack here, so this place is nothing but happy and positive for me."

I place the box next to Poppy, sitting on the warm dock and dipping my feet into the cool water.

"That was a fun summer. I remember you chose to ride with me, and we went on backroads with the windows rolled down, screaming to music at the top of our lungs. My dad called us when we didn't show up after a couple of hours." Poppy's laugh echoes across the lake.

"They weren't mad. They laughed on the phone and told us to be careful. Your mom waited to go to the store for me, because she wanted to make sure I had everything I needed." Poppy grabs a garlic bite. "I also remember you throwing me into the lake after dinner."

She narrows her eyes, taking a big bite of her bread, moaning a little.

"You looked like a drowned puppy when you came back up, but I still thought you were cute." I grab a large slice of my supreme pizza with extra cheese and extra peppers.

"Do you think we will come back after we move for our careers?" Poppy looks down at the water. Her voice is small, almost sad.

"Hell yes! This place will always be here when we want to come back." I shove a huge bite of pizza in my mouth. "So, what is this amazing idea you came up with when we left the store?"

"I thought you would catch on, but we haven't done scary stories around the campfire in quite some time. I was thinking of waiting until everyone else gets here to do it. I wanted to make smores tonight, but I see you brought one of my brownies and I didn't eat it while we were shopping, so I want one tonight."

"We can save these for tomorrow or do smores tomorrow. I want to do whatever you want to do." I pop one of the garlic bites in my mouth.

My mom will love these. I'll have to make her order some when we come this summer. Poppy and I eat dinner as the sun slowly sets. This is the best first lake trip I could have ever asked for.

Poppy lies on her back, looking up at the rest of the sunset when she finishes her second slice of pizza. One of my favorite things about Oklahoma is the painted sky at sunset, and Poppy has said the same thing many times. I take the food inside, and when I come back, I see Poppy still hasn't moved. I lay on the dock next to her.

I feel Poppy's small hand grab mine. "I love you," Poppy whispers into the darkening sky as stars slowly start to pepper the dark blue night.

I lean up on my elbow, looking down at Poppy. She is smiling, but the rest of her face is relaxed. She looks so at peace here, and my heart soars at the thought of one day this will be all ours. This isn't the first time I've thought of Poppy as my wife since we've been together.

"I love you too." I lean down, kissing Poppy senseless.

The fire crackles, and the sound of the bugs singing into the darkness calms me as I sit around a campfire with my whole family, minus Hawk and Harley, because they are sleeping. Nova is even here, and she looks genuinely happy as she talks to Roxi.

"Okay, who wants to tell the first ghost story?" Jax asks, sitting in the chair right next to me.

I love this, but I'm also scared, because Jax can tell a good story and spook me.

"I can," Nova says, looking at Violet with tears welling in her eyes. "I think you should finally learn what happened to Noelle."

Even though it is dark outside, I can see Violet swallow hard. "Are you sure?"

"It is part of my recovery, but I'm afraid you're going to hate me after I tell you." This time, Nova looks down, folding her arms around herself.

Violet looks at Otis, and I see him mouth something, but I have no clue what he is saying to her.

"I can't promise to forgive you, but I promise we'll try to work past this, together," Violet says, glancing around the fire with her lips pressed into a thin line.

Nova nods, and I can see the uncertainty dancing in her eyes, but something in her is compelled to tell a story I'm sure no one here is ready to hear.

"I don't remember much about the first day of the trip you invited me on. All I remember is being so mad at you for choosing to go camping with your loser boyfriend of yours and, of course, Noelle." Nova's breathing becomes labored. "I was furious, and nothing would make the furry in me calm. I wanted you to myself. I was hoping you would want to go on a sister's trip with me, and you know, since we were finally old enough to go without mom. I never told you what I wanted, and after talking to my therapist, I know I was wrong and my anger was misplaced. We could have gone when you got back or something, but I didn't want to go camping."

I stand from my chair, moving to sit on Jax's lap. Something in the pit of my stomach drops, making this story feel wrong to listen to.

"You, okay?" Jax asks, wrapping me in his arms.

I nod my head, because I don't know whether I am or not.

Nova looks toward the water. "I don't know where we were, but being back at this lake brings back some of those same feelings. The best way to describe the violent anger was coursing through my body is blinding rage. I saw Noelle standing on the deck about thirty minutes before sunrise. I swear, I didn't mean to hurt her. I went over there to talk to her, and she said something, and it felt like a rubber band snapped, and I lost control of everything."

Violet is shaking her head almost like she can't believe what she's hearing right now, but honestly, neither can I. "What did she say?"

Violet finally asks through her clenched jaw.

"She told me," Nova huffs. "I'd better not do anything to ruin your camping trip, or she would make me regret it. I laughed in her face and grabbed her by the hair on the back of her head. I pushed her forward and told her she would be the one who would be sorry. I only meant to scare her by pushing her in the water, but she grabbed onto me, and we both went into the water. My blood was boiling, and I felt like I was watching myself as I surfaced, almost like an out-of-body experience. Noelle began swimming to the shore, but I caught up with her and pushed her under the water. I still remember the feeling of her fighting me, trying to come up for air, but I wouldn't let her. I kept holding her under the water until she stopped moving, and I held her there more." Violet stands from her chair with her hands balled into fists. "I didn't let go even when she clawed at me, and I didn't let go until the sun started to peak over the water."

"You murdered my best friend!" she shrieks. "Then you attempted kill me twice. What else do I have to look past, so you don't come after me or anyone else I love?"

"Violet," Nova sniffles. "I've done so many bad things, but I want you in my life so bad, and if I have to have these people in mine to have you then I will, but I can't lose you. I won't survive it."

"Why are you telling me now?" Violet stomps her foot in the dirt.

"I need to come clean. I need you to know everything." Nova looks up at Violet from under her lashes. She looks like a villain with the shadows dancing across her face from the glow of the crackling fire. "I've never meant to hurt anyone, especially you."

"We can talk about this in therapy, but I'm going to drop this, but not for you. "Violet looks at the lake as the fire gleams off her tears.

I can see she is crying, mourning the loss of her friend again. I know now things are never going to be the same between them again, but Violet is strong and a woman of her word, so she will talk about this in therapy, but she will never forgive and never forget.

After learning about how far Nova is willing to go to keep Violet to herself, I'm not sure I feel safe with her being her, but Violet didn't tell her to leave, so I am going to trust her. That means the scary story Jax told me about the girl who drowned here one morning is true.

I shiver, leaning back into Jax's hold. "So, who else has a scary story?"

CHAPTER 30

POPPY

I can't believe I'm going to do this. I say as I'm hunched in one of those hot cardboard cakes strippers pop out of. Jax has joked for several years about wanting to have a stripper jump out of a giant cake on his birthday during our senior year of college, so here we are. I'm trying to make his dreams come true, since I wasn't comfortable hiring a stripper. I worked with Walsh and Lidia to make it possible for me to be the one to make my man's fantasies come to life.

I told him we had to get the cake ready.

"Are you ready for this?" Walsh asks while lifting me over the top of the fake cake.

"As ready as I'm going to be." I smile weakly.

I bend my legs and hover over the opening of the cake. My feet find the bottom first, and I drop into a quick crouch, tucking myself down inside.

"Alright, let's go." Walsh closes the top of the cake, and I am trapped in darkness.

I feel them wheel me across the floor as the whole bar starts singing happy birthday poorly.

The cake stops, and I hear Jax ask over the drunken singing, "Where's Poppy?"

No one answers him, but when they stop singing, I jump up with my arms fanning up and over my head. I know Jax will like the little outfit I changed into. I am wearing a jersey I had made, and it is completely bedazzled. The shirt is long enough for me to wear it as a dress, and I have a sexy lingerie set underneath in the same colors as the jersey. I have black stockings connected to a garter belt, and a fun surprise for Jax. I'll whisper to him when I'm done with my little birthday song.

With the help of Walsh, I get out of the big cardboard cake, and I begin singing to him as a couple of Lidia's friends bring out the real cake.

Jax blows out the candles with the biggest smile I have ever seen on his face.

"Thank you," he says, kissing me deeply. "This is better than anything I could have imagined."

I grab a hold of his shirt, and I blindly reach for his phone with my other hand. When he pulls back from me, he is breathing hard.

"Fuck, Poppy, you made every dirty fantasy of mine come true, but even better than my sick mind could ever come up with." Jax leans down, kissing my neck, tickling me.

"I'm happy you're not mad about me being the one to come out of the cake instead of a real stripper." I feel Jax's body shake as he laughs, but he doesn't stop kissing my neck. "I have another surprise for you."

Jax moves away from my neck, resting his forehead on mine. "This is more than enough. By the way, I can't wait to see what is under this jersey." I feel Jax's hand move up the back of my thigh. "I got a little peek when you were getting out of the cake."

"If you like that, then you will like my next surprise." I give Jax his phone with what he says is his favorite app. "You can play before I take you home, and show you exactly what is under this jersey, but don't get too drunk." I wink, handing him his phone.

"You are the best fucking girlfriend ever. I definitely won't get too drunk. I want to remember everything from tonight." Jax looks down at his phone with a crooked smile. "Thank you for making this the best birthday ever."

Jax moves his fingers across the screen of his phone. I gasp, grabbing a tighter hold on his shirt as the vibrations send shock waves of pleasure through me. Jax takes his hand off the phone, and I faintly hear the locking sound of his phone before it disappears into his pocket. He leans down, kissing me again, making the hunger I have for him triple.

The crowd cheers, chanting, "SHOT! SHOT! SHOT!"

A few trays of shots in little red plastic cups are being brought around. Jax grabs two when they get close enough.

"You want one?" Jax holds the mini cup to me.

I look into the shot glass and wrinkle my nose. "It's whiskey," I whisper, shaking my head.

Another tray comes around, and Jax looks to see what's on it. I know they're safe when he sets the first two; he grabbed down, trading them for the new ones.

"Tequila." Jax winks, handing me the shot glass.

I look at the full cup. There is no way I can down this whole shot, but whatever I don't drink, Jax will finish for me.

"ONE! TWO! THREE! SHOT!" Someone yells.

I tip the cup back, taking as much of the shot as I can. My nose wrinkles at the strong taste coating my tongue. I hold the shot glass up to Jax, and he tosses it back like burning liquor is nothing. His tongue darts out, licking a couple of stray drops off his lip. My mouth drops as the thought of what he can do with his tongue fills my head.

Jax pulls me close to his body. "Come on, let's go dance."

The last thing I want is to dance with Jax right now. I want to find the first empty room and let him have his way with me, but I know he wants to stay and party more, so off to the dance floor I go.

"Pops, wake up," Jax says my nickname in a soft, calming tone, but he is shaking me awake after partying last night is a little alarming.

"Jax," I groan. "What's wrong?" I blink several times, trying to get rid of the sleep from my eyes.

"Coach Harrison called and asked me to come to his office. I think this is about me going pro."

If this is about him going pro, he would have a couple of weeks before he has to leave for whatever team wants him, because Oklahoma doesn't have a pro team. I didn't think this would happen so soon, but again, I am not surprised. Jax has worked his ass off for this.

"Whatever he says, I want you to know how I'm so proud of you." I kiss Jax before he leaves me alone.

I haven't asked Jax to move in with me, because I wasn't ready to live with him as boyfriend and girlfriend yet, even though we spend every night together. If he does get invited into the NFL, what will it mean for our relationship?

My hands begin to shake as anxious waves make me sick to my stomach. I know Jax said he would do long distance, because no matter what, ending our relationship is not an option.

I roll out of bed, standing on the soft rug with shaky legs. I need to get my mind off of this until Jax comes home. I walk with slow steps to the piano, and when I sit down, I lift the fallboard, and a sense of comfort washes over me, but my heart is still pounding. Music always helps me through what I am feeling. I know as soon as my fingers touch the keys, I will get lost in what I'm doing until he finally walks through the door.

I didn't think I could survive the heartbreak from Lewis, but Jax put me back together like I was never broken. He is my home, and no matter where we are, if he is there, I will be safe and complete.

My hands shake as I press the first note to the song I wrote for Jax. I never played it for him because I wrote this song the summer after high school. It is about the love I have for him, but not the romantic kind. This love is for the guy who saved me.

I play note after note slowly, feeling any of the anxiety I was feeling slip away from me. I shift from one song to another, and Jax is still not home, which I'm hoping is a good sign, like he got great news or something.

I stand up, lifting the lid of the wooden bench seat, and I grab two notebooks. One is full of lyrics, and the other is a notebook of music sheets I'm using to compose a new song. I grab my favorite pencil and my guitar. I loop my guitar strap, which Jax had customized for me, around my shoulder and sit back down on the bench. I open the notebooks to the bright white pages of the song I am currently working on. There are a bunch of scribbles all over the pages, some arrows, and doodles. This page would look disorganized and wouldn't make sense to anyone else, but to me, I see a beautiful story in the chaos.

I begin playing my guitar because I have the piano part of the song done, but I hit a snag in the same spot as I always do. I think if I can hear the melody on the piano and the lyrics out loud, I may be able to figure out what isn't working. Before I can stand up from the piano bench, the door to my apartment swings open. I scream at the top of my lungs, almost like you hear in scary movies. I wobble on the piano bench, trying not to fall off. My heart begins pounding hard in my chest as black spots begin to pepper my vision.

"Shit!" I hear Jax curse. "I didn't mean to scare you."

"It's alright, I needed a good jolt to wake me up." I laugh despite my whole body shaking.

"Pops, come sit down," Jax says, taking large steps to the couch. "I want to talk to you about my meeting with Coach Harrison."

I watch as he sits down, patting the cushion next to him. I walk with heavy steps to the couch. Dread fills me, making my heart pound hard. Jax is smiling, almost bouncing in his seat, so I know whatever he is fixing to say is good news, at least it will be for him. I'm not so sure if what he has to say will be good for me.

"Coach Harrison called me right after he got off the phone with one of the coaches out of Tennessee. He said they have been watching me for a while but wanted to wait until next year to draft me." Jax stops talking, taking a huge breath as he tries to talk fast. "Well, one of their players wants to retire earlier than he originally planned, and they called Coach Harrison to see if I wanted the spot. I'm their first choice. Can you believe it?"

"Jax, that is so amazing!" I shriek, tackling him on the couch, hugging him tightly. "Is this one of the teams you were wanting to play for?"

"I mean, this is my door to go pro. There is no guarantee I will get another opportunity." Jax pulls me onto his lap until I'm straddling him. "But while I was there, he got another call, and he said good news, you were offered a spot in both New England and Seattle."

JAX! Three teams want you!" I put my hands on his cheeks, kissing him deeply. "We have to celebrate!" I say when I come up for air.

Jax chuckles. "I have to commit before we can celebrate."

My eyebrows scrunch together. This doesn't sound like Jax. He is the type of guy who will celebrate anything, no matter what it is.

"Who says! This is huge. Jax, you are invited to play on three NFL teams! I put my hands on his shoulders, looking down at him.

Jax puts his forehead on mine, where our noses are still touching. "I think I need to talk to my dad about what I need to do. I am supposed to meet up with someone to talk about contracts. So, I guess we will celebrate, because my parents will want to take me out to dinner."

"That's great. I would love to go to dinner with your parents, but in the meantime…" I kiss Jax, moving my hands down his chest until I get to the button on his jeans.

"Pops, what are you doing?" Jax asks, moving his hands to my hips, but I shake my head, taking his warm touch off of me.

I tilt my head to the left, but my eyes still travel all over Jax even though he is fully clothed. "Oh, you know, just admiring my soon-to-be pro football boyfriend."

"Is that all you're doing?" Jax raises his eyebrow at me with a silly, lopsided grin.

I love it when he looks up at me like that, because it reminds me of the guy from high school who became my best friend. I remember Jax used to smile like that all the time. He was once a carefree, laidback guy until he jumped in front of the bullet for me. I know he told me saving me was worth it, but I watched one of the best parts of him harden over time.

"Would you object if I planned on doing more?" I giggle under my breath.

"Fuck no." Jax puts his large hand under my ass. I feel him shift as he stands up. "Let's take this to your room."

I giggle again at the thrill of being lifted into the air and carried to my room. Jax kisses my neck as he walks blindly to our destination.

CHAPTER 31

JAX

"JAX!" Poppy yells from my bedroom as she packs up my stuff to take with me when I move in a few days.

After a lot of consideration and looking at the contracts with my dad and our lawyers, I decided on New England. The hardest part about choosing a team was Poppy. I didn't want to lose her in all this.

I leave my mom in the kitchen to finish sorting things to keep, donate, and trash as I walk to my room, where Poppy is.

"Yeah?" I ask, walking into my room, seeing Poppy facing the door with three thongs dangling off her finger.

"Why do you have so many?" She bites her lip as her shoulders shake from her silent laugh.

"Well, I had to buy the pink one for rush week, and it was cheaper to buy a set instead of a single." I shrug.

She can act like she didn't enjoy seeing me in those things, but we both know it turned her on. I pull her into my arms, and she giggles. The underwear falls off Poppy's finger and onto the floor.

"Do you like seeing me in the stripper underwear?" I ask, leaning down until I'm inches from her face.

I inhale Poppy's sweet shampoo. Her smell is so addicting.

"They're not bad," she says in a breathy whisper.

I pull back, finding Poppy's beautiful face is as red as the flower she is named after. I laugh so hard my whole body shakes. I love she still gets embarrassed about stuff like this after all we've done together.

"I'm good with getting rid of them unless you don't want me to. I can strip them off for you anytime you want." I straighten back up, looking down at Poppy as her blush deepens.

Poppy looks up at me with her lips in a large "O" shape. My mind is quick to think of plenty of filthy things I could do with her mouth.

"JAX! We need to get the kitchen finished!" My mom hollers, breaking the spell I was put under.

I kiss Poppy on the forehead. "We will finish this later."

"Alright, but one last thing. Do you think the app will work when we are states apart?" She holds up the box has the little toy I got her for Halloween.

"Only one way to find out." I kiss her on the forehead again.

I walk back into the kitchen, and my mom looks at me with a wide smile. "Everything alright?"

Shit, my mom is looking at me like she knows what Poppy and I were talking about.

"Yeah, why?" I ask my mom as I look at the stuff she has been putting on the counter for me to look at.

"I am so happy to see you so grown up and in love with a wonderful woman." My mom walks over to me, wrapping her arms around me. "I'm so sorry I thought you guys being together was a bad thing. I was wrong."

I put my hand on my mom's back, rubbing up and down. "It's okay. We all handled the change wrong, but we got past it. Do you remember when you told me I need to consider if I am willing to marry Poppy before pursuing this any further, so neither of us ends up heartbroken?"

My mom pulls back a little, looking up at me with her brows pushed together. "Yeah…" she whispers.

"Well, one day I am going to ask her to be my wife, and I hope you and Dad will give us your blessings."

My mom hugs me, and I can hear her sniffling a little.

"This is something I am 100 percent certain of. I can see how much Poppy loves you, and I would love nothing more than for her to be your wife."

"Thanks, mom." I hug her before we get back to packing up my kitchen. "Can I be the one to tell dad?"

My mom nods, but I get a little peak of her face, and I can see tears falling from her cheeks. She is crying, but not from being sad, but from the overwhelming happiness filling her heart. This is the same look she had when she was at our high school graduation, and when I told my parents about the pro teams wanting me.

While we pack the rest of my things, my mom keeps looking over her shoulder at me with tears in her eyes. I guess I am going to have to tell my dad sooner than I wanted, because I don't know how long my mom will be able to keep this a secret from him.

My parents are staying at Poppy's apartment, because we still have so much packing to do tomorrow, but I know Poppy is naked, waiting for me in my bed. I adjust myself in my underwear before I step out of the bathroom with a little gift I got for Poppy a while back, and I couldn't think of a better night to try out a pair of fuzzy red handcuffs.

I turn on a song on my phone is connected to the speakers in my room. I let the music play for a couple of seconds before I open the door.

"I got you a gift." I twirl the handcuffs around my pointer finger.

"Jax, hope you don't think I am going to be the one to wear those?" Poppy is under my sheet with it pulled up to her armpits, but her shoulders are bare, so I know she doesn't have any clothes on.

"You want to cuff me to the bed. Kinky, I like it." I laugh, walking to the bed, stripping out of my underwear before Poppy can get a good look at me in the thong I have hidden under my boxer briefs, I'm busting out of.

Poppy moves the sheet in front of her face, muffling her loud giggles. I love it when she laughs at my jokes, especially the dirty ones. I have always said my future wife needs to think I am funny and is always down to have a good time. This is the second time tonight I have thought about my future wife, and in my head, I can see Poppy walking down the aisle in a beautiful white gown, with a veil over her face, clutching onto a bouquet of poppies like her mom had.

I crawl onto the bed until I am inches in front of Poppy's face. I pull the sheet down, and when I can see her pink face, I cup her chin in my hand, kissing her deeply.

Poppy's arms wrap around my neck, holding me to her. I get lost in the spell of her kiss. I put my hands under her ass, holding her body close to mine as I move her with me until I am sitting on the bed with my back propped up against the headboard, and she is straddling me with only the thin sheet between us.

She pulls back, resting her forehead. "Have I told you how proud I am of you?" Her warm breath fans my face.

"I think you've said it once or twice." We both laugh.

"I can't wait to watch you play. It is so hot seeing you in your uniform." Poppy giggles as she runs her hands down my chest.

"How hot does it make you?" I ask slowly, trying to move the sheet out from under Poppy.

"Why don't you find out?" Poppy winks.

"It will be my pleasure." I kiss Poppy, moving my hands from her ass over her thighs.

I may not know what is going to happen when I move, but I will not let anything come between Poppy and me, because I will make her my wife one day.

EPILOGUE 1

JAX

I'm standing on the balcony of my penthouse apartment, surrounded by twinkly lights and dozens of poppy flowers. I don't know exactly how many my mom ordered, but the setup is perfect.

I remember how nervous I was when I told my parents I wanted to ask Poppy to marry me, but this evening I feel calm and ready to ask this wonderful woman to be my wife. She was invited to co-write a song in Nashville, and I am waiting for her to come home. I may have lied and told her I couldn't pick her up, but I would have a car waiting for her.

The florist helped me set up all the flowers. She went as far as to make a path leading Poppy right to me, with some flameless candles giving everything a soft, romantic glow. I have a candlelit dinner set up under the stars for us to eat from the first restaurant I took Poppy to when she came to visit me before she moved here.

I check Poppy's location one last time, and I curse under my breath. There is no backing out now, even if I wanted to, but I don't. I want Poppy to be my wife more than anything in this world. I think waiting for Poppy is what is getting to me right now, but either way, I like the feel of the adrenaline is pumping through my veins right now.

I get down on one knee as I watch the front door slowly open through the wall of windows connecting my living room to the balcony.

Poppy wheels her suitcase in. "JAX! "I'm home!" she shouts, not looking up yet.

She shuts the door, slips her shoes off, and still does not notice the changes made to the apartment. I watch Poppy continue to put her things away as my hands begin to sweat.

If you had asked me when I was in high school if I would have

Poppy as my wife, I would have laughed in your face and called you a liar, because she was off limits, and I didn't stand a chance against Lewis.

Poppy finally turns around, seeing the room filled with flowers and lights. She looks around, and when she sees me on one knee, her hands fly to her mouth. She walks slowly, dragging out the moment for me to ask her to be mine for the rest of our lives.

When she steps out onto the balcony, I can hear the sobs, making her shake. She stops right in front of me, and the comforting smell of her perfume fills my nose, making me feel intoxicated.

"Poppy Fae Monroe, I have loved you in secret, and I have loved you as family, but now I get to love you out loud and with no complications and zero shame. Now I want to love you as your husband and you as my wife. I want to love you in every way I can and bring you the same happiness you bring me. Will you marry me?"

Tears rush down Poppy's face, staining her cheeks black with mascara. Her head is bobbing up and down, "Yes!" She cries.

I stand up, grab her hand, and put my grandmother's engagement ring on her finger. When we say I do, I will add her grandmother's ring too, because when I asked Grams if she would give me her blessing to marry Poppy, she began crying and said of course, but she also gave me the wedding ring she got from her husband, so when we get married, I will slip the ring on her finger. I wanted to tell Grams I didn't want to take anything from Wells and Otis, but she wouldn't hear what I had to say. She told me she already gave them the rings that were promised to them. She said that when she passes, she will leave her engagement ring to me to give to Poppy on one of our anniversaries, but she is not ready to part with it yet. I asked her why she didn't leave them her rings, and she said she had always wanted to be buried with them, but when she learned she had a granddaughter, she wished one day Poppy would like to have them.

I pick Poppy up and twirl her in a circle before I kiss her breathlessly. I can't wait to spend the rest of my life with my best friend.

EPILOGUE 2

JAX

I have been waiting for this day for two years. Today is the day I finally get to make Poppy my wife. This is a little bittersweet for me, because I had always thought Lewis would be my best man, and he isn't. However, I do have a good group of men by my side.

"Jax, are you ready?" My mom asks, knocking on the door.

My dad goes to answer the door while my best man, Walsh, and my groomsmen, Wells and Otis, chat and drink some bourbon. I'm ready. I would have gone to the courthouse the night I proposed, but Poppy has always wanted a wedding. She said she used to talk about what she would wear and who the man her mom wanted her.

"How is she?" I ask my mom.

"Well, she asked me not to tell you until after the wedding, but Lewis showed up." My hands ball into fists. "He gave her a gift, and he told her it is for both of you, and he is happy she has chosen you to be her prince, because you're the only man who deserves her."

"He didn't want to see me?" I ask between my teeth.

The sting of my old friend not wanting to say anything after showing up to see my bride on my wedding day burns in my chest.

"He didn't want you to think he was here to fight, or he was trying to ruin your wedding when he wasn't. I do think he wanted to see you, because he gave me this." My mom holds out a silver envelope with my name on it in Lewis's sloppy handwriting.

I put the card in my bag. I will read this later, because the last thing I want to do is read something that could ruin my mood.

"Thanks." I turn and put my jacket on. "How do I look?"

"You look handsome," my mom's voice cracks.

"I'm going to go to Poppy's room now. I'm proud of you for the woman you chose to spend life with." My dad hugs me.

"Shane," my mom says, stopping my father. "Can you see if Poppy will eat a cracker or drink some water before you walk her down the aisle?"

My dad nods, leaving me alone.

"Poppy's not feeling well?" I walk to the door. "Why didn't she tell me?"

"I think it's nerves." My mom turns to the groomsmen. "Now, which one of you is going to escort me to my seat?"

Otis steps forward with his arm extended in her direction. "I would be honored."

My mom hugs me one more time. "I'm so happy. My baby gets to marry the love of his life today."

We chose to have a small wedding in the same church where both of our parents got married. I asked her if this is what she wanted, and she said she could feel her mom here. I wasn't going to ask again, because I could tell how serious she was.

I walk down the aisle and to the altar with excited butterflies dancing in my stomach. As soon as the pastor takes his place, I feel a wave of nausea take over.

The instrumental song Poppy composed begins to play, and my back straightens as Lidia walks out arm in arm with Walsh. A lot of my college teammates came, and my whole pro team is here to support us. We had the guests sit wherever, especially since Poppy doesn't have as many people here as I do, even though she has some celebrities here she works with pretty regularly and has built a good friendship with.

Violet and Otis walk out, followed by Freya and Wells. Our colors are red and navy for Poppy since those are our favorite colors. The music changes again, and I recognize the opening music of the song she wrote for me. The doors open, and Poppy walks in a beautiful, white, flowy gown with a long veil, and Poppies clutched tightly in her hand. She looks like an angel walking toward me. I have never seen anyone so beautiful.

Poppy stops at the bottom of the stairs, and when I hear Grams and my dad answer the pastor when he asks who gives this woman away, I feel my own cheeks become wet even though I'm sure I've been crying this whole time.

The ceremony flies by in a blur, but when I'm asked to kiss the bride, my heart pounds hard in my chest as I kiss Poppy as my wife for the first time. The world fades away, and the only thing I feel is the love Poppy and I have for each other.

"Alright, ladies and gentlemen!" The DJ says, cutting the music off. "The bride would like the groom, Shane, Roxi, and Grams to come sit down in the middle of the dance floor." I watch as Violet, Wells, Otis, and Freya bring a chair onto the dance floor.

"Well, I'm guessing this isn't a lap dance." I joke.

"Nope, she said she has a surprise, but I don't know anything else." my mom whispers.

Poppy walks to the center of the floor with Otis, Wells, Freya, Hawk, Harley, Violet, and even Nova by her side. Poppy has a box in her hand. She is smiling, but I can tell she is nervous from the slight shaking of the box in her trembling hands.

The DJ comes onto the dance floor. "Ladies and gentlemen, the bride has a present for her groom. If you would gather around."

Poppy hands me the box, takes the mic from the DJ. "Family and friends, I have a gift for Jax I would like to share with you," Poppy says, confusing me even more. "On the count of three, you can lift the lid." Poppy leans down, kissing my cheek. "ONE! TWO THREE!" Poppy and the crowd roar cheerfully.

I open the lid and pull out a tiny version of my team's jersey with my number and Taylor's on the back. I look at it, holding it up for my parents and Grams to see. The crowd cheers, and I sit here, either too stunned to realize what this means, or I am too stupid.

"I'm going to be a grandma!" My mom cries, hugging my dad.

All at once, the crowd erupts in loud congratulations.

I slowly stand up, walking to my wife as tears stream down her face. I pull her into my arms, leaning down to her ear. "We're having a baby?" I whisper close to her.

She shivers from the feeling of my breath fanning down on her. "I mean, you shouldn't be surprised with how often we have sex." Poppy giggles, leaning in, kissing my jaw.

"You made me a husband and a dad in one day. I can't wait to get you back to our room to show you how happy I am." I kiss Poppy, and the crowd goes wild.

When we break apart, our families give us tearful congratulations, and the photographer comes over to get pictures of Poppy and I with our families while I hold the little jersey. Our families walk away from us with smiles and tears. Poppy and I take some photos by ourselves.

I wanted to be a dad one day, but not as soon as I got married; in the end, I couldn't ask for anything better than having a mini-Poppy to love just as much as I will love his or her mom. After all, Poppy is and has always been my endgame. I just needed to listen to my heart and not my head to get the girl a boy has liked since the beginning.

Saving
POPPY
Jennifer Froh

ALL
for
VIOLET
JENNIFER FROH

ACKNOWLEDGEMENTS

Somehow, time has flown, and I am now publishing the third book. This all started as a dream of a character that represented resilience—a story where you can find beauty and love even in the darkness of life. When I received feedback on this book, I was told by my closest friends that they didn't like Poppy with Lewis, but they preferred her with Jax instead. So… as a good friend, I wrote them a little novella, thinking it would stay between us, but I ended up falling in love with this story! I can't thank them enough for sparking the creative fire that fueled the start of this book. I also want to thank my family for always supporting me on my journey to follow my dreams. They never question the time I spend writing or working on my books at coffee shops or showing up at my events! I also must thank everyone who has read my books, come to see me at events, or told me they love my work. I wouldn't be where I am without you! Thanks to my Aunt Beverly Siegmun, my artist for the book cover of this story—the hand-painted art is the perfect touch.

ABOUT THE AUTHOR

Jennifer Froh is back for book three, but slightly more experienced, slightly more chaotic, and still fueled by daydreaming and questionable ideas.

When she is not writing stories full of messy hearts, forbidden tension, and a little bit of spice, she can be found reading, binge-watching shows, and overthinking fictional characters.

If there's one thing to expect from Jennifer Froh, it's chaos, chemistry, and characters who don't always make the best decisions—but you'll love them anyway.